AMERICAN FAMILIES
28 Short Stories

A UNIQUE COLLECTION BY
AMERICAN WRITERS

THE SORROWS OF GIN by John Cheever—a little girl experiences "the pitiful corruption of the adult world"

AFLOAT by Ann Beattie—an insecure second wife faces a visit from her critical adolescent stepdaughter

WEDDING DAY by Roberta Silman—amid religious ritual and family tradition, a young bride ponders her future

VIOLATION by Mary Gordon—a young woman endures the lasting shame of a beloved uncle's unwanted attentions

STILL OF SOME USE by John Updike—a family project of cleaning out the attic becomes a bittersweet rem

And twenty-thre . . .

AMER S

BARBARA H. SOLOMON, Professor of English at Iona College, is the editor of five other anthologies available in Mentor editions: *The Awakening and Selected Stories of Kate Chopin, The Short Fiction of Sarah Orne Jewett and Mary Wilkins Freeman, The Experience of the American Woman, A Mary Wollstonecraft Reader*, and *American Wives: Thirty Short Stories by Women.*

he doesn't pay you, I'll pay you. But he'll pay you. Don't worry. He says he will, and he will."

"I don't want to worry," she said. "But I worry anyway. I worry about my boys, and after that I worry about myself. I never thought I'd see one of my boys in this shape. I'm just glad your dad isn't alive to see it."

In three months my brother gave her fifty dollars of what he owed me and was supposed to pay to her. Or maybe it was seventy-five dollars he gave her. There are conflicting stories—two conflicting stories, his and hers. But that's all he paid her of the five hundred—fifty dollars or else seventy-five dollars, according to whose story you want to listen to. I had to make up the rest to her. I had to keep shelling out, same as always. My brother was finished. That's what he told me—that he was finished—when I called to see what was up, after my mother had phoned, looking for her money.

My mother said, "I made the mailman go back and check inside his truck, to see if your letter might have fallen down behind the seat. Then I went around and asked the neighbors did they get any of my mail by mistake. I'm going crazy with worry about this situation, honey." Then she said, "What's a mother supposed to think?" Who was looking out for her best interests in this business? She wanted to know that, and she wanted to know when she could expect her money.

So that's when I got on the phone to my brother to see if this was just a simple delay or a full-fledged collapse. But, according to Billy, he was a goner. He was absolutely done for. He was putting his house on the market immediately. He just hoped he hadn't waited too long to try and move it. And there wasn't anything left inside the house that he could sell. He'd sold off everything except the kitchen table and chairs. "I wish I could sell my blood," he said. "But who'd buy it? With my luck, I probably have an incurable disease." And, naturally, the investment thing hadn't worked out. When I asked him about it over the phone, all he said was that it hadn't materialized. His tax refund didn't make it, either—the I.R.S. had some kind of lien on his return. "When it rains it pours," he said. "I'm sorry, brother. I didn't mean for this to happen."

"I understand," I said. And I did. But it didn't make it any easier. Anyway, one thing and the other, I didn't get my money from him, and neither did my mother. I had to keep on sending her money every month.

I was sore, yes. Who wouldn't be? My heart went out to him, and I wished trouble hadn't knocked on his door. But my own back was against the wall now. At least, though, whatever happens to him from here on, he won't come back to me for more money—seeing as how he still owes me. Nobody would do that to you. That's how I figured, anyway, But that's how little I knew.

I kept my nose to the grindstone. I got up early every morning and went to work and worked hard all day. When I came home I plopped into the big chair and just sat there. I was so tired it took me a while to get around to unlacing my shoes. Then I just went on sitting there. I was too tired to even get up and turn on the TV.

I was sorry about my brother's troubles. But I had troubles of my own. In addition to my mother, I had several other people on my payroll. I had a former wife I was sending money to every month. I had to do that. I didn't want to, but the court said I had to. And I had a daughter with two kids in Bellingham, and I had to send her something every month. Her kids had to eat, didn't they? She was living with a swine who wouldn't even *look* for work, a guy who couldn't hold a job if they handed him one. The time or two he did find something, he overslept, or his car broke down on the way in to work, or else he'd just be let go, no explanation, and that was that.

Once, long ago, when I used to think like a man about these things, I threatened to kill that guy. But that's neither here nor there. Besides, I was drinking in those days. In any case, the bastard is still hanging around.

My daughter would write these letters and say how they were living on oatmeal, she and her kids. (I guess he was starving, too, but she knew better than to mention that guy's name in her letters to me.) She'd tell me that if

I could just carry her until summer things would pick up for her. Things would turn around for her, she was sure, in the summer. If nothing else worked out—but she was sure it would; she had several irons in the fire—she could always get a job in the fish cannery that was not far from where she lived. She'd wear rubber boots and rubber clothes and gloves and pack salmon into cans. Or else she might sell root beer from a vending stand beside the road to people who lined up in their cars at the border, waiting to get into Canada. People sitting in their cars in the middle of summer were going to be thirsty, right? They were going to be crying out for cold drinks. Anyway, one thing or the other, whatever line of work she decided on, she'd do fine in the summer. She just had to make it until then, and that's where I came in.

My daughter said she knew she had to change her life. She wanted to stand on her own two feet like everyone else. She wanted to quit looking at herself as a victim. "I'm not a victim," she said to me over the phone one night. "I'm just a young woman with two kids and a son-of-a-bitch bum who lives with me. No different from lots of other women. I'm not afraid of hard work. Just give me a chance. That's all I ask of the world." She said she could do without for herself. But until her break came, until opportunity knocked, it was the kids she worried about. The kids were always asking her when Grandpop was going to visit, she said. Right this minute they were drawing pictures of the swing sets and swimming pool at the motel I'd stayed in when I'd visited a year ago. But summer was the thing, she said. If she could make it until summer, her troubles would be over. Things would change then—she knew they would. And with a little help from me she could make it. "I don't know what I'd do without you, Dad." That's what she said. It nearly broke my heart. Sure I had to help her. I was glad to be even halfway in a position to help her. I had a job, didn't I? Compared to her and everyone else in my family, I had it made. Compared to the rest, I lived on Easy Street.

I sent the money she asked for. I sent money every time she asked. And then I told her I thought it'd be simpler if I just sent a sum of money, not a whole lot, but money even so, on the first of each month. It would be money she could count on, and it would be *her* money, no one else's—hers and the kids'. That's what I hoped for, anyway. I wished there was some way I could be sure the bastard who lived with her couldn't get his hands on so much as an orange or a piece of bread that my money bought. But I couldn't. I just had to go ahead and send the money and stop worrying about whether he'd soon be tucking into a plate of my eggs and biscuits.

My mother and my daughter and my former wife. That's three people on the payroll right there, not counting my brother. But my son needed money, too. After he graduated from high school, he packed his things, left his mother's house, and went to a college back East. A college in New Hampshire, of all places. Who's ever heard of New Hampshire? But he was the first kid in the family, on either side of the family, to even *want* to go to college, so everybody thought it was a good idea. I thought so, too, at first. How'd I know it was going to wind up costing me an arm and a leg? He borrowed left and right from the banks to keep himself going. He didn't want to have to work a job and go to school at the same time. That's what he said. And, sure, I guess I can understand it. In a way, I can even sympathize. Who likes to work? I don't. But after he'd borrowed everything he could, everything in sight, including enough to finance a junior year in Germany, I had to begin sending him money, and a lot of it. When, finally, I said I couldn't send any more, he wrote back and said if that was the case, if that was really the way I felt, he was going to deal drugs or else rob a bank—whatever he had to do to get money to live on. I'd be lucky if he wasn't shot or sent to prison.

I wrote back and said I'd changed my mind and I could send him a little more after all. What else could I do? I didn't want his blood on my hands. I didn't want to think of my kid being packed off to prison, or something even worse. I had plenty on my conscience as it was.

That's four people, right? Not counting my brother, who wasn't a regular yet. I was going crazy with it. I worried night and day. I couldn't sleep over it. I was paying out nearly as much money every month as I was bringing in. You don't have to be a genius, or know anything about economics, to understand that this state of affairs couldn't keep on. I had to get a loan to keep up my end of things. That was another monthly payment.

So I started cutting back. I had to quit eating out, for instance. Since I lived alone, eating out was something I liked to do, but it became a thing of the past. And I had to watch myself when it came to thinking about movies. I couldn't buy clothes or get my teeth fixed. The car was falling apart. I needed new shoes, but forget it.

Once in a while I'd get fed up with it and write letters to all of them, threatening to change my name and telling them I was going to quit my job. I'd tell them I was planning a move to Australia. And the thing was, I was serious when I'd say that about Australia, even though I didn't know the first thing about Australia. I just knew it was on the other side of the world, and that's where I wanted to be.

But when it came right down to it, none of them really believed I'd go to Australia. They had me, and they knew it. They knew I was desperate, and they were sorry and they said so. But they counted on it all blowing over before the first of the month, when I had to sit down and make out the checks.

After one of my letters where I talked about moving to Australia, my mother wrote that she didn't want to be a burden any longer. Just as soon as the swelling went down in her legs, she said, she was going out to look for work. She was seventy-five years old, but maybe she could go back to waitressing, she said. I wrote her back and told her not to be silly. I said I was glad I could help her. And I was. I was glad I could help. I just needed to win the lottery.

My daughter knew Australia was just a way of saying to everybody that I'd had it. She knew I needed a break and something to cheer me up. So she wrote that she was going to leave her kids with somebody and take the cannery job when the season rolled around. She was young and strong, she said. She thought she could work the twelve-to-fourteen-hour-a-day shifts, seven days a week, no problem. She'd just have to tell herself she could do it, get herself psyched up for it, and her body would listen. She just had to line up the right kind of babysitter. That'd be the big thing. It was going to require a special kind of sitter, seeing as how the hours would be long and the kids were hyper to begin with, because of all the Popsicles and Tootsie Rolls, M&M's, and the like that they put away every day. It's the stuff kids like to eat, right? Anyway, she thought she could find the right person if she kept looking. But she had to buy the boots and clothes for the work, and that's where I could help.

My son wrote that he was sorry for his part in things and thought he and I would both be better off if he ended it once and for all. For one thing, he'd discovered he was allergic to cocaine. It made his eyes stream and affected his breathing, he said. This meant he couldn't test the drugs in the transactions he'd need to make. So, before it could even begin, his career as a drug dealer was over. No, he said, better a bullet in the temple and end it all right here. Or maybe hanging. That would save him the trouble of borrowing a gun. And save us the price of bullets. That's actually what he said in his letter, if you can believe it. He enclosed a picture of himself that somebody had taken last summer when he was in the study-abroad program in Germany. He was standing under a big tree with thick limbs hanging down a few feet over his head. In the picture, he wasn't smiling.

My former wife didn't have anything to say on the matter. She didn't have to. She knew she'd get her money the first of each month, even if it had to come all the way from Sydney. If she didn't get it, she just had to pick up the phone and call her lawyer.

This is where things stood when my brother called one Sunday afternoon in early May. I had the windows open, and a nice breeze moved through the house. The radio was playing. The hillside behind the house was in bloom. But I began to sweat when I heard his voice on the line. I hadn't heard from him since the dispute over the five hundred, so I couldn't believe he was going to try and touch me for more money now. But I began to sweat anyway. He asked how things stood with me, and I launched into the payroll thing and all. I talked about oatmeal, cocaine, fish canneries, suicide, bank jobs, and how I couldn't go to the movies or eat out. I said I had a hole in my shoe. I talked about the payments that went on and on to my former wife. He knew all about this, of course. He knew everything I was telling him. Still, he said he was sorry to hear it. I kept talking. It was his dime. But as he talked I started thinking, *How are you going to pay for this call, Billy?* Then it came to me that *I* was going to pay for it. It was only a matter of minutes, or seconds, until it was all decided.

I looked out the window. The sky was blue, with a few white clouds in it. Some birds clung to a telephone wire. I wiped my face on my sleeve. I didn't know what else I could say. So I suddenly stopped talking and just stared out the window at the mountains, and waited. And that's when my brother said, "I hate to ask you this, but—" When he said that, my heart did this sinking thing. And then he went ahead and asked.

This time it was a thousand. A thousand! He was worse off than when he'd called that other time. He let me have some details. The bill collectors were at the door—the door! he said—and the windows rattled, the house shook, when they hammered with their fists. *Blam, blam, blam,* he said. There was no place to hide from them. His house was about to be pulled out from under him. "Help me, brother," he said.

Where was I going to raise a thousand dollars? I took a good grip on the receiver, turned away from the window, and said, "But you didn't pay me back the last time you borrowed money. What about that?"

"I didn't?" he said, acting surprised. "I guess I thought I had. I wanted to, anyway. I tried to, so help me God."

"You were supposed to pay that money to Mom," I said. "But you didn't. I had to keep giving her money every month, same as always. There's no end to it, Billy. Listen, I take one step forward and I go two steps back. I'm going under. You're all going under, and you're pulling me down with you."

"I paid her *some* of it," he said. "I did pay her a little. Just for the record," he said, "I paid her something."

"She said you gave her fifty dollars and that was all."

"No," he said. "I gave her seventy-five. She forgot about the other twenty-five. I was over there one afternoon, and I gave her two tens and a five. I gave her some cash, and she just forgot about it. Her memory's going. Look," he said, "I promise I'll be good for it this time, I swear to God. Add up what I still owe you and add it to this money here I'm trying to borrow, and I'll send you a check. We'll exchange checks. Hold on to my check for two months, that's all I'm asking. I'll be out of the woods in two months' time. Then you'll have your money. July 1st, I promise, no later, and this time I *can* swear to it. We're in the process of selling this little piece of property that Irma Jean inherited a while back from her uncle. It's as good as sold. The deal has closed. It's just a question now of working out a couple of minor details and signing the papers. Plus, I've got this job lined up. It's definite. I'll have to drive fifty miles round trip every day, but that's no problem—hell, no. I'd drive a hundred and fifty if I had to, and be glad to do it. I'm saying I'll have money in the bank in two months' time. You'll get your money, all of it, by July 1st, and you can count on it."

"Billy, I love you," I said. "But I've got a load to carry. I'm carrying a very heavy load these days, in case you didn't know."

"That's why I won't let you down on this," he said. "You have my word of honor. You can trust me on this absolutely. I promise you my check will be good in two months, no later. Two months is all I'm asking for. Brother, I don't know where else to turn. You're my last hope."

I did it, sure. To my surprise, I still had some credit with the bank, so I borrowed the money, and I sent it to him. Our checks crossed in the mail. I stuck a thumbtack through his check and put it up on the kitchen wall next to the calendar and the picture of my son standing under that tree. And then I waited.

I kept waiting. My brother wrote and asked me not to cash the check on the day we'd agreed to. Please wait a while longer is what he said. Some things had come up. The job he'd been promised had fallen through at the last minute. That was one thing that came up. And that little piece of property belonging to his wife hadn't sold after all. At the last minute, she'd had a change of heart about selling it. It had been in her family for generations. What could he do? It was her land, and she wouldn't listen to reason, he said.

My daughter telephoned around this time to say that somebody had broken into her trailer and ripped her off. Everything in the trailer. Every stick of furniture was gone when she came home from work after her first night at the cannery. There wasn't even a chair left for her to sit down on. Her bed had been stolen, too. They were going to have to sleep on the floor like Gypsies, she said.

"Where was what's-his-name when this happened?" I said.

She said he'd been out looking for work earlier in the day. She guessed he was with friends. Actually, she didn't know his whereabouts at the time of the crime, or even right now, for that matter. "I hope he's at the bottom of the river," she said. The kids had been with the sitter when the ripoff happened. But, anyway, if she could just borrow enough from me to buy some secondhand furniture she'd pay me back, she said, when she got her first check. If she had some money from me before the end of the week—I could wire it, maybe—she could pick up some essentials. "Somebody's violated my space," she said. "I feel like I've been raped."

My son wrote from New Hampshire that it was essential he go back to Europe. His life hung in the balance, he said. He was graduating at the end of summer session, but he couldn't stand to live in America a day longer after that. This was a materialist society, and he simply couldn't take it anymore. People over here, in the U.S., couldn't hold a conversation unless *money* figured in it some way, and he was sick of it. He wasn't a Yuppie, and didn't want to become a Yuppie. That wasn't his thing. He'd get out of my hair, he said, if he could just borrow enough from me, this one last time, to buy a ticket to Germany.

I didn't hear anything from my former wife. I didn't have to. We both knew how things stood there.

My mother wrote that she was having to do without support hose and wasn't able to have her hair tinted. She'd thought this would be the year she could put some money back for the rainy days ahead, but it wasn't working out that way. She could see it wasn't in the cards. "How are you?" she wanted to know. "How's everybody else? I hope you're okay."

I put more checks in the mail. Then I held my breath and waited.

While I was waiting, I had this dream one night. Two dreams, really. I dreamt them on the same night. In the first dream, my dad was alive once more, and he was giving me a ride on his shoulders. I was this little kid, maybe five or six years old. *Get up here,* he said, and he took me by the hands and swung me onto his shoulders. I was high off the ground, but I wasn't afraid. He was holding on to me. We were holding on to each other. Then he began to move down the sidewalk. I brought my hands up from his shoulders and put them around his forehead. *Don't muss my hair,* he said. *You can let go,* he said, *I've got you. You won't fall.* When he said that, I became aware of the strong grip of his hands around my ankles. Then I did let go. I turned loose and held my arms out on either side of me. I kept them out there like that for balance. My dad went on walking while I rode on his shoulders. I pretended he was an elephant. I don't know where we were going. Maybe we were going to the store, or else to the park so he could push me in the swing.

I woke up then, got out of bed, and used the bathroom. It was starting to get light out, and it was only an hour or so until I had to get up. I thought about making coffee and getting dressed. But then I decided to go back to bed. I didn't plan to sleep, though. I thought I'd just lie there for a while with my hands behind my neck and watch it turn light out and maybe think about my dad a little, since I hadn't thought about him in a long time. He just wasn't part of my life any longer, waking or sleeping. Anyway, I got back in bed. But it couldn't have been more than a minute before I fell asleep once more, and when I did I got into this other dream. My former wife was in it, though she wasn't my former wife in the dream. She was still my wife. My kids were in it, too. They were little, and they were eating potato chips. In my dream, I thought I could smell the potato chips and hear them being eaten. We were on a blanket, and we were close to some water. There was a sense of satisfaction and well-being in the dream. Then, suddenly, I found myself in the company of some other people—people I didn't know—and the next thing that happened was that I was kicking the window out of my son's car and threatening his life, as I did once, a long time ago. He was inside the car as my shoe smashed through the glass. That's when my eyes flew open, and I woke up. The alarm was going off. I reached over and pushed the switch and lay there for a few minutes more, my heart racing. In the second dream, somebody had offered me some whiskey, and I drank it. Drinking that whiskey was the thing that scared me. That was the worst thing that could have happened. That was rock bottom. Compared to that, everything else was a picnic. I lay there for a minute longer, trying to calm down. Then I got up.

I made coffee and sat at the kitchen table in front of the window. I pushed my cup back and forth in little circles on the table and began to think seriously about Australia again. And then, all of a sudden, I could imagine how it must have sounded to my family when I'd threatened them with a move to Australia. They would have been shocked at first, and even a little scared. Then, because they knew me, they'd probably started laughing. Now, thinking about their laughter, I had to laugh, too. *Ha, ha, ha.* That was exactly the sound I made there at the table—*ha, ha, ha*—as if I'd read somewhere how to laugh.

What was it I planned to do in Australia, anyway? The truth was, I wouldn't be going there any more than I'd be going to Timbuktu, the moon, or the North Pole. Hell, I didn't want to go to Australia. But once I understood this, once I understood I wouldn't be going there—or anywhere else, for that matter—I began to feel better. I lit another cigarette and poured some more coffee. There wasn't any milk for the coffee, but I didn't care. I could skip having milk in my coffee for a day and it wouldn't kill me. Pretty soon I packed the lunch and filled the thermos and put the thermos in the lunch pail. Then I went outside.

It was a fine morning. The sun lay over the mountains behind the town, and a flock of birds was moving from one part of the valley to another. I didn't bother to lock the door. I remembered what had happened to my daughter, but decided I didn't have anything worth stealing anyway. There was nothing in the house I couldn't live without. I had the TV, but I was sick of watching TV. They'd be doing me a favor if they broke in and took it off my hands.

I felt pretty good, all things considered, and I decided to walk to work. It wasn't all that far, and I had time to spare. I'd save a little gas, sure, but that wasn't the main consideration. It was summer, after all, and before long summer would be over. Summer, I couldn't help thinking, had been the time everybody's luck had been going to change.

I started walking alongside the road, and it was then, for some reason, I began to think about my son. I wished him well, wherever he was. If he'd made it back to Germany by now—and he should have—I hoped he was happy. He hadn't written yet to give me his address, but I was sure I'd hear something before long. And my daughter, God love her and keep her. I hoped she was doing okay. I decided to write her a letter that evening and tell her I was rooting for her. My mother was alive and more or less in good health, and I felt lucky there, too. If all went well, I'd have her for several more years.

Birds were calling, and some cars passed me on the highway. Good luck to you, too, brother, I thought. I hope your ship comes in. Pay me back when you get it. And my former wife, the woman I used to love so much. She was alive, and she was well, too—so far as I knew, anyway. I wished her happiness. When all was said and done, I decided things could be a lot worse. Just now, of course, things were hard for everyone. People's luck had gone south on them was all. But things were bound to change soon. Things would pick up in the fall maybe. There was lots to hope for.

I kept on walking. Then I began to whistle. I felt I had the right to whistle if I wanted to. I let my arms swing as I walked. But the lunch pail kept throwing me off balance. I had sandwiches, an apple, and some cookies in there, not to mention the thermos. I stopped in front of Smitty's, an old café that had gravel in the parking area and boards over the windows. The place had been boarded up for as long as I could remember. I decided to put the lunch pail down for a minute. I did that, and then I raised my arms—raised them up level with my shoulders. I was standing there like that, like a goof, when somebody tooted a car horn and pulled off the highway into the parking area. I picked up my lunch pail and went over to the car. It was a guy I knew from work whose name was George. He reached over and opened the door on the passenger's side. "Hey, get in, buddy," he said.

"Hello, George," I said. I got in and shut the door, and the car sped off, throwing gravel from under the tires.

"I saw you," George said. "Yeah, I did, I saw you. You're in training for something, but I don't know what." He looked at me and then looked at the road again. He was going fast. "You always walk down the road with your arms out like that?" He laughed—*ha, ha, ha*—and stepped on the gas.

"Sometimes," I said. "It depends, I guess. Actually, I was standing," I said. I lit a cigarette and leaned back in the seat.

"So what's new?" George said. He put a cigar in his mouth, but he didn't light it.

"Nothing's new," I said. "What's new with you?"

George shrugged. Then he grinned. He was going very fast now. Wind buffeted the car and whistled by outside the windows. He was driving as if we were late for work. But we weren't late. We had lots of time, and I told him so.

Nevertheless, he cranked it up. We passed the turnoff

and kept going. We were moving by then, heading straight toward the mountains. He took the cigar out of his mouth and put it in his shirt pocket. "I borrowed some money and had this baby overhauled," he said. Then he said he wanted me to see something. He punched it and gave it everything he could. I fastened my seat belt and held on.

"*Go,*" I said. "What are you waiting for, George?" And that's when we really flew. Wind howled outside the windows. He had it floored, and we were going flat out. We streaked down that road in his big unpaid-for car.

ACKNOWLEDGMENTS

From *Free and Other Stories* by Theodore Dreiser. Copyright 1918 by Boni & Liverwright, Inc.; Copyright © 1945 by Theodore Dreiser. Reprinted by permission of the Dreiser Trust.

From *The Stories of John Cheever* by John Cheever. Copyright © 1953 by John Cheever. Reprinted by permission of Alfred A. Knopf, Inc.

From *Tell Me a Riddle* by Tillie Olsen. Copyright © 1956 by Tillie Olson. Reprinted by permission of Delacorte Press/ Seymour Lawrence. All rights reserved.

From *The Best of Simple* by Langston Hughes. Copyright © 1961 by Langston Hughes. Reprinted by permission of Hill and Wang, a division of Farrar, Straus & Giroux, Inc.

From *Bloodline* by Ernest J. Gaines. Copyright © 1963 by Ernest J. Gaines. Reprinted by permission of Doubleday, a division of Bantam, Doubleday, Dell Publishing Group, Inc.

From *Nights in the Gardens of Brooklyn* by Harvey Swados. Copyright © 1964 by Harvey Swados. Reprinted by permission of Viking Penguin, Inc.

"My Son the Murderer" by Bernard Malamud. Copyright, © 1968. Originally published in *Esquire*. Reprinted by permission of Russell & Volkening, Inc.

From *Shifting Landscape* by Henry Roth. Copyright © 1969 by Henry Roth. Permission granted by the Jewish Publication Society.

From *Rites of Passage* by Joanne Greenberg. Copyright © 1972 by Joanne Greenberg. Reprinted by permission of Henry Holt and Company, Inc.

From *Inventing the Abbotts* by Sue Miller. Copyright © 1987 by Sue Miller. Reprinted by permission of Harper & Row.

From *The Melting Pot* by Lynne Sharon Schwartz. Copyright © 1987 by Lynne Sharon Schwartz. Reprinted by permission of Harper & Row.

From *Trust Me* by John Updike. Copyright © 1987 by John Updike. Reprinted by permission of Alfred A. Knopf, Inc.

From *Where I'm Calling From* by Raymond Carver. Copyright © 1988 by Raymond Carver. Reprinted by permission of Atlantic Monthly Press.

American Families

28 Short Stories

EDITED AND WITH
AN INTRODUCTION BY

Barbara H. Solomon

A MENTOR BOOK

MENTOR
Published by the Penguin Group
Penguin Books USA Inc., 375 Hudson Street,
New York, New York 10014, U.S.A.
Penguin Books Ltd, 27 Wrights Lane,
London W8 5TZ, England
Penguin Books Australia Ltd, Ringwood,
Victoria, Australia
Penguin Books Canada Ltd, 10 Alcorn Avenue,
Toronto, Ontario, Canada M4V 3B2
Penguin Books (N.Z.) Ltd, 182–190 Wairau Road,
Auckland 10, New Zealand

Penguin Books Ltd, Registered Offices:
Harmondsworth, Middlesex, England

Published by Mentor, an imprint of Dutton Signet,
a division of Penguin Books USA Inc.

First Printing, November, 1989
11 10 9 8 7 6 5

Library of Congress Catalog Card Number: 89-62120

Printed in the United States of America

PUBLISHER'S NOTE
This is a work of fiction. Names, characters, places, and incidents either are the product of the author's imagination or are used fictitiously, and any resemblance to actual persons, living or dead, events, or locales is entirely coincidental.

This book is for
Jennifer, Nancy, and Stanley,
for THE FAMILY,
and
for Anna Thurer, who nurtured it

Contents

ACKNOWLEDGMENTS

I would like to express my appreciation to Professor Michael Palma for introducing me to the fiction of Marian Thurm and to Maryellen Fanelli, Iona College English major, for introducing me to the fiction of Roberta Silman. To Iona College, I am indebted for a Faculty Enrichment Grant which enabled me to do much of the research for this collection. At the College, a great deal of assistance was offered by Mary A. Bruno and the staff of the Secretarial Services Center: Patti Besen, Michelle Curry, Adrianna DiLello, Nancy Girardi, Teresa Martin, and Dorota Warren as well as the following Department of English student assistants: Mark Campisi, Jeanie Carstensen, Luisa Ferreira, and Eileen Moore.

Introduction

American short stories offer a very detailed and insightful history of American family life. They reflect our ideals of shared values and goals, of domestic comfort, of supportive relationships which are characterized by nurturing intimacy, and of economic interdependence. Even more interestingly, they depict our disillusionment with failed marriages, our disappointment with parent-child relationships which are difficult or which have soured, our dismay at the burdens which are sometimes imposed by family members, and our despair at the insensitivity with which relatives treat one another. Essentially they dramatize the disparity between the ideal family relationships we want to enjoy and strive to achieve and the imperfect and troubled relationships with which we are faced.

In viewing the stories as a social history, readers can see that a major change has occurred in the way American authors portray family life. Most often in nineteenth-century fiction, the enemies of familial happiness are external forces such as poverty or illness. In much twentieth-century fiction, however, particularly that of the last two decades, characters who critically examine their minor discontents, persistent unhappiness, or even anguish, are likely to discover that their problems stem from destructive relationships or patterns of behavior which are embedded in the fabric of their family life. As the emphasis within the fiction has shifted from a dramatization of external to internal conflicts during the past century, we can see that ideals about family values have not changed greatly, but that the priorities of these values depend upon historical or cultural circumstances, which do change.

Even a brief comparison of the lifestyles of the typical nineteenth-century American families with those in the second half of the twentieth century will demonstrate the gulf between the experience of the two. Many of the decisions faced by modern families were never matters of choice for a family in the 1890s. For example, a nineteenth-century family might live on a farm with each member contributing services to a tightly knit economic unit. Although the marriages of young people were only occasionally arranged by parents, marital choices were frequently and strongly influenced by familial pressures. Lacking birth-control methods, a young couple never expected to decide whether or not to have children or how many children they wished to have. The children regularly performed daily chores and looked to their parents as role models who would teach them the skills needed for adult success.

A farmer father would instruct his sons in the maintenance or repair of a house, a barn, or farm equipment, and in the selection and care of livestock as well as in actual farming. The mother would instruct her daughters in growing and preserving fruits and vegetables for family use, in cooking and baking, in the processing of milk and the making of butter and cheese, and in the sewing or knitting of a considerable portion of the family's wardrobe.

In the cities, turn-of-the-century lower- and middle-class families often rented rooms to immigrant or newly arrived workers to supplement the family income. The wives and children who worked at housekeeping and food preparation in such households contributed valuable services to enable the family to succeed.

Frequent religious and social celebrations augmented the family's shared economic bonds. Families attended church services together on the sabbath. During the evenings they often gathered to read biblical selections or fiction aloud. Increasingly, they celebrated Thanksgiving with a turkey, Christmas with a decorated tree, and birthdays with a birthday cake—all family "traditions" which at that time had only recently gained wide popularity.

Significantly, the family tradition which has grown steadily in the twentieth century has been the family reunion, the planned and well-organized gathering of family members, many of whom travel great distances to visit with relatives they rarely see or, perhaps, have never met before.

The somewhat idealized but typical stories of family life in the second half of the nineteenth century were intended to inculcate moral views in the reader. By and large, this fiction is based on the conviction that home life is essentially harmonious and that relatives are motivated by good will and a desire to be helpful. The stability and perpetuation of the family is a structure upon which the characters can depend.

The security and importance of family life are portrayed in Mary Wilkins Freeman's turn-of-the-century story "The Lombardy Poplar." It depicts two female cousins who greatly resemble each other in appearance, who share many attitudes and experiences, and who even have the same name. Clearly family solidarity has been at the core of the protagonist's entire life, but a dispute between the cousins brings some interesting insights to this woman. Family relationships that are too close may impede an individual's ability to develop an autonomous identity.

One note of change from the somewhat idealized nineteenth-century view of family harmony to the twentieth-century indictments against the pain of family life was sounded in 1893 with the appearance of Stephen Crane's novella *Maggie: A Girl of the Streets*. It depicted the New York ghetto existence of the Johnsons: violent and drunken parents who abuse their three battered and fearful children, Jimmy, Maggie, and Tommie. Crane traces Maggie's pathetic fate as the inevitable result of this degrading and destructive environment on a simple, good-hearted girl who lacks the special powers of imagination, strength, and intelligence needed to combat the overwhelming horrors of her family life.

The realistic twentieth-century stories of which Crane's tale was a precursor, however, do not concentrate on the sort of extreme situations which he chose to describe, although they often dramatize the failures of family life which are debilitating and destructive. In chronicling contemporary family experience, American authors reflect the enormous social changes of an urban, technological, and geographically mobile nation as they realistically depict familial conflicts and crises. At the very time when we crave a rich, satisfying family experience as an antidote to the stressful work situations often endured by adults in an indifferent—or even hostile—corporate world, family life seems fraught with its own series of stressful demands and demoralizing conflicts.

A number of significant changes have precipitated some of the current pressures on American families. First, the stigma historically associated with divorce has largely been replaced by a non-judgmental view; and revised legislation has made the process of getting a divorce—once difficult and costly—simpler and quicker. Perhaps Bobbie Ann Mason's "Old Things" is a quintessential story about changing attitudes toward marriage and divorce in the second half of the twentieth century. Cleo Watkins, a fifty-two-year-old widow, is dismayed when her daughter Linda leaves her husband and moves, with her children Tammy and Davey, into Cleo's small house. Fond of her son-in-law, Cleo can't understand Linda's complaints about her husband and tells her daughter, "These children need a daddy." She worries about how Linda, a cashier at a local K-Mart, will be able to support her children, who are extravagant and spoiled by Cleo's standards. During a discussion about a family friend, Cleo tells her daughter: "People can't just have everything they want, all the time." Linda's response is "But people don't have to do what they don't want to as much now as they used to." Cleo, who regularly watches TV talk shows featuring discussions of men as single parents, teenage alcoholism, and drug addiction, concludes that she "should know that," because "it's all over television."

Next, the higher divorce rate has resulted in a growing number of single-parent households. In Tillie Olsen's powerful story "I Stand Here Ironing," an impoverished single mother must make bitter decisions which cause her to feel powerless and inadequate. Then, too, the problems of child custody after a divorce are complex and wrenching. In "Starlight," Marian Thurm dramatizes the situation of Elaine, a mother who is about to be visited by her sons, aged nine and eleven, who had chosen to live with their father after the divorce which he had initiated.

> At first she had felt an overwhelming grief when the boys told her they preferred to live with their father; the humiliation had come later, along with a sudden cold anger. She got over her anger soon enough—how could you be angry at children who were too young to know they had hurt you?

Another result of divorce is the growing number of households in which a stepparent must help with the rearing of the spouse's children. Even brief visits may prove stressful as a divorced father or mother tries to maintain a loving relationship with a child who may have ambivalent feelings toward the parent who has severed the daily connection of family life and who has remarried. Ann Beattie captures much of this kind of strain in "Afloat," which describes the annual visit of an adolescent daughter from the perspective of the second wife, a woman painfully conscious of the fact that she can not have children.

Other relatives also have experienced severe dislocation as grandparents, uncles, aunts, and cousins have diminishing contact with children to whom they are related through the parent who has not received custody in a divorce. Conversely, there are step grandparents, step aunts and uncles, and step cousins who now find that there are members of the family whom they do not know very well and to whom they are not bonded by shared experiences.

Complicating these situations are other major changes. A considerable number of women with young children are now employed outside the home. Although much has been made of the increasing family responsibilities undertaken by men, women working outside the home frequently find themselves under considerable pressure to respond to the needs of children, husband, and parents while performing in demanding jobs or competitive careers. Greater geographic mobility has led to the separation from family members who might have supplied them with help in emergencies.

Another change of recent decades concerns the number of couples who now live together in relationships which may or may not lead to marriage. Their companions may be treated as potential family members, attending gatherings as participants or as outsiders whose presence offends other relatives.

A result of the longer lives enjoyed by Americans is that all of us must, at some time, expect to assume some responsibility for the actual care or supervision of care for aging parents. In "Tuesdays," Mary Hedin depicts the conflicting emotions typically experienced in these relationships as a middle-aged daughter pays a weekly visit to her elderly parents. Dismayed by their restricted circumstances and sorrowed by her mother's illness and deterioration, she pities them. But she is also irritated as she consumes the meal her father has prepared—the foods of the aged which she doesn't like or want—and then is forced to listen to his criticism of her adult son.

Increasingly we have become aware that building and maintaining good family relationships are not merely matters of being loving, of following our instincts, or of seeking advice from other family members. There are skills we need to learn in communicating our emotions or needs, in dealing with conflicts, or in attempting to get family members to modify behavior that is distasteful or hurtful.

For example, we have discovered that success in marriage often has little to do with the depth of the spouses' love for each other before marriage or with their sexual compatibility. Instead, a crucial factor seems to be the couple's ability to deal with incompatibility, that is, to resolve their disputes. Happily married couples are able to communicate, to talk over problems, to sense stress, and to share the events of their day. Some even seemed to have developed a "private language," a group of words or phrases with a special meaning for them. In "And

Sarah Laughed" by Joanne Greenberg, a farm wife of twenty-five years has experienced a terrible void in her life because her husband, Matthew, and all four of their sons are deaf. Again and again Sarah attempts to rationalize the qualms she has about her silent household:

> If she ever hungered for laughter from him or the little meaningless talk that confirms existence and affection, she told herself angrily that Matthew talked through his work. Words die in the air; they can be turned one way or another, but Matthew's work prayed and laughed for him.

Additionally, we have learned that loving parents—with all good intentions—will be inadequate parents if they have not learned how to channel their anger, how to criticize their children's behavior rather than attack their character, and how to create daily routines which provide an opportunity for shared experiences in which family members can discuss their feelings, describe their problems, be congratulated on their successes, or just generally sense the warmth and supportive atmosphere of home. When an older, unmarried woman, Aurélie, in Kate Chopin's "Regret," finds that she must temporarily care for her neighbor's four young children, she hasn't the faintest idea of the tasks which such a responsibility will entail. Fortunately, the children instruct her in the rituals which are necessary, for example, in putting them to bed. The baby, of course, must be sung to and rocked and a favorite bedtime story must be supplied.

As one might expect, the majority of stories in this collection are concerned with relationships between parents and children. The strains in these relationships may be comic ones, such as the tension created when a controlling father tries to give a bottle of hair conditioner to his visiting son in Stephen Wolf's "The Legacy of Beau Kremel," or tragic as when in Tillie Olsen's "I Stand Here Ironing," a mother regrets the ways in which she failed to fulfill the needs of one of her daughters. The strains between parent and child may be inevitable, as they are in Theodore Dreiser's "Old Rogaum and His Theresa" in which an immigrant father desperately attempts to maintain parental authority over his adolescent daughter, or as in Gloria Naylor's "Kiswana Browne," in which a twenty-three-year-old black activist daughter wants to impress her middle-class mother—whose values she scorns—with her own ability to lead an independent life away from home. The strains may be temporary, such as those occasioned by a nervous family's desire to be helpful on a special day in Roberta Silman's "Wedding Day," or, as in Henry Roth's "Final Dwarf," the strains will continually recur in every ordinary situation—such as an errand to the A&P—because the antagonism between a middle-aged son and his elderly father will never diminish.

Yet another tense relationship is depicted in Bernard Malamud's "My Son the Murderer," in which a bewildered and helpless father spies on his twenty-two-year-old, uncommunicative son who is about to be drafted. Leo, the father, feels he is living with a stranger and observes that the worst kind of worry is that in which "you can't get inside the other person and find out why. You don't know where's the switch to turn off. All you can do is worry more."

John Updike describes a very different situation in "Still of Some Use," as a divorced father returns to help his former wife and their two sons clear out the house which they once shared as a family. Both the father and his younger son experience an unexpected sense of loss as they discard the possessions which once knitted them together.

In two additional stories about fathers and sons, "The Writer in the Family" by E. L. Doctorow and "My Legacy" by Don Zacharia, an adult son reminisces about his father's character as well as his own boyhood experiences. As he recalls family relationships and activities, each son grows to understand and value more fully his father's dreams, needs, and distinctive identity. In another story, David Low's "Winterblossom Garden," told from the perspective of an adult son, the young man, a photographer, puzzles over the marriage of his father and mother which was arranged by relatives in China as well as about the alienation experienced by a Chinese-American family in the borough of Queens in New York.

A story from a mother's point of view, "What I Did for Love" by Lynne Sharon Schwartz, also chronicles family relationships over an extended period of time. Schwartz's story concerns urban parents—once political activists against the establishment—and their changing aspirations as they raise their young daughter.

In two stories concerning parents and adult children, Mary Gordon's "Violation" and Sue Miller's "Appropriate Affect," women who have been hurt or betrayed by a male family member have to deal with anger which does not subside with time. Although both women have chosen to protect other members of the family by concealing their experiences, and although both have led largely fulfilling lives, a family visit in Gordon's story revives a painful memory of the behavior of an uncle, and an illness in Miller's story releases the bitter recollection of a husband's infidelity.

"The Sorrows of Gin" by John Cheever and "The Sky Is Gray" by Ernest J. Gaines, two stories told from the perspective of a child, depict family problems in extremely different circumstances. The affluent but discontented Lawsons of Cheever's story live in the suburbs, where they hire a succession of unsatisfactory cooks who also function as babysitters for their daughter, Amy. The members of the black farm family in Gaines's story are struggling to survive while the father is away in the army and the oldest child, James, who is about eight, valiantly tries to be the "man of the family."

Matters of welcoming or rejecting family responsibility are at the center of many of the stories which follow, including three about the financial arrangements between parents and children or between brothers: Charlotte Perkins Gilman's "The Widow's Might," Raymond Carver's "Elephant," and Tobias Wolff's "The Rich Brother." In Gilman's tale, a son and two daughters—all married—are clearly reluctant to be inconvenienced by or contribute very much toward the support of their newly widowed mother. The wealthy son knows that his wife would not want his mother to live with them, but each of her daughters would share the "care and trouble" of having her live with them, only on the condition that their husbands would not have to pay for her food, clothing, or expenses. In Carver's story the narrator has been sending monthly checks to his mother, his former wife, his daughter and her children as well as to his college-aged son, when his brother loses his job and telephones to say that without a loan, he and his family will lose their house. In Wolff's story, the deeply felt tension between two adult brothers is exacerbated by the fact that one is highly successful, practical, and cynical while the other is penniless, inept, gullible, and idealistic. The drain on Pete, the rich brother, goes far beyond the temporary need to support his younger brother, Donald.

In two stories about more distant relations, a nephew and uncle in Harvey Swados's "My Coney Island Uncle," and about two cousins in Langston Hughes's "Simple and Cousin F. D. Roosevelt Brown," each adult welcomes the responsibility of temporarily looking after a younger relative and providing a kind of initiation to a wider world for the visiting boy.

When American writers hold up, in the mirror of their art, scenes of family solidarity, of loyalty, unselfishness, and understanding, they help us to focus on the intimate experiences we long to share with our own families. When they dramatize the disparity between the ideals we have and the realities of family behavior, they help us to understand the situations and character traits which lead to disappointment or failure. As they explore the changing nature of the American family, they remind us of the unchanged needs we all share and of the paradox of family life: it is simultaneously the source of so much frustration and pain as well as of such great comfort and pleasure.

—Barbara H. Solomon

Kate Chopin
(1851–1904)

In 1879, Chopin, her husband, Oscar, and five sons moved from New Orleans to Cloutierville, a small town in Louisiana where she gave birth to the last of her children, her daughter, Lelia. Occupied with family concerns, she had never written a single word for publication, and her literary career, which was to begin when she was thirty-eight years old, was still a decade away. After the death of Oscar, she returned to her native St. Louis, and several years later, in 1889, two of her stories and a poem appeared. The following year, her first novel, *At Fault,* was published, and within a short period of time she had established herself as a short story writer of national reputation. Most of her stories were collected in two volumes, *Bayou Folk* (1894) and *A Night in Acadie* (1897). Amid a storm of abuse from literary critics, her masterpiece, the novel *The Awakening,* was published in 1899.

REGRET

Mamzelle Aurélie possessed a good strong figure, ruddy cheeks, hair that was changing from brown to gray, and a determined eye. She wore a man's hat about the farm, and an old blue army overcoat when it was cold, and sometimes topboots.

Mamzelle Aurélie had never thought of marrying. She had never been in love. At the age of twenty she had received a proposal, which she had promptly declined, and at the age of fifty she had not yet lived to regret it.

So she was quite alone in the world, except for her dog Ponto, and the negroes who lived in her cabins and worked her crops, and the fowls, a few cows, a couple of mules, her gun (with which she shot chicken-hawks), and her religion.

One morning Mamzelle Aurélie stood upon her gallery, contemplating, with arms akimbo, a small band of very small children who, to all intents and purposes, might have fallen from the clouds, so unexpected and bewildering was their coming, and so unwelcome. They were the children of her nearest neighbor, Odile, who was not such a near neighbor, after all.

The young woman had appeared but five minutes before, accompanied by these four children. In her arms she carried little Elodie; she dragged Ti Nomme by an unwilling hand; while Marcéline and Marcélette followed with irresolute steps.

Her face was red and disfigured from tears and excitement. She had been summoned to a neighboring parish by the dangerous illness of her mother; her husband was away in Texas—it seemed to her a million miles away; and Valsin was waiting with the mule-cart to drive her to the station.

"It's no question, Mamzelle Aurélie; you jus' got to keep those youngsters fo' me tell I come back. Dieu sait,[1] I wouldn' botha you with 'em if it was any otha way to do! Make 'em mine you, Mamzelle Aurélie; don' spare 'em. Me, there, I'm half crazy between the chil'ren, an' Léon not home, an' maybe not even to fine po' maman alive encore!"—a harrowing possibility which drove Odile to take a final hasty and convulsive leave of her disconsolate family.

She left them crowded into the narrow strip of shade on the porch of the long, low house; the white sunlight was beating in on the white old boards; some chickens were scratching in the grass at the foot of the steps, and one had boldly mounted, and was stepping heavily, sol-

[1]God knows.

emnly, and aimlessly across the gallery. There was a pleasant odor of pinks in the air, and the sound of negroes' laughter was coming across the flowering cotton-field.

Mamzelle Aurélie stood contemplating the children. She looked with a critical eye upon Marcéline, who had been left staggering beneath the weight of the chubby Elodie. She surveyed with the same calculating air Marcélette mingling her silent tears with the audible grief and rebellion of Ti Nomme. During those few contemplative moments she was collecting herself, determining upon a line of action which should be identical with a line of duty. She began by feeding them

If Mamzelle Aurélie's responsibilities might have begun and ended there, they could easily have been dismissed; for her larder was amply provided against an emergency of this nature. But little children are not little pigs; they require and demand attentions which were wholly unexpected by Mamzelle Aurélie, and which she was ill prepared to give.

She was, indeed, very inapt in her management of Odile's children during the first few days. How could she know that Marcélette always wept when spoken to in a loud and commanding tone of voice? It was a peculiarity of Marcélette's. She became acquainted with Ti Nomme's passion for flowers only when he had plucked all the choicest gardenias and pinks for the apparent purpose of critically studying their botanical construction.

" 'Tain't enough to tell 'em, Mamzelle Aurélie," Marcéline instructed her; "you got to tie 'im in a chair. It's w'at maman all time do w'en he's bad: she tie 'im in a chair." The chair in which Mamzelle Aurélie tied Ti Nomme was roomy and comfortable, and he seized the opportunity to take a nap in it, the afternoon being warm.

At night, when she ordered them one and all to bed as she would have shooed the chickens into the hen-house, they stayed uncomprehending before her. What about the little white nightgowns that had to be taken from the pillow-slip in which they were brought over, and shaken by some strong hand till they snapped like ox-whips? What about the tub of water which had to be brought and set in the middle of the floor, in which the little tired, dusty, sunbrowned feet had every one to be washed sweet and clean? And it made Marcéline and Marcélette laugh merrily—the idea that Mamzelle Aurélie should for a moment have believed that Ti Nomme could fall asleep without being told the story of *Croquemitaine*[2] or *Loup-garou,*[3] or both; or that Elodie could fall asleep at all without being rocked and sung to.

"I tell you, Aunt Ruby," Mamzelle Aurélie informed her cook in confidence; "me, I'd rather manage a dozen plantation' than fo' chil'ren. It's terrassent! Bonté![4] Don't talk to me about chil'ren!"

" 'Tain' ispected sich as you would know airy thing 'bout 'em, Mamzelle Aurélie. I see dat plainly yistiddy w'en I spy dat li'le chile playin' wid yo' baskit o' keys. You don' know dat makes chillun grow up hard-headed, to play wid keys? Des like it make 'em teeth hard to look in a lookin'-glass. Them's the things you got to know in the raisin' an' manigement o' chillun."

Mamzelle Aurélie certainly did not pretend or aspire to such subtle and far-reaching knowledge on the subject as Aunt Ruby possessed, who had "raised five an' bared (buried) six" in her day. She was glad enough to learn a few little mother-tricks to serve the moment's need.

Ti Nomme's sticky fingers compelled her to unearth white aprons that she had not worn for years, and she had to accustom herself to his moist kisses—the expressions of an affectionate and exuberant nature. She got down her sewing-basket, which she seldom used, from the top shelf of the armoire, and placed it within the ready and easy reach which torn slips and buttonless waists demanded. It took her some days to become accustomed to the laughing and crying, the chattering that echoed through the house and around it all day long. And it was not the first or the second night that she could sleep comfortably with little Elodie's hot, plump body pressed close against her, and the little one's warm breath beating her cheek like the fanning of a bird's wing.

[2]The "Bogeyman."
[3]The "Werewolf."
[4]"It's exhausting! Goodness."

But at the end of two weeks Mamzelle Aurélie had grown quite used to these things, and she no longer complained.

It was also at the end of two weeks that Mamzelle Aurélie, one evening, looking away toward the crib where the cattle were being fed, saw Valsin's blue cart turning the bend of the road. Odile sat beside the mulatto, upright and alert. As they drew near, the young woman's beaming face indicated that her homecoming was a happy one.

But this coming, unannounced and unexpected, threw Mamzelle Aurélie into a flutter that was almost agitation. The children had to be gathered. Where was Ti Nomme? Yonder in the shed, putting an edge on his knife at the grindstone. And Marcéline and Marcélette? Cutting and fashioning doll-rags in the corner of the gallery. As for Elodie, she was safe enough in Mamzelle Aurélie's arms; and she had screamed with delight at sight of the familiar blue cart which was bringing her mother back to her.

The excitement was all over, and they were gone. How still it was when they were gone! Mamzelle Aurélie stood upon the gallery, looking and listening. She could no longer see the cart; the red sunset and the blue-gray twilight had together flung a purple mist across the fields and road that hid it from her view. She could no longer hear the wheezing and creaking of its wheels. But she could still faintly hear the shrill, glad voices of the children.

She turned into the house. There was much work awaiting her, for the children had left a sad disorder behind them; but she did not at once set about the task of righting it. Mamzelle Aurélie seated herself beside the table. She gave one slow glance through the room, into which the evening shadows were creeping and deepening around her solitary figure. She let her head fall down upon her bended arm, and began to cry. Oh, but she cried! Not softly, as women often do. She cried like a man, with sobs that seemed to tear her very soul. She did not notice Ponto licking her hand.

Mary Wilkins Freeman
(1852–1930)

At the age of thirty, Mary Wilkins Freeman succeeded in selling two adult stories to magazines after almost a decade of failing to publish her work, which included numerous children's poems and stories. During the next two decades she wrote prolifically and successfully, drawing on small New England towns as the background for her depictions of the lives of varied women characters. Among the almost forty volumes of her published work are the novels *Jane Field* (1893), *Pembroke* (1894), and *The Shoulders of Atlas* (1908), as well as collections of her short stories: *A Humble Romance and Other Stories* (1887), *A New England Nun and Other Stories* (1891), and *Six Trees* (1903). In 1908 she participated in an unusual joint fiction-writing project with authors such as William Dean Howells and Henry James, which resulted in the publication of *The Whole Family: A Novel by Twelve Authors.*

THE LOMBARDY POPLAR

There had been five in the family of the Lombardy poplar. Formerly he had stood before the Dunn house in a lusty row of three brothers and a mighty father, from whose strong roots, extending far under the soil, they had all sprung.

Now they were all gone, except this one, the last of the sons of the tree. He alone remained, faithful as a sentinel before the onslaught of winter storms and summer suns; he yielded to neither. He was head and shoulders above the other trees—the cherry and horse-chestnuts in the square front yard behind him. Higher than the house, piercing the blue with his broad truncate of green, he stood silent, stiff, and immovable. He seldom made any sound with his closely massed foliage, and it required a mighty and concentrated gust of wind to sway him ever so little from his straight perpendicular.

As the tree was the last of his immediate family, so the woman who lived in the house was the last of hers. Sarah Dunn was the only survivor of a large family. No fewer than nine children had been born to her parents; now father, mother, and eight children were all dead, and this elderly woman was left alone in the old house. Consumption had been in the Dunn family. The last who had succumbed to it was Sarah's twin-sister Marah, and she had lived until both had gray hair.

After that last funeral, where she was the solitary real mourner, there being only distant relatives of the Dunn name, Sarah closed all the house except a few rooms, and resigned herself to living out her colorless life alone. She seldom went into any other house; she had few visitors, with the exception of one woman. She was a second cousin, of the same name, being also Sarah Dunn. She came regularly on Thursday afternoons, stayed to tea, and went to the evening prayer-meeting. Besides the sameness of name, there was a remarkable resemblance in personal appearance between the two women. They were of about the same age; they both had gray-blond hair, which was very thin, and strained painfully back from the ears and necks into tiny rosettes at the backs of their heads, below little, black lace caps trimmed with bows of purple ribbon. The cousin Sarah had not worn the black lace cap until the other Sarah's twin-sister Marah had died. Then all the dead woman's wardrobe had been given to her, since she was needy. Sarah and her twin had always dressed alike, and there were many in the village who never until the day of her death had been able to distinguish Marah from Sarah. They were alike not only in appearance, but in character. The resemblance was so absolute as to produce a feeling of something at fault in the beholder. It was difficult, when looking from one to the other, to believe that the second was a vital fact; it was like seeing double. After Marah was dead it was the same with the cousin, Sarah Dunn. The clothes of the deceased twin completed all that had been necessary to make the resemblance perfect. There was in the whole Dunn family a curious endurance of characteristics. It was said in the village that you could tell a Dunn if you met him at the ends of the earth. They were all described as little, and sloping-shouldered, and peak-chinned, and sharp-nosed, and light-livered. Sarah and Cousin Sarah were all these. The family tricks of color and form and feature were represented to their fullest extent in both. People said that they were Dunns from the soles of their feet to the crowns of their heads. They did not even use plurals in dealing with them. When they set out together for evening meeting in the summer twilight, both moving with the same gentle, mincing step, the same slight sway of shoulders, draped precisely alike with little, knitted, white wool shawls, the same deprecating cant of heads, identically bonneted, as if they were perpetually avoiding some low-hanging bough of life in their way of progress, the neighbors said, "There's Sarah Dunn goin' to meetin'."

When the twin was alive it was, "There's Sarah and Marah goin' to meetin'." Even the very similar names had served as a slight distinction, as formerly the different dress of the cousins had made it easier to distinguish between them. Now there was no difference between the outward charactertistics of the two Sarah Dunns, even to a close observer. Name, appearance, dress, all were identical. And the minds of the two seemed to partake of this similarity. Their conversation consisted mainly of a peaceful monotony of agreement. "For the Lord's sake, Sarah Dunn, 'ain't you got any mind of your own?" cried a neighbor of an energetic and independent turn, once when she had run in of a Thursday afternoon when the cousin was there. Sarah looked at the cousin before replying, and the two minds seemed to cogitate the problem through the medium of mild, pale eyes, set alike under faint levels of eyebrow. "For the Lord's sake, if you ain't lookin' at each other to find out!" cried the neighbor, with a high sniff, while the two other women stared at each other in a vain effort to understand.

The twin had been dead five years, and the cousin had come every Thursday afternoon to see Sarah before any point of difference in their mental attitudes was evident. They regarded the weather with identical emotions, they relished the same food, they felt the same degree of heat or cold, they had the same likes and dislikes for other people, but at last there came a disagreement. It was on a Thursday in summer, when the heat was intense. The cousin had come along the dusty road between the white-powdered weeds and flowers, holding above her head an umbrella small and ancient, covered with faded green silk, which had belonged to Marah, wearing an old purple muslin of the dead woman's, and her black lace mitts. Sarah was at home, rocking in the south parlor window, dressed in the mate to the purple muslin, fanning herself with a small black fan edged with feathers which gave out a curious odor of mouldy roses.

When the cousin entered, she laid aside her bonnet and mitts, and seated herself opposite Sarah, and fanned herself with the mate to the fan.

"It is dreadful warm," said the cousin.

"Dreadful!" said Sarah.

"Seems too me it 'ain't been so warm since that hot Sabbath the summer after Marah died," said the cousin, with gentle reminiscence.

"Just what I was thinking," said Sarah.

"An' it's dusty too, just as it was then."

"Yes, it was dreadful dusty then. I got my black silk so full of dust it was just about ruined, goin' to meetin' that Sabbath," said Sarah.

"An' I was dreadful afraid I had sp'ilt Marah's, an' she always kept it so nice."

"Yes, she had always kept it dreadful nice," assented Sarah.

"Yes, she had. I 'most wished, when I got home that afternoon, and saw how dusty it was, that she'd kept it and been laid away in it, instead of my havin' it, but I knew she'd said to wear it, and get the good of it, and never mind."

"Yes, she would."

"And I got the dust all off it with a piece of her old black velvet bunnit," said the cousin, with mild deprecation.

"That's they way I got the dust off mine, with a piece of my old black velvet bunnit," said Sarah.

"It's better than anything else to take the dust off black silk."

"Yes, 'tis."

"I saw Mis' Andrew Dunn as I was comin' past," said the cousin.

"I saw her this mornin' down to the store," said Sarah.

"I thought she looked kind of pindlin', and she coughed some."

"She did when I saw her. I thought she looked real miserable. Shouldn't wonder if she was goin' in the same way as the others."

"Just what I think."

"It was funny we didn't get the consumption, ain't it, when all our folks died with it?"

"Yes, it is funny."

"I s'pose we wa'n't the kind to."

"Yes, I s'pose so."

Then the two women swayed peacefully back and forth in their rocking-chairs, and fluttered their fans gently before their calm faces.

"It is too hot to sew to-day," remarked Sarah Dunn.

"Yes, it is," assented her cousin.

"I thought I wouldn't bake biscuit for supper, long as it was so dreadful hot."

"I was hopin' you wouldn't. It's too hot for hot biscuit. They kind of go against you."

"That's what I said. Says I, now I ain't goin' to heat up the house bakin' hot bread to-night. I know she won't want me to."

"No, you was just right. I don't."

"Says I, I've got some good cold bread and butter, and blackberries that I bought of the little Whitcomb boy this mornin', and a nice custard-pie, and two kinds of cake besides cookies, and I guess that'll do."

"That's just what I should have picked out for supper."

"And I thought we'd have it early, so as to get it cleared away, and take our time walkin' to meetin', it's so dreadful hot."

"Yes, it's a good idea."

"I s'pose there won't be so many to meetin', it's so hot," said Sarah.

"Yes, I s'pose so."

"It's queer folks can stay away from meetin' on account of the weather."

"It don't mean much to them that do," said the cousin, with pious rancor.

"That's so," said Sarah. "I guess it don't. I guess it ain't the comfort to them that it is to me. I guess if some of them had lost as many folks as I have they'd go whether 'twas hot or cold."

"I guess they would. They don't know much about it."

Sarah gazed sadly and reflectively out of the window at the deep yard, with its front gravel walk bordered with wilting pinks and sprawling peonies, its horse-chestnut and cherry trees, and its solitary Lombardy poplar set in advance, straight and stiff as a sentinel of summer. "Speakin' of losin' folks," she said, "you 'ain't any idea what a blessin' that popple-tree out there has been to me, especially since Marah died."

Then, for the first time, the cousin stopped waving her fan in unison, and the shadow of a different opinion darkened her face. "That popple-tree?" she said, with harsh inquiry.

"Yes, that popple-tree." Sarah continued gazing at the tree, standing in majestic isolation, with its long streak of shadow athwart the grass.

The cousin looked, too; then she turned towards Sarah with a frown of puzzled dissent verging on irritability and scorn. "That popple-tree! Land! How do you talk!" said she. "What sort of blessin' can an old tree be when your folks are gone, Sarah Dunn?"

Sarah faced her with stout affirmation: "I've seen that popple there ever since I can remember, and it's all I've got left that's anyways alive, and it seems like my own folks, and I can't help it."

The cousin sniffed audibly. She resumed fanning herself, with violent jerks. "Well," said she, "if you can feel as if an old popple-tree made up to you, in any fashion, for the loss of your own folks, and if you can feel as if it was them, all I've got to say is, I can't."

"I'm thankful I can," said Sarah Dunn.

"Well, I can't. It seems to me as if it was almost sacrilegious."

"I can't help how it seems to you." There was a flush of nervous indignation on Sarah Dunn's pale, flaccid cheeks; her voice rang sharp. The resemblance between the two faces, which had in reality been more marked in expression, as evincing a perfect accord of mental action, than in feature, had almost disappeared.

"An old popple-tree!" said the cousin, with a fury of sarcasm. "If it had been any other tree than a popple, it wouldn't strike anybody as quite so bad. I've always thought a popple was about the homeliest tree that grows. Much as ever as it does grow. It just stays, stiff and pointed, as if it was goin' to make a hole in the sky; don't give no shade worth anything; don't seem to have much to do with the earth and folks, anyhow. I was thankful when I got mine cut down. Them three that was in front of our house were always an eyesore to me, and I talked till I got father to cut them down. I always wondered why you hung on to this one so."

"I wouldn't have that popple-tree cut down for a hundred dollars," declared Sarah Dunn. She had closed her fan, and she held it up straight like a weapon.

"My land! Well, if I was goin' to make such a fuss over a tree I'd have taken something different from a popple. I'd have taken a pretty elm or a maple. They look something like trees. This don't look like anything on earth besides itself. It ain't a tree. It's a stick tryin' to look like one."

"That's why I like it," replied Sarah Dunn, with a high lift of her head. She gave a look of sharp resentment at her cousin. Then she gazed at the tree again, and her whole face changed indescribably. She seemed like another person. The tree seemed to cast a shadow of likeness over her. She appeared straighter, taller; all her lines of meek yielding, or scarcely even anything so strong as yielding, of utter passiveness, vanished. She looked stiff and uncompromising. Her mouth was firm, her chin high, her eyes steady, and, more than all, there was over her an expression of individuality which had not been there before. "That's why I like the popple," she said, in an incisive voice. "That's just why. I'm sick of things and folks that are just like everything and everybody else. I'm sick of trees that are just trees. I like one that ain't."

"My land!" ejaculated the cousin, in a tone of contempt not unmixed with timidity. She stared at the other woman with shrinking and aversion in her pale-blue eyes. "What has come over you, Sarah Dunn?" said she, at last, with a feeble attempt to assert herself.

"Nothin' has come over me. I always felt that way about that popple."

"Marah wa'n't such a fool about that old popple."

"No, she wa'n't, but maybe she would have been if I had been taken first instead of her. Everybody has got to have something to lean on."

"Well, I 'ain't got anything any more than you have, but I can stand up straight without an old popple."

"You 'ain't no call to talk that way," said Sarah.

"I hate to hear folks that I've always thought had common-sense talk like fools," said the cousin, with growing courage.

"If you don't like to hear me talk, it's always easy enough to get out of hearin' distance."

"I'd like to know what you mean by that, Sarah Dunn."

"I mean it just as you want to take it."

"Maybe you mean that my room is better than my company."

"Just as you are a mind to take it."

The cousin sat indeterminately for a few minutes. She thought of the bread and the blackberries, the pie and the two kinds of cake.

"What on earth do you mean goin' on so queer?" said she, in a hesitating and somewhat conciliatory voice.

"I mean just what I said. That tree is a blessin' to me, it's company, and I think it's the handsomest tree anywheres around. That's what I meant, and if you want to take me up for it, you can."

The cousin hesitated. She further reflected that she had in her solitary house no bread at all; she had not baked for two days. She would have to make a fire and bake biscuits in all that burning heat, and she had no cake nor berries. In fact, there was nothing whatever in her larder, except two cold potatoes, and a summer-squash pie, which she suspected was sour. She wanted to bury the hatchet, she wanted to stay, but her slow blood was up. All her strength of character lay in inertia. One inertia of acquiescence was over, the other of dissent was triumphant. She could scarcely yield for all the bread and blackberries and cake. She shut up her fan with a clap.

"That fan was Marah's," said Sarah, meaningly, with a glance of reproach and indignation.

"I know it was Marah's," returned the cousin, rising with a jerk. "I know it was Marah's. 'Most everything I've got was hers, and I know that too. I ought to know it; I've been twitted about it times enough. If you think I ain't careful enough with her things, you can take them back again. If presents ain't mine after they've been give me, I don't want 'em."

The cousin went out of the room with a flounce of her purple muslin skirts. She passed into Sarah's little room where her cape and bonnet lay carefully placed on the snowy hill of the feather bed. She put them on, snatched up her green silk parasol, and passed through the sitting-room to the front entry.

"If you are a mind to go off mad, for such a thing as that, you can," said Sarah, rocking violently.

"You can feel just the way you want to," returned the cousin, with a sniff, "but you can't expect anybody with a mite of common-sense to fall in with such crazy ideas." She was out of the room and the house then with a switch, and speeding down the road with the green parasol bobbing overhead.

Sarah gave a sigh; she stared after her cousin's retreating form, then at the poplar-tree, and nodded as in confirmation of some resolution within her own mind. Presently she got up, looked on the table, then on the bed and bureau in the bedroom. The cousin had taken the fan.

Sarah returned to her chair, and sat fanning herself absent-mindedly. She gazed out at the yard and the poplar-tree. She had not resumed her wonted expression; the shadow of the stately, concentrated tree seemed still over her. She held her faded blond head stiff and high, her pale-blue eyes were steady, her chin firm above the lace ruffle at her throat. But there was sorrow in her heart. She was a creature of as strong race-ties as the tree. All her kin were dear to her, and the cousin had been the dearest after the death of her sister. She felt as if part of herself had been cut away, leaving a bitter ache of vacancy, and yet a proud self-sufficiency was over her. She could exist and hold her head high in the world without her kindred, as well as the poplar. When it was teatime she did not stir. She forgot. She did not rouse herself until the meeting-bell began to ring. Then she rose hurriedly, put on her bonnet and cape, and hastened down the road. When she came in sight of the church, with its open vestry windows, whence floated already singing voices, for she was somewhat late, she saw the cousin coming from the opposite direction. The two met at the vestry door, but neither spoke. They entered side by side; Sarah seated herself, and the cousin passed to the seat in front of her. The congregation, who were singing "Sweet Hour of Prayer," stared. There was quite a general turning of heads. Everybody seemed to notice that Sarah Dunn and her cousin Sarah Dunn were sitting in separate settees. Sarah opened her hymn-book and held it before her face. The cousin sang in a shrill tremolo. Sarah hesitated a moment, then she struck in and sang louder. Her voice was truer and better. Both had sung in the choir when young.

The singing ceased. The minister, who was old, offered prayer, and then requested a brother to make remarks, then another to offer prayer. Prayer and remarks alike were made in a low, inarticulate drone. Above it sounded the rustle of the trees outside in a rising wind, and the shrill reiteration of the locusts invisible in their tumult of sound. Sarah Dunn, sitting fanning, listening, yet scarcely comprehending the human speech any more than she comprehended the voices of the summer night outside, kept her eyes fastened on the straining surface of gray hair surmounted by the tiny black triangle of her cousin's bonnet. Now and then she gazed instead at the narrow black shoulders beneath. There was something rather pitiful as well as uncompromising about those narrow shoulders, suggesting as they did the narrowness of the life-path through which they moved, and also the stiff-neckedness in petty ends, if any, of their owner; but Sarah did not comprehend that. They were for her simply her cousin's shoulders, the cousin who had taken exception to her small assertion of her own individuality, and they bore for her an expression of arbitrary criticism as marked as if they had been the cousin's face. She felt an animosity distinctly vindictive towards the shoulders; she had an impulse to push and crowd in her own. The cousin sat fanning herself quite violently. Presently a short lock of hair on Sarah's forehead became disengaged from the rest, and blew wildly in the wind from the fan. Sarah put it back with an impatient motion, but it flew out again. Then Sarah shut up her own fan, and sat in stern resignation, holding to the recreant lock of hair to keep it in place, while the wind from the cousin's fan continued to smite her in the face. Sarah did not fan herself until the cousin laid down her fan for a moment, then she resumed hers with an angry sigh. When the cousin opened her fan again, Sarah dropped hers in her lap, and sat with one hand pressed against her hair, with an expression of bitter long-suffering drawing down the corners of her mouth.

After the service was over Sarah rose promptly and went out, almost crowding before the others in her effort to gain the door before her cousin. The cousin did the same; thus each defeated her own ends, and the two passed through the door shoulder to shoulder. Once out in the night air, they separated speedily, and each went her way to her solitary home.

Sarah, when she reached her house, stopped beside the poplar-tree and stood gazing up at its shaft of solitary vernal majesty. Its outlines were softened in the dim light. Sarah thought of the "pillar of cloud" in the Old Testament. As she gazed the feeling of righteous and justified indignation against the other Sarah Dunn grew and strengthened. She looked at the Lombardy poplar, one of a large race of trees, all with similar characteristics which determined kinship, yet there was this tree as separate and marked among its kind as if of another name and family. She could see from where she stood the pale tremulousness of a silver poplar in the corner of the next yard. "Them trees is both poplars," she reflected, "but each of 'em is its own tree." Then she reasoned by analogy. "There ain't any reason why if Sarah Dunn and I are both Dunns, and look alike, we should be just alike." She shook her head fiercely. "I ain't goin' to be Sarah Dunn, and she needn't try to make me," said she, quite aloud. Then she went into the house, and left the Lombardy poplar alone in the dark summer night.

It was not long before people began to talk about the quarrel between the two Sarah Dunns. Sarah Dunn proper said nothing, but the cousin told her story right and left; how Sarah had talked as if she didn't have common-sense, putting an old, stiff popple-tree on a par with the folks she'd lost, and she, the cousin, had told her she didn't have common-sense, and then Sarah had ordered her out of her house, and wouldn't speak to her comin' out of meetin'. People began to look askance at Sarah Dunn, but she was quite unaware of it. She had formed her own plan of action, and was engaged in carrying it out. The day succeeding that of the dispute with the cousin was the hottest of a hot trio, memorable long after in that vicinity, but Sarah dressed herself in one of her cool old muslins, took her parasol and fan, and started to walk to Atkins, five miles distant, where all the stores were. She had to pass the cousin's house. The cousin, peering between the slats of a blind in the sitting-room, watched her pass, and wondered with angry curiosity where she could be going. She watched all the forenoon for her to return, but it was high noon before Sarah came in sight. She was walking at a good pace, her face was composed and unflushed. She held her head high, and walked past, her starched white petticoat rattling and her purple muslin held up daintily in front, but trailing in the back in a cloud of dust. Her white-stockinged ankles and black cloth shoes were quite visible as she advanced, stepping swiftly and precisely. She had a number of large parcels pressed closely to her sides under her arms and dangling by the strings from her hands. The cousin wondered unhappily what she had bought in Atkins. Sarah, passing, knew that she wondered, and was filled with childish triumph and delight. "I'd like to know what she'd say if she knew what I'd got," she said to herself.

The next morning the neighbors saw Annie Doane, who went out dressmaking by the day, enter Sarah Dunn's yard with her bag of patterns. It was the first time for years that she had been seen to enter there, for Sarah and Marah had worn their clothes with delicate care, and they had seldom needed replenishing, since the fashions had been ignored by them.

The neighbors wondered. They lay in wait for Annie Doane on her way home that night, but she was very close. They discovered nothing, and could not even guess with the wildest imagination what Sarah Dunn was having made. But the next Sunday a shimmer of red silk and a toss of pink flowers were seen at the Dunn gate, and Sarah Dunn, clad in a gown of dark-red silk and a bonnet tufted with pink roses, holding aloft a red parasol, passed down the street to meeting. No Dunn had ever worn, within the memory of man, any colors save purple and black and faded green or drab, never any but purple or white or black flowers in her bonnet. No woman of half her years, and seldom a young girl, was ever seen in the village clad in red. Even the old minister hesitated a second in his discourse, and recovered himself with a hem of embarrassment when Sarah entered the meeting-house. She had waited until the sermon was begun before she sailed up the aisle. There were many of her name in the church. The pale, small, delicate faces in the neutral-colored bonnets stared at her as if a bird of another feather had gotten into their nest; but the cousin, who sat across the aisle from Sarah, caught her breath with an audible gasp.

After the service Sarah Dunn walked with her down the aisle, pressing close to her side. "Good-mornin'," said she, affably. The cousin in Marah's old black silk, which was matched by the one which Sarah would naturally have worn that Sunday, looked at her, and said, feebly, "Good-mornin'." There seemed no likeness whatever between the two women as they went down the aisle. Sarah was a Dunn apart. She held up her dress as she had seen young girls, drawing it tightly over her back and hips, elevating it on one side.

When they emerged from the meeting-house, Sarah spoke. "I should be happy to have you come over and spend the day to-morrow," she said, "and have a chicken dinner. I'm goin' to have the Plymouth Rock crower killed. I've got too many crowers. He'll weigh near five pounds, and I'm goin' to roast him."

"I'll be happy to come," replied the cousin, feebly. She was vanquished.

"And I'm goin' to give you my clothes like Marah's," said Sarah, calmly. "I'm goin' to dress different."

"Thank you," said the cousin.

"I'll have dinner ready about twelve. I want it early, so as to get it out of the way," said Sarah.

"I'll be there in time," said the cousin.

Then they went their ways. Sarah, when she reached home, paused at the front gate, and stood gazing up at the poplar. Then she nodded affirmatively and entered the house, and the door closed after her in her red silk dress. And the Lombardy poplar-tree stood in its green majesty before the house, and its shadow lengthened athwart the yard to the very walls.

Charlotte Perkins Gilman
(1860–1935)

Divorced from her first husband, Charles Stetson, at the age of thirty, Charlotte Perkins Gilman moved to California, where she supported herself by lecturing on the status of women and on socialism, teaching school, running a boarding house, editing newspapers, and writing. Among her works on social and feminist issues are *Women and Economics* (1898), *Concerning Children* (1900), *Human Work* (1904), and *The Man-made World; or Our Androcentric Culture* (1911). Among her novels are: *The Crux* (1911) and *What Diantha Did* (1912), as well as three feminist, Utopian works, *Moving the Mountain* (1911), *Herland* (1915), and *With Her in Ourland* (1916). *The Living of Charlotte Perkins Gilman,* her autobiography, was published in 1935. Terminally and painfully ill with cancer, she chose to end her own life.

THE WIDOW'S MIGHT

James had come on to the funeral, but his wife had not; she could not leave the children—that is what he said. She said, privately, to him, that she would not go. She never was willing to leave New York except for Europe or for summer vacations; and a trip to Denver in November—to attend a funeral—was not a possibility to her mind.

Ellen and Adelaide were both there: they felt it a duty—but neither of their husbands had come. Mr. Jennings could not leave his classes in Cambridge, and Mr. Oswald could not leave his business in Pittsburgh—that is what they said.

The last services were over. They had had a cold, melancholy lunch and were all to take the night train home again. Meanwhile, the lawyer was coming at four to read the will.

"It is only a formality. There can't be much left," said James.

"No," agreed Adelaide, "I suppose not."

"A long illness eats up everything," said Ellen, and sighed. Her husband had come to Colorado for his lungs years before and was still delicate.

"Well," said James rather abruptly, "what are we going to do with Mother?"

"Why, of course—" Ellen began, "we *could* take her. It would depend a good deal on how much property there is—I mean, on where she'd want to go. Edward's salary is more than needed now." Ellen's mental processes seemed a little mixed.

"She can come to see me if she prefers, of course," said Adelaide. "But I don't think it would be very pleasant for her. Mother never did like Pittsburgh."

James looked from one to the other.

"Let me see—how old is Mother?"

"Oh she's all of fifty," answered Ellen, "and much broken, I think. It's been a long strain, you know." She turned plaintively to her brother. "I should think you could make her more comfortable than either of us, James—with your big house."

"I think a woman is always happier living with a son than with a daughter's husband," said Adelaide. "I've always thought so."

"That is often true," her brother admitted. "But it depends." He stopped, and the sisters exchanged glances. They knew upon what it depended.

"Perhaps if she stayed with me, you could—help some," suggested Ellen.

"Of course, of course, I could do that," he agreed with evident relief. "She might visit between you—take turns—

and I could pay her board. About how much ought it to amount to? We might as well arrange everything now."

"Things cost awfully in these days," Ellen said with a crisscross of fine wrinkles on her pale forehead. "But of course it would be only just *what* it costs. I shouldn't want to *make* anything."

"It's work and care, Ellen, and you may as well admit it. You need all your strength—with those sickly children and Edward on your hands. When she comes to me, there need be no expense, James, except for clothes. I have room enough and Mr. Oswald will never notice the difference in the house bills—but he does hate to pay out money for clothes."

"Mother must be provided for properly," her son declared. "How much ought it to cost—a year—for clothes?"

"You know what your wife's cost," suggested Adelaide, with a flicker of a smile about her lips.

"Oh, *no*," said Ellen. "That's no criterion! Maude is in society, you see. Mother wouldn't *dream* of having so much."

James looked at her gratefully. "Board—and clothes—all told; what should you say, Ellen?"

Ellen scrabbled in her small black handbag for a piece of paper, and found none. James handed her an envelope and a fountain pen.

"Food—just plain food materials—costs all of four dollars a week now—for one person," said she. "And heat—and light—and extra service. I should think six a week would be the *least*, James. And for clothes and carfare and small expenses—I should say—well, three hundred dollars!"

"That would make over six hundred a year," said James slowly. "How about Oswald sharing that, Adelaide?"

Adelaide flushed. "I do not think he would be willing, James. Of course, if it were absolutely necessary—"

"He has money enough," said her brother.

"Yes, but he never seems to have any outside of his business—and he has his own parents to carry now. No—I can give her a home, but that's all."

"You see, you'd have none of the care and trouble, James," said Ellen. "We—the girls—are each willing to have her with us, while perhaps Maude wouldn't care to, but if you could just pay the money—"

"Maybe there's some left, after all," suggested Adelaide. "And this place ought to sell for something."

"This place" was a piece of rolling land within ten miles of Denver. It had a bit of river bottom, and ran up towards the foothills. From the house the view ran north and south along the precipitous ranks of the "Big Rockies" to westward. To the east lay the vast stretches of sloping plain.

"There ought to be at least six or eight thousand dollars from it, I should say," he concluded.

"Speaking of clothes," Adelaide rather irrelevantly suggested, "I see Mother didn't get any new black. She's always worn it as long as I can remember."

"Mother's a long time," said Ellen. "I wonder if she wants anything. I'll go up and see."

"No," said Adelaide. "She said she wanted to be let alone—and rest. She said she'd be down by the time Mr. Frankland got here."

"She's bearing it pretty well," Ellen suggested, after a little silence.

"It's not like a broken heart," Adelaide explained. "Of course Father meant well—"

"He was a man who always did his duty," admitted Ellen. "But we none of us—loved him—very much."

"He is dead and buried," said James. "We can at least respect his memory."

"We've hardly seen Mother—under that black veil," Ellen went on. "It must have aged her. This long nursing."

"She had help toward the last—a man nurse," said Adelaide.

"Yes, but a long illness is an awful strain—and Mother never was good at nursing. She has surely done her duty," pursued Ellen.

"And now she's entitled to a rest," said James, rising and walking about the room. "I wonder how soon we can close up affairs here—and get rid of this place. There might be enough in it to give her almost a living—properly invested."

Ellen looked out across the dusty stretches of land.

"How I did hate to live here!" she said.

"So did I," said Adelaide.

"So did I," said James.

And they all smiled rather grimly.

"We don't any of us seem to be very—affectionate, about Mother," Adelaide presently admitted. "I don't know why it is—we never were an affectionate family, I guess."

"Nobody could be affectionate with Father," Ellen suggested timidly.

"And Mother—poor Mother! She's had an awful life."

"Mother has always done her duty," said James in a determined voice, "and so did Father, as he saw it. Now we'll do ours."

"Ah," exclaimed Ellen, jumping to her feet, "here comes the lawyer. I'll call Mother."

She ran quickly upstairs and tapped at her mother's door.

"Mother, oh Mother," she cried. "Mr. Frankland's come."

"I know it," came back a voice from within. "Tell him to go ahead and read the will. I know what's in it. I'll be down in a few minutes."

Ellen went slowly back downstairs with the fine criss-cross of wrinkles showing on her pale forehead again, and delivered her mother's message.

The other two glanced at each other hesitatingly, but Mr. Frankland spoke up briskly.

"Quite natural, of course, under the circumstances. Sorry I couldn't get to the funeral. A case on this morning."

The will was short. The estate was left to be divided among the children in four equal parts, two to the son and one each to the daughters after the mother's legal share had been deducted, if she were still living. In such case they were furthermore directed to provide for their mother while she lived. The estate, as described, consisted of the ranch, the large, rambling house on it, with all the furniture, stock, and implements, and some five thousand dollars in mining stocks.

"That is less than I had supposed," said James.

"This will was made ten years ago," Mr. Frankland explained. "I have done business for your father since that time. He kept his faculties to the end, and I think that you will find that the property has appreciated. Mrs. McPherson has taken excellent care of the ranch, I understand—and has had some boarders."

Both the sisters exchanged pained glances.

"There's an end to all that now," said James.

At this moment, the door opened and a tall black figure, cloaked and veiled, came into the room.

"I'm glad to hear you say that Mr. McPherson kept his faculties to the end, Mr. Frankland," said the widow. "It's true. I didn't come down to hear that old will. It's no good now."

They all turned in their chairs.

"Is there a later will, madam?" inquired the lawyer.

"Not that I know of. Mr. McPherson had no property when he died."

"No property! My dear lady—four years ago he certainly had some."

"Yes, but three years and a half ago he gave it all to me. Here are all the deeds."

There they were, in very truth—formal and correct, and quite simple and clear—for deeds. James R. McPherson, Sr., had assuredly given to his wife the whole estate.

"You remember that was the panic year," she continued. "There was pressure from some of Mr. McPherson's creditors; he thought it would be safer so."

"Why—yes," remarked Mr. Frankland. "I do remember now his advising with me about it. But I thought the step unnecessary."

James cleared his throat.

"Well, Mother, this does complicate matters a little. We were hoping that we could settle up all the business this afternoon—with Mr. Frankland's help—and take you back with us."

"We can't be spared any longer, you see, Mother," said Ellen.

"Can't you deed it back again, Mother," Adelaide

suggested, "to James, or to—all of us, so we can get away?"

"Why should I?"

"Now, Mother," Ellen put in persuasively, "we know how badly you feel, and you are nervous and tired, but I told you this morning when we came, that we expected to take you back with us. You know you've been packing—"

"Yes, I've been packing," replied the voice behind the veil.

"I dare say it was safer—to have the property in your name—technically," James admitted, "but now I think it would be the simplest way for you to make it over to me in a lump, and I will see that Father's wishes are carried out to the letter."

"Your father is dead," remarked the voice.

"Yes, Mother, we know—we know how you feel," Ellen ventured.

"I am alive," said Mrs. McPherson.

"Dear Mother, it's very trying to talk business to you at such a time. We all realize it," Adelaide explained with a touch of asperity. "But we told you we couldn't stay as soon as we got here."

"And the business has to be settled," James added conclusively.

"It is settled."

"Perhaps Mr. Frankland can make it clear to you," went on James with forced patience.

"I do not doubt that your mother understands perfectly," murmured the lawyer. "I have always found her a woman of remarkable intelligence."

"Thank you, Mr. Frankland. Possibly you may be able to make my children understand that this property—such as it is—is mine now."

"Why assuredly, assuredly, Mrs. McPherson. We all see that. But we assume, as a matter of course, that you will consider Mr. McPherson's wishes in regard to the disposition of the estate."

"I have considered Mr. McPherson's wishes for thirty years," she replied. "Now, I'll consider mine. I have done my duty since the day I married him. It is eleven thousand days—today." The last with sudden intensity.

"But madam, your children—"

"I have no children, Mr. Frankland. I have two daughters and a son. These two grown persons here, grown up, married, having children of their own—or ought to have—were my children. I did my duty by them, and they did their duty by me—and would yet, no doubt." The tone changed suddenly. "But they don't have to. I'm tired of duty."

The little group of listeners looked up, startled.

"You don't know how things have been going on here," the voice went on. "I didn't trouble you with my affairs. But I'll tell you now. When your father saw fit to make over the property to me—to save it—and when he knew that he hadn't many years to live, I took hold of things. I had to have a nurse for your father—and a doctor coming; the house was a sort of hospital, so I made it a little more so. I had half a dozen patients and nurses here—and made money by it. I ran the garden—kept cows—raised my own chickens—worked out-of-doors—slept out-of-doors. I'm a stronger woman today than I ever was in my life!"

She stood up, tall, strong and straight, and drew a deep breath.

"Your father's property amounted to about eight thousand dollars when he died," she continued. "That would be two thousand dollars to James and one thousand dollars to each of the girls. That I'm willing to give you now—each of you—in your own name. But if my daughters will take my advice, they'd better let me send them the yearly income—in cash—to spend as they like. It is good for a woman to have some money of her own."

"I think you are right, Mother," said Adelaide.

"Yes indeed," murmured Ellen.

"Don't you need it yourself, Mother?" asked James, with a sudden feeling of tenderness for the stiff figure in black.

"No, James, I shall keep the ranch, you see. I have good reliable help. I've made two thousand dollars a year—clear—off it so far, and now I've rented it for that to a doctor friend of mine—woman doctor."

"I think you have done remarkably well, Mrs. McPherson—wonderfully well," said Mr. Frankland.

"And you'll have an income of two thousand dollars a year," said Adelaide incredulously.

"You'll come and live with me, won't you?" ventured Ellen.

"Thank you, my dear, I will not."

"You're more than welcome in my big house," said Adelaide.

"No thank you, my dear."

"I don't doubt Maude will be glad to have you," James rather hesitatingly offered.

"I do. I doubt it very much. No thank you, my dear."

"But what *are* you going to do?"

Ellen seemed genuinely concerned.

"I'm going to do what I never did before. I'm going to *live*!"

With a firm swift step, the tall figure moved to the windows and pulled up the lowered shades. The brilliant Colorado sunshine poured into the room. She threw off the long black veil.

"That's borrowed," she said. "I didn't want to hurt your feelings at the funeral."

She unbuttoned the long black cloak and dropped it at her feet, standing there in the full sunlight, a little flushed and smiling, dressed in a well-made traveling suit of dull mixed colors.

"If you want to know my plans, I'll tell you. I've got six thousand dollars of my own. I earned it in three years—off my little rancho-sanitarium. One thousand I have put in the savings bank—to bring me back from anywhere on earth, and to put me in an old lady's home if it is necessary. Here is an agreement with a cremation company. They'll import me, if necessary, and have me duly—expurgated—or they don't get the money. But I've got five thousand dollars to play with, and I'm going to play."

Her daughters looked shocked.

"Why, Mother—"

"At your age—"

James drew down his upper lip and looked like his father.

"I knew you wouldn't any of you understand," she continued more quietly. "But it doesn't matter any more. Thirty years I've given you—and your father. Now I'll have thirty years of my own."

"Are you—are you sure you're—well, Mother?" Ellen urged with real anxiety.

Her mother laughed outright.

"Well, really well, never was better, have been doing business up to today—good medical testimony that. No question of my sanity, my dears! I want you to grasp the fact that your mother is a Real Person with some interests of her own and half a lifetime yet. The first twenty didn't count for much—I was growing up and couldn't help myself. The last thirty have been—hard. James perhaps realizes that more than you girls, but you all know it. Now, I'm free."

"Where *do* you mean to go, Mother?" James asked.

She looked around the little circle with a serene air of decision and replied.

"To New Zealand. I've always wanted to go there," she pursued. "Now I'm going. And to Australia—and Tasmania—and Madagascar—and Terra del Fuego. I shall be gone some time."

They separated that night—three going east, one west.

Theodore Dreiser
(1871–1945)

Son of a stern German Catholic father and an affectionate Mennonite mother, Dreiser, who was born in Terre Haute, Indiana, recalled among his earliest impressions his overwhelming pity at the sight of the holes in his mother's badly worn shoes. Himself a "have-not," he felt the enormous temptations of American materialist society, having, as a young man, withheld money from his employer in order to buy the overcoat he desperately wanted. Dreiser's advanced education consisted of a single year at the University of Indiana, which was financed by Mildred Fielding, a high school teacher who believed he had great potential. Essentially, he developed as a writer through studying on his own such theorists as Huxley, Tyndall, and Spencer, and through practical experience as a reporter for newspapers in St. Louis, Chicago, Pittsburgh, and New York. His first novel, *Sister Carrie* (1900), received virtually no distribution since the publisher, Doubleday, Page and Co., after signing a contract with Dreiser, developed reservations about the novel's morality. Among the novels subsequently published were *Jennie Gerhardt* (1911), *The Financier* (1912), *The Titan* (1914), *An American Tragedy* (1925), which was filmed in 1951 as *A Place in the Sun,* and *The Bulwark* (1946).

OLD ROGAUM AND HIS THERESA

In all Bleecker Street was no more comfortable doorway than that of the butcher Rogaum, even if the first floor was given over to meat market purposes. It was to one side of the main entrance, which gave ingress to the butcher shop; and from it led up a flight of steps, at least five feet wide, to the living rooms above. A little portico stood out in front of it, railed on either side, and within was a second or final door, forming, with the outer or storm door, a little area, where Mrs. Rogaum and her children frequently sat of a summer's evening. The outer door was never locked, owing to the inconvenience it would inflict on Mr. Rogaum, who had no other way of getting upstairs. In winter, when all had gone to bed, there had been cases in which belated travelers had taken refuge there from the snow or sleet. One or two newsboys occasionally slept there, until routed out by Officer Maguire, who, seeing it half open one morning at two o'clock, took occasion to look in. He jogged the newsboys sharply with his stick, and then, when they were gone, tried the inner door, which was locked.

"You ought to keep that outer door locked, Rogaum," he observed to the phlegmatic butcher the next evening, as he was passing, "people might get in. A couple o' kids was sleepin' in there last night."

"Ach, dot iss no difference," answered Rogaum pleasantly. "I haf der inner door locked, yet. Let dem sleep. Dot iss no difference."

"Better lock it," said the officer, more to vindicate his authority than anything else. "Something will happen there yet."

The door was never locked, however, and now of a summer evening Mrs. Rogaum and the children made pleasant use of its recess, watching the rout of street cars and occasionally belated trucks go by. The children played on the sidewalk, all except the budding Theresa (eighteen just turning), who, with one companion of the neighborhood, the pretty Kenrihan girl, walked up and down the block, laughing, glancing, watching the boys. Old Mrs. Kenrihan lived in the next block, and there, sometimes, the two stopped. There, also, they most frequently pretended to be when talking with the boys in the intervening side street. Young "Connie" Almerting and George Goujon were the bright particular mashers who held the attention of the maidens in this block. These two made their acquaintance in the customary bold, boyish way, and thereafter the girls had an urgent desire to be out in the street together after eight, and to linger where the boys could see and overtake them.

Old Mrs. Rogaum never knew. She was a particularly fat, old German lady, completely dominated by her liege and portly lord, and at nine o'clock regularly, as he had long ago deemed meet and fit, she was wont to betake her way upward and so to bed. Old Rogaum himself, at that hour, closed the market and went to his chamber.

Before that all the children were called sharply, once from the doorstep below and once from the window above, only Mrs. Rogaum did it first and Rogaum last. It had come, because of a shade of lenience, not wholly apparent in the father's nature, that the older of the children needed two callings and sometimes three. Theresa, now that she had "got in" with the Kenrihan maiden, needed that many calls and even more.

She was just at that age for which mere thoughtless, sensory life holds its greatest charm. She loved to walk up and down in the as yet bright street where were voices and laughter, and occasionally moonlight streaming down. What a nuisance it was to be called at nine, anyhow. Why should one have to go in then, anyhow. What old fogies her parents were, wishing to go to bed so early. Mrs. Kenrihan was not so strict with her daughter. It made her pettish when Rogaum insisted, calling as he often did, in German, "Come you now," in a very hoarse and belligerent voice.

She came, eventually, frowning and wretched, all the moonlight calling her, all the voices of the night urging her to come back. Her innate opposition due to her urgent youth made her coming later and later, however, until now, by August of this, her eighteenth year, it was nearly ten when she entered, and Rogaum was almost invariably angry.

"I vill lock you oudt," he declared, in strongly accented English, while she tried to slip by him each time. "I vill show you. Du sollst come ven I say, yet. Hear now."

"I'll not," answered Theresa, but it was always under her breath.

Poor Mrs. Rogaum troubled at hearing the wrath in her husband's voice. It spoke of harder and fiercer times which had been with her. Still she was not powerful enough in the family councils to put in a weighty word. So Rogaum fumed unrestricted.

There were other nights, however, many of them, and now that the young sparks of the neighborhood had enlisted the girls' attention, it was a more trying time than ever. Never did a street seem more beautiful. Its shabby red walls, dusty pavements and protruding store steps and iron railings seemed bits of the ornamental paraphernalia of heaven itself. These lights, the cars, the moon, the street lamps! Theresa had a tender eye for the dashing Almerting, a young idler and loafer of the district, the son of a stationer farther up the street. What a fine fellow he was, indeed! What a handsome nose and chin! What eyes! What authority! His cigarette was always cocked at a high angle, in her presence, and his hat had the least suggestion of being set to one side. He had a shrewd way of winking one eye, taking her boldly by the arm, hailing her as, "Hey, Pretty!" and was strong and athletic and worked (when he worked) in a tobacco factory. His was a trade, indeed, nearly acquired, as he said, and his jingling pockets attested that he had money of his own. Altogether he was very captivating.

"Aw, whaddy ya want to go in for?" he used to say to her, tossing his head gayly on one side to listen and holding her by the arm, as old Rogaum called. "Tell him yuh didn't hear."

"No, I've got to go," said the girl, who was soft and plump and fair—a Rhine maiden type.

"Well, yuh don't have to go just yet. Stay another minute. George, what was that fellow's name that tried to sass us the other day?"

"Theresa!" roared old Rogaum forcefully. "If you do not now come! Ve vill see!"

"I've got to go," repeated Theresa with a faint effort at starting. "Can't you hear? Don't hold me. I haf to."

"Aw, whaddy ya want to be such a coward for? Y' don't have to go. He won't do nothin' tuh yuh. My old man was always hollerin' like that up tuh a couple years ago. Let him holler! Say, kid, but yuh got sweet eyes! They're as blue! An' your mouth—"

"Now stop! You hear me!" Theresa would protest softly, as swiftly, he would slip an arm about her waist and draw her to him, sometimes in a vain, sometimes in a successful effort to kiss her.

As a rule she managed to interpose an elbow between her face and his, but even then he would manage to touch an ear or a cheek or her neck—sometimes her mouth, full and warm—before she would develop sufficient energy to push him away and herself free. Then she would protest mock earnestly or sometimes run away.

"Now, I'll never speak to you any more, if that's the way you're going to do. My father don't allow me to kiss boys, anyhow," and then she would run, half ashamed, half smiling to herself as he would stare after her, or if she lingered, develop a kind of anger and even rage.

"Aw, cut it! Whaddy ya want to be so shy for? Dontcha like me? What's gettin' into yuh, anyhow? Hey?"

In the meantime George Goujon and Myrtle Kenrihan, their companions, might be sweeting and going through a similar contest, perhaps a hundred feet up the street or near at hand. The quality of old Rogaum's voice would by now have become so raucous, however, that Theresa would have lost all comfort in the scene and, becoming frightened, hurry away. Then it was often that both Almerting and Goujon as well as Myrtle Kenrihan would follow her to the corner, almost in sight of the irate old butcher.

"Let him call," young Almerting would insist, laying a

final hold on her soft white fingers and causing her to quiver thereby.

"Oh, no," she would gasp nervously. "I can't."

"Well, go on, then," he would say, and with a flip of his heel would turn back, leaving Theresa to wonder whether she had alienated him forever or no. Then she would hurry to her father's door.

"Muss ich all my time spenden calling, mit you on de streeds oudt?" old Rogaum would roar wrathfully, the while his fat hand would descend on her back. "Take dot now. Vy don'd you come ven I call? In now. I vill show you. Und come you yussed vunce more at dis time—ve vill see if I am boss in my own house, aber! Komst du vun minute nach ten to-morrow und you vill see vot you vill get. I vill der door lock. Du sollst not in kommen. Mark! Oudt sollst du stayen—oudt!" and he would glare wrathfully at her retreating figure.

Sometimes Theresa would whimper, sometimes cry or sulk. She almost hated her father for his cruelty, "the big, fat, rough thing," and just because she wanted to stay out in the bright streets, too! Because he was old and stout and wanted to go to bed at ten, he thought every one else did. And outside was the dark sky with its stars, and the street lamps, the cars, the tinkle and laughter of eternal life!

"Oh!" she would sigh as she undressed and crawled into her small neat bed. To think that she had to live like this all her days! At the same time old Rogaum was angry and equally determined. It was not so much that he imagined that his Theresa was in bad company as yet, but he wished to forefend against possible danger. This was not a good neighborhood by any means. The boys around here were tough. He wanted Theresa to pick some nice sober youth from among the other Germans he and his wife knew here and there—at the Lutheran Church, for instance. Otherwise she shouldn't marry. He knew she only walked from his shop to the door of the Kenrihans and back again. Had not his wife told him so? If he had thought upon what far pilgrimage her feet had already ventured, or had even seen the dashing Almerting hanging near, then had there been wrath indeed. As it was, his mind was more or less at ease.

On many, many evenings it was much the same. Sometimes she got in on time, sometimes not, but more and more "Connie" Almerting claimed her for his "steady," and bought her ice-cream. In the range of the short block and its confining corners it was all done, lingering by the curbstone and strolling a half block either way in the side streets, until she had offended seriously at home, and the threat was repeated anew. He often tried to persuade her to go on picnics or outings of various kinds, but this, somehow, was not to be thought of at her age—at least with him. She knew her father would never endure the thought, and never even had the courage to mention it, let alone run away. Mere lingering with him at the adjacent street corners brought stronger and stronger admonishments—even more blows and the threat that she should not get in at all.

Well enough she meant to obey, but on one radiant night late in June the time fled too fast. The moon was so bright, the air so soft. The feel of far summer things was in the wind and even in this dusty street. Theresa, in a newly starched white summer dress, had been loitering up and down with Myrtle when as usual they encountered Almerting and Goujon. Now it was ten, and the regular calls were beginning.

"Aw, wait a minute," said "Connie." "Stand still. He won't lock yuh out."

"But he will, though," said Theresa. "You don't know him."

"Well, if he does, come on back to me. I'll take care of yuh. I'll be here. But he won't though. If you stayed out a little while he'd letcha in all right. That's the way my old man used to try to do me but it didn't work with me. I stayed out an' he let me in, just the same. Don'tcha let him kidja." He jingled some loose change in his pocket.

Never in his life had he had a girl on his hands at any unseasonable hour, but it was nice to talk big, and there was a club to which he belonged, The Varick Street Roosters, and to which he had a key. It would be closed and empty at this hour, and she could stay there until morning, if need be or with Myrtle Kenrihan. He would take her there if she insisted. There was a sinister grin on the youth's face.

By now Theresa's affections had carried her far. This youth with his slim body, his delicate strong hands, his fine chin, straight mouth and hard dark eyes—how wonderful he seemed! He was but nineteen to her eighteen but cold, shrewd, daring. Yet how tender he seemed to her, how well worth having! Always, when he kissed her now, she trembled in the balance. There was something in the iron grasp of his fingers that went through her like fire. His glance held hers at times when she could scarcely endure it.

"I'll wait, anyhow," he insisted.

Longer and longer she lingered, but now for once no voice came.

She began to feel that something was wrong—a greater strain than if old Rogaum's voice had been filling the whole neighborhood.

"I've got to go," she said.

"Gee, but you're a coward, yuh are!" said he derisively. "What 'r yuh always so scared about? He always says he'll lock yuh out, but he never does."

"Yes, but he will," she insisted nervously. "I think he has this time. You don't know him. He's something awful when he gets real mad. Oh, Connie, I must go!" For the sixth or seventh time she moved, and once more he caught her arm and waist and tried to kiss her, but she slipped away from him.

"Ah, yuh!" he exclaimed. "I wish he would lock yuh out!"

At her own doorstep she paused momentarily, more to soften her progress than anything. The outer door was open as usual, but not the inner. She tried it, but it would not give. It was locked! For a moment she paused, cold fear racing over her body, and then knocked.

No answer.

Again she rattled the door, this time nervously, and was about to cry out.

Still no answer.

At last she heard her father's voice, hoarse and indifferent, not addressed to her at all, but to her mother.

"Let her go, now," it said savagely, from the front room where he supposed she could not hear. "I vill her a lesson teach."

"Hadn't you better let her in now, yet?" pleaded Mrs. Rogaum faintly.

"No," insisted Mr. Rogaum. "Nefer! Let her go now. If she vill alvays stay oudt, let her stay now. Ve vill see how she likes dot."

His voice was rich in wrath, and he was saving up a good beating for her into the bargain, that she knew. She would have to wait and wait and plead, and when she was thoroughly wretched and subdued he would let her in and beat her—such a beating as she had never received in all her born days.

Again the door rattled, and still she got no answer. Not even her call brought a sound.

Now, strangely, a new element, not heretofore apparent in her nature but nevertheless wholly there, was called into life, springing in action as Diana, full formed. Why should he always be so harsh? She hadn't done anything but stay out a little later than usual. He was always so anxious to keep her in and subdue her. For once the cold chill of her girlish fears left her, and she wavered angrily.

"All right," she said, some old German stubbornness springing up, "I won't knock. You don't need to let me in, then."

A suggestion of tears was in her eyes, but she backed firmly out onto the stoop and sat down, hesitating. Old Rogaum saw her, lowering down from the lattice, but said nothing. He would teach her for once what were proper hours!

At the corner, standing, Almerting also saw her. He recognized the simple white dress, and paused steadily, a strange thrill racing over him. Really they had locked her out! Gee, this was new. It was great, in a way. There she was, white, quiet, shut out, waiting at her father's doorstep.

Sitting thus, Theresa pondered a moment, her girlish rashness and anger dominating her. Her pride was hurt and she felt revengeful. They would shut her out, would they? All right, she would go out and they should look to it how they would get her back—the old curmudgeons. For the moment the home of Myrtle Kenrihan came to her as a possible refuge, but she decided that she need not go there yet. She had better wait about awhile and see—or walk and frighten them. He would beat her, would he? Well, maybe he would and maybe he wouldn't. She might come back, but still that was a thing afar off. Just now it didn't matter so much. "Connie" was still there on the corner. He loved her dearly. She felt it.

Getting up, she stepped to the now quieting sidewalk and strolled up the street. It was a rather nervous procedure, however. There were street cars still, and stores lighted and people passing, but soon these would not be, and she was locked out. The side streets were already little more than long silent walks and gleaming rows of lamps.

At the corner her youthful lover almost pounced upon her.

"Locked out, are yuh?" he asked, his eyes shining.

For the moment she was delighted to see him, for a nameless dread had already laid hold of her. Home meant so much. Up to now it had been her whole life.

"Yes," she answered feebly.

"Well, let's stroll on a little," said the boy. He had not as yet quite made up his mind what to do, but the night was young. It was so fine to have her with him—his.

At the farther corner they passed Officers Maguire and Delahanty, idly swinging their clubs and discussing politics.

" 'Tis a shame," Officer Delahanty was saying, "the way things are run now," but he paused to add, "Ain't that old Rogaum's girl over there with young Almerting?"

"It is," replied Maguire, looking after.

"Well, I'm thinkin' he'd better be keepin' an eye on her," said the former. "She's too young to be runnin' around with the likes o' him."

Maguire agreed. "He's a young tough," he observed. "I never liked him. He's too fresh. He works over here in Myer's tobacco factory, and belongs to The Roosters. He's up to no good, I'll warrant that."

"Teach 'em a lesson, I would," Almerting was saying to Theresa as they strolled on. "We'll walk around a while an' make 'em think yuh mean business. They won't lock yuh out any more. If they don't let yuh in when we come back I'll find yuh a place, all right."

His sharp eyes were gleaming as he looked around into her own. Already he had made up his mind that she should not go back if he could help it. He knew a better place than home for this night, anyhow—the club room of The Roosters, if nowhere else. They could stay there for a time, anyhow.

By now old Rogaum, who had seen her walking up the street alone, was marveling at her audacity, but thought she would soon come back. It was amazing that she should exhibit such temerity, but he would teach her! Such a whipping! At half-past ten, however, he stuck his head out of the open window and saw nothing of her. At eleven, the same. Then he walked the floor.

At first wrathful, then nervous, then nervous and wrathful, he finally ended all nervous, without a scintilla of wrath. His stout wife sat up in bed and began to wring her hands.

"Lie down!" he commanded. "You make me sick. I know vot I am doing!"

"Is she still at der door?" pleaded the mother.

"No," he said. "I don't tink so. She should come ven I call."

His nerves were weakening, however, and now they finally collapsed.

"She vent de stread up," he said anxiously after a time. "I vill go after."

Slipping on his coat, he went down the stairs and out into the night. It was growing late, and the stillness and gloom of midnight were nearing. Nowhere in sight was his Theresa. First one way and then another he went, looking here, there, everywhere, finally groaning.

"Ach, Gott!" he said, the sweat bursting out on his brow, "vot in Teufel's name iss dis?"

He thought he would seek a policeman, but there was none. Officer Maguire had long since gone for a quiet game in one of the neighboring saloons. His partner had temporarily returned to his own beat. Still old Rogaum hunted on, worrying more and more.

Finally he bethought him to hasten home again, for she must have got back. Mrs. Rogaum, too, would be frantic if she had not. If she were not there he must go to the police. Such a night! And his Theresa—— This thing could not go on.

As he turned into his own corner he almost ran, coming up to the little portico wet and panting. At a puffing step he turned, and almost fell over a white body at his feet, a prone and writhing woman.

"Ach, Gott!" he cried aloud, almost shouting in his distress and excitement. "Theresa, vot iss dis? Wilhelmina, a light now. Bring a light now, I say, for himmel's sake! Theresa hat sich *umgebracht.* Help!"

He had fallen to his knees and was turning over the writhing, groaning figure. By the pale light of the street, however, he could make out that it was not his Theresa, fortunately, as he had at first feared, but another and yet there was something very like her in the figure.

"Um!" said the stranger weakly. "Ah!"

The dress was gray, not white as was his Theresa's, but the body was round and plump. It cut the fiercest cords of his intensity, this thought of death to a young woman, but there was something else about the situation which made him forget his own troubles.

Mrs. Rogaum, loudly admonished, almost tumbled down the stairs. At the foot she held the light she had brought—a small glass oil-lamp—and then nearly dropped it. A fairly attractive figure, more girl than woman, rich in all the physical charms that characterize a certain type, lay near to dying. Her soft hair had fallen back over a good forehead, now quite white. Her pretty hands, well decked with rings, were clutched tightly in an agonized grip. At her neck a blue silk shirtwaist and light lace collar were torn away where she had clutched herself, and on the white flesh was a yellow stain as of one who had been burned. A strange odor reeked in the area, and in one corner was a spilled bottle.

"Ach, Gott!" exclaimed Mrs. Rogaum. "It iss a vooman!

She haf herself gekilt. Run for der police! Oh, my! oh, my!"

Rogaum did not kneel for more than a moment. Somehow, this creature's fate seemed in some psychic way identified with that of his own daughter. He bounded up, and jumping out his front door, began to call lustily for the police. Officer Maguire, at his social game nearby, heard the very first cry and came running.

"What's the matter here, now?" he exclaimed, rushing up full and ready for murder, robbery, fire, or, indeed, anything in the whole roster of human calamities.

"A vooman!" said Rogaum excitedly. "She haf herself *umgebracht*. She iss dying. Ach, Gott! in my own doorstep, yet!"

"Vere iss der hospital?" put in Mrs. Rogaum, thinking clearly of an ambulance, but not being able to express it. "She iss gekilt, sure. Oh! Oh!" and bending over her the poor old motherly soul stroked the tightened hands, and trickled tears upon the blue shirtwaist. "Ach, vy did you do dot?" she said. "Ach, for vy?"

Officer Maguire was essentially a man of action. He jumped to the sidewalk, amid the gathering company, and beat loudly with his club upon the stone flagging. Then he ran to the nearest police phone, returning to aid in any other way he might. A milk wagon passing on its way from the Jersey ferry with a few tons of fresh milk aboard, he held it up and demanded a helping.

"Give us a quart there, will you?" he said authoritatively. "A woman's swallowed acid in here."

"Sure," said the driver, anxious to learn the cause of the excitement. "Got a glass, anybody?"

Maguire ran back and returned, bearing a measure. Mrs. Rogaum stood looking nervously on, while the stocky officer raised the golden head and poured the milk.

"Here, now, drink this," he said. "Come on. Try an' swallow it."

The girl, a blonde of the type the world too well knows, opened her eyes and looked, groaning a little.

"Drink it," shouted the officer fiercely. "Do you want to die? Open your mouth!"

Used to a fear of the law in all her days, she obeyed

now, even in death. The lips parted, the fresh milk was drained to the end, some spilling on neck and cheek.

While they were working old Rogaum came back and stood looking on, by the side of his wife. Also Officer Delahanty, having heard the peculiar wooden ring of the stick upon the stone in the night, had come up.

"Ach, ach," exclaimed Rogaum rather distractedly, "und she iss oudt yet. I could not find her. Oh, oh!"

There was a clang of a gong up the street as the racing ambulance turned rapidly in. A young hospital surgeon dismounted, and seeing the woman's condition, ordered immediate removal. Both officers and Rogaum, as well as the surgeon, helped place her in the ambulance. After a moment the lone bell, ringing wildly in the night, was all the evidence remaining that a tragedy had been here.

"Do you know how she came here?" asked Officer Delahanty, coming back to get Rogaum's testimony for the police.

"No, no," answered Rogaum wretchedly. "She vass here alretty. I vass for my daughter loog. Ach, himmel, I haf my daughter lost. She iss avay."

Mrs. Rogaum also chattered, the significance of Theresa's absence all the more painfully emphasized by this.

The officer did not at first get the import of this. He was only interested in the facts of the present case.

"You say she was here when you come? Where was you?"

"I say I vass for my daughter loog. I come here, und der vooman vass here now alretty."

"Yes. What time was this?"

"Only now yet. Yussed a half-hour."

Officer Maguire had strolled up, after chasing away a small crowd that had gathered with fierce and unholy threats. For the first time now he noticed the peculiar perturbation of the usually placid German couple.

"What about your daughter?" he asked, catching a word as to that.

Both old people raised their voices at once.

"She haf gone. She haf run avay. Ach, himmel, ve must for her loog. Quick—she could not get in. Ve had der door shut."

"Locked her out, eh?" inquired Maguire after a time, hearing much of the rest of the story.

"Yes," explained Rogaum. "It was to schkare her a liddle. She vould not come ven I called."

"Sure, that's the girl we saw walkin' with young Almerting, do ye mind? The one in the white dress," said Delahanty to Maguire.

"White dress, yah!" echoed Rogaum, and then the fact of her walking with some one came home like a blow.

"Did you hear dot?" he exclaimed even as Mrs. Rogaum did likewise. *"Mein Got, hast du das gehoert?"*

He fairly jumped as he said it. His hands flew up to his stout and ruddy head.

"Whaddy ya want to let her out for nights?" asked Maguire roughly, catching the drift of the situation. "That's no time for young girls to be out, anyhow, and with these toughs around here. Sure, I saw her, nearly two hours ago."

"Ach," groaned Rogaum. "Two hours yet. Ho, ho, ho!" His voice was quite hysteric.

"Well, go on in," said Officer Delahanty. "There's no use yellin' out here. Give us a description of her an' we'll send out an alarm. You won't be able to find her walkin' around."

Her parents described her exactly. The two men turned to the nearest police box and then disappeared, leaving the old German couple in the throes of distress. A time-worn old church-clock nearby now chimed out one and then two. The notes cut like knives. Mrs. Rogaum began fearfully to cry. Rogaum walked and blustered to himself.

"It's a queer case, that," said Officer Delahanty to Maguire after having reported the matter of Theresa, but referring solely to the outcast of the doorway so recently sent away and in whose fate they were much more interested. She being a part of the commercialized vice of the city, they were curious as to the cause of her suicide. "I think I know that woman. I think I know where she came from. You do, too—Adele's, around the corner, eh? She didn't come into that doorway by herself, either. She was put there. You know how they do."

"You're right," said Maguire. "She was put there, all right, and that's just where she come from, too."

The two of them now tipped up their noses and cocked their eyes significantly.

"Let's go around," added Maguire.

They went, the significant red light over the transom at 68 telling its own story. Strolling leisurely up, they knocked. At the very first sound a painted denizen of the half-world opened the door.

"Where's Adele?" asked Maguire as the two, hats on as usual, stepped in.

"She's gone to bed."

"Tell her to come down."

They seated themselves deliberately in the gaudy mirrored parlor and waited, conversing between themselves in whispers. Presently a sleepy-looking woman of forty in a gaudy robe of heavy texture, and slippered in red, appeared.

"We're here about that suicide case you had tonight. What about it? Who was she? How'd she come to be in that doorway around the corner? Come, now," Maguire added, as the madam assumed an air of mingled injured and ignorant innocence, "you know. Can that stuff! How did she come to take poison?"

"I don't know what you're talking about," said the woman with the utmost air of innocence. "I never heard of any suicide."

"Aw, come now," insisted Delahanty, "the girl around the corner. You know. We know you've got a pull, but we've got to know about this case, just the same. Come across now. It won't be published. What made her take the poison?"

Under the steady eyes of the officers the woman hesitated, but finally weakened.

"Why—why—her lover went back on her—that's all. She got so blue we just couldn't do anything with her. I tried to, but she wouldn't listen."

"Lover, eh?" put in Maguire as though that were the most unheard-of thing in the world. "What was his name?"

"I don't know. You never can tell that."

"What was her name—Annie?" asked Delahanty wisely,

as though he knew but was merely inquiring for form's sake.

"No—Emily."

"Well, how did she come to get over there, anyhow?" inquired Maguire most pleasantly.

"George took her," she replied, referring to a man-of-all-work about the place.

Then little by little as they sat there the whole miserable story came out, miserable as all the willfulness and error and suffering of the world.

"How old was she?"

"Oh, twenty-one."

"Well, where'd she come from?"

"Oh, here in New York. Her family locked her out one night, I think."

Something in the way the woman said this last brought old Rogaum and his daughter back to the policemen's minds. They had forgotten all about her by now, although they had turned in an alarm. Fearing to interfere too much with this well-known and politically controlled institution, the two men left, but outside they fell to talking of the other case.

"We ought to tell old Rogaum about her some time," said Maguire to Delahanty cynically. "He locked his kid out to-night."

"Yes, it might be a good thing for him to hear that," replied the other. "We'd better go round there an' see if his girl's back yet. She may be back by now," and so they returned but little disturbed by the joint miseries.

At Rogaum's door they once more knocked loudly.

"Is your daughter back again?" asked Maguire when a reply was had.

"Ach, no," replied the hysterical Mrs. Rogaum, who was quite alone now. "My husband he haf gone oudt again to loog vunce more. Oh, my! Oh, my!"

"Well, that's what you get for lockin' her out," returned Maguire loftily, the other story fresh in his mind. "That other girl downstairs here tonight was locked out too, once." He chanced to have a girl-child of his own and somehow he was in the mood for pointing a moral.

"You oughtn't to do anything like that. Where d'yuh expect she's goin' to if you lock her out?"

Mrs. Rogaum groaned. She explained that it was not her fault, but anyhow it was carrying coals to Newcastle to talk to her so. The advice was better for her husband.

The pair finally returned to the station to see if the call had been attended to.

"Sure," said the sergeant, "certainly. Whaddy ya think?" and he read from the blotter before him:

" 'Look out for girl, Theresa Rogaum. Aged 18; height, about 5, 3; light hair, blue eyes, white cotton dress, trimmed with blue ribbon. Last seen with lad named Almerting, about 19 years of age, about 5, 9; weight 135 pounds.' "

There were other details even more pointed and conclusive. For over an hour now, supposedly, policemen from the Battery to Harlem, and far beyond, had been scanning long streets and dim shadows for a girl in a white dress with a youth of nineteen,—supposedly.

Officer Halsey, another of this region, which took in a portion of Washington Square, had seen a good many couples this pleasant summer evening since the description of Theresa and Almerting had been read to him over the telephone, but none that answered to these. Like Maguire and Delahanty, he was more or less indifferent to all such cases, but idling on a corner near the park at about three a.m., a brother officer, one Paisly by name, came up and casually mentioned the missing pair also.

"I bet I saw that couple, not over an hour ago. She was dressed in white, and looked to me as if she didn't want to be out. I didn't happen to think at the time, but now I remember. They acted sort o' funny. She did, anyhow. They went in this park down at the Fourth Street end there."

"Supposing we beat it, then," suggested Halsey, weary for something to do.

"Sure," said the other quickly, and together they began a careful search, kicking around in the moonlight under the trees. The moon was leaning moderately toward the west, and all the branches were silvered with light and dew. Among the flowers, past clumps of bushes, near the fountain, they searched, each one going his way alone. At last, the wandering Halsey paused beside a thick clump of flaming bushes, ruddy, slightly, even in the light. A murmur of voices greeted him, and something very much like the sound of a sob.

"What's that?" he said mentally, drawing near and listening.

"Why don't you come on now?" said the first of the voices heard. "They won't let you in any more. You're with me, ain't you? What's the use cryin'?"

No answer to this, but no sobs. She must have been crying silently.

"Come on. I can take care of yuh. We can live in Hoboken. I know a place where we can go to-night. That's all right."

There was a movement as if the speaker were patting her on the shoulder.

"What's the use cryin'? Don't you believe I love yuh?"

The officer who had stolen quietly around to get a better view now came closer. He wanted to see for himself. In the moonlight, from a comfortable distance, he could see them seated. The tall bushes were almost all about the bench. In the arms of the youth was the girl in white, held very close. Leaning over to get a better view, he saw him kiss her and hold her—hold her in such a way that she could but yield to him, whatever her slight disinclination.

It was a common affair at earlier hours, but rather interesting now. The officer was interested. He crept nearer.

"What are you two doin' here?" he suddenly inquired, rising before them, as though he had not seen.

The girl tumbled out of her compromising position, speechless and blushing violently. The young man stood up, nervous, but still defiant.

"Aw, we were just sittin' here," he replied.

"Yes? Well, say, what's your name? I think we're lookin' for you two, anyhow. Almerting?"

"That's me," said the youth.

"And yours?" he added, addressing Theresa.

"Theresa Rogaum," replied the latter brokenly, beginning to cry.

"Well, you two'll have to come along with me," he added laconically. "The Captain wants to see both of you," and he marched them solemnly away.

"What for?" young Almerting ventured to inquire after a time, blanched with fright.

"Never mind," replied the policeman irritably. "Come along, you'll find out at the station house. We want you both. That's enough."

At the other end of the park Paisly joined them, and, at the station-house, the girl was given a chair. She was all tears and melancholy with a modicum possibly of relief at being thus rescued from the world. Her companion, for all his youth, was defiant if circumspect, a natural animal defeated of its aim.

"Better go for her father," commented the sergeant, and by four in the morning old Rogaum, who had still been up and walking the floor, was rushing stationward. From an earlier rage he had passed to an almost killing grief, but now at the thought that he might possibly see his daughter alive and well once more he was overflowing with a mingled emotion which contained rage, fear, sorrow, and a number of other things. What should he do to her if she were alive? Beat her? Kiss her? Or what? Arrived at the station, however, and seeing his fair Theresa in the hands of the police, and this young stranger lingering near, also detained, he was beside himself with fear, rage, affection.

"You! You!" he exclaimed at once, glaring at the imperturbable Almerting, when told that this was the young man who was found with his girl. Then, seized with a sudden horror, he added, turning to Theresa, "Vot haf you done? Oh, oh! You! You!" he repeated again to Almerting angrily, now that he felt that his daughter was safe. "Come not near my tochter any more! I vill preak your effery pone, du teufel, du!"

He made a move toward the incarcerated lover, but here the sergeant interfered.

"Stop that, now," he said calmly. "Take your daughter out of here and go home, or I'll lock you both up. We don't want any fighting here. D'ye hear? Keep your daughter off the streets hereafter, then she won't get into trouble. Don't let her run around with such young toughs as this." Almerting winced. "Then there won't anything happen to her. We'll do whatever punishing's to be done."

"Aw, what's eatin' him!" commented Almerting dourly, now that he felt himself reasonably safe from a personal encounter. "What have I done? He locked her out, didn't he? I was just keepin' her company till morning."

"Yes, we know all about that," said the sergeant, "and about you, too. You shut up, or you'll go downtown to Special Sessions. I want no guff out o' you." Still he ordered the butcher angrily to be gone.

Old Rogaum heard nothing. He had his daughter. He was taking her home. She was not dead—not even morally injured in so far as he could learn. He was a compound of wondrous feelings. What to do was beyond him.

At the corner near the butcher shop they encountered the wakeful Maguire, still idling, as they passed. He was pleased to see that Rogaum had his Theresa once more. It raised him to a high, moralizing height.

"Don't lock her out any more," he called significantly. "That's what brought the other girl to your door, you know!"

"Vot iss dot?" said Rogaum.

"I say the other girl was locked out. That's why she committed suicide."

"Ach, I know," said the husky German under his breath, but he had no intention of locking her out. He did not know what he would do until they were in the presence of his crying wife, who fell upon Theresa, weeping. Then he decided to be reasonably lenient.

"She vass like you," said the old mother to the wandering Theresa, ignorant of the seeming lesson brought to their very door. "She vass loog like you."

"I vill not vip you now," said the old butcher solemnly, too delighted to think of punishment after having feared every horror under the sun, "aber, go not oudt any more. Keep off de streads so late. I von't haf it. Dot loafer, aber—let him yussed come here some more! I fix him!"

"No, no," said the fat mother tearfully, smoothing her daughter's hair. "She vouldn't run avay no more yet, no, no." Old Mrs. Rogaum was all mother.

"Well, you wouldn't let me in," insisted Theresa, "and I didn't have any place to go. What do you want me to do? I'm not going to stay in the house all the time."

"I fix him!" roared Rogaum, unloading all his rage now on the recreant lover freely. "Yussed let him come some more! Der penitentiary he should haf!"

"Oh, he's not so bad," Theresa told her mother, almost a heroine now that she was home and safe. "He's Mr. Almerting, the stationer's boy. They live here in the next block."

"Don't you ever bother that girl again," the sergeant was saying to young Almerting as he turned him loose an hour later. "If you do, we'll get you, and you won't get off under six months. Y' hear me, do you?"

"Aw, I don't want 'er," replied the boy truculently and cynically. "Let him have his old daughter. What'd he want to lock 'er out for? They'd better not lock 'er out again though, that's all I say. I don't want 'er."

"Beat it!" replied the sergeant, and away he went.

John Cheever
(1912–1982)

Born and raised in Quincy, Massachusetts, John Cheever published his first story, "Expelled," in *The New Republic* at the age of eighteen, using some details of his own expulsion from Thayer Academy in South Braintree, Massachusetts. Best known as a short fiction writer, his story collections include: *The Way Some People Live: A Book of Stories* (1943), *The Enormous Radio and Other Stories* (1953), *The Housebreaker of Shady Hill and Other Stories* (1958), *Some People, Places, and Things That Will Not Appear in My Next Novel* (1961), *The Brigadier and the Golf Window* (1964), *The World of Apples* (1973), and *The Stories of John Cheever* (1978), a retrospective collection. The author of five novels, *The Wapshot Chronicle* (1957), *The Wapshot Scandal* (1964), *Bullet Park* (1969), *Falconer* (1977), and *Oh What a Paradise It Seems* (1982), Cheever won the National Book Award, the Pulitzer Prize, and received the Howells Medal for Fiction from the National Academy of Arts and Letters.

THE SORROWS OF GIN

It was Sunday afternoon, and from her bedroom Amy could hear the Beardens coming in, followed a little while later by the Farquarsons and the Parminters. She went on reading *Black Beauty* until she felt in her bones that they might be eating something good. Then she closed her book and went down the stairs. The living-room door was shut, but through it she could hear the noise of loud talk and laughter. They must have been gossiping or worse, because they all stopped talking when she entered the room.

"Hi, Amy," Mr. Farquarson said.

"Mr. Farquarson spoke to you, Amy," her father said.

"Hello, Mr. Farquarson," she said. By standing outside the group for a minute, until they had resumed their conversation, and then by slipping past Mrs. Farquarson, she was able to swoop down on the nut dish and take a handful.

"Amy!" Mr. Lawton said.

"I'm sorry, Daddy," she said, retreating out of the circle, toward the piano.

"Put those nuts back," he said.

"I've handled them, Daddy," she said.

"Well, pass the nuts, dear," her mother said sweetly. "Perhaps someone else would like nuts."

Amy filled her mouth with the nuts she had taken, returned to the coffee table, and passed the nut dish.

"Thank you, Amy," they said, taking a peanut or two.

"How do you like your new school, Amy?" Mrs. Bearden asked.

"I like it," Amy said. "I like private schools better than public schools. It isn't so much like a factory."

"What grade are you in?" Mrs. Bearden asked.

"Fourth," she said.

Her father took Mr. Parminter's glass and his own, and got up to go into the dining room to refill them. She fell into the chair he had left vacant.

"Don't sit in your father's chair, Amy," her mother said, not realizing that Amy's legs were worn out from riding a bicycle, while her father had done nothing but sit down all day.

As she walked toward the French doors, she heard her mother beginning to talk about the new cook. It was a good example of the interesting things they found to talk about.

"You'd better put your bicycle in the garage," her

father said, returning with the fresh drinks. "It looks like rain."

Amy went out onto the terrace and looked at the sky, but it was not very cloudy, it wouldn't rain, and his advice, like all the advice he gave her, was superfluous. They were always at her. "Put your bicycle away." "Open the door for Grandmother, Amy." "Feed the cat." "Do your homework." "Pass the nuts." "Help Mrs. Bearden with her parcels." "Amy, please try and take more pains with your appearance."

They all stood, and her father came to the door and called her. "We're going over to the Parminters' for supper," he said. "Cook's here, so you won't be alone. Be sure and go to bed at eight like a good girl. And come and kiss me good night."

After their cars had driven off, Amy wandered through the kitchen to the cook's bedroom beyond it and knocked on the door. "Come in," a voice said, and when Amy entered, she found the cook, whose name was Rosemary, in her bathrobe, reading the Bible. Rosemary smiled at Amy. Her smile was sweet and her old eyes were blue. "Your parents have gone out again?" she asked. Amy said that they had, and the old woman invited her to sit down. "They do seem to enjoy themselves, don't they? During the four days I've been here, they've been out every night, or had people in." She put the Bible face down on her lap and smiled, but not at Amy. "Of course, the drinking that goes on here is all sociable, and what your parents do is none of my business, is it? I worry about drink more than most people because of my poor sister. My poor sister drank too much. For ten years, I went to visit her on Sunday afternoons, and most of the time she was *non compos mentis.* Sometimes I'd find her huddled up on the floor with one or two sherry bottles empty beside her. Sometimes she'd seem sober enough to a stranger, but I could tell in a second by the way she spoke her words that she'd drunk enough not to be herself any more. Now my poor sister is gone, I don't have anyone to visit at all."

"What happened to your sister?" Amy asked.

"She was a lovely person, with a peaches-and-cream

complexion and fair hair," Rosemary said. "Gin makes some people gay—it makes them laugh and cry—but with my sister it only made her sullen and withdrawn. When she was drinking, she would retreat into herself. Drink made her contrary. If I'd say the weather was fine, she'd tell me I was wrong. If I'd say it was raining, she'd say it was clearing. She'd correct me about everything I said, however small it was. She died in Bellevue Hospital one summer while I was working in Maine. She was the only family I had."

The directness with which Rosemary spoke had the effect on Amy of making her feel grown, and for once politeness came to her easily. "You must miss your sister a great deal," she said.

"I was just sitting here now thinking about her. She was in service, like me, and it's lonely work. You're always surrounded by a family, and yet you're never a part of it. Your pride is often hurt. The Madams seem condescending and inconsiderate. I'm not blaming the ladies I've worked for. It's just the nature of the relationship. They order chicken salad, and you get up before dawn to get ahead of yourself, and just as you've finished the chicken salad, they change their minds and want crab-meat soup."

"My mother changes her mind all the time," Amy said.

"Sometimes you're in a country place with nobody else in help. You're tired, but not too tired to feel lonely. You go out onto the servants' porch when the pots and pans are done, planning to enjoy God's creation, and although the front of the house may have a fine view of the lake or the mountains, the view from the back is never much. But there is the sky and the trees and the stars and the birds singing and the pleasure of resting your feet. But then you hear them in the front of the house, laughing and talking with their guests and their sons and daughters. If you're new and they whisper, you can be sure they're talking about you. That takes all the pleasure out of the evening."

"Oh," Amy said.

"I've worked all kinds of places—places where there

were eight or nine in help and places where I was expected to burn the rubbish myself, on winter nights, and shovel the snow. In a house where there's a lot of help, there's usually some devil among them—some old butler or parlormaid—who tries to make your life miserable from the beginning. 'The Madam doesn't like it this way,' and 'The Madam doesn't like it that way,' and "I've been with the Madam for twenty years," they tell you. It takes a diplomat to get along. Then there is the rooms they give you, and every one of them I've ever seen is cheerless. If you have a bottle in your suitcase, it's a terrible temptation in the beginning not to take a drink to raise your spirits. But I have a strong character. It was different with my poor sister. She used to complain about nervousness, but, sitting here thinking about her tonight, I wonder if she suffered from nervousness at all. I wonder if she didn't make it all up. I wonder if she just wasn't meant to be in service. Toward the end, the only work she could get was out in the country, where nobody else would go, and she never lasted much more than a week or two. She'd take a little gin for her nervousness, then a little for her tiredness, and when she'd drunk her own bottle and everything she could steal, they'd hear about it in the front part of the house. There was usually a scene, and my poor sister always liked to have the last word. Oh, if I had had my way, they'd be a law against it! It's not my business to advise you to take anything from your father, but I'd be proud of you if you'd empty his gin bottle into the sink now and then—the filthy stuff! But it's made me feel better to talk with you, sweetheart. It's made me not miss my poor sister so much. Now I'll read a little more in my Bible, and then I'll get you some supper."

The Lawtons had had a bad year with cooks—there had been five of them. The arrival of Rosemary had made Marcia Lawton think back to a vague theory of dispensations; she had suffered, and now she was being rewarded. Rosemary was clean, industrious, and cheerful, and her table—as the Lawtons said—was just like the Chambord. On Wednesday night after dinner, she took the train to New York, promising to return on the evening train Thursday. Thursday morning, Marcia went into the cook's room. It was a distasteful but a habitual precaution. The absence of anything personal in the room—a package of cigarettes, a fountain pen, an alarm clock, a radio, or anything else that could tie the old woman to the place—gave her the uncanny feeling that she was being deceived, as she had so often been deceived by cooks in the past. She opened the closet door and saw a single uniform hanging there and, on the closet floor, Rosemary's old suitcase and the white shoes she wore in the kitchen. The suitcase was locked, but when Marcia lifted it, it seemed to be nearly empty.

Mr. Lawton and Amy drove to the station after dinner on Thursday to meet the eight-sixteen train. The top of the car was down, and the brisk air, the starlight, and the company of her father made the little girl feel kindly toward the world. The railroad station in Shady Hill resembled the railroad stations in old movies she had seen on television, where detectives and spies, bluebeards and their trusting victims, were met to be driven off to remote country estates. Amy liked the station, particularly toward dark. She imagined that the people who traveled on the locals were engaged on errands that were more urgent and sinister than commuting. Except when there was a heavy fog or a snowstorm, the club car that her father traveled on seemed to have the gloss and the monotony of the rest of his life. The locals that ran at odd hours belonged to a world of deeper contrasts, where she would like to live.

They were a few minutes early, and Amy got out of the car and stood on the platform. She wondered what the fringe of string that hung above the tracks at either end of the station was for, but she knew enough not to ask her father, because he wouldn't be able to tell her. She could hear the train before it came into view, and the noise excited her and made her happy. When the train drew in to the station and stopped, she looked in the lighted windows for Rosemary and didn't see her. Mr. Lawton got out of the car and joined Amy on the platform. They could see the conductor bending over someone in a seat, and finally the cook arose. She clung to the conductor as he led her out on the platform of the car, and she was crying. "Like peaches and cream," Amy heard her sob. "A lovely, lovely person." The conductor spoke to her kindly, put his arm around her shoulders, and eased her down the steps. Then the train pulled out, and she stood there drying her tears. "Don't say a word, Mr. Lawton," she said, "and I won't say anything." She held out a small paper bag. "Here's a present for you, little girl."

"Thank you, Rosemary," Amy said. She looked into the paper bag and saw that it contained several packets of Japanese water flowers.

Rosemary walked toward the car with the caution of someone who can hardly find her way in the dim light. A sour smell came from her. Her best coat was spotted with mud and ripped in the back. Mr. Lawton told Amy to get in the back seat of the car, and made the cook sit in front, beside him. He slammed the car door shut after her angrily, and then went around to the driver's seat and drove home. Rosemary reached into her handbag and took out a Coca-Cola bottle with a cork stopper and took a drink. Amy could tell by the smell that the Coca-Cola bottle was filled with gin.

"Rosemary!" Mr. Lawton said.

"I'm lonely," the cook said. "I'm lonely, and I'm afraid, and it's all I've got."

He said nothing more until he had turned into their drive and brought the car around to the back door. "Go and get your suitcase, Rosemary," he said. "I'll wait here in the car."

As soon as the cook had staggered into the house, he told Amy to go in by the front door. "Go upstairs to your room and get ready for bed."

Her mother called down the stairs when Amy came in, to ask if Rosemary had returned. Amy didn't answer. She went to the bar, took an open gin bottle, and emptied it into the pantry sink. She was nearly crying when she encountered her mother in the living room, and told her that her father was taking the cook back to the station.

When Amy came home from school the next day, she

found a heavy, black-haired woman cleaning the living room. The car Mr. Lawton usually drove to the station was at the garage for a checkup, and Amy drove to the station with her mother to meet him. As he came across the station platform, she could tell by the lack of color in his face that he had had a hard day. He kissed her mother, touched Amy on the head, and got behind the wheel.

"You know," her mother said, "there's something terribly wrong with the guest-room shower."

"Damn it, Marcia," he said. "I wish you wouldn't always greet me with bad news!"

His grating voice oppressed Amy, and she began to fiddle with the button that raised and lowered the window.

"Stop that, Amy!" he said.

"Oh, well, the shower isn't important," her mother said. She laughed weakly.

"When I got back from San Francisco last week," he said, "you couldn't wait to tell me that we need a new oil burner."

"Well, I've got a part-time cook. That's good news."

"Is she a lush?" her father asked.

"Don't be disagreeable, dear. She'll get us some dinner and wash the dishes and take the bus home. We're going to the Farquarsons'."

"I'm really too tired to go anywhere," he said.

"Who's going to take care of me?" Amy asked.

"You always have a good time at the Farquarsons'," her mother said.

"Well, let's leave early," he said.

"Who's going to take care of me?" Amy asked.

"Mrs. Henlein," her mother said.

When they got home, Amy went over to the piano.

Her father washed his hands in the bathroom off the hall and then went to the bar. He came into the living room holding the empty gin bottle. "What's her name?" he asked.

"Ruby," her mother said.

"She's exceptional. She's drunk a quart of gin on her first day."

"Oh dear!" her mother said. "Well, let's not make any trouble now."

"Everybody is drinking my liquor," her father shouted, "and I am God-damned sick and tired of it!"

"There's plenty of gin in the closet," her mother said. "Open another bottle."

"We paid that gardener three dollars an hour and all he did was sneak in here and drink up my Scotch. The sitter we had before we got Mrs. Henlein used to water my bourbon, and I don't have to remind you about Rosemary. The cook before Rosemary not only drank everything in my liquor cabinet but she drank all the rum, kirsch, sherry, and wine that we had in the kitchen for cooking. Then, there's that Polish woman we had last summer. Even that old laundress. *And* the painters. I think they must have put some kind of mark on my door. I think the agency must have checked me off as an easy touch."

"Well, let's get through dinner, and then you can speak to her."

"The hell with that!" he said. "I'm not going to encourage people to rob me. *Ruby!*" He shouted her name several times, but she didn't answer. Then she appeared in the dining-room doorway anyway, wearing her hat and coat.

"I'm sick," she said. Amy could see that she was frightened.

"I should think that you would be," her father said.

"I'm sick," the cook mumbled, "and I can't find anything around here, and I'm going home."

"Good," he said. "Good! I'm through with paying people to come in here and drink my liquor."

The cook started out the front way, and Marcia Lawton followed her into the front hall to pay her something. Amy had watched this scene from the piano bench, a position that was withdrawn but that still gave her a good view. She saw her father get a fresh bottle of gin and make a shaker of Martinis. He looked very unhappy.

"Well," her mother said when she came back into the room. "You know, she didn't look drunk."

"Please don't argue with me, Marcia," her father said.

He poured two cocktails, said "Cheers," and drank a little. "We can get some dinner at Orpheo's," he said.

"I suppose so," her mother said. "I'll rustle up something for Amy." She went into the kitchen, and Amy opened her music to "Reflets d'Automne." "COUNT," her music teacher had written. "COUNT and lightly, lightly . . ." Amy began to play. Whenever she made a mistake, she said "Darn it!" and started at the beginning again. In the middle of "Reflets d'Automne" it struck her that *she* was the one who had emptied the gin bottle. Her perplexity was so intense that she stopped playing, but her feelings did not go beyond perplexity, although she did not have the strength to continue playing the piano. Her mother relieved her. "Your supper's in the kitchen, dear," she said. "And you can take a popsicle out of the deep freeze for dessert. Just one."

Marcia Lawton held her empty glass toward her husband, who filled it from the shaker. Then she went upstairs. Mr. Lawton remained in the room, and, studying her father closely, Amy saw that his tense look had begun to soften. He did not seem so unhappy any more, and as she passed him on her way to the kitchen, he smiled at her tenderly and patted her on the top of the head.

When Amy had finished her supper, eaten her popsicle, and exploded the bag it came in, she returned to the piano and played "Chopsticks" for a while. Her father came downstairs in his evening clothes, put his drink on the mantelpiece, and went to the French doors to look at his terrace and his garden. Amy noticed that the transformation that had begun with a softening of his features was even more advanced. At last, he seemed happy. Amy wondered if he was drunk, although his walk was not unsteady. If anything, it was more steady.

Her parents never achieved the kind of rolling, swinging gait that she saw impersonated by a tightrope walker in the circus each year while the band struck up "Show Me the Way to Go Home" and that she liked to imitate herself sometimes. She liked to turn round and round and round on the lawn, until, staggering and a little sick, she would whoop, "I'm drunk! I'm a drunken man!" and reel over the grass, righting herself as she was about to fall and finding herself not unhappy at having lost for a second her ability to see the world. But she had never seen her parents like that. She had never seen them hanging on to a lamppost and singing and reeling, but she had seen them fall down. They were never indecorous—they seemed to get more decorous and formal the more they drank—but sometimes her father would get up to fill everybody's glass and he would walk straight enough but his shoes would seem to stick to the carpet. And sometimes, when he got to the dining-room door, he would miss it by a foot or more. Once, she had seen him walk into the wall with such force that he collapsed onto the floor and broke most of the glasses he was carrying. One or two people laughed, but the laughter was not general or hearty, and most of them pretended that he had not fallen down at all. When her father got to his feet, he went right on to the bar as if nothing had happened. Amy had once seen Mrs. Farquarson miss the chair she was about to sit in, by a foot, and thump down onto the floor, but nobody laughed then, and they pretended that Mrs. Farquarson hadn't fallen down at all. They seemed like actors in a play. In the school play, when you knocked over a paper tree you were supposed to pick it up without showing what you were doing, so that you would not spoil the illusion of being in a deep forest, and that was the way *they* were when somebody fell down.

Now her father had that stiff, funny walk that was so different from the way he tramped up and down the station platform in the morning, and she could see that he was looking for something. He was looking for his drink. It was right on the mantelpiece, but he didn't look there. He looked on all the tables in the living room. Then he went out onto the terrace and looked there, and then he came back into the living room and looked on all the tables again. Then he went back onto the terrace, and then back over the living-room tables, looking three times in the same place, although he was always telling her to look intelligently when she lost her sneakers or her raincoat. "Look for it, Amy," he was always saying. "Try and remember where you left it. I can't buy you a new raincoat every time it rains." Finally he gave up and poured himself a cocktail in another glass. "I'm going to get Mrs. Henlein," he told Amy, as if this were an important piece of information.

Amy's only feeling for Mrs. Henlein was indifference, and when her father returned with the sitter, Amy thought of the nights, stretching into weeks—the years, almost—when she had been cooped up with Mrs. Henlein. Mrs. Henlein was very polite and was always telling Amy what was ladylike and what was not. Mrs. Henlein also wanted to know where Amy's parents were going and what kind of party it was, although it was none of her business. She always sat down on the sofa as if she owned the place, and talked about people she had never been introduced to, and asked Amy to bring her the newspaper, although she had no authority at all.

When Marcia Lawton came down, Mrs. Henlein wished her good evening. "Have a lovely party," she called after the Lawtons as they went out the door. Then she turned to Amy. "Where are your parents going, sweetheart?

"But you must know, sweetheart. Put on your thinking cap and try to remember. Are they going to the club?"

"No," Amy said.

"I wonder if they could be going to the Trenchers'," Mrs. Henlein said. "The Trenchers' house was lighted up when we came by."

"They're not going to the Trenchers'," Amy said. "They hate the Trenchers."

"Well, where are they going, sweetheart?" Mrs. Henlein asked.

"They're going to the Farquarsons'," Amy said.

"Well, that's all I wanted to know, sweetheart," Mrs. Henlein said. "Now get me the newspaper and hand it to me politely. *Politely,*" she said, as Amy approached her with the paper. "It doesn't mean anything when you do things for your elders unless you do them politely." She put on her glasses and began to read the paper.

Amy went upstairs to her room. In a glass on her table were the Japanese flowers that Rosemary had brought her, blooming stalely in water that was colored pink from the dyes. Amy went down the back stairs and through the kitchen into the dining room. Her father's cocktail things were spread over the bar. She emptied the gin bottle into the pantry sink and then put it back where she had found it. It was too late to ride her bicycle and too early to go to bed, and she knew that if she got anything interesting on the television, like a murder, Mrs. Henlein would make her turn it off. Then she remembered that her father had brought her home from his trip West a book about horses, and she ran cheerfully up the back stairs to read her new book.

It was after two when the Lawtons returned. Mrs. Henlein, asleep on the living-room sofa dreaming about a dusty attic, was awakened by their voices in the hall. Marcia Lawton paid her, and thanked her, and asked if anyone had called, and then went upstairs. Mr. Lawton was in the dining room, rattling the bottles around. Mrs. Henlein, anxious to get into her own bed and back to sleep, prayed that he wasn't going to pour himself another drink, as they so often did. She was driven home night after night by drunken gentlemen. He stood in the door of the dining room, holding an empty bottle in his hand. "You must be stinking, Mrs. Henlein," he said.

"Hmm," she said. She didn't understand.

"You drank a full quart of gin," he said.

The lackluster old woman—half between wakefulness and sleep—gathered together her bones and groped for her gray hair. It was in her nature to collect stray cats, pile the bathroom up to the ceiling with interesting and valuable newspapers, rouge, talk to herself, sleep in her underwear in case of fire, quarrel over the price of soup bones, and have it circulated around the neighborhood that when she finally died in her dusty junk heap, the mattress would be full of bankbooks and the pillow stuffed with hundred-dollar bills. She had resisted all these rich temptations in order to appear a lady, and she was repaid by being called a common thief. She began to scream at him.

"You take that back, Mr. Lawton! You take back every one of those words you just said! I never stole anything in my whole life, and nobody in my family ever stole anything, and I don't have to stand here and be insulted by a drunk man. Why, as for drinking, I haven't drunk enough to fill an eyeglass for twenty-five years. Mr. Henlein took me to a place of refreshment twenty-five years ago, and I drank two Manhattan cocktails that made me so sick and dizzy that I've never liked the stuff ever since. How dare you speak to me like this! Calling me a thief and a drunken woman! Oh, you disgust me—you disgust me in your ignorance of all the trouble I've had. Do you know what I had for Christmas dinner last year? I had a bacon sandwich. Son of a bitch!" She began to weep. "I'm glad I said it!" she screamed. "It's the first time I've used a dirty word in my whole life and I'm glad I said it. Son of a bitch!" A sense of liberation, as if she stood at the bow of a great ship, came over her. "I lived in this neighborhood my whole life. I can remember when it was full of good farming people and there was fish in the rivers. My father had four acres of sweet meadowland and a name that was known far and wide, and on my mother's side I'm descended from patroons, Dutch nobility. My mother was the spit and image of Queen Wilhelmina. You think you can get away with insulting me, but you're very, very, very much mistaken." She went to the telephone and, picking up the receiver, screamed, "Police! Police! Police! This is Mrs. Henlein, and I'm over at the Lawtons'. He's drunk, and he's calling me insulting names, and I want you to come over here and arrest him!"

The voices woke Amy, and, lying in her bed, she perceived vaguely the pitiful corruption of the adult world; how crude and frail it was, like a piece of worn burlap, patched with stupidities and mistakes, useless and ugly, and yet they never saw its worthlessness, and when you pointed it out to them, they were indignant. But as the voices went on and she heard the cry "Police! Police!" she was frightened. She did not see how they could arrest her, although they could find her fingerprints on the empty bottle, but it was not her own danger that frightened her but the collapse, in the middle of the night, of her father's house. It was all her fault, and when she heard her father speaking into the extension telephone in the library, she felt sunk in guilt. Her father tried to be good and kind—and, remembering the expensive illustrated book about horses that he had brought her from the West, she had to set her teeth to keep from crying. She covered her head with a pillow and realized miserably that she would have to go away. She had plenty of friends from the time when they used to live in New York, or she could spend the night in the Park or hide in a museum. She would have to go away.

"Good Morning," her father said at breakfast. "Ready for a good day!" Cheered by the swelling light in the sky, by the recollection of the manner in which he had handled Mrs. Henlein and kept the police from coming, refreshed by his sleep, and pleased at the thought of playing golf, Mr. Lawton spoke with feeling, but the words seemed to Amy offensive and fatuous; they took away her appetite, and she slumped over her cereal bowl, stirring it with a spoon. "Don't slump, Amy," he said. Then she remembered the night, the screaming, the resolve to go. His cheerfulness refreshed her memory. Her decision was settled. She had a ballet lesson at ten, and she was going to have lunch with Lillian Towele. Then she would leave.

Children prepare for a sea voyage with a toothbrush and a Teddy bear; they equip themselves for a trip around the world with a pair of odd socks, a conch shell, and a thermometer; books and stones and peacock feathers, candy bars, tennis balls, soiled handkerchiefs, and skeins of old string appear to them to be the necessities of travel, and Amy packed, that afternoon, with the impulsiveness of her kind. She was late coming home from lunch, and her getaway was delayed, but she didn't mind. She could catch one of the late-afternoon locals; one of the cooks' trains. Her father was playing golf and her mother was off somewhere. A part-time worker was cleaning the living room. When Amy had finished packing, she went into her parents' bedroom and flushed the toilet. While the water murmured, she took a twenty-dollar bill from her mother's desk. Then she went downstairs and left the house and walked around Blenhollow Circle and down Alewives Lane to the station. No regrets or goodbyes formed in her mind. She went over the names of the friends she had in the city, in case she decided not to spend the night in a museum. When she opened the door of the waiting room, Mr. Flanagan, the stationmaster, was poking his coal fire.

"I want to buy a ticket to New York," Amy said.

"One-way or round-trip?"

"One-way, please."

Mr. Flanagan went through the door into the ticket office and raised the glass window. "I'm afraid I haven't got a half-fare ticket for you, Amy," he said. "I'll have to write one."

"That's all right," she said. She put the twenty-dollar bill on the counter.

"And in order to change that," he said, "I'll have to go over to the other side. Here's the four-thirty-two coming in now, but you'll be able to get the five-ten." She didn't protest, and went and sat beside her cardboard suitcase, which was printed with European hotel and place names. When the local had come and gone, Mr. Flanagan shut his glass window and walked over the footbridge to the northbound platform and called the Lawtons'. Mr. Lawton had just come in from his game and was mixing himself a cocktail. "I think your daughter's planning to take some kind of a trip," Mr. Flanagan said.

It was dark by the time Mr. Lawton got down to the station. He saw his daughter through the station window. The girl sitting on the bench, the rich names on her paper suitcase, touched him as it was in her power to touch him only when she seemed helpless or when she was very sick. Someone had walked over his grave! He shivered with longing, he felt his skin coarsen as when, driving home late and alone, a shower of leaves on the wind crossed the beam of his headlights, liberating him for a second at the most from the literal symbols of his life—the buttonless shirts, the vouchers and bank statements, the order blanks, and the empty glasses. He seemed to listen—God knows for what. Commands, drums, the crackle of signal fires, the music of the glockenspiel—how sweet it sounds on the Alpine air—singing from a tavern in the pass, the honking of wild swans; he seemed to smell the salt air in the churches of Venice. Then, as it was with the leaves, the power of her figure to trouble him was ended: his gooseflesh vanished. He was himself. Oh, why should she want to run away? Travel—and who knew better than a man who spent three days of every fortnight on the road—was a world of overheated plane cabins and repetitious magazines, where even the coffee, even the champagne, tasted of plastics. How could he teach her that home sweet home was the best place of all?

Tillie Olsen
(b. 1913)

"Tell Me a Riddle," the title story of a volume of four of Olsen's tales, won the O. Henry Award for the best American short story in 1961. Currently a resident of San Francisco, she edited Rebecca Harding Davis's *Life in the Iron Mills* (1972) and published a novel, *Yonnondio: From the Thirties* (1974). The title refers to the fact that the manuscript for this novel was rediscovered by Olsen almost forty years after she had been forced to set it aside for lack of time to complete it. In 1978 she published *Silences,* a feminist, nonfiction work. She has taught at Amherst, Stanford, M.I.T., and the University of Massachusetts at Boston and is the recipient of fellowships from the Guggenheim Foundation and the National Endowment for the Humanities.

I STAND HERE IRONING

I stand here ironing, and what you asked me moves tormented back and forth with the iron.

"I wish you would manage the time to come in and talk with me about your daughter. I'm sure you can help me understand her. She's a youngster who needs help and whom I'm deeply interested in helping."

"Who needs help." Even if I came, what good would it do? You think because I am her mother I have a key, or that in some way you could use me as a key? She has lived for nineteen years. There is all that life that has happened outside of me, beyond me.

And when is there time to remember, to sift, to weigh, to estimate, to total? I will start and there will be an interruption and I will have to gather it all together again. Or I will become engulfed with all I did or did not do, with what should have been and what cannot be helped.

She was a beautiful baby. The first and only one of our five that was beautiful at birth. You do not guess how new and uneasy her tenancy in her now-loveliness. You did not know her all those years she was thought homely, or see her poring over her baby pictures, making me tell her over and over how beautiful she had been—and would be, I would tell her—and was now, to the seeing eye. But the seeing eyes were few or non-existent. Including mine.

I nursed her. They feel that's important nowadays. I nursed all the children, but with her, with all the fierce rigidity of first motherhood, I did like the books then said. Though her cries battered me to trembling and my breasts ached with swollenness, I waited till the clock decreed.

Why do I put that first? I do not even know if it matters, or if it explains anything.

She was a beautiful baby. She blew shining bubbles of sound. She loved motion, loved light, loved color and music and textures. She would lie on the floor in her blue overalls patting the surface so hard in ecstasy her hands and feet would blur. She was a miracle to me, but when she was eight months old I had to leave her daytimes with the woman downstairs to whom she was no miracle at all, for I worked or looked for work and for Emily's father, who "could no longer endure" (he wrote in his good-bye note) "sharing want with us."

I was nineteen. It was the pre-relief, pre-WPA world of the depression. I would start running as soon as I got off the streetcar, running up the stairs, the place smelling sour, and awake or asleep to startle awake, when she saw me she would break into a clogged weeping that could not be comforted, a weeping I can hear yet.

After a while I found a job hashing at night so I could be with her days, and it was better. But it came to where I had to bring her to his family and leave her.

It took a long time to raise the money for her fare back. Then she got chicken pox and I had to wait longer. When she finally came, I hardly knew her, walking quick and nervous like her father, looking like her father, thin, and dressed in a shoddy red that yellowed her skin and glared at the pockmarks. All the baby loveliness gone.

She was two. Old enough for nursery school they said, and I did not know then what I know now—the fatigue of the long day, and the lacerations of group life in the nurseries that are only parking places for children.

Except that it would have made no difference if I had known. It was the only place there was. It was the only way we could be together, the only way I could hold a job.

And even without knowing, I knew. I knew the teacher that was evil because all these years it has curdled into my memory, the little boy hunched in the corner, her rasp, "why aren't you outside, because Alvin hits you? that's no reason, go out, scaredy." I knew Emily hated it even if she did not clutch and implore "don't go Mommy" like the other children, mornings.

She always had a reason why she should stay home. Momma, you look sick, Momma. I feel sick. Momma, the teachers aren't there today, they're sick. Momma, we can't go, there was a fire there last night. Momma, it's a holiday today, no school, they told me.

But never a direct protest, never rebellion. I think of our others in their three-, four-year-oldness—the explosions, the tempers, the denunciations, the demands—and I feel suddenly ill. I put the iron down. What in me demanded that goodness in her? And what was the cost, the cost to her of such goodness?

The old man living in the back once said in his gentle way: "You should smile at Emily more when you look at her." What *was* in my face when I looked at her? I loved her. There were all the acts of love.

It was only with the others I remembered what he said, and it was the face of joy, and not of care or tightness or worry I turned to them—too late for Emily. She does not smile easily, let alone almost always as her brothers and sisters do. Her face is closed and sombre, but when she wants, how fluid. You must have seen it in her pantomimes, you spoke of her rare gift for comedy on the stage that rouses a laughter out of the audience so dear they applaud and applaud and do not want to let her go.

Where does it come from, that comedy? There was none of it in her when she came back to me that second time, after I had had to send her away again. She had a new daddy now to learn to love, and I think perhaps it was a better time.

Except when we left her alone nights, telling ourselves she was old enough.

"Can't you go some other time, Mommy, like tomorrow?" she would ask. "Will it be just a little while you'll be gone? Do you promise?"

The time we came back, the front door open, the clock on the floor in the hall. She rigid awake. "It wasn't just a little while. I didn't cry. Three times I called you, just three times, and then I ran downstairs to open the door so you could come faster. The clock talked loud. I threw it away, it scared me what it talked."

She said the clock talked loud again that night I went to the hospital to have Susan. She was delirious with the fever that comes before red measles, but she was fully conscious all the week I was gone and the week after we were home when she could not come near the new baby or me.

She did not get well. She stayed skeleton thin, not wanting to eat, and night after night she had nightmares. She would call for me, and I would rouse from exhaustion to sleepily call back: "You're all right, darling, go to sleep, it's just a dream," and if she still called, in a sterner voice, "now go to sleep, Emily, there's nothing to hurt you." Twice, only twice, when I had to get up for Susan anyhow, I went in to sit with her.

Now when it is too late (as if she would let me hold and comfort her like I do the others) I get up and go to her at once at her moan or restless stirring. "Are you awake, Emily? Can I get you something?" And the answer is always the same: "No, I'm all right, go back to sleep, Mother."

They persuaded me at the clinic to send her away to a convalescent home in the country where "she can have the kind of food and care you can't manage for her, and you'll be free to concentrate on the new baby." They still send children to that place. I see pictures on the society page of sleek young women planning affairs to raise money for it, or dancing at the affairs, or decorating Easter eggs or filling Christmas stockings for the children.

They never have a picture of the children so I do not know if the girls still wear those gigantic red bows and the ravaged looks on the every other Sunday when parents can come to visit "unless otherwise notified"—as we were notified the first six weeks.

Oh it is a handsome place, green lawns and tall trees and fluted flower beds. High up on the balconies of each cottage the children stand, the girls in their red bows and white dresses, the boys in white suits and giant red ties. The parents stand below shrieking up to be heard and the children shriek down to be heard, and between them the invisible wall "Not To Be Contaminated by Parental Germs or Physical Affection."

There was a tiny girl who always stood hand in hand with Emily. Her parents never came. One visit she was gone. "They moved her to Rose College," Emily shouted in explanation. "They don't like you to love anybody here."

She wrote once a week, the labored writing of a seven-year-old. "I am fine. How is the baby. If I write my leter nicly I will have a star. Love." There never was a star. We wrote every other day, letters she could never hold or keep but only hear read—once. "We simply do not have room for children to keep any personal possessions," they patiently explained when we pieced one Sunday's shrieking together to plead how much it would mean to Emily, who loved so to keep things, to be allowed to keep her letters and cards.

Each visit she looked frailer. "She isn't eating," they told us.

(They had runny eggs for breakfast or mush with lumps,

Emily said later, I'd hold it in my mouth and not swallow. Nothing ever tasted good, just when they had chicken.)

It took us eight months to get her released home, and only the fact that she gained back so little of her seven lost pounds convinced the social worker.

I used to try to hold and love her after she came back, but her body would stay stiff, and after a while she'd push away. She ate little. Food sickened her, and I think much of life too. Oh she had physical lightness and brightness, twinkling by on skates, bouncing like a ball up and down up and down over the jump rope, skimming over the hill; but these were momentary.

She fretted about her appearance, thin and dark and foreign-looking at a time when every little girl was supposed to look or thought she should look a chubby blonde replica of Shirley Temple. The doorbell sometimes rang for her, but no one seemed to come and play in the house or be a best friend. Maybe because we moved so much.

There was a boy she loved painfully through two school semesters. Months later she told me how she had taken pennies from my purse to buy him candy. "Licorice was his favorite and I brought him some every day, but he still liked Jennifer better'n me. Why, Mommy?" The kind of question for which there is no answer.

School was a worry to her. She was not glib or quick in a world where glibness and quickness were easily confused with ability to learn. To her overworked and exasperated teachers she was an overconscientious "slow learner" who kept trying to catch up and was absent entirely too often.

I let her be absent, though sometimes the illness was imaginary. How different from my now-strictness about attendance with the others. I wasn't working. We had a new baby, I was home anyhow. Sometimes, after Susan grew old enough, I would keep her home from school, too, to have them all together.

Mostly Emily had asthma, and her breathing, harsh and labored, would fill the house with a curiously tranquil sound. I would bring the two old dresser mirrors and her boxes of collections to her bed. She would select beads and single earrings, bottle tops and shells, dried flowers and pebbles, old postcards and scraps, all sorts of oddments; then she and Susan would play Kingdom, setting up landscapes and furniture, peopling them with action.

Those were the only times of peaceful companionship between her and Susan. I have edged away from it, that poisonous feeling between them, that terrible balancing of hurts and needs I had to do between the two, and did so badly, those earlier years.

Oh there are conflicts between the others too, each one human, needing, demanding, hurting, taking—but only between Emily and Susan, no, Emily toward Susan that corroding resentment. It seems so obvious on the surface, yet it is not obvious. Susan, the second child, Susan, golden- and curly-haired and chubby, quick and articulate and assured, everything in appearance and manner Emily was not; Susan, not able to resist Emily's precious things, losing or sometimes clumsily breaking them; Susan telling jokes and riddles to company for applause while Emily sat silent (to say to me later: that was *my* riddle, Mother, I told it to Susan); Susan, who for all the five years' difference in age was just a year behind Emily in developing physically.

I am glad for that slow physical development that widened the difference between her and her contemporaries, though she suffered over it. She was too vulnerable for that terrible world of youthful competition, of preening and parading, of constant measuring of yourself against every other, of envy, "If I had that copper hair," "If I had that skin. . . ." She tormented herself enough about not looking like the others, there was enough of the unsureness, the having to be conscious of words before you speak, the constant caring—what are they thinking of me? without having it all magnified by the merciless physical drives.

Ronnie is calling. He is wet and I change him. It is rare there is such a cry now. That time of motherhood is almost behind me when the ear is not one's own but must always be racked and listening for the child cry, the child call. We sit for a while and I hold him, looking out over the city spread in charcoal with its soft aisles of light "*Shoogily,*" he breathes and curls closer. I carry him back to bed, asleep. *Shoogily.* A funny word, a family word, inherited from Emily, invented by her to say: *comfort.*

In this and other ways she leaves her seal, I say aloud. And startle at my saying it. What do I mean? What did I start to gather together, to try and make coherent? I was at the terrible, growing years. War years. I do not remember them well. I was working, there were four smaller ones now, there was not time for her. She had to help be a mother, and housekeeper, and shopper. She had to set her seal. Mornings of crisis and near hysteria trying to get lunches packed, hair combed, coats and shoes found, everyone to school or Child Care on time, the baby ready for transportation. And always the paper scribbled on by a smaller one, the book looked at by Susan then mislaid, the homework not done. Running out to that huge school where she was one, she was lost, she was a drop; suffering over the unpreparedness, stammering and unsure in her classes.

There was so little time left at night after the kids were bedded down. She would struggle over books, always eating (it was in those years she developed her enormous appetite that is legendary in our family) and I would be ironing, or preparing food for the next day, or writing V-mail to Bill, or tending the baby. Sometimes, to make me laugh, or out of her despair, she would imitate happenings or types at school.

I think I said once: "Why don't you do something like this in the school amateur show?" One morning she phoned me at work, hardly understandable through the weeping: "Mother, I did it. I won, I won; they gave me first prize; they clapped and clapped and wouldn't let me go."

Now suddenly she was Somebody, and as imprisoned in her difference as she had been in anonymity.

She began to be asked to perform at other high schools, even in colleges, then at city and statewide affairs. The first one we went to, I only recognized her that first moment when thin, shy, she almost drowned herself into the curtains. Then: Was this Emily? The control, the command, the convulsing and deadly clowning, the spell, then the roaring, stamping audience, unwilling to let this rare and precious laughter out of their lives.

Afterwards: You ought to do something about her with a gift like that—but without money or knowing how, what does one do? We have left it all to her, and the gift has as often eddied inside, clogged and clotted, as been used and growing.

She is coming. She runs up the stairs two at a time with her light graceful step, and I know she is happy tonight. Whatever it was that occasioned your call did not happen today.

"Aren't you ever going to finish the ironing, Mother? Whistler painted his mother in a rocker. I'd have to paint mine standing over an ironing board." This is one of her communicative nights and she tells me everything and nothing as she fixes herself a plate of food out of the icebox.

She is so lovely. Why did you want me to come in at all? Why were you concerned? She will find her way.

She starts up the stairs to bed. "Don't get me up with the rest in the morning." "But I thought you were having midterms." "Oh, those," she comes back in, kisses me, and says quite lightly, "in a couple of years when we'll all be atom-dead they won't matter a bit."

She has said it before. She *believes* it. But because I have been dredging the past, and all that compounds a human being is so heavy and meaningful in me, I cannot endure it tonight.

I will never total it all. I will never come in to say: She was a child seldom smiled at. Her father left me before she was a year old. I had to work her first six years when there was work, or I sent her home and to his relatives. There were years she had care she hated. She was dark and thin and foreign-looking in a world where the prestige went to blondeness and curly hair and dimples, she was slow where glibness was prized. She was a child of anxious, not proud, love. We were poor and could not afford for her the soil of easy growth. I was a young mother, I was a distracted mother. There were the other children pushing up, demanding. Her younger sister seemed all that she was not. There were years she did not want me to touch her. She kept too much in herself, her life was such she had to keep too much in herself. My wisdom came too late. She has much to her and probably nothing will come of it. She is a child of her age, of depression, of war, of fear.

Let her be. So all that is in her will not bloom—but in how many does it? There is still enough left to live by. Only help her to know—help make it so there is cause for her to know—that she is more than this dress on the ironing board, helpless before the iron.

Langston Hughes

(1902–1967)

Born in Joplin, Missouri, Langston Hughes spent most of his youth in the Midwest before coming to New York City in 1921 to attend Columbia University. After an unsuccessful year there, he signed on a tramp steamer to Africa and Europe as a seaman and cook's helper; later he earned a B.A. at Lincoln University in Pennsylvania, an all-black college. He returned to New York, where he became a leader of the group of Harlem writers of the Black Literary Renaissance of the 1920s. Among his numerous collections of poetry are *The Weary Blues* (1926), *The Dream Keeper and Other Poems* (1932), *Shakespeare in Harlem* (1942), *Montage of a Dream Deferred* (1951), and *The Selected Poems of Langston Hughes* (1959 and 1965), a retrospective collection. The author of works in a wide range of literary forms, he published a novel, *Not Without Laughter* (1930), children's books, plays, nonfiction, opera libretti, lyrics for musicals such as Kurt Weill's *Street Scene* (1940), and the short-story collections *The Ways of the White Folks* (1934) and *Laughing to Keep from Crying* (1952). His most popular works were the "Simple" newspaper sketches written for the *Chicago Defender* in the 1940s and collected in *Simple Speaks His Mind* (1950), *Simple Takes a Wife* (1953), *Simple Stakes a Claim* (1957), and *The Best of Simple* (1961).

SIMPLE AND COUSIN F. D. ROOSEVELT BROWN

(Selected Sketches)

Feet Live Their Own Life

"If you want to know about my life," said Simple as he blew the foam from the top of the newly filled glass the bartender put before him, "don't look at my face, don't look at my hands. Look at my feet and see if you can tell how long I been standing on them."

"I cannot see your feet through your shoes," I said.

"You do not need to see through my shoes," said Simple. "Can't you tell by the shoes I wear—not pointed, not rocking-chair, not French-toed, not nothing but big, long, broad, and flat—that I been standing on these feet a long time and carrying some heavy burdens? They ain't flat from standing at no bar, neither, because I always sets at a bar. Can't you tell that? You know I do not hang out in a bar unless it has stools, don't you?"

"That I have observed," I said, "but I did not connect it with your past life."

"Everything I do is connected up with my past life," said Simple. "From Virginia to Joyce, from my wife to Zarita, from my mother's milk to this glass of beer, everything is connected up."

"I trust you will connect up with that dollar I just loaned you when you get paid," I said. "And who is Virginia? You never told me about her."

"Virginia is where I was borned," said Simple. "I *would* be borned in a state named after a woman. From that day on, women never give me no peace."

"You, I fear, are boasting. If the women were running after you as much as you run after them, you would not be able to sit here on this bar stool in peace. I don't see any women coming to call you out to go home, as some of these fellows' wives do around here."

"Joyce better not come in no bar looking for me," said Simple. "That is why me and my wife busted up—one reason. I do not like to be called out of no bar by a female. It's a man's perogative to just set and drink sometimes."

"How do you connect that prerogative with your past?" I asked.

"When I was a wee small child," said Simple, "I had no place to set and think in, being as how I was raised up with three brothers, two sisters, seven cousins, one married aunt, a common-law uncle, and the minister's grandchild—and the house only had four rooms. I never had no place just to set and think. Neither to set and drink—not even much my milk before some hongry child snatched it out of my hand. I were not the youngest, neither a girl, nor the cutest. I don't know why, but I don't think nobody liked me much. Which is why I was afraid to like anybody for a long time myself. When I did like somebody, I was full-grown and then I picked out the wrong woman because I had no practice in liking anybody before that. We did not get along."

"Is that when you took to drink?"

"Drink took to me," said Simple. "Whiskey just naturally likes me but beer likes me better. By the time I got married I had got to the point where a cold bottle was almost as good as a warm bed, especially when the bottle could not talk and the bed-warmer could. I do not like a woman to talk to me too much—I mean about me. Which is why I like Joyce. Joyce most in generally talks about herself."

"I am still looking at your feet," I said, "and I swear they do not reveal your life to me. Your feet are no open book."

"You have eyes but you see not," said Simple. "These feet have stood on every rock from the Rock of Ages to 135th and Lenox. These feet have supported everything from a cotton bale to a hongry woman. These feet have walked ten thousand miles working for white folks and another ten thousand keeping up with colored. These feet have stood at altars, crap tables, free lunches, bars, graves, kitchen doors, betting windows, hospital clinics, WPA desks, social security railings, and in all kinds of lines from soup lines to the draft. If I just had four feet, I could have stood in more places longer. As it is, I done wore out seven hundred pairs of shoes, eighty-nine tennis shoes, twelve summer sandals, also six loafers. The socks that these feet have bought could build a knitting mill. The corns I've cut away would dull a German razor. The bunions I forgot would make you ache from now till Judgment Day. If anybody was to write the history of my life, they should start with my feet."

"Your feet are not all that extraordinary," I said. "Besides, everything you are saying is general. Tell me specifically some one thing your feet have done that makes them different from any other feet in the world, just one."

"Do you see that window in that white man's store across the street?" asked Simple. "Well, this right foot of mine broke out that window in the Harlem riots right smack in the middle. Didn't no other foot in the world break that window but mine. And this left foot carried me off running as soon as my right foot came down. Nobody else's feet saved me from the cops that night but these *two* feet right here. Don't tell me these feet ain't had a life of their own."

"For shame," I said, "going around kicking out windows. Why?"

"Why?" said Simple. "You have to ask my great-great-grandpa why. He must of been simple—else why did he let them capture him in Africa and sell him for a slave to breed my great-grandpa in slavery to breed my grandpa in slavery to breed my pa to breed me to look at that window and say, 'It ain't mine! Bam-mmm-mm-m!' and kick it out?"

"This bar glass is not yours either," I said. "Why don't you smash it?"

"It's got my beer in it," said Simple.

Just then Zarita came in wearing her Thursday-night rabbit-skin coat. She didn't stop at the bar, being dressed up, but went straight back to a booth. Simple's hand went up, his beer went down, and the glass back to its wet spot on the bar.

"Excuse me a minute," he said, sliding off the stool.

Just to give him pause, the dozens, that old verbal

game of maligning a friend's female relatives, came to mind. "Wait," I said. "You have told me about what to ask your great-great-grandpa. But I want to know what to ask your great-great-grand*ma*."

"I don't play the dozens that far back," said Simple, following Zarita into the smokey juke-box blue of the back room.

Landladies

The next time I saw him, he was hot under the collar, but only incidentally about Zarita. Before the bartender had even put the glasses down he groaned, "I do not understand landladies."

"Now what?" I asked. "A landlady is a woman, isn't she? And, according to your declarations, you know how to handle women."

"I know how to handle women who act like ladies, but my landlady ain't no lady. Sometimes I even wish I was living with my wife again so I could have my own place and not have no landladies," said Simple.

"Landladies are practically always landladies," I said.

"But in New York they are landladies *plus!*" declared Simple.

"For instance?"

"For a instant, my landlady said to me one night when I come in, said, 'Third Floor Rear?'

"I said, 'Yes'm.'

"She says, 'You pays no attention to my notices I puts up, does you?'

"I said, 'No'm.'

"She says, 'I know you don't. You had company in your room after ten o'clock last night in spite of my rule.'

" 'No, ma'am. That was in the room next to mine.'

" 'Yes, but you was in there with your company, Mr. Simple.' Zarita can't keep her voice down when she goes calling. 'You and you-all's company and Mr. Boyd's was raising sand. I heard you way down here.'

" 'What you heard was the Fourth Floor Back snoring,

madam. We went out of here at ten-thirty and I didn't come back till two and I came back alone.'

" 'Four this morning, you mean! And you slammed the door!'

" 'Madam, you sure can hear good that late.'

" 'I am not deef. I also was raised in a decent home. And I would like you to respect my place.'

" 'Yes, ma'am,' I said, because I owed her a half week's rent and I did not want to argue right then, although I was mad. But when I went upstairs and saw that sign over them little old pink towels she hangs there in the bathroom, Lord knows for what, I got madder. Sign says:

GUEST TOWELS—ROOMERS DO NOT USE

"But when even a guest of mine uses them, she jumps salty. So for what are they there? Then I saw that other little old sign up over the sink

WASH FACE ONLY IN BOWL—NO SOX

And a sign over the tub says:

DO NOT WASH CLOTHES IN HEAR

Another sign out in the hall says:

TURN OUT LIGHT—COSTS MONEY

As if it wasn't money I'm paying for my rent! And there's still and yet another sign in my room which states:

NO COOKING, DRINKING, NO ROWDYISMS

As if I can cook without a stove or be rowdy by myself. And then right over my bed:

NO CO. AFTER 10

Just like a man can get along in this world alone. But it were part Zarita's fault talking so loud. Anyhow when I saw all them signs I got madder than I had ever been before, and I tore them all down.

"Landladies must think roomers is uncivilized and don't know how to behave themselves. Well, I do. I was also raised in a decent home. My mama made us respect our home. And I have never been known yet to wash my socks in no face bowl. So I tore them signs down.

"The next evening when I come in from work, before I even hit the steps, the landlady yells from the parlor, 'Third Floor Rear?'

"I said, "Yes, this is the Third Floor Rear.'

"She says, 'Does you know who tore my signs down in the bathroom and in the hall? Also your room?'

"I said, 'I tore your signs down, madam. I have been looking at them signs for three months, so I know 'em by heart.'

"She says, 'You will put them back, or else move.'

"I said, 'I not only tore them signs down, I also tore them *up!*'

"She says, 'When you have paid me my rent, you move.'

"I said, 'I will move now.'

"She said, 'You will not take your trunk now.'

"I said, 'What's to keep me?'

"She said, 'Your room door is locked.'

"I said, 'Lady, I got a date tonight. I got to get in to change my clothes.'

"She says, 'You'll get in when you pay your rent.'

"So I had to take the money for my date that night—that I was intending to take out Joyce—and pay up my room rent. The next week I didn't have enough to move, so I am still there."

"Did you put back the signs?" I asked.

"Sure," said Simple. "I even writ a new sign for her which says:

DON'T NOBODY NO TIME TEAR DOWN
THESE SIGNS—ELSE MOVE"

They Come and They Go

"Do you know what happened to me last night when I got home?" said Simple.

"How could I—when I haven't seen you since?"

"F. D. was setting in my room."

"Who in the world is F. D.?"

"Franklin D. Roosevelt Brown."

"I haven't the least idea whom you are talking about," I said.

"I am talking about the fact I never did think I would be being a father to a son who is not my son, but it looks like that is what is about to happen to me."

"A son?"

"Same as," said Simple. "I've been adopted."

"It's beyond my comprehension."

"Mine, too," said Simple. "But his name ought to make you remember what I told you once about my Cousin Mattie Mae's baby being born down in Virginia a long time ago when she were working for them rich white folks, and she named that baby Franklin D. Roosevelt Brown. Them rich old Southerners got mad when they heard it, and told Mattie Mae she better take that white name off that black child. Mattie Mae told them she'd quit first, which she did.

"Well, when I got home high last night at one-two A.M.—having fell off my budget—and come creeping up the steps not to disturb my old landlady, I saw a light under the crack of my door. I thought maybe Zarita had got in my room by mistake, since sometimes she do inveigle my landlady. But when I opened the door, I hollered out loud, also damn near turned pale. I had not expected to see no Negro sitting on my bed. I thought he were a robber. Every hair on my head turned to wire. But it were not no robber. It were a boy.

"When he riz up grinning, instead of fighting, I yelled, 'If I knowed who you was I'd grab my pistol out of that drawer and shook you before you could speak your name, but I do not want to kill nobody I don't know. Who *in the hell* is you?"

" 'F. D.'

" 'F. D. who?' I said, still shaking.

" 'Don't you remember me? I'm your Cousin Mattie Mae's boy, Franklin D. Roosevelt Brown. You saw me when I was five years old.'

" 'You sure ain't five now,' I said, 'and you done scared the hell out of me, setting on *my* chair in *my* room at this time of night, and I ain't seen you since you was a baby. You big as I am. How old are you?'

" 'Seventeen, going on eighteen,' he said.

" 'What are you doing out so late?'

" 'I'm not just out, Cousin Jess. I'm gone.'

" 'Gone! From where?'

" 'Home. I left.'

" 'Left what home? I ain't heard tell of you, nor Mattie Mae neither, in ten years. Where do you live, Brooklyn?'

" 'Virginia,' he said.

" 'Your mother sent you here?'

" 'My mama does not know I am gone,' he said. 'I ran away.'

" 'Well, how come you run *here*?'

" 'Because you're my favorite cousin. I got your address from Uncle George William. I've heard tell of you all my life, Cousin Jess. Folks at home're always talking about you. And I never will forget that hard big-league ball you bought me when I was five years old, and you came home on that visit. I broke my mama's lamp with it and got whipped within an inch of my life. But I never did blame you for it—like the rest of them did. I sure am glad to see you now, Cousin Jess. Howdy!'

" 'Set down,' I said. He set. 'On what did you come here—hitch-hike?'

" 'No, sir. Train. I didn't dream of getting to New York, Cousin Jess, wasn't even thinking of it. But I've been wanting to come, ever since my step-father rawhided me. Then when Mama Mattie just keeps on telling me I'm just like my father, no-good, I was thinking of running away to Norfolk and joining the navy, till somebody told me I wasn't old enough without my parents' consent. Then I thought I'd run as far as Baltimore maybe before frost sets in. But all this was just kind of vague in my mind. Then, last night, I was hanging around the station watching the trains come in and the girls eating ice-cream cones when a colored man got off the streamliner from the North and he said to me, *Here, boy, here is a ticket for you. The rest of this here round-trip, I do not want it. Use it, sell it, tear it up, or give it away. I don't care.*

" 'I looked at it and saw that it was a ticket to New York—a great long yellow ticket. I said, *Aren't you going back up North*?

" 'The man said, *I been up North. They comes and they goes. You go.*

" 'He cut out and left me standing there on the train platform with the ticket in my hand. So when the night train came along in a few minutes heading North, I got on. Here I am.'

" 'Here you is, all right,' I said.

" 'I always did want to come North, Cousin Jess, so I come to you—'

" 'Don't get *me* confused with the North! I ain't the North.'

" 'And I always wanted to see New York and—'

" 'My room ain't New York. Out yonder is New York.'

" 'You are all the Harlem I knew to come to, so—'

" 'Excuse me from being Harlem, because I ain't. Where are you going to sleep? Also eat?' I said. 'How are you going to live?'

"Then that kid took his eyes off me for the first time. He looked down. In fact he looked like he were going to cry.

" 'O.K.,' he said, 'I guess I can't sleep here. And I'm not hungry. So so long, Cousin Jess.'

"He got up and reached for his hat which were on my dresser. In my mind I was going to say, 'Go on back home.'

"Instead I heard my mouth say, 'Hey, you. F. D.! Hang your clothes on the back of that chair. You can sleep over there next to the wall—I got to jump out early when the alarm goes off. I'm telling you, though, I'm a man that snores when I'm in my licker, so if you can sleep through—'

" 'If you don't mind a fellow that kicks in his sleep, Cousin Jess—'

" 'Did you bring your toothbrush?'

" 'No sir, just the clothes on my back.'

" 'Well, you can get a toothbrush tomorrow.'

"So that's the way it were. My big old landlady let F. D. in to wait for me when I wasn't home. Now, what am I gonna do?"

"You say he's going on eighteen. He's practically a man, isn't he? So he'll know his way around soon."

"I don't know my way around yet," said Simple.

A Million—And One

"When I first come to Harlem, I remember, some of them folks that was here then are gone now. It's true, all right, as that man told F. D., 'They come and they go.' New York is too much for them. Some can't make the riffle, just can't stand the pace. Some go to Sea View, some to Lawnside Cemetery, some to Riker's Island, and some go back home. Some get off trains back down South where they come from—and stay. They *been* North, like that man said.

"If I had not told so many lies myself in my time, I would believe F. D. was lying. But I know that sometimes a lie is the truth. And some things that really happen are more like lies than some things that don't. F. D. couldn't make up nothing like his story about that ticket that would be *that* true. So I know it was true. That boy wanted to come to New York so bad he wished himself up on a ticket. Then he had sense enough to believe the ticket was real. It were real. And here he is!

"Do you think I will tell F. D. to go home? I would not!" said Simple. "I remember when I first come to Harlem, nobody had better not tell me to return back home. I do not know if I looked like that kid or not. But I can see F. D. now setting there last night on that chair with one million dreams in his eyes and a million more in his heart. Could I tell him to go home?"

"What kind of kid is F. D.?"

"About the darkest *young* boy I ever seen. And he has the whitest teeth which, when he smiles, lights up the room. He also looks like he has always just taken a bath, he is so clean. Fact is, I would say F. D. is a handsome black boy, but my judgment might be wrong. I want you and Joyce to meet him. He's a husky young cat, done picked so much tobacco he's built like a boxer. Also plays basketball, says his high-school team were the county champeens last spring. He's graduated and got a diploma, too. I know he's smart because the first thing he asked me for this morning when that alarm clock went off, was, 'Cousin Jess, you got any books I can read while you're at work?'

"You know, I couldn't find nothing but a comic book. But I borrowed a dollar from my landlady and told him, 'Go out and look at Harlem today—till I find my books. There ain't but about a million Negroes in Harlem. You will make One Million and *One*. Get acquainted with your brothers.'

"You mean you turned him loose on the town unaccompanied, just like that, and he's never been here before?"

"Could I stay off from work just to go sightseeing with F. D.?"

"I suppose not, but—"

"And do I know anybody else rich enough to be off from work in the daytime? I do not. That young boy did not want to be cooped up in that hot room in the warm summertime with nobody there. And it was a good thing I turned him loose this morning, too, because do you know what he did?"

"No."

"F. D. found himself a job the *first* day he was here. I'm telling you the Semple family is smart even on the Brown side."

"How did he accomplish that miraculous feat?"

"He asked a boy running for the subway if he knew where a job was. The boy said, 'I'm running to my job now. If you can keep up with me, there might be another one down where I am.'

"So F. D. run, too. He like to lost that boy in the subway rush, but he pushed and scrooged along with him, and ended up in the garment center. When that boy run in and grabbed a hand-truck loaded with ladies' garments, F. D. grabbed a hand-truck, too. So the man thought he was working there all the time and give him a invoice to deliver. When he come back, he give him another one. And they put F. D. down on the payroll as hired. That boy just went to work on his nerve."

"It runs in the family," I said. "That's the way you drink, on your nerve—and your friends."

"Come Saturday, I can borrow from F. D.," said Simple.

"Where is he now while you're supporting the bar?"

"I sent him to the movies. He is too young to invite in a bar. But if it was left up to me, I would rather have him in this nice noisy café which ain't no more immoral than them jitterbug candy stores where they sell reefers and write numbers for kids. More junkies hang around a candy store than in a bar, also dope pushers, which I hope F. D. do not meet. What am I going to do with that boy when he starts getting around? Harlem is a blip. He cannot just go to movies every night."

"What you are going to do about sending him back home or, at least, getting in touch with his parents, is the problem it seems to me you should be considering."

"I should?" asked Simple. "I took for granted F. D. were here to stay. I ain't none of his close relations that I have to correspond with his ma. And from what he told me tonight whilst we was eating in the Do-Right Lunch, in my opinion, he just as well not be with Mattie Mae. She's married again and got seven children by another man, not F. D.'s father. They got more mouths than they can feed now. Which is maybe why that boy is so smart. He's been working since he were eight-nine years old. So if he has to look out for his self anyhow, it might as well be in New York where the color line will not choke him to death. I ain't even thought about F. D. going back home."

"Don't you suppose his mother will worry about where he is?"

"I will tell F. D. to drop Mattie Mae a card tonight when I get in. I do not intend to stay out until A.M. and set a bad example for that boy. And he better be home when I get there."

"Do you intend to start bossing the boy around immediately?"

"I intend to start keeping him straight," said Simple. "I know some of the ropes in New York, and if I find him pulling on the wrong ones, I will pull him back."

"Do you intend to keep him with you in that small room of yours?" I asked. "That will cramp your style slightly for entertaining, will it not?"

"Zarita better not light around that room while F. D. is there," said Simple. "I will ask Joyce to take him to church to meet some nice young girls what attends Christian Endeavor or B.Y.P.U. Since I am F. D.'s favorite cousin, he is going to meet some of Harlem's *favorite* people, you know, society, *up there*—the kind I do not know very well myself, but which Joyce knows. I will not let a fine boy like F. D. down. I might even try to meet a few undrinking folks myself—just to have somebody to introduce F. D. to. He ain't got around to the point of asking me yet where I go when I go out. But if he gets curious I'm liable to end up at Abyssinia's prayer meeting some night."

"For you," I said, "I think that would be carrying things a little far. That boy will like you just as well when he finds out your true character. With young people, just be yourself, and you'll get along. Kids don't like four-flushers, nor false fronts, you can be sure of that. Take my advice and just be yourself with F. D."

"There's something else you can give me tonight besides advice, daddy-o. Maybe you'll lend—"

"My good man, please don't start that again. Always borrowing—"

"You thought I was going to say money, didn't you? Uh-uh! Fooled you for once. I was going to say, lend me some extra books you got around your place for that boy to look at."

"Happy to, of course. When?"

"Right now, tonight," said Simple. "I don't want that boy to wake up nary another morning and I ain't got a single book in the house. He will think I am ignorant. Give me some books now."

"Suppose I am not going home now?"

"I very seldom ask of you a favor outside a bar."

"You have *never* asked me for one like this before. Come on, let's go get the books. The Lord must have sent that boy up North to bring a little culture into your life. Joyce has been trying all these years without success. Thank God for Franklin D. Roosevelt Brown!"

"Mattie Mae had a point when she gave that boy that powerful name," said Simple. "It has done took effect on me. I might even read one of them books you are going to lend me. I got to have something to talk about with my cousin. He's educated. Virginia schools for colored ain't as bad as they used to be, so he has learned a lot more than I. Of course, I can talk with you because when you drink beer you come down to my level. But F. D. is too young to drink, so I got to come *up* to his. Am I right?"

"I think you are very right."

"Then pick me out a book I can read *now* this evening," said Simple.

"They say *Knowledge cannot be assimilated overnight,*" I reminded him.

"I don't care what they say," said Simple. "It can be laying there ready to assimilate in the morning."

All in the Family

"F. D. says he don't know which one is the biggest, my landlady or Joyce's. And don't you know both of them evil old landladies is just crazy about that boy!"

"So you took F. D. around to meet Joyce?"

"I did. And Joyce said, 'Jess, when we get married, we're going to adopt F. D.'

"I said, 'In another year F. D. will be big enough to adopt you. He's mighty near grown now.'

" 'We will need a big brother for our babies,' says Joyce. 'And F. D. is a fine boy. He likes culture.'

"Joyce were referring to the fact that he read one of them books you lent us. I ain't read mine yet. But F. D. has done read one and started on mine, too. So when he gets through and tells me what it's all about, I won't have to read mine. He is a very nice young boy, and polite to womens. Southern folks raises their kids better than Northerners, I do believe. F. D. has got manners—even if he is got the nerve to call me *coz* already—short for cousin. One thing, he is about the most pleasantest young fellow I been around, always talking and smiling that big old bright smile of his. I do not mind having him in my room at all. In facts, he is company for me. Also he has offered to pay half the rent."

"Did you accept?"

"What do you mean, did I accept? F. D. has not been here hardly a week yet. He is a young boy just getting started in New York, and I am his kinfolks. You know I would not accept no rent from that boy. What good is relatives if they can't do a little something for you once in a while? None of mine never helped me since Aunt Lucy died. But if somebody had of helped me just a little bit when I were in my young manhood, I might of gotten somewhere further by now, not just laboring from hand to mouth. I am going to help this boy, and he is going to get somewhere. F. D. is already helping me."

"How do you mean, helping you?"

"With somebody around to talk to, I don't spend so much dough in bars any more, as early as Joyce goes to bed."

"You don't mean to tell me you keep that young man up all night long talking to you after you get home from your rounds?"

"I get home early now—to see if he has got home. I done commanded F. D. to be in the house by midnight. Just so he won't think I'm spying on him, I comes home about twelve-thirty or one. He's laying on his side of the bed reading a book. I do not want to put the light out while he's reading—also I am not sleepy so early—so I start talking to him. And we talks sometimes till two-three in the morning."

"It must run in the family," I said, "both of you are night-owls. What can you find to talk about with a youngster like F. D.?"

"Life," said Simple.

"That covers a very wide range of subjects," I said.

"F. D. ain't no baby. When you are going on eighteen now, it is just like going on twenty-eight when I were a child. Besides, he were raised by Mattie Mae, and even though she's my cousin, she never was known to be no lily."

"You don't need to tell everything you know about your Cousin Mattie Mae," I said.

"I say that to this," said Simple, "Mattie were not bashful with nobody. So I know she did not raise F. D. on Sunday school cards alone. He knows the facts of life. You know what he asked me already? I were telling him about the reason I have started putting Five or Ten dollars in the leaves of the Bible every week is because I am preparing to pay for my divorce.

"F. D. says, 'Then you were married legally, and not common law?'

" 'I regrets it, but I were,' I said.

"F. D. said, 'But coz, I always heard common law is better since it doesn't cost so much to get loose.'

"I did not think it would be good morals to agree with F. D., so I said, 'Boy, where did you hear that?'

" 'From mama,' said F. D.

" 'Mattie Mae said that?' I asked like I was surprised.

" 'Yes, but mama didn't really believe it herself, after she saw the results,' said F. D., 'because after my third brother and sister came, she told my step-father he had *better* marry her—or she would get out an injunction to keep him from rooming at our house. So they got married. Which was all right by me,' says F. D., 'except that he thought his fatherly duty was to tan *my* hide, which I never did like, not being his child. And you know I am too big to whip now. But look at these scars on my legs.'

"F. D. stretched one leg out from under the sheet and raised it up, then he pulled the other one out. Both of them were whelped up.

" 'Mama should not have let him whip me like this, should she? But she is crazy about that Negro.'

" 'I will whip you myself,' I said, 'if you talk to anybody else that way about your mama, F. D. After all she is *my* cousin. 'Course, you can talk to me—since it's all in the family. But let's keep it there.'

" 'Naturally,' says F. D."

Kick for Punt

" 'Did you know who my father was, Cousin Jess?' F. D. asked me last night, 'because I never even as much as laid eyes on him.'

" 'I knowed the Negro,' I said. 'I met him once when I were home on a visit before I settled permanent in the North. He were a big black handsome man. Folks called him John Henry because he worked on the railroad and were just passing through with the construction.'

" 'I wonder where the construction gang went on to?' asked F. D.

" 'That, son, I do not know,' I said. I meant *coz.* But not being around that boy since he was five, he seemed more like a son to me than a cousin, even a third or fourth cousin. I always think of cousins as being around my age. Anyhow, I told him I did not know much more about his father than his mother did, except that he were a great one for bawling and brawling, laughing and joke-telling, drinking and not thinking. I wanted to say, 'F. D., I am surprised at you taking to books because all your father could read were the spots on the cards. But he really could play skin, blackjack, and poker. How I know is he beat me out of my fare back to Baltimore, then laughed, and took me out and bought me all I could drink.' But I did not tell that boy that about his father. I said, 'Coz, he were a right nice fellow, always smiling and good-natured just like you, so you come by it naturally. And if he had ever seen you, he would have been crazy about you because you were sure a lively boy-baby. It is too bad that construction gang moved on before you were born. They was working Northwards. I wouldn't be surprised if your daddy warn't somewhere in Harlem by now.'

" 'I wish I could find him," said F. D. 'But he wouldn't know me and I wouldn't know him, we never having seen each other. But I wish I would find him.'

" 'Wishing that hard, I expect you will find him,' I said, 'just like you wished up a ticket to come to New York.'

" 'I wish I would,' he said, half asleep by that time,

and he went on to sleep. So I turned out the light—but not before I jumped into my shirt and pants, and come on out here to the bar to grab myself a couple of more beers. You see I ain't got on nothing now but house shoes, don't you?"

"That boy is liable to wake up and wonder where in the hell you have gone," I said.

"If he do, it won't be the first time he has missed a relative in the middle of the night, I bet. I have been behaving myself right good since I had F. D. under my wing. At least I do come home, even if I might maybe sneak right out again soon as he goes to sleep."

"Why you think you have to deceive that boy about your night-prowl habits, I don't know," I said. "You do nothing vicious or wrong, and I am sure he's not the kind of boy who would look down on a man for imbibing a bit of beer, would he?"

"No, he would not," said Simple. "But I do not want him to think because I am out all night, he should maybe be out, too. So I come in—and come out again when he is unconscious. Just like it took Joyce two or three years to find out I did not go *right* home to bed when I used to leave her house. She knows it now, though."

"And she loves you right on. Just as this boy will still like you when he finds out you don't need more than three or four hours' sleep. He'll probably admire you just for that."

"Next week will be time enough for him to find out, though, won't it? This week lemme set a good example."

"Good examples are not set by deceit," I argued.

"Oh, but sometimes they are," said Simple. "A congressman is a good example until somebody catches him with a deep freeze. A minister is a good example until he gets caught with the deacon's wife. I am a good example as long as F. D. *thinks* I am in my bed asleep. I don't have to always be there in person, do I?"

"Getting your proper rest would do you no harm, however."

"Vacation's coming up. I'll rest then. So don't worry about me."

"Last year you went to Saratoga, didn't you? Where are you going this time?"

"I know where I *ain't* going—and that is to the country. Yes, I know the poem says, 'Only God can make a tree.' But I sure am glad God let Edison make street lights, too, also electric signs. I like electric signs better than I do trees. And neon signs over a bar, man, I love! A bar can shelter me better than any tree. And a tall stool beats short grass any time. Grass is full of chiggers. It is too dark in the country at night, and sunrise comes too early. In the daytime you don't see nothing but animals. Horses, pigs, cows, sheep, birds, chickens. Not a one of them animals ever said one interesting word to me. Animals is no company. I like them in zoos better. Trees I like in parks, birds in somebody else's cages, chickens in frozen-food bins, and sunrise in bed. No, daddy-o, I will not go to the country this summer. I like lights too well."

"You see Tony flashing these lights off and on, don't you? He is about to close the bar. We'd better get out or there won't be any light—except daylight."

"Doggone if it ain't four A.M.," said Simple. "Yonder is dawn breaking. Dawn never was as pretty in the country as it is sneaking over Lenox Avenue. Lemme get on home and see is F. D. done kicked the pillow out from under his own head. That is the kickingest boy! Punt formation! He dreams he's playing football in his sleep—drop-kicks, place-kicks, punts, goals. Dream on, coz, but damn if I want to be the ball! If you kick me this morning, I sure will kick you back."

"You won't get much sleep anyhow, going to bed this late."

"Yes, I will, too," said Simple. "I sleep quick."

Subway to Jamaica

"F. D. were not there when I got back home last night in spite of the fact that it were 12:30, past P.M., so I came back out. I did not see you, so I went back in—and I come back out again. I broke my money-savings rule not to drink more than one beer on myself so I can pay for that divorce. I bought four, also a drink of whiskey. I was worried about that boy being a new boy in the block and a stranger in town—some of them young hellions might of ganged him.

"I stood on the corner of Lenox Avenue and looked up and down. No F. D. I walked to Seventh Avenue and looked up and down. No F. D. All the movies was closed. Nothing but bars open, so I went in a bar I had never been in before.

"Then I said, 'To hell with F.D.! He's big as me, so I ain't responsible. I do not care where he's at. What right has he got to worry me like this? I ain't his daddy.'

"I returned back to my Third Floor Rear. He still were not there—going on four in the morning. So I took off my clothes and went to bed. I did not sleep.

"F. D. come in later than me by twice. But I give that boy credit he did not try to tiptoe. If he just had come in with his shoes in his hands sneaking up the steps, I would have riz up mad and caught him with 'Where the damnation you been, arriving back this time of night?'

"But when F. D. come walking in loud like nothing had happened, creaking every step and hitting on his heels, I pretended to be asleep. F. D. set down on the bed to take his shoes off. I grunted and groaned, "Uh-er-ummm-uh! Man, why don't you turn on the light so you can see?'

" 'Cousin Jess, I've been having a ball,' he said. 'Listen! We've been to the Savoy. It's fine up there! Two bands and a rainbow chandelier that goes around. I'm learning the mambo. I had to take a girl all the way home to Brooklyn.'

"I could not help it but say, 'Late as it is, I thought maybe you had gone to Georgia.'

" 'No, I got on the wrong subway coming back and forgot to change. I went all the way to some place called Jamaica.'

" 'That happens to every Negro what ever comes to New York, at least once,' I said. 'I think they just made that Jamaica line to confuse Negroes, because everybody knows somebody that lives in Brooklyn, and the first time you start back to Harlem you *always* end up in Jamaica. Don't you have to work in the morning, F. D.?'

" 'Yes, sir.'

"Then fall on over in this bed and get your rest.'

" 'She's a sweet little number, coz.'

" 'Um-hummmm, well, tell me about her tomorrow.'

" 'Were you asleep, coz?'

" 'Yes, I were asleep—till you woke me up.'

" 'I got her phone number.'

" 'Um-hum! Well, I suppose you'll be running to Brooklyn every night now.'

" 'Not every night. I couldn't get a date in edgewise till Sunday. That girl is popular. Sunday we're going to Coney Island.'

" 'I want you to bring that girl up here and let me look her over before you-all get too thick. You hear me, F. D.?'

" 'Yes, sir, but I'll bet you're gonna like her, Cousin Jess. Her name is Gloria. She's eighteen and keen. Dresses crazy—had on a big wide leather belt with green shoe strings in the front and a little tiny waist about the size of this bed post. You gonna like her.'

" 'Turn over and go to sleep, boy. And next time, don't get mixed up on no subway to Jamaica. What you due to take is the *A Train* to Harlem. Otherwise, you will arrive at nowhere, square.'

" 'She don't think I'm a square, Cousin Jess.'

"I made out like I was snoring so that boy would stop talking. Next thing I knew, we was both asleep. F. D. must have been sleeping real good because in a few minutes he hauled off and kicked me, which woke me up. In another half-hour the alarm went off. So I didn't get much rest last night. But I'm glad the boy had fun, though. If you do not have a good time in your young years, you might not know how when you get old. And the sooner you find out what train to take to get where you are going in the world, the better. The Jamaica train does *not* run to Harlem. It goes somewhere else."

Boys, Birds, and Bees

"Joyce is gone," said Simple.

"Where?"

"That is just it. I do not know where. She must of left right from work yesterday, which were Friday, because when I rung them seven bells last night, her big old fat landlady waddled to the door and hollered, 'Joyce is gone.'

" 'Gone where?' I says.

" 'You ought to know. You closer than her shadow.'

" 'Madam, I am asking you a question.'

" 'You know her vacation has started. She told me to tell you she would be away for a fortnight, whatever that is.'

" 'A fourth-night?'

" 'Them is her words, not mine, so figure it out for yourself.'

"And she waddled on back through them double doors. What is a fourth-night?"

"Two weeks," I said.

"Well, why didn't Joyce say so? That girl is been around that Maxwell-Reeves woman too much. She's talking in tongues. Two weeks! Well, she can stay gone *two years* for all I care. Facts is, Joyce can *stay* gone. She do not need to come back to me."

"Consider well what you are saying, old boy."

"Don't worry about what I am saying. When she returns, I will close my door against her. I'm a good mind to go home right now and get that money out of that sock I been saving and blow it all in, every damn penny."

"Before I let you do that," I said, "I'll treat you to a whole bottle of beer myself. Bartender, set 'em up! And you, I do not want to hear you talking like that just because Joyce is a little piqued."

"I wish I could peek on her wherever she is at now. Relaxing! I would unlax her."

"Let that girl relax alone and get herself together, calm her nerves, think things over, and come back refreshed. You'll be so glad to see her you won't know what to do."

"She better let me know where she's at by Monday

morning," said Simple. "If she do not drop me a line at once *now*, she will find herself dropped. Joyce is embarrassing me. F. D. thinks I know all about womens, and here I don't even know where my own woman is at.

"Last night I took F. D. upstairs to see Carlyle who has come back to his wife and baby. I told F. D., 'Carlyle is a young man a year or two older than yourself. He can give you some good advice which has got me stumped to talk over with you. You been running over to Brooklyn a mighty lot these nights lately, spending time with that keen kitty with the leather belt. Carlyle is a married man. He can tell you *how* he got married.' "

" 'Midsummer madness,' " I started quoting.

"That's right," said Simple. "Now, you take F. D. These young peoples nowadays know a plenty and they act like they knows more. But when you come right down to it, sometimes they don't know B from bullfoot—especially when it comes to subtracting the result from the cause. Sometimes it does not even take nine months to have the answer on your hands. Then they are surprised. F. D. is at the age where a boy needs somebody to talk to him."

"Why don't you talk to him? He seems to respect you."

"That's just it. He *do* respect me. And I don't know how to talk about them things without using bad words. That is all right amongst grown men. But F. D. ain't old enough yet to be drafted. Still and yet, he's old enough to do what the Bible says Adam did—and which has been going on ever since. I don't know what to say to a young boy at that age. I gets somewhatly embarrassed."

"So you turn F. D. over to Carlyle for the birds and bees, eh?"

"Carlyle is more near about his same age. But Carlyle's done had experience with which he walks the floor each and every night."

"Do you expect Carlyle's sex vocabulary to be any cleaner than yours?"

"Dirtier," said Simple. "But F. D. do not respect Carlyle."

On the Warpath

"Have you met F. D.'s girl yet?"

"I did," said Simple. "My landlady did also. She passed comment on her, 'Cute as a bug in a rug! Your cousin has better taste than you have, Mr. Semple, being seen in public with streak-haired characters like Zarita.'

"I reminded my landlady that I also knows Joyce.

" 'Which helps a little bit,' she said. 'But I give that young boy, F. D., credit. He did not take up with no trash when he come to New York. Gloria is a real sweet kid. Brooklyn girls is raised. They don't just grow, like they do here in New York. If I was to rear a family,' she continues, 'I would move to Brooklyn—which is a quiet suburb—and leave all you loud-mouthed roomers behind here in Harlem to make out the best way you can. Harlem is no place for a child.'

"Not wishing to carry on the conversation, I did not reply. I were not feeling talkative. Do you know what Joyce wrote me?"

"No."

"Just one word scrawled across the middle of the card like she were in a hurry—*Greetings*! No address, no nothing, but the picture of a beach and some white folks in swimming."

"You could tell from the postmark where it was, couldn't you?"

"It were so pale all I could make out was *AT*—and the rest was hardly there. But it must be Atlantic City, which is where I know Joyce has been before and likes."

"The Paradise, the Harlem, there are some fine night clubs there. Bars, music, dancing."

"I better not go down there and find Joyce setting up in no night club."

"What have you got against night clubs?"

"Nothing. It's what I got against guys who take girls to night clubs. I would not take no woman to a cabaret and spend all that loot on her that I did not intend to take further. A man is always thinking ahead of a woman."

"You have a suspicious mind," I said. "But I am sure Joyce would know how to resist any too intimate encroachments, even if she did accept some handsome stranger's bid for a date."

"'*Bang-up good time—I intend to relax*,' were the last words she said. It's that very last word, *relax*, that keeps running through my mind. On a vacation, you have to relax *with* somebody. If I go down to Atlantic City Sunday, I better not catch Joyce relaxing on the Boardwalk with no other joker. I will run him dead in the ocean. And he better know how to walk the water because he darest not come back to shore with me on the warpath."

"I am sure an exhibition of that nature would perturb Joyce," I said, "and do no credit to your own intelligence."

"About myself I do not care," said Simple. "As for Joyce, it would be worth a round-trip ticket to Atlantic City just to put the fear of God into her heart. Joyce do not realize who she is messing with, upsetting me like this. Here I am ready to give her the best years of my life, soon as that decree comes, and she cuts out on me for a fourth-night leaving no address whatsoever. *Greetings*! Don't she know no more words than that to write to me? She could say, *Dear Jess*. She could say, *Having a wonderful time, but something is missing—you*! She could say, *Hope you are well*! How much do it cost to go to Atlantic City?"

"Damned if I know."

"Lend me a dime," said Simple. "I am going to phone the bus station and find out. Don't let me catch no other Negro down there on no beach relaxing with Joyce when I get there, either!"

"Think carefully, old man," I said, "before starting on a wild goose chase."

"Wild goose, nothing!" cried Simple. "He'll be a dead duck."

Four Rings

"I have not seen you for a few days," I said. "Where've you been?"

"Working," said Simple.

"Same place, your old job back?"

"Not yet—but the same place. I'm helping to reconvert. I went down there Monday and said, 'Look here, don't you need somebody to maintain while you converts?'

"The man said, 'I believe they are short-handed, but I don't believe they're employing any colored boys in the reconversion jobs.'

"I said, 'What makes you think I'm colored? They done took such words off of jobs in New York State by law.'

"I know he wanted to say, 'But they ain't took the black off of your face.'

"But he did not. He just looked kind of surprised when I said, 'What makes you think I'm colored?' Then he grinned. And I grinned. He is a right good-natured white man.

"He said, 'Go see the foreman.'

"I did. And I got took on. I got tired of waiting for them to reconvert that plant, so I am reconverting along with them. In six or eight weeks, they'll be ready to open up again. I will know a lots more about the new machines and things they are putting in because I'm watching every move they make and every screw they turn. Maybe I might even get a better job when the plant opens up. We got a good shop steward in my department. I believe he will look out for me."

"I hope so," I said. "You've been there long enough to deserve some upgrading."

"I'm on the up-and-up," said Simple. "I was so happy last night, I kissed Joyce all over the parlor. When we set down on the sofa she thought there was a bear next to her. I were so rambunctious, Joyce says, 'There's an end to this sofa—and you have got me right up against the end. Unhand me, Jess Semple. I'm going to make you something to drink.'

"Now that surprised me so that I let her go. Joyce had not ever made me a drink before—knowing how I drink in the street—except she's giving a party and serving guests and such, which must include me. Well, sir, Joyce went on back in the kitchen, and in a few minutes she comes out with two cups and a pot just steaming, something with a spicy smell.

" 'Whiskey toddy?'

" 'Guess again.'

" 'Hot rum punch?'

" 'No!' she says, 'Sassafras tea.'

" 'What?' I hollers. 'Sassafras tea?'

" 'To cool the blood,' she says. 'You remember down home, old folks used to give it to the young folks in the spring? Well, spring is on its way, dear. And I think you need this.'

"It did look right good, and smelled delicious, steaming pink and rosy as wine. I had not had no sassafras tea since I left Virginia when us kids used to strip the bark and bring it home to Grandma Arcie to dry. Trust Joyce to think up something different.

" 'You know we got to have our health tested before we can get married,' she said.

" 'I know it,' I says. 'Let's go tomorrow.' Not really meaning that, but don't you know that girl took time off from work and went. Me, too. And we'll have the certifications by the end of this week."

"This is only March," I said. "June is a long way off. Aren't you rushing matters a bit?"

"Them little details we wants to get out of the way," said Simple. "We is busy people. We got to start looking for an apartment. No more rooming from our wedding night on. Then soon as we can, we gonna start buying a house. Maybe next fall. Do you want to room with us in our house?"

"What my situation next fall will be, I cannot tell. So may I delay my answer?"

"You may, just so you're standing up there beside me at my wedding. You're supposed to hand me the rings. Ain't that what the best man does?"

"I think he does. But I'm rather backward about being your best man. After all, we are only bar acquaintances. A best man is usually a *close* friend, somebody with whom you grew up or with whom you went to college, somebody you know very well."

"I did not grow up with nobody, my folks moved so much. I stayed with fifty-eleven relatives in seven different towns. I did not go to college, and I do not know anybody very well but you. I bull-jive around with lots of cats in bars, and I sometimes cast an eye on different womens now and then. I drinks with anybody from Zarita to Watermelon Joe. But, excusing Zarita, I don't know none of them other folks very well. With them I just jives. Maybe I don't even know you, but with you at least I talk. No doubt, you got some friends you know better. But don't nobody know *me* better. So you be my best man."

"Then I'm supposed to give you a bachelor's party a night or two before the ceremony. Your wedding is going to cost me money, too, Jess! I'm certainly glad you're drinking less these days, so I won't have to stock up so heavy on liquors."

"Just a keg of beer," said Simple. "I mean one *private* one with my name on it. What you give the other jokers, I do not care. And the young folks will need some refreshments. F. D. is also getting married."

"At the same time as you and Joyce?"

"Yes," said Simple. "So he writ me to get him two rings just like ours. Him and Gloria wants everything to be just like me and Joyce's."

"Has that young boy gone and committed another Carlyle?" I asked.

"I asked him that, too," said Simple. "He said, 'No.' Him and Gloria do not want to have no children at all until he comes back from the army."

"From the army?"

"Didn't I tell you F. D. got his draft call? Soon as this college term is over, he has to go to his service. So them kids is gonna get married so F. D. can go with a clear conscience. F. D. and Gloria are marrying to separate—and me and Joyce are marrying to stay together. There's some advantage in being in a high age bracket after all."

"Love will find a way," I said, "whatever the age. God bless all of you—F. D. and Gloria, and you and—"

"Joyce—my honey in the evening!"

"Yes, all four of you."

Ernest J. Gaines
(b. 1933)

Born in Oscar, Louisiana, Ernest J. Gaines was educated at Vallejo Junior College, San Francisco State University, and Stanford University, where he was a Wallace Stegner Fellow. He has been a writer-in-residence at Denison University, Stanford University, University of Southwestern Louisiana, and Whittier College, and is a recipient of awards from the National Endowment for the Arts, from the American Academy and Institute of Arts and Letters, and from the Black Academy of Arts and Letters, as well as a Guggenheim Fellowship and a Rockefeller grant. His novels include *Catherine Carmier* (1964), *Of Love and Dust* (1967), *The Autobiography of Miss Jane Pittman* (1971), *In My Father's House* (1978), and *A Gathering of Old Men* (1983); a collection of his stories, *Bloodline,* was published in 1968. *The Autobiography of Miss Jane Pittman,* starring Cicely Tyson, was adapted for television in 1974; an adaptation of *A Gathering of Old Men,* starring Lou Gossett, Jr., and Richard Widmark, appeared on television in 1987; and "The Sky Is Gray" was dramatized on public television in 1980.

THE SKY IS GRAY

I

Go'n be coming in a few minutes. Coming round that bend down there full speed. And I'm go'n get out my handkerchief and wave it down, and we go'n get on it and go.

I keep on looking for it, but Mama don't look that way no more. She's looking down the road where we just come from. It's a long old road, and far's you can see you don't see nothing but gravel. You got dry weeds on both sides, and you got trees on both sides, and fences on both sides, too. And you got cows in the pastures and they standing close together. And when we was coming out here to catch the bus I seen the smoke coming out of the cows's noses.

I look at my mama and I know what she's thinking. I been with Mama so much, just me and her, I know what she's thinking all the time. Right now it's home—Auntie and them. She's thinking if they got enough wood—if she left enough there to keep them warm till we get back. She's thinking if it go'n rain and if any of them go'n have to go out in the rain. She's thinking 'bout the hog—if he go'n get out, and if Ty and Val be able to get him back in. She always worry like that when she leaves the house. She don't worry too much if she leave me there with the smaller ones, 'cause she know I'm go'n look after them and look after Auntie and everything else. I'm the oldest and she say I'm the man.

I look at my mama and I love my mama. She's wearing that black coat and that black hat and she's looking sad. I love my mama and I want to put my arm around her and tell her. But I'm not supposed to do that. She say that's weakness and that's crybaby stuff, and she don't want no crybaby round her. She don't want you to be scared, either. 'Cause Ty's scared of ghosts and she's always whipping him. I'm scared of the dark, too, but I make 'tend I ain't. I make 'tend I ain't 'cause I'm the oldest, and I got to set a good sample for the rest. I can't ever be scared and I can't ever cry. And that's why I never said nothing 'bout my teeth. It's been hurting me and hurting me close to a month now, but I never said it. I didn't say it 'cause I didn't want act like a crybaby, and 'cause I know we didn't have enough money to go have it pulled. But, Lord, it been hurting me. And look like it wouldn't start till at night when you was trying to get yourself little sleep. Then soon's you shut your eyes—ummm-ummm, Lord, look like it go right down to your heartstring.

"Hurting, hanh?" Ty'd say.

I'd shake my head, but I wouldn't open my mouth for nothing. You open your mouth and let that wind in, and it almost kill you.

I'd just lay there and listen to them snore. Ty there, right 'side me, and Auntie and Val over by the fireplace. Val younger than me and Ty, and he sleeps with Auntie. Mama sleeps round the other side with Louis and Walker.

I'd just lay there and listen to them, and listen to that wind out there, and listen to that fire in the fireplace. Sometimes it'd stop long enough to let me get little rest. Sometimes it just hurt, hurt, hurt. Lord, have mercy.

2

Auntie knowed it was hurting me. I didn't tell nobody but Ty, 'cause we buddies and he ain't go'n tell anybody. But some kind of way Auntie found out. When she asked me, I told her no, nothing was wrong. But she knowed it all the time. She told me to mash up a piece of aspirin and wrap it in some cotton and jugg it down in that hole. I did it, but it didn't do no good. It stopped for a little while, and started right back again. Auntie wanted to tell Mama, but I told her, "Uh-uh." 'Cause I knowed we didn't have any money, and it just was go'n make her mad again. So Auntie told Monsieur Bayonne, and Monsieur Bayonne came over to the house and told me to kneel down 'side him on the fireplace. He put his finger in his mouth and made the Sign of the Cross on my jaw. The tip of Monsieur Bayonne's finger is some hard, 'cause he's always playing on that guitar. If we sit outside at night we can always hear Monsieur Bayonne playing on his guitar. Sometimes we leave him out there playing on the guitar.

Monsieur Bayonne made the Sign of the Cross over and over on my jaw, but that didn't do no good. Even when he prayed and told me to pray some, too, that tooth still hurt me.

"How you feeling?" he say.

"Same," I say.

He kept on praying and making the Sign of the Cross and I kept on praying, too.

"Still hurting?" he say.

"Yes, sir."

Monsieur Bayonne mashed harder and harder on my jaw. He mashed so hard he almost pushed me over on Ty. But then he stopped.

"What kind of prayers you praying, boy?" he say.

"Baptist," I say.

"Well, I'll be—no wonder that tooth still killing him. I'm going one way and he pulling the other. Boy, don't you know any Catholic prayers?"

"I know 'Hail Mary,' " I say.

"Then you better start saying it."

"Yes, sir."

He started mashing on my jaw again, and I could hear him praying at the same time. And, sure enough, after awhile it stopped hurting me.

Me and Ty went outside where Monsieur Bayonne's two hounds was and we started playing with them. "Let's go hunting," Ty say. "All right," I say; and we went on back in the pasture. Soon the hounds got on a trail, and me and Ty followed them all 'cross the pasture and then back in the woods, too. And then they cornered this little old rabbit and killed him, and me and Ty made them get back, and we picked up the rabbit and started on back home. But my tooth had started hurting me again. It was hurting me plenty now, but I wouldn't tell Monsieur Bayonne. That night I didn't sleep a bit, and first thing in the morning Auntie told me to go back and let Monsieur Bayonne pray over me some more. Monsieur Bayonne was in his kitchen making coffee when I got there. Soon's he seen me he knowed what was wrong.

"All right, kneel down there 'side that stove," he say. "And this time make sure you pray Catholic. I don't know nothing 'bout that Baptist, and I don't want to know nothing 'bout him."

3

Last night Mama say, "Tomorrow we going to town."

"It ain't hurting me no more," I say. "I can eat anything on it."

"Tomorrow we going to town," she say.

And after she finished eating, she got up and went to bed. She always go to bed early now. 'Fore Daddy went in the Army, she used to stay up late. All of us sitting out on the gallery or round the fire. But now, look like soon's she finish eating she go to bed.

This morning when I woke up, her and Auntie was standing 'fore the fireplace. She say: "Enough to get there and back. Dollar and a half to have it pulled. Twenty-five for me to go, twenty-five for him. Twenty-five for me to come back, twenty-five for him. Fifty cents left. Guess I get little piece of salt meat with that."

"Sure can use it," Auntie say. "White beans and no salt meat ain't white beans."

"I do the best I can," Mama say.

They was quiet after that, and I made 'tend I was still asleep.

"James, hit the floor," Auntie say.

I still made 'tend I was asleep. I didn't want them to know I was listening.

"All right," Auntie say, shaking me by the shoulder. "Come on. Today's the day."

I pushed the cover down to get out, and Ty grabbed it and pulled it back.

"You, too, Ty," Auntie say.

"I ain't getting no teef pulled," Ty say.

"Don't mean it ain't time to get up," Auntie say. "Hit it, Ty."

Ty got up grumbling.

"James, you hurry up and get in your clothes and eat your food," Auntie say. "What time y'all coming back?" she say to Mama.

"That 'leven o'clock bus," Mama say. "Got to get back in that field this evening."

"Get a move on you, James," Auntie say.

I went in the kitchen and washed my face, then I ate

my breakfast. I was having bread and syrup. The bread was warm and hard and tasted good. And I tried to make it last a long time.

Ty came back there grumbling and mad at me.

"Got to get up," he say. "I ain't having no teefs pulled. What I got to be getting up for?"

Ty poured some syrup in his pan and got a piece of bread. He didn't wash his hands, neither his face, and I could see that white stuff in his eyes.

"You the one getting your teef pulled," he say. "What I got to get up for. I bet if I was getting a teef pulled, you wouldn't be getting up. Shucks; syrup again. I'm getting tired of this old syrup. Syrup, syrup, syrup. I'm go'n take with the sugar diabetes. I want me some bacon sometime."

"Go out in the field and work and you can have your bacon," Auntie say. She stood in the middle door looking at Ty. "You better be glad you got syrup. Some people ain't got that—hard's time is."

"Shucks," Ty say. "How can I be strong."

"I don't know too much 'bout your strength," Auntie say; "but I know where you go'n be hot at, you keep that grumbling up. James, get a move on you; your mama waiting."

I ate my last piece of bread and went in the front room. Mama was standing 'fore the fireplace warming her hands. I put on my coat and cap, and we left the house.

4

I look down there again, but it still ain't coming. I almost say, "It ain't coming yet," but I keep my mouth shut. 'Cause that's something else she don't like. She don't like for you to say something just for nothing. She can see it ain't coming. I can see it ain't coming, so why say it ain't coming. I don't say it, I turn and look at the river that's back of us. It's so cold the smoke's just raising up from the water. I see a bunch of pool-doos not too far out—just on the other side the lilies. I'm wondering if you can eat pool-doos. I ain't too sure, 'cause I ain't never ate none. But I done ate owls and blackbirds, and I done ate redbirds, too. I didn't want to kill the redbirds, but she made me kill them. They had two of them back there. One in my trap, one in Ty's trap. Me and Ty was go'n play with them and let them go, but she made me kill them 'cause we needed the food.

"I can't," I say. "I can't."

"Here," she say. "Take it."

"I can't," I say. "I can't. I can't kill him, Mama, please."

"Here," she say. "Take this fork, James."

"Please, Mama, I can't kill him," I say.

I could tell she was go'n hit me. I jerked back, but I didn't jerk back soon enough.

"Take it," she say.

I took it and reached in for him, but he kept on hopping to the back.

"I can't, Mama," I say. The water just kept on running down my face. "I can't," I say.

"Get him out of there," she say.

I reached in for him and he kept on hopping to the back. Then I reached in farther, and he pecked me on the hand.

"I can't, Mama," I say.

She slapped me again.

I reached in again, but he kept on hopping out my way. Then he hopped to one side and I reached there. The fork got him on the leg and I heard his leg pop. I pulled my hand out 'cause I had hurt him.

"Give it here," she say, and jerked the fork out of my hand.

She reached in and got the little bird right in the neck. I heard the fork go in his neck, and I heard it go in the ground. She brought him out and helt him right in front of me.

"That's one," she say. She shook him off and gived me the fork. "Get the other one."

"I can't, Mama," I say. "I'll do anything, but don't make me do that."

She went to the corner of the fence and broke the

biggest switch over there she could find. I knelt 'side the trap, crying.

"Get him out of there," she say.

"I can't, Mama."

She started hitting me 'cross the back. I went down on the ground, crying.

"Get him," she say.

"Octavia?" Auntie say.

'Cause she had come out of the house and she was standing by the tree looking at us.

"Get him out of there," Mama say.

"Octavia," Auntie say, "explain to him. Explain to him. Just don't beat him. Explain to him."

But she hit me and hit me and hit me.

I'm still young—I ain't no more than eight; but I know now; I know why I had to do it. (They was so little, though. They was so little. I 'member how I picked the feathers off them and cleaned them and helt them over the fire. Then we all ate them. Ain't had but a little bitty piece each, but we all had a little bitty piece, and everybody just looked at me 'cause they was so proud.) Suppose she had to go away? That's why I had to do it. Suppose she had to go away like Daddy went away? Then who was go'n look after us? They had to be somebody left to carry on. I didn't know it then, but I know it now. Auntie and Monsieur Bayonne talked to me and made me see.

5

Time I see it I get out my handkerchief and start waving. It's still 'way down there, but I keep waving anyhow. Then it come up and stop and me and Mama get on. Mama tell me to go sit in the back while she pay. I do like she say, and the people look at me. When I pass the little sign that say "White" and "Colored," I start looking for a seat. I just see one of them back there, but I don't take it, 'cause I want my mama to sit down herself. She comes in the back and sit down, and I lean on the seat. They got seats in the front, but I know I can't sit there, 'cause I have to sit back of the sign. Anyhow, I don't want to sit there if my mama go'n sit back here.

They got a lady sitting 'side my mama and she looks at me and smiles little bit. I smile back, but I don't open my mouth, 'cause the wind'll get in and make that tooth ache. The lady take out a pack of gum and reach me a slice, but I shake my head. The lady just can't understand why a little boy'll turn down gum, and she reach me a slice again. This time I point to my jaw. The lady understands and smiles little bit, and I smile little bit, but I don't open my mouth, though.

They got a girl sitting 'cross from me. She got on a red overcoat and her hair's plaited in one big plait. First, I make 'tend I don't see her over there, but then I start looking at her little bit. She make 'tend she don't see me, either, but I catch her looking that way. She got a cold, and every now and then she h'ist that little handkerchief to her nose. She ought to blow it, but she don't. Must think she's too much a lady or something.

Every time she h'ist that little handkerchief, the lady 'side her say something in her ear. She shakes her head and lays her hands in her lap again. Then I catch her kind of looking where I'm at. I smile at her little bit. But think she'll smile back? Uh-uh. She just turn up her little old nose and turn her head. Well, I show her both of us can turn us head. I turn mine too and look out at the river.

The river is gray. The sky is gray. They have pool-doos on the water. The water is wavy, and the pool-doos go up and down. The bus go round a turn, and you got plenty trees hiding the river. Then the bus go round another turn, and I can see the river again.

I look toward the front where all the white people sitting. Then I look at that little old gal again. I don't look right at her, 'cause I don't want all them people to know I love her. I just look at her little bit, like I'm looking out that window over there. But she knows I'm looking that way, and she kind of look at me, too. The lady sitting 'side her catch her this time, and she leans over and says something in her ear.

"I don't love him nothing," that little old gal says out loud.

Everybody back there hear her mouth, and all of them look at us and laugh.

"I don't love you, either," I say. "So you don't have to turn up your nose, Miss."

"You the one looking," she say.

"I wasn't looking at you," I say. "I was looking out that window, there."

"Out that window, my foot," she say. "I seen you. Everytime I turned round you was looking at me."

"You must of been looking yourself if you seen me all them times," I say.

"Shucks," she say, "I got me all kind of boyfriends."

"I got girlfriends, too," I say.

"Well, I just don't want you getting your hopes up," she say.

I don't say no more to that little old gal 'cause I don't want have to bust her in the mouth. I lean on the seat where Mama sitting, and I don't even look that way no more. When we get to Bayonne, she jugg her little old tongue out at me. I make 'tend I'm go'n hit her, and she duck down 'side her mama. And all the people laugh at us again.

6

Me and Mama get off and start walking in town. Bayonne is a little bitty town. Baton Rouge is a hundred times bigger than Bayonne. I went to Baton Rouge once—me, Ty, Mama, and Daddy. But that was 'way back yonder, 'fore Daddy went in the Army. I wonder when we go'n see him again. I wonder when. Look like he ain't ever coming back home. . . . Even the pavement all cracked in Bayonne. Got grass shooting right out the sidewalk. Got weeds in the ditch, too; just like they got at home.

It's some cold in Bayonne. Look like it's colder than it is home. The wind blows in my face, and I feel that stuff running down my nose. I sniff. Mama says use that handkerchief. I blow my nose and put it back.

We pass a school and I see them white children playing

in the yard. Big old red school, and them children just running and playing. Then we pass a café, and I see a bunch of people in there eating. I wish I was in there 'cause I'm cold. Mama tells me keep my eyes in front where they belong.

We pass stores that's got dummies, and we pass another café, and then we pass a shoe shop, and that bald-head man in there fixing on a shoe. I look at him and I butt into that white lady, and Mama jerks me in front and tells me to stay there.

We come up to the courthouse, and I see the flag waving there. This flag ain't like the one we got at school. This one here ain't got but a handful of stars. One at school got a big pile of stars—one for every state. We pass it and we turn and there it is—the dentist office. Me and Mama go in, and they got people sitting everywhere you look. They even got a little boy in there younger than me.

Me and Mama sit on that bench, and a white lady come in there and ask me what my name is. Mama tells her and the white lady goes on back. Then I hear somebody hollering in there. Soon's that little boy hear him hollering, he starts hollering, too. His mama pats him and pats him, trying to make him hush up, but he ain't thinking 'bout his mama.

The man that was hollering in there comes out holding his jaw. He is a big old man and he's wearing overalls and a jumper.

"Got it, hanh?" another man asks him.

The man shakes his head—don't want open his mouth.

"Man, I thought they was killing you in there," the other man says. "Hollering like a pig under a gate."

The man don't say nothing. He just heads for the door, and the other man follows him.

"John Lee," the white lady says. "John Lee Williams."

The little boy juggs his head down in his mama's lap and holler more now. His mama tells him go with the nurse, but he ain't thinking 'bout his mama. His mama tells him again, but he don't even hear her. His mama picks him up and takes him in there, and even when the white lady shuts the door I can still hear little old John Lee.

"I often wonder why the Lord let a child like that suffer," a lady says to my mama. The lady's sitting right in front of us on another bench. She's got on a white dress and a black sweater. She must be a nurse or something herself, I reckon.

"Not us to question," a man says.

"Sometimes I don't know if we shouldn't," the lady says.

"I know definitely we shouldn't," the man says. The man looks like a preacher. He's big and fat and he's got on a black suit. He's got a gold chain, too.

"Why?" the lady says.

"Why anything?" the preacher says.

"Yes," the lady says. "Why anything?"

"Not us to question," the preacher says.

The lady looks at the preacher a little while and looks at Mama again.

"And look like it's the poor who suffers the most," she says. "I don't understand it."

"Best not to even try," the preacher says. "He works in mysterious ways—wonders to perform."

Right then little John Lee bust out hollering, and everybody turn they head to listen.

"He's not a good dentist," the lady says. "Dr. Robillard is much better. But more expensive. That's why most of the colored people come here. The white people go to Dr. Robillard. Y'all from Bayonne?"

"Down the river," my mama says. And that's all she go'n say, 'cause she don't talk much. But the lady keeps on looking at her, and so she says, "Near Morgan."

"I see," the lady says.

7

"That's the trouble with the black people in this country today," somebody else says. This one here's sitting on the same side me and Mama's sitting, and he is kind of sitting in front of that preacher. He looks like a teacher or somebody that goes to college. He's got on a suit, and he's got a book that he's been reading. "We don't question is exactly our problem," he says. "We should question and question and question—question everything."

The preacher just looks at him a long time. He done put a toothpick or something in his mouth, and he just keeps on turning it and turning it. You can see he don't like that boy with that book.

"Maybe you can explain what you mean," he says.

"I said what I meant," the boy says. "Question everything. Every stripe, every star, every word spoken. Everything."

"It 'pears to me that this young lady and I was talking 'bout God, young man," the preacher says.

"Question Him, too," the boy says.

"Wait," the preacher says, "Wait now."

"You heard me right," the boy says. "His existence as well as everything else. Everything."

The preacher just looks across the room at the boy. You can see he's getting madder and madder. But mad or no mad, the boy ain't thinking 'bout him. He looks at that preacher just's hard's the preacher looks at him.

"Is this what they coming to?" the preacher says. "Is that what we educating them for?"

"You're not educating me," the boy says. "I wash dishes at night so that I can go to school in the day. So even the words you spoke need questioning."

The preacher just looks at him and shakes his head.

"When I come in this room and seen you there with your book, I said to myself, 'There's an intelligent man.' How wrong a person can be."

"Show me one reason to believe in the existence of a God," the boy says.

"My heart tells me," the preacher says.

" 'My heart tells me,' " the boy says. " 'My heart tells me.' Sure, 'My heart tells me.' And as long as you listen to what your heart tells you, you will have only what the white man gives you and nothing more. Me, I don't listen to my heart. The purpose of the heart is to pump blood throughout the body, and nothing else."

"Who's your paw, boy?" the preacher says.

"Why?"

"Who is he?"

"He's dead."

"And your mom?"

"She's in Charity Hospital with pneumonia. Half killed herself, working for nothing."

"And 'cause he's dead and she's sick, you mad at the world?"

"I'm not mad at the world. I'm questioning the world. I'm questioning it with cold logic sir. What do words like Freedom, Liberty, God, White, Colored mean? I want to know. That's why *you* are sending us to school, to read and to ask questions. And because we ask these questions, you call us mad. No sir, it is not us who are mad."

"You keep saying 'us'?"

" 'Us.' Yes—us. I'm not alone."

The preacher just shakes his head. Then he looks at everybody in the room—everybody. Some of the people look down at the floor, keep from looking at him. I kind of look 'way myself, but soon's I know he done turn his head, I look that way again.

"I'm sorry for you," he says to the boy.

"Why?" the boy says. "Why not be sorry for yourself? Why are you so much better off than I am? Why aren't you sorry for these other people in here? Why not be sorry for the lady who had to drag her child into the dentist office? Why not be sorry for the lady sitting on that bench over there? Be sorry for them. Not for me. Some way or the other I'm going to make it."

"No, I'm sorry for you," the preacher says.

"Of course, of course," the boy says, nodding his head. "You're sorry for me because I rock that pillar you're leaning on."

"You can't ever rock the pillar I'm leaning on, young man. It's stronger than anything man can ever do."

"You believe in God because a man told you to believe in God," the boy says. "A white man told you to believe in God. And why? To keep you ignorant so he can keep his feet on your neck."

"So now we the ignorant?" the preacher says.

"Yes," the boy says. "Yes." And he opens his book again.

The preacher just looks at him sitting there. The boy done forgot all about him. Everybody else make 'tend they done forgot the squabble, too.

Then I see that preacher getting up real slow. Preacher's great big old man and he got to brace himself to get up. He comes over where the boy is sitting. He just stands there a little while looking down at him, but the boy don't raise his head.

"Get up, boy," preacher says.

The boy looks up at him, then he shuts his book real slow and stands up. Preacher just hauls back and hit him in the face. The boy falls back 'gainst the wall, but he straightens himself up and looks right back at that preacher.

"You forgot the other cheek," he says.

The preacher hauls back and hit him again on the other side. But this time the boy braces himself and don't fall.

"That hasn't changed a thing," he says.

The preacher just looks at the boy. The preacher's breathing real hard like he just run up a big hill. The boy sits down and opens his book again.

"I feel sorry for you," the preacher says. "I never felt so sorry for a man before."

The boy makes 'tend he don't even hear that preacher. He keeps on reading his book. The preacher goes back and gets his hat off the chair.

"Excuse me," he says to us. "I'll come back some other time. Y'all, please excuse me."

And he looks at the boy and goes out the room. The boy h'ist his hand up to his mouth one time to wipe 'way some blood. All the rest of the time he keeps on reading. And nobody else in there say a word.

8

Little John Lee and his mama come out the dentist office, and the nurse calls somebody else in. Then little bit later they come out, and the nurse calls another name. But fast's she calls somebody in there, somebody else comes in the place where we sitting, and the room stays full.

The people coming in now, all of them wearing big coats. One of them says something 'bout sleeting, another one says he hope not. Another one says he think it ain't nothing but rain. 'Cause, he says, rain can get awful cold this time of year.

All round the room they talking. Some of them talking to people right by them, some of them talking to people clear 'cross the room, some of them talking to anybody'll listen. It's a little bitty room, no bigger than us kitchen, and I can see everybody in there. The little old room's full of smoke, 'cause you got two old men smoking pipes over by that side door. I think I feel my tooth thumping me some, and I hold my breath and wait. I wait and wait, but it don't thump me no more. Thank God for that.

I feel like going to sleep, and I lean back 'gainst the wall. But I'm scared to go to sleep. Scared 'cause the nurse might call my name and I won't hear her. And Mama might go to sleep, too, and she'll be mad if neither one of us heard the nurse.

I look up at Mama. I love my mama. I love my mama. And when cotton come I'm go'n get her a new coat. And I ain't go'n get a black one, either. I think I'm go'n get her a red one.

"They got some books over there," I say. "Want read one of them?"

Mama looks at the books, but she don't answer me.

"You got yourself a little man there," the lady says.

Mama don't say nothing to the lady, but she must've smiled, 'cause I seen the lady smiling back. The lady looks at me a little while, like she's feeling sorry for me.

"You sure got that preacher out here in a hurry," she says to that boy.

The boy looks up at her and looks in his book again. When I grow up I want be just like him. I want clothes like that and I want keep a book with me, too.

"You really don't believe in God?" the lady says.

"No," he says.

"But why?" the lady says.

"Because the wind is pink," he says.

"What?" the lady says.

The boy don't answer her no more. He just reads in his book.

"Talking 'bout the wind is pink," that old lady says. She's sitting on the same bench with the boy and she's trying to look in his face. The boy makes 'tend the old lady ain't even there. He just keeps on reading. "Wind is pink," she says again. "Eh, Lord, what children go'n be saying next?"

The lady 'cross from us bust out laughing.

"That's a good one," she says. "The wind is pink. Yes sir, that's a good one."

"Don't you believe the wind is pink?" the boy says. He keep his head down in the book.

"Course I believe it, honey," the lady says. "Course I do." She looks at us and winks her eye. "And what color is grass, honey?"

"Grass? Grass is black."

She bust out laughing again. The boy looks at her.

"Don't you believe grass is black?" he says.

The lady quits her laughing and looks at him. Everybody else looking at him, too. The place quiet, quiet.

"Grass is green, honey," the lady says. "It was green yesterday, it's green today, and it's go'n be green tomorrow."

"How do you know it's green?"

"I know because I know."

"You don't know it's green," the boy says. "You believe it's green because someone told you it was green. If someone had told you it was black you'd believe it was black."

"It's green," the lady says. "I know green when I see green."

"Prove it's green," the boy says.

"Sure, now," the lady says. "Don't tell me it's coming to that."

"It's coming to just that," the boy says. "Words mean nothing. One means no more than the other."

"That's what it all coming to?" the old lady says. That old lady got on a turban and she got on two sweaters.

She got a green sweater under a black sweater. I can see the green sweater 'cause some of the buttons on the other sweater's missing.

"Yes ma'am," the boy says. "Words mean nothing. Action is the only thing. Doing. That's the only thing."

"Other words, you want the Lord to come down here and show Hisself to you?" she says.

"Exactly, ma'am," he says.

"You don't mean that, I'm sure?" she says.

"I do, ma'am," he says.

"Done, Jesus," the old lady says, shaking her head.

"I didn't go 'long with that preacher at first," the other lady says; "but now—I don't know. When a person say the grass is black, he's either a lunatic or something's wrong."

"Prove to me that it's green," the boy says.

"It's green because the people say it's green."

"Those same people say we're citizens of these United States," the boy says.

"I think I'm a citizen," the lady says.

"Citizens have certain rights," the boy says. "Name me one right that you have. One right, granted by the Constitution, that you can exercise in Bayonne."

The lady don't answer him. She just looks at him like she don't know what he's talking 'bout. I know I don't.

"Things changing," she says.

"Things are changing because some black men have begun to think with their brains and not their hearts," the boy says.

"You trying to say these people don't believe in God?"

"I'm sure some of them do. Maybe most of them do. But they don't believe that God is going to touch these white people's hearts and change things tomorrow. Things change through action. By no other way."

Everybody sit quiet and look at the boy. Nobody says a thing. Then the lady 'cross the room from me and Mama just shakes her head.

"Let's hope that not all your generation feel the same way you do," she says.

"Think what you please, it doesn't matter," the boy says. "But it will be men who listen to their heads and not their hearts who will see that your children have a better chance than you had."

"Let's hope they ain't all like you, though," the old lady says. "Done forgot the heart absolutely."

"Yes ma'am, I hope they aren't all like me," the boy says. "Unfortunately, I was born too late to believe in your God. Let's hope that the ones who come after will have your faith—if not in your God, then in something else, something definitely that they can lean on. I haven't anything. For me, the wind is pink, the grass is black."

9

The nurse comes in the room where we all sitting and waiting and says the doctor won't take no more patients till one o'clock this evening. My mama jumps up off the bench and goes up to the white lady.

"Nurse, I have to go back in the field this evening," she says.

"The doctor is treating his last patient now," the nurse says. "One o'clock this evening."

"Can I at least speak to the doctor?" my mama asks.

"I'm his nurse," the lady says.

"My little boy's sick," my mama says. "Right now his tooth almost killing him."

The nurse looks at me. She's trying to make up her mind if to let me come in. I look at her real pitiful. The tooth ain't hurting me at all, but Mama says it is, so I make 'tend for her sake.

"This evening," the nurse says, and goes on back in the office.

"Don't feel 'jected, honey," the lady says to Mama. "I been round them a long time—they take you when they want to. If you was white, that's something else; but we the wrong color."

Mama don't say nothing to the lady, and me and her go outside and stand 'gainst the wall. It's cold out there. I can feel that wind going through my coat. Some of the other people come out of the room and go up the street. Me and Mama stand there a little while and we start walking. I don't know where we going. When we come to the other street we just stand there.

"You don't have to make water, do you?" Mama says.

"No, ma'am," I say.

We go on up the street. Walking real slow. I can tell Mama don't know where she's going. When we come to a store we stand there and look at the dummies. I look at a little boy wearing a brown overcoat. He's got on brown shoes, too. I look at my old shoes and look at his'n again. You wait till summer, I say.

Me and Mama walk away. We come up to another store and we stop and look at them dummies, too. Then we go on again. We pass a café where the white people in there eating. Mama tells me keep my eyes in front where they belong, but I can't help for seeing them people eat. My stomach starts to growling 'cause I'm hungry. When I see people eating, I get hungry; when I see a coat, I get cold.

A man whistles at my mama when we go by a filling station. She makes 'tend she don't even see him. I look back and I feel like hitting him in the mouth. If I was bigger, I say; if I was bigger, you'd see.

We keep on going. I'm getting colder and colder, but I don't say nothing. I feel that stuff running down my nose and I sniff.

"That rag," Mama says.

I get it out and wipe my nose. I'm getting cold all over now—my face, my hands, my feet, everything. We pass another little café, but this'n for white people, too, and we can't go in there, either. So we just walk. I'm so cold now I'm 'bout ready to say it. If I knowed where we was going I wouldn't be so cold, but I don't know where we going. We go, we go, we go. We walk clean out of Bayonne. Then we cross the street and we come back. Same thing I seen when I got off the bus this morning. Same old trees, same old walk, same old weeds, same old cracked pave—same old everything.

I sniff again.

"That rag," Mama says.

I wipe my nose real fast and jugg that handkerchief back in my pocket 'fore my hand gets too cold. I raise my head and I can see David's hardware store. When we come up to it, we go in. I don't know why, but I'm glad.

It's warm in there. It's so warm in there you don't ever want to leave. I look for the heater, and I see it over by them barrels. Three white men standing round the heater talking in Creole. One of them comes over to see what my mama want.

"Got any axe handles?" she says.

Me, Mama and the white man start to the back, but Mama stops me when we come up to the heater. She and the white man go on. I hold my hands over the heater and look at them. They go all the way to the back, and I see the white man pointing to the axe handles 'gainst the wall. Mama takes one of them and shakes it like she's trying to figure how much it weighs. Then she rubs her hand over it from one end to the other end. She turns it over and looks at the other side, then she shakes it again, and shakes her head and puts it back. She gets another one and she does it just like she did the first one, then she shakes her head. Then she gets a brown one and do it that, too. But she don't like this one, either. Then she gets another one, but 'fore she shakes it or anything, she looks at me. Look like she's trying to say something to me, but I don't know what it is. All I know is I done got warm now and I'm feeling right smart better. Mama shakes this axe handle just like she did the others, and shakes her head and says something to the white man. The white man just looks at his pile of axe handles, and when Mama pass him to come to the front, the white man just scratch his head and follows her. She tells me come on and we go on and start walking again.

We walk and walk, and no time at all I'm cold again. Look like I'm colder now 'cause I can still remember how good it was back there. My stomach growls and I suck it in to keep Mama from hearing it. She's walking right 'side me, and it growls so loud you can hear it a mile. But Mama don't say a word.

10

When we come up to the courthouse, I look at the clock. It's got quarter to twelve. Mean we got another hour and a quarter to be out here in the cold. We go and stand 'side a building. Something hits my cap and I look up at the sky. Sleet's falling.

I look at Mama standing there. I want stand close 'side her, but she don't like that. She say that's crybaby stuff. She say you got to stand for yourself, by yourself.

"Let's go back to that office," she says.

We cross the street. When we get to the dentist office I try to open the door, but I can't. I twist and twist, but I can't. Mama pushes me to the side and she twist the knob, but she can't open the door, either. She turns 'way from the door. I look at her, but I don't move and I don't say nothing. I done seen her like this before and I'm scared of her.

"You hungry?" she says. She says it like she's mad at me, like I'm the cause of everything.

"No, ma'am," I say.

"You want eat and walk back, or you rather don't eat and ride?"

"I ain't hungry," I say.

I ain't just hungry, but I'm cold, too. I'm so hungry and cold I want to cry. And look like I'm getting colder and colder. My feet done got numb. I try to work my toes, but I don't even feel them. Look like I'm go'n die. Look like I'm go'n stand right here and freeze to death. I think 'bout home. I think 'bout Val and Auntie and Ty and Louis and Walker. It's 'bout twelve o'clock and I know they eating dinner now. I can hear Ty making jokes. He done forgot 'bout getting up early this morning and right now he's probably making jokes. Always trying to make somebody laugh. I wish I was right there listening to him. Give anything in the world if I was home round the fire.

"Come on," Mama says.

We start walking again. My feet so numb I can't hardly feel them. We turn the corner and go on back up the street. The clock on the courthouse starts hitting for twelve.

The sleet's coming down plenty now. They hit the pave and bounce like rice. Oh, Lord; oh, Lord, I pray. Don't let me die, don't let me die, don't let me die, Lord.

11

Now I know where we going. We going back of town where the colored people eat. I don't care if I don't eat. I been hungry before. I can stand it. But I can't stand the cold.

I can see we go'n have a long walk. It's 'bout a mile down there. But I don't mind. I know when I get there I'm go'n warm myself. I think I can hold out. My hands numb in my pockets and my feet numb, too, but if I keep moving I can hold out. Just don't stop no more, that's all.

The sky's gray. The sleet keeps on falling. Falling like rain now—plenty, plenty. You can hear it hitting the pave. You can see it bouncing. Sometimes it bounces two times 'fore it settles.

We keep on going. We don't say nothing. We just keep on going, keep on going.

I wonder what Mama's thinking. I hope she ain't mad at me. When summer come I'm go'n pick plenty cotton and get her a coat. I'm go'n get her a red one.

I hope they'd make it summer all the time. I'd be glad if it was summer all the time—but it ain't. We got to have winter, too. Lord, I hate the winter. I guess everybody hate the winter.

I don't sniff this time. I get out my handkerchief and wipe my nose. My hands's so cold I can hardly hold the handkerchief.

I think we getting close, but we ain't there yet. I wonder where everybody is. Can't see a soul but us. Look like we the only two people moving round today. Must be too cold for the rest of the people to move round in.

I can hear my teeth. I hope they don't knock together

too hard and make that bad one hurt. Lord, that's all I need, for that bad one to start off.

I hear a church bell somewhere. But today ain't Sunday. They must be ringing for a funeral or something.

I wonder what they doing at home. They must be eating. Monsieur Bayonne might be there with his guitar. One day Ty played with Monsieur Bayonne's guitar and broke one of the strings. Monsieur Bayonne was some mad with Ty. He say Ty wasn't go'n ever 'mount to nothing. Ty can go just like Monsieur Bayonne when he ain't there. Ty can make everybody laugh when he starts to mocking Monsieur Bayonne.

I used to like to be with Mama and Daddy. We used to be happy. But they took him in the Army. Now, nobody happy no more. . . . I be glad when Daddy comes home.

Monsieur Bayonne say it wasn't fair for them to take Daddy and give Mama nothing and give us nothing. Auntie say, "Shhh, Etienne. Don't let them hear you talk like that." Monsieur Bayonne say, "It's God truth. What they giving his children? They have to walk three and a half miles to school hot or cold. That's anything to give for a paw? She's got to work in the field rain or shine just to make ends meet. That's anything to give for a husband?" Auntie say, "Shhh, Etienne, shhh." "Yes, you right," Monsieur Bayonne say. "Best don't say it in front of them now. But one day they go'n find out. One day." "Yes, I suppose so," Auntie say. "Then what, Rose Mary?" Monsieur Bayonne say. "I don't know, Etienne," Auntie say. "All we can do is us job, and leave everything else in His hand . . ."

We getting closer, now. We getting closer. I can even see the railroad tracks.

We cross the tracks, and now I see the café. Just to get in there, I say. Just to get in there. Already I'm starting to feel little better.

12

We go in. Ahh, it's good. I look for the heater; there 'gainst the wall. One of them little brown ones. I just stand there and hold my hands over it. I can't open my hands too wide 'cause they almost froze.

Mama's standing right 'side me. She done unbuttoned her coat. Smoke rises out of the coat, and the coat smells like a wet dog.

I move to the side so Mama can have more room. She opens out her hands and rubs them together. I rub mine together, too, 'cause this keep them from hurting. If you let them warm too fast, they hurt you sure. But if you let them warm just little bit at a time, and you keep rubbing them, they be all right every time.

They got just two more people in the café. A lady back of the counter, and a man on this side the counter. They been watching us ever since we come in.

Mama gets out the handkerchief and count up the money. Both of us know how much money she's got there. Three dollars. No, she ain't got three dollars 'cause she had to pay us way up here. She ain't got but two dollars and a half left. Dollar and a half to get my tooth pulled, and fifty cents for us to go back on, and fifty cents worth of salt meat.

She stirs the money round with her finger. Most of the money is change 'cause I can hear it rubbing together. She stirs it and stirs it. Then she looks at the door. It's still sleeting. I can hear it hitting 'gainst the wall like rice.

"I ain't hungry, Mama," I say.

"Got to pay them something for they heat," she says.

She takes a quarter out the handkerchief and ties the handkerchief up again. She looks over her shoulder at the people, but she still don't move. I hope she don't spend the money. I don't want her spending it on me. I'm hungry, I'm almost starving I'm so hungry, but I don't want her spending the money on me.

She flips the quarter over like she's thinking. She's must be thinking 'bout us walking back home. Lord, I sure don't want walk home. If I thought it'd do any good to say something, I'd say it. But Mama makes up her own mind 'bout things.

She turns 'way from the heater right fast, like she better hurry up and spend the quarter 'fore she change her mind. I watch her go toward the counter. The man and the lady look at her. She tells the lady something and the lady walks away. The man keeps on looking at her. Her back's turned to the man, and she don't even know he's standing there.

The lady puts some cakes and a glass of milk on the counter. Then she pours up a cup of coffee and sets it 'side the other stuff. Mama pays her for the things and comes on back where I'm standing. She tells me sit down at the table 'gainst the wall.

The milk and the cakes's for me; the coffee's for Mama. I eat slow and I look at her. She's looking outside at the sleet. She's looking real sad. I say to myself, I'm go'n make all this up one day. You see, one day, I'm go'n make all this up. I want say it now; I want tell her how I feel right now; but Mama don't like for us to talk like that.

"I can't eat all this," I say.

They ain't got but just three little old cakes there. I'm so hungry right now, the Lord knows I can eat a hundred times three, but I want my mama to have one.

Mama don't even look my way. She knows I'm hungry, she knows I want it. I let it stay there a little while, then I get it and eat it. I eat just on my front teeth, though, 'cause if cake touch that back tooth I know what'll happen. Thank God it ain't hurt me at all today.

After I finish eating I see the man go to the juke box. He drops a nickel in it, then he just stand there a little while looking at the record. Mama tells me keep my eyes in front where they belong. I turn my head like she say, but then I hear the man coming toward us.

"Dance, pretty?" he says.

Mama gets up to dance with him. But 'fore you know it, she done grabbed the little man in the collar and done heaved him 'side the wall. He hit the wall so hard he stop the juke box from playing.

"Some pimp," the lady back of the counter says. "Some pimp."

The little man jumps up off the floor and starts toward my mama. 'Fore you know it, Mama done sprung open her knife and she's waiting for him.

"Come on," she says. "Come on. I'll gut you from your neighbo to your throat. Come on."

I go up to the little man to hit him, but Mama makes me come and stand 'side her. The little man looks at me and Mama and goes on back to the counter.

"Some pimp," the lady back of the counter says. "Some pimp." She starts laughing and pointing at the little man. "Yes sir, you a pimp, all right. Yes sir-ree."

13

"Fasten that coat, let's go," Mama says.

"You don't have to leave," the lady says. Mama don't answer the lady, and we right out in the cold again. I'm warm right now—my hands, my ears, my feet—but I know this ain't go'n last too long. It done sleet so much now you got ice everywhere you look.

We cross the railroad tracks, and soon's we do, I get cold. That wind goes through this little old coat like it ain't even there. I got on a shirt and a sweater under the coat, but that wind don't pay them no mind. I look up and I can see we got a long way to go. I wonder if we go'n make it 'fore I get too cold.

We cross over to walk on the sidewalk. They got just one sidewalk back here, and it's over there.

After we go just a little piece, I smell bread cooking. I look, then I see a baker shop. When we get closer, I can smell it more better. I shut my eyes and make 'tend I'm eating. But I keep them shut too long and I butt up 'gainst a telephone post. Mama grabs me and see if I'm hurt. I ain't bleeding or nothing and she turns me loose.

I can feel I'm getting colder and colder, and I look up to see how far we still got to go. Uptown is 'way up yonder. A half mile more, I reckon. I try to think of something. They say think and you won't get cold. I think of that poem, "Annabel Lee." I ain't been to school in so long—this bad weather—I reckon they done passed "Annabel Lee" by now. But passed it or not, I'm sure Miss Walker go'n make me recite it when I get there. That woman don't never forget nothing. I ain't never seen nobody like that in my life.

I'm still getting cold. "Annabel Lee" or no "Annabel Lee," I'm still getting cold. But I can see we getting closer. We getting there gradually.

Soon's we turn the corner, I seen a little old white lady up in front of us. She's the only lady on the street. She's all in black and she's got a long black rag over her head.

"Stop," she says.

Me and Mama stop and look at her. She must be crazy to be out in all this bad weather. Ain't got but a few other people out there, and all of them's men.

"Y'all done ate?" she says.

"Just finish," Mama says.

"Y'all must be cold then?" she says.

"We headed for the dentist," Mama says. "We'll warm up when we get there."

"What dentist?" the old lady says. "Mr. Bassett?"

"Yes, ma'am," Mama says.

"Come on in," the old lady says. "I'll telephone him and tell him y'all coming."

Me and Mama follow the old lady in the store. It's a little bitty store, and it don't have much in there. The old lady takes off her head rag and folds it up.

"Helena?" somebody calls from the back.

"Yes, Alnest?" the old lady says.

"Did you see them?"

"They're here. Standing beside me."

"Good. Now you can stay inside."

The old lady looks at Mama. Mama's waiting to hear what she brought us in here for. I'm waiting for that, too.

"I saw y'all each time you went by," she says. "I came out to catch you, but you were gone."

"We went back of town," Mama says.

"Did you eat?"

"Yes, ma'am."

The old lady looks at Mama a long time, like she's thinking Mama might just be saying that. Mama looks right back at her. The old lady looks at me to see what I have to say. I don't say nothing. I sure ain't going 'gainst my mama.

"There's food in the kitchen," she says to Mama. "I've been keeping it warm."

Mama turns right around and starts for the door.

"Just a minute," the old lady says. Mama stops. "The boy'll have to work for it. It isn't free."

"We don't take no handout," Mama says.

"I'm not handing out anything," the old lady says. "I need my garbage moved to the front. Ernest has a bad cold and can't go out there."

"James'll move it for you," Mama says.

"Not unless you eat," the old lady says. "I'm old, but I have my pride, too, you know."

Mama can see she ain't go'n beat this old lady down, so she just shakes her head.

"All right," the old lady says. "Come into the kitchen."

She leads the way with that rag in her hand. The kitchen is a little bitty little old thing, too. The table and the stove just 'bout fill it up. They got a little room to the side. Somebody in there layin 'cross the bed—'cause I can see one of his feet. Must be the person she was talking to: Ernest or Alnest—something like that.

"Sit down," the old lady says to Mama. "Not you," she says to me. "You have to move the cans."

"Helena?" the man says in the other room.

"Yes, Alnest?" the old lady says.

"Are you going out there again?"

"I must show the boy where the garbage is, Alnest," the old lady says.

"Keep your shawl over your head," the old man says.

"You don't have to remind me, Alnest. Come, Boy," the old lady says.

We go out in the yard. Little old back yard ain't no bigger than the store or the kitchen. But it can sleet here just like it can sleet in any big back yard. And 'fore you know it, I'm trembling.

"There," the old lady says, pointing to the cans. I pick up one of the cans and set it right back down. The can's so light. I'm go'n see what's inside of it.

"Here," the old lady says. "Leave that can alone."

I look back at her standing there in the door. She's got

that black rag wrapped round her shoulders, and she's pointing one of her little old fingers at me.

"Pick it up and carry it to the front," she says. I go by her with the can, and she's looking at me all the time. I'm sure the can's empty. I'm sure she could've carried it herself—maybe both of them at the same time. "Set it on the sidewalk by the door and come back for the other one," she says.

I go and come back, and Mama looks at me when I pass her. I get the other can and take it to the front. It don't feel a bit heavier than that first one. I tell myself I ain't go'n be nobody's fool, and I'm go'n look inside this can to see just what I been hauling. First, I look up the street, then down the street. Nobody coming. Then I look over my shoulder toward the door. That little old lady done slipped up there quiet's a mouse, watching me again. Look like she knowed what I was go'n do.

"Ehh, Lord," she says. "Children, children. Come in here, boy, and go wash your hands."

I follow her in the kitchen. She points toward the bathroom, and I go in there and wash up. Little bitty old bathroom, but it's clean, clean. I don't use any of her towels; I wipe my hands on my pants legs.

When I come back in the kitchen, the old lady done dished up the food. Rice, gravy, meat—and she even got some lettuce and tomato in a saucer. She even got a glass of milk and a piece of cake there, too. It looks so good, I almost start eating 'fore I say my blessing.

"Helena?" the old man says.

"Yes, Alnest?"

"Are they eating?"

"Yes," she says.

"Good," he says. "Now you'll stay inside."

The old lady goes in there where he is and I can hear them talking. I look at Mama. She's eating slow like she's thinking. I wonder what's the matter now. I reckon she's thinking 'bout home.

The old lady comes back in the kitchen.

"I talked to Dr. Bassett's nurse," she says. "Dr. Bassett will take you as soon as you get there."

"Thank you, ma'am," Mama says.

"Perfectly all right," the old lady says. "Which one is it?"

Mama nods toward me. The old lady looks at me real sad. I look sad, too.

"You're not afraid, are you?" she says.

"No, ma'am," I say.

"That's a good boy," the old lady says. "Nothing to be afraid of. Dr. Bassett will not hurt you."

When me and Mama get through eating, we thank the old lady again.

"Helena, are they leaving?" the old man says.

"Yes, Alnest."

"Tell them I say good-bye."

"They can hear you, Alnest."

"Good-bye both mother and son," the old man says. "And may God be with you."

Me and Mama tell the old man good-bye, and we follow the old lady in the front room. Mama opens the door to go out, but she stops and comes back in the store.

"You sell salt meat?" she says.

"Yes."

"Give me two bits worth."

"That isn't very much salt meat," the old lady says.

"That's all I have," Mama says.

The old lady goes back of the counter and cuts a big piece off the chunk. Then she wraps it up and puts it in a paper bag.

"Two bits," she says.

"That looks like awful lot of meat for a quarter," Mama says.

"Two bits," the old lady says. "I've been selling salt meat behind this counter twenty-five years. I think I know what I'm doing."

"You got a scale there," Mama says.

"What?" the old lady says.

"Weigh it," Mama says.

"What?" the old lady says. "Are you telling me how to run my business?"

"Thanks very much for the food," Mama says.

"Just a minute," the old lady says.

"James," Mama says to me. I move toward the door.

"Just one minute, I said," the old lady says.

Me and Mama stop again and look at her. The old lady takes the meat out of the bag and unwraps it and cuts 'bout half of it off. Then she wraps it up again and juggs it back in the bag and gives the bag to Mama. Mama lays the quarter on the counter.

"Your kindness will never be forgotten," she says. "James," she says to me.

We go out, and the old lady comes to the door to look at us. After we go a little piece I look back, and she's still there watching us.

The sleet's coming down heavy, heavy now, and I turn up my coat collar to keep my neck warm. My mama tells me turn it right back down.

"You not a bum," she says. "You a man."

Harvey Swados
(1920–1972)

Born in Buffalo, New York, Harvey Swados worked as a riveter in an airplane plant and as a metal finisher for the Ford Motor Company in the early 1940s. A socialist, whose fiction reflected his deep sympathy and concern for the working class, he published five novels, *Out Went the Candle* (1955), *False Coin* (1959), *The Will* (1963), *Standing Fast* (1970) and—posthumously—*Celebration* (1975). His stories are collected in *On the Line* (1957), *Nights in the Gardens of Brooklyn* (1961 and 1986), and *A Story for Teddy and Others* (1965). Among his nonfiction are *A Radical's America* (1962) and *Standing Up for the People: The Life and Work of Estes Kefauver*. He was a recipient of a Hudson Review Fellowship, a Guggenheim Fellowship, a National Institute of Arts and Letters Award, and a National Endowment for the Arts grant.

MY CONEY ISLAND UNCLE

Inevitably our parents are the bearers of our disillusion. After they have ushered us into the world, they must bring word that Santa does not exist, that camp is out of the question, that Grandma is dying, and that they themselves are flawed by spite and unreason. Sometimes it falls to another grownup to renew in us for a time, through disinterested kindliness, that original seamless innocence, the very notion of which can otherwise become a sour mockery. The lucky ones among us can be grateful for a childhood graced by an unencumbered relative—a bachelor uncle, perhaps—who enjoys us not for what we may become, or may one day owe to him, but simply because we exist. I had such an uncle.

We lived, my parents and I, in a small frame house not far off Main Street in Dunkirk, New York, which is on Lake Erie about halfway between Buffalo and Erie, Pennsylvania. My father had inherited a hardware and agricultural-implements store to and from which he walked every day, and where my mother joined him to keep the books and wait on customers during the hours when I was in school.

My mother was a good sport, I think now, about a life that she could not have foreseen when she fell in love with my father on a summer vacation at Lake Chautauqua. She had been a New York girl with musical ambitions; she often exercised her light and agreeable soprano voice of an evening during my boyhood, accompanying herself at the Aeolian Duo-Art piano father had given her on the occasion of the arrival of her firstborn—me, Charley Morrison, who also turned out to be her lastborn. Mother solaced herself with introducing me to "the better things" (Friday-night poetry readings at her Sorosis Club, piano lessons with Miss Letts, and reproductions of the Great Masters), traveling to an occasional concert in Buffalo, and taking me to New York every year to visit her three brothers, my uncles Al, Eddie, and Dan.

Uncle Dan was the one who mattered. I can't remember why he happened to be visiting us when I entered kindergarten on the very morning of my fifth birthday. What I do remember, so vividly that the sunlit-noonday thrill of it is still almost painful, is the sight of Uncle Dan coming toward my mother and me on the cracked sidewalk before our little house, which sagged, a bit askew, like my father, as we returned from that terrifying first day of school. He was leading an Irish-setter puppy by a braided leather leash.

Aside from our family doctor, who had bad breath and wore high-top shoes, Uncle Dan was the only real doctor I knew. He might not have been an outstanding physician, but he did know, even though he never married or fathered a son, what could turn the trick with a small boy. As I ran up to him, still trembling from the strange lonely newness of the classroom, he unwound the leash from his fingers and flipped it at me.

"Here you go, Charley boy," he said. "Here's a puppy dog for a good student."

And he stood there, stocky and self-possessed, smiling around his cigar, ignoring my mother's shocked surprise and nudging amusedly at my bottom with his toes as I dropped to my knees to caress my new dog. "Just treat him right, Charley boy," he said, "and you'll have a real friend."

I didn't know how to tell Uncle Dan that he was my favorite. The other New York uncles were all right, but they had wives and children of their own; he was the one who I felt belonged to me. People said that I looked like him, which was beyond my understanding—he was a burly man with an impudent mop of reddish-brown hair (my father had almost none that I can recall even from my earliest childhood, and I couldn't even tell you the color of the fringe around his ears), and an even more unlikely mustache, full, square, and bristling. How could I resemble a middle-aged man—he must have been in his thirties at that time—with a big thick mustache? It was enough that he would give me a dog, and an occasional boot in the behind, to show me that he appreciated what I didn't dare to tell him.

As the years passed, I came to believe that he would have understood, had he been around, far more than my parents. Not that they didn't try, in that dull and drowsy community. But in the cruel way of children, I often felt, particularly as the depression invaded our lives like a prolonged state of mourning, that they—immured in their dark semibankrupt store that smelled of iron filings and bird seed—had no notion of how they ought to treat me. Else why would they have lied to me after they had my dog put away when he went into distemper convulsions? And why did they take it for a kindness to let me oversleep the grand opening night of the circus, the only halfway exciting event of the year in Dunkirk, after I had worked to the point of exhaustion for a pass, a ticket which they could never have afforded, in those lean days, to buy me?

I was going on thirteen that summer, sullen and rebellious after the circus fiasco, when my father informed me with clumsily evasive tact that, as a reward for having done well in school and helped out at the store, I was to be sent to New York. Alone.

I was old enough to know that my parents could not have come to this decision by themselves. Mother's family had to be consulted, if only because they would have to put me up. My mother had already forgone her annual visit home, but this, as well as the matter of who was paying for my ticket, was something that simply went unmentioned in our household; to bring it up would have been like asking if you were going to get a Christmas present, and how much would be spent on it.

Besides, I had a strong hunch that it was my Uncle Dan who was footing the bill. He was the one with the fewest responsibilities, and it was he who scrawled me the postcard (he never could manage a whole letter) asking if I'd like to batch it with him for a while.

If they had fixed it up not with my Coney Island uncle but with the Manhattan uncles, Al or Eddie, I probably wouldn't even have wanted to go at all. Not that I was spoiled or blasé about New York. But mother and I had always stayed with Uncle Al and Aunt Clara, mother sleeping on the studio couch, me bunking with their boys. They were all right, but as far as I was concerned there was nothing glamorous or big-city about them. Uncle Al was seldom home except Sunday evenings, when he'd slump down morosely before the radio to listen to Ed Wynn, and Aunt Clara was in the kitchen baking all day, gabbing with mother. She wouldn't let my cousins own bicycles, they didn't even know how to ride, and they never ceased needling me monotonously as a hick. We'd stand around in the concrete courtyard of the apartment house, not a blade of grass in sight, bouncing a sponge-rubber ball back and forth in the little clear space to one side of the corroded green fountain of a nymph with jug that never worked anyway, and taunting each other out of boredom and aimlessness.

"Is this all you guys ever do?" I'd ask. "Isn't there anything else to do in New York, except follow the horseballs in the bridle path in Central Park?"

"Horseballs yourself. Is it true you still got Indians running around loose in Dunkirk? Aren't you afraid of getting scalped? Why do you always say faw-rest and George War-shington?"

And then my mother, with her relentless passion for intellectual improvement, would haul us off on the bus to the Museum of the City of New York to look at dolls costumed as dead mayors' wives, or to the Museum of Natural History to study the pasted-together bones of brontosauruses and tyrannosauruses. After five or six days I was more than ready to go home.

I just knew that it would be different now, staying with my Coney Island uncle. From the moment that father bade me goodbye in the unwashed bus depot that smelled of depression and defeat, stowing his rusty Gladstone in the rack over my head, shaking hands with me shyly, and smiling a reassurance that did not conceal his perpetual somberness, I settled into the new mood of freedom and adventure. All through the long ride down across Pennsylvania, Erie to Warren to Coudersport to Towanda to Scranton to New York, I pitched and rolled on the torn leather seat with the stuffing oozing out, exalted as though I strode the deck of a Yankee clipper. Even the discovery that my uncle was not at the Manhattan Greyhound Terminal to meet me, as he had promised, was exhilarating. I kept a good grip on the valise, as father had advocated, and while I was looking about for Uncle Dan, a lady from Travelers Aid came up and asked if I was Charley Morrison.

"Your uncle is tied up in an emergency. He says to come right out to his place. Now you can take any line of the BMT, can you remember that? Don't take the IRT, you'll get all mixed up."

It was like Uncle Dan, I thought, not to send some stooge relative after me, but to trust me, even though it was already well into the night, to find my way out to Coney Island. I got there without trouble, hauled the valise down the steps of the elevated into the street at

Surf Avenue, and walked straight up the block, milling and restless as Times Square, even at midnight, to the corner where Uncle Dan's signs hung in all his second-floor windows. Just as I was reaching out to punch his night bell I heard my uncle's familiar voice behind me, deep and drawling.

"Charley boy! Have a nice ride?"

I swung around. Uncle Dan was standing there smiling, medical bag in his left hand, cigar and door key in his right. His hat was shoved back on his head, and his Palm Beach suit was wrinkled at the crotch; he had put on some weight and seemed tired, but otherwise he looked the same.

"Let's just throw our bags in the hall, so we can go out and grab a bite."

He led me around the corner and up the ramp, gritty with sand, to the boardwalk. Above us the looped wires of bulbs drooped like heavy necklaces, the neon lights of stores and stands slashed on and off, some hurling their arrows hopelessly after each other, others stabbing into the sky like red-hot sparks, and the night was so illumined by them all that you could follow the smoke from the skillets of the hamburger joints high into the air before it disappeared into the darkness, along with the hot steam of the coffee urns. Amidst the acrid smell of burning molasses, before salt-water-taffy machines swaying rhythmically as they pulled the fat, creamy ribbons to and fro, girls opened cupid's-bow mouths to receive huge wobbling cones of cotton candy extended eagerly by their sailor boy friends. The ground shook beneath me with the thudding of thousands of feet on the wooden boardwalk, stained in spots from the wet footprints of late bathers and the spilled soda pop of boys my age who shook up the open bottles and released their thumbs to aim the spray at the unsuspecting before they fled. And over it all the intermittent roar of the plunging roller coaster across the way at Steeplechase Park, its electric controls rattling as it raced down below the horizon like an express train to hell.

Uncle Dan led the way to Nathan's hot-dog stand and said to a Greek counterman, "Two franks well done,

Chris, for me and my nephew." He turned to me. "You take yours with sauerkraut? I forget."

I said boldly, "I like mine with everything." Mother would never have let me eat a spicy hot dog in the middle of the night, much less with all that junk smeared, rubbed, and squeezed on it.

"That's your nephew, hey, Doc?"

"Come in from the West to keep me company for a while. We're going to have some fun, us two bachelors." My uncle took a huge bite; I had never before seen anyone handle a hot dog, a cigar, and a toothpick all at once. "And listen, Chris, if this boy comes by with a hungry look during the day, his credit is good."

"I got you." The counterman extended his bare arm, hairy as a gorilla's. "Have a knish, kid."

We washed down the hot dogs and knishes with big shupers of root beer. The glass mugs were heavy as sin, frosty, with foam running down the sides; Uncle Dan blew off some of the suds at me as if we were drinking beer, which was just what I had been secretly pretending. As we strolled on he asked, "What time do they make you go to bed back home?"

I hesitated. I wanted to add thirty minutes to my weekend late limit, but then something made me answer honestly.

Uncle Dan screwed up his face. "That sounds awful damn early to me. At least, it is for Coney Island. Tell you what, if you promise not to snitch to your mother, we'll just forget that curfew stuff while you're staying with me."

I could hardly trust myself to reply.

"Your mother's a good woman," Uncle Dan remarked, in a thoughtful tone that I had never heard him use before. He took me by the elbow and led me to his apartment through the midnight crowds, thicker than we had even for circuses back home. "She's got her troubles, you know, like all of us. But she's my favorite. I mean, your uncles are all right, they're not bad fellows, but they've made a couple mistakes. Number one was when they got married."

As he threw away his cigar, he added, "Number two

was when Al and Eddie left Brooklyn. In Manhattan, you don't even realize that you're living on the shore, on the edge of the ocean, the way you do here."

He fell silent, and I, matching my step to his, could not remember when Uncle Dan had ever talked to me so much all at once. After a while he went on, "This is a good place to live. You'll see."

In the two minutes that it took me to fall asleep, I observed that Uncle Dan came to bed beside me in his drawers. It was a practice that my mother condemned as disgusting, but I resolved to put my pajamas back into father's Gladstone next morning. Mother thought too that you couldn't get really clean in a shower, and at home we had a monstrous old claw-legged tub that we filled part way with kettles of boiling water from the kitchen stove, in a bathroom so drafty that we stuffed the casement with rags and plugged in two electric heaters from the store ten minutes before bathtime. But Uncle Dan's shower stall, into which I leaped when I awoke, with Uncle Dan already halfway through his office hours down the corridor, had a ripply-glass door with a chrome handle, the first I'd ever seen outside of the movies, and water that kept coming out hot, forever.

I did get a rather haphazard tourist's view of New York in the days that followed—waiting in line with the other out-of-towners on Sixth Avenue to see a Marlene Dietrich movie about the Russian Revolution at Radio City Music Hall, riding the elevator to the top of the Empire State Building to peer down at the tiny pedestrians who might be Uncle Al or Uncle Eddie ("from up here your uncles look like ants")—but what entered deep into my being was a sense of the variety and richness of possibility in the city, a sense of how one could, if one only wished, enter any of a number of communities, each as unique as the single one in the small town I had left behind.

Uncle Dan did this for me, and without even realizing it. All he knew was that it might be fun for me to tag along with him for a while. It never occurred to him that just by exposing me to his daily round, which to him was not particularly exciting but pleasant enough so that he had no deep incentive to change it, he was presenting me with motives for persisting in this confounding, fascinating world.

If my father knew everyone who came into his store, everyone knew Uncle Dan when he stepped out onto the street. But there was a difference. On our way to his Buick, which he kept garaged a few blocks away, on Neptune Avenue—I cannot remember whether it was the first or the second day of my visit, for by now everything has blended into a generalized memory of that liberating week, as if the revolution I was experiencing was far more than the sum of its insurrectionary incidents—we were suddenly stopped by a pleading woman.

"Doctor, doctor!" she cried, gasping for breath, holding out her empty reddened hands as though she were extending something precious and hot, like a freshly baked cake. It occurred to me that if she had been carrying something, anything, even a little purse, in those swollen hands, she wouldn't have looked so wild.

"Let's take it easy," my uncle said. He addressed her by some Polish or Slavic name. "Is it your husband? Casper?"

She nodded, trotting alongside us as we approached the car. "He beat up on Mrs. Polanyi. He knock her down, he try to kill her."

"I warned you it was going to happen, didn't I?"

"What I can do? I can send him away? How we going to eat?"

"Well, now you'll have to do it. No two ways." He held open the front door of the car. "Hop in."

She shook her head vigorously. What was this? Why wouldn't she get in? My heart thumping, I stared at the frightened woman, who stood there with her chest heaving, refusing to sit in the front seat.

But Uncle Dan understood. With a sigh he yanked open the rear door. "OK, let's not waste time."

She crawled into the back, and as I settled myself beside my uncle, he muttered, "She thinks it's not polite to sit up front next to the doctor. It's a wonder she'll ride with us at all."

In a few minutes we had pulled up in front of her

house, a red-brick tenement indistinguishable from all the others on the block except for the crowd gathered before it. Uncle Dan leaned on the horn with one hand to clear the way as he reached back with the other for his satchel. "Come on, Clara," he said to the woman, who had been crouched on the edge of the seat as if afraid that she might soil it, "we'll go take care of Mrs. Polanyi. Charley boy, you keep an eye on the car."

I couldn't just sit there on that baking Brooklyn street, not with the neighborhood kids staring at me. So I got out and thrust myself into the crowd.

In its midst a girl of about my age, one of her twin braids half unwound, was crying against the bosom of a gray-haired woman.

"What happened?" I asked boldly.

A boy answered wisely, "It was her mother." "Huh muddah" was the way he pronounced it, and it took me a second or two to understand. "The nut stomped on huh. He's a real nut. You the doctor's son?"

Before I could answer, a thin-faced sallow man came out the front door and sauntered down the stoop, pausing only to light a cigarette with a wooden kitchen match. Although he was tieless, he wore a sharp striped suit with a grease stain big as a campaign button on his left lapel; his fly was open. The crowd moved off even while the flame of the match still flickered, before he blew it out. He came directly to me, placing his face so close to mine that I could see the pores on his fleshy nose, and fixed me with his very pale, almost colorless blue eyes. I had the feeling that he was looking through me, at something just behind my head, rather than at me.

"You the doctor's boy?"

"I'm his nephew." I heard mutters from the crowd, which had drifted back to either side of us.

"He's a great man. Man of science. You know science?"

"Not much."

"It powers the world. You know science, you got hidden power. Mrs. Polanyi, she was tuned in. She was wired for sound. They send her messages against me. Man, she could have destroyed everybody. You know Mrs. Polanyi?"

I shook my head wordlessly. I knew, suddenly, who he was, and what was wrong, but I was not frightened. I was simply curious and fascinated. After a few moments of odd disjointed talk my uncle tramped out in his heavy, solid way, lugging his satchel and blowing on a prescription blank. He beckoned to the crying girl.

"Hey, Jeanette! Take this to Rudnicki's drugstore and get it filled. Your mother'll be all right—I'll stop by tomorrow." He winked at me as he shoved a fresh cigar into his mouth, then turned to the man who had been talking with me. "Casper, you got to go for a ride. You met my nephew already?"

"Sure. He's a smart one. Science, like you. It powers the world." His pupils were the merest pinpoints; his jaws were clamped as if with a wrench; when he smiled it was like a dog baring his fangs.

"Amen. Come on, Casper, let's go. Here comes your wife."

Her handkerchief to her face, she stumbled down the steps and through the ranks of the curious.

"I'm going to need you to sign the commitment papers, Clara. . . . Close that door, will you, Charley boy?"

And we were off to the hospital, my uncle making easy talk with the wife, and me sitting beside the demented husband who had almost murdered a defenseless woman. It did not take long for him to be removed to the barred retreat where for all I know he still paces, hunting for the secret wires of science.

After we had finally left his wife, in the charge of a sister, weeping in terror at the prospect of feeding her family without her husband's wages, Uncle Dan took me into the precinct house, where he had to make out a report. Then we drove across the length of Coney Island, from the hump of Sea Gate, sticking out into Gravesend Bay, over to Brighton Beach, to that corner of it which encloses Sheepshead Bay, and there, on a street of bayfront cottages smelling not of traffic exhaust, dumbwaiters, and dark metallic elevators, but of clams, salt marshes, oakum, and rotting bait, I met a sword swallower.

Mr. and Mrs. Alvarez might have been, superficially, customers of my father's. She was a childless but motherly woman with the bosom of a pigeon, but her flashing eyes were those of an opera singer. When we arrived she was just removing a sheet of cookies from the oven. While her husband, who greeted us in his bathrobe with the *Daily News* dangling from his left fist, was squeezing my hand so hard that it brought tears to my eyes, Mrs. Alvarez was already pouring me a glass of milk and setting the cookies before me.

She stood over me and stroked my hair while I ate and drank, saying, "You come from a nice part of the country, kiddo. Many's the time Alfredo and I played the fairground circuit all in through there."

"What did you do?"

She laughed, her bosom shaking. "You wouldn't think it to look at me, but I used to be a bareback rider. Since I got too heavy, we settled here, and Al works the shows on the island."

Her husband, the examination of his throat and chest completed, returned to the kitchen from the bedroom without bothering to throw his robe over his undershirt and trousers. I was impressed by his shoulders, which were embroidered like tapestry with writhing tattooed dragons, their tails looping up around his wiry corded neck.

"How you like it here, kid?" he demanded.

"I like it fine."

"Doc says I'm going to live for a while," he announced to his wife and to me.

"Not if you don't change jobs," my uncle grunted, but that seemed to make no particular impression. Mr. Alvarez stepped jerkily to the closet and fetched out a long package, a broom handle maybe, wrapped in flannel.

"You didn't take the boy to the sideshow yet, did you, Doc?"

Uncle Dan shook his head. "Give us a chance. He hasn't even been to Bedloe's Island yet, to the Statue of Liberty."

"Aw, the Statue of Liberty. Let me show you something, kid." He unwrapped the flannel with a flourish and exposed a glittering sword, wonderfully filigreed all along the blade.

Before any of us could say a word Mr. Alvarez snapped to attention as though he were presenting arms at court, then raised his walnut-brown sinewy arms and brought the point of the sword to his lips. He bent his grizzled head back farther than I had ever seen anyone do and slipped the sword into his open mouth and down his gullet, inch by inch, then foot by foot. You could actually see it going down from the outside, his bare neck working and swelling as it contained the cold steel.

Mrs. Alvarez sat at the kitchen table, placid and proud. "Pretty good, huh? Here, take along some cookies in wax paper. You'll get hungry later."

Mr. Alvarez brought up the sword as deliberately and delicately as he had slid it down, clicked his heels, and bowed. "You get the point?" he asked, and laughed with a hoarse bark.

"That's the most amazing thing I ever saw," I said honestly.

"I can do that with almost any type sword. Except one that's too curved, like a scimitar." Skimitar, he pronounced it. "I can do it with a rapier, even with a saber. You got to keep a straight passage, see, the head has got to be straight back. It's all in the head, am I right or wrong, Doc?"

Mr. Alvarez gave me the sword to examine. "You come to the show, kid, and you'll be able to see right through me. I swallow an electrified sword, it's got little bulbs on it. I stand in front of a black curtain and you can see the bulbs inside me just like my backbone was lit up."

He was chuckling all the way to the door. "See you in the freak show."

In the car my uncle sighed, his hands hanging over the steering wheel for a moment before he stepped on the starter. "Nice people, aren't they?"

"You bet."

"He's got an ulcerated throat. It's a precancerous condition, really. You can't go on insulting the body indefinitely, Charley boy. But his wife can't work anymore, and he doesn't know how to do anything else. Well, I thought you'd enjoy meeting them."

We did visit the freak show a few nights later. I gaped at the tattooed lady's bluish hide, blurred like an old map, and stared in uncomfortable awe at the seminude form of the half man, half woman, not wholly convinced by Uncle Dan's explanation of glandular pathology. My parents would never have taken me there, either as a favor or an object lesson, and I did not dare to ask Uncle Dan what he had in mind, if anything, besides entertainment.

The Fat Lady was off that night because of a toothache. But since she too was a patient of Uncle Dan's, next morning I found myself riding with her and my uncle in an old panel truck from her flat in Brighton over to the dentist's, on Linden Boulevard in Flatbush. Uncle Dan and I sat in front with the driver, her brother-in-law, who was all business; Smiling Sally herself was spread out, like some giant growth, all over a plank fixed to the bed of the truck for her. From time to time a groan would issue from that vast heap of flesh, and her massive arm would rise slowly, alarmingly, reaching out to my uncle for comfort.

Uncle Dan was to give her the anesthetic, but before the extraction we had to get her into the office of his colleague, Dr. Otto Reinitz, whose first-floor office fortunately had French windows. No sooner had we begun preparations to transport Sally through the window to the dentist than the envious neighborhood kids began to gather, picking their noses and pointing at the groaning circus queen.

First we had to rig up a kind of staging with a block and tackle, like the bos'n's chair used by sign painters, and then, supervised by her sweating but experienced brother-in-law, we hoisted unsmiling Sally aboard and on into the office of the waiting Dr. Reinitz, a skinny man with an eyeshade and the biggest Adam's apple I had ever seen. We pushed the sofa from the waiting room into the office so that Sally could recline on it within reach of the dentist's forceps.

When the job was done and Sally came back to life, she became a person for me. I had no idea how old she was, maybe twenty-five, maybe forty-five, but beneath all of that fat there beat the heart of a flirt. She smiled winsomely, bravely making light of her pain, she looked sidelong at me, she squeezed my hand.

"That's some assistant, Doc," she said to my uncle. "A regaleh doll. How old are you, sonny? Old enough for the girls?"

I knew the answer to the first question, if not to the second, and she rewarded me with an inscribed postcard photo in a glassine envelope,displaying her in a grotesque tentlike puffed-sleeve party dress, bobby socks, and Mary Janes, which she took from the purse that dangled like a toy doll's from the rings of flesh at her wrist. SMILING SALLY, 649 LBS. OF JOLLITY, it said.

"I get a quarter for these at the freak show," she told me. "For you, nothing. Someday you'll grow up to be a big doctor like your uncle."

That morning, I thought maybe I would. There were others my uncle attended whose lives had also been tarnished, some in ways I would not dare to mention when I returned home. In Greenpoint, just across the East River from Lower Manhattan, on Noble Street (the name has stuck in my mind), I waited in a candy store while Uncle Dan administered sedation in the flat upstairs to a screaming woman whose son's body had just been brought back from Red Hook, where rival mobsters had put three bullets in the back of his head. From there we drove in silence, around the Navy Yard, over to a portion of Sands Street which no longer even exists, teetering shacks aswarm with prostitutes.

I waited in the car, my face on fire, trying not to stare back at the bored, gum-chewing girls waving at me from behind lace-curtained windows. When my uncle came out, he tossed his satchel on the back seat and gave my bony shoulder a squeeze.

"The more trouble I see," he said, "the hungrier I get. Let's grab a bite in Borough Hall before I get stuck with my office hours."

He had to file some papers and pick up vaccines in downtown Brooklyn too, so we parked on Montague Street and had a businessman's lunch in a real bar, where I watched salesmen matching each other for drinks by rolling dice from a cup.

"Nothing like that in Dunkirk," I assured my uncle.

"Charley boy," he laughed, "you could say the same thing about Sands Street, in spades."

On the way back to the car, cutting across the open square in front of Borough Hall, we came upon a circle of lunch-hour loungers listening to a sidewalk speaker. I thought at first that he was selling razor blades or carrot slicers, the kind of pitchman that my father always referred to as cheap, cutthroat competition, but then as I pushed my way through I saw that he was black, and that he displayed nothing but a stick of yellow chalk.

He was a skinny, solemn man, conservatively dressed, but with eyes bulbous and roving like those of a rearing stallion. The bony, imperious hand that held the chalk slid occasionally to his mouth to wipe the spittle from his lips

"Ich bin a shvartser id!" he cried.

Out of the corner of his mouth Uncle Dan explained, "He's telling them he's a black Jew."

"I do not preach the New Testament," the orator shouted in English. "Let us speak only of the wonders concealed in the Old. Let us confine ourselves only to the Pentateuch. Those of you who paid attention in *heder* will recall where it says . . ." and he lapsed into Hebrew.

His accent brought grins from the crowd; but suddenly he squatted and began to print characters on the street, in the space before us. His calligraphy, stark and sharp and yellow, stood out on the black street like the brilliant mysterious border of an Oriental rug. Drawing with nervous rapidity, he continued to scream at us as he stooped over his chalk, lecturing in English, quoting in Hebrew. Swiftly a pattern emerged as he whirled and twisted on his haunches: The mysterious phrases intersected at their center to form—"Inevitably!" he cried out, enraptured, the sweat of persuasion dripping down his cheeks—a cross.

"What I tell you?" a tubby man beside me demanded of his companion. "He's a *meshummad,* like I said."

"To be a *meshummad,* you got to be a Jew to start out. Otherwise, how can you change over? Nah, he's a missionary, an agitator. He comes downtown to convert."

Some of the crowd were muttering angrily, others turning their backs in disgust, a few (like Uncle Dan) chuckling, as the black orator called after us, flailing his long arms, white cuffs dangling over his wrists, "It is written in our own Book! We must admit the Christ to our hearts!"

And in the course of that week I saw signs and portents, cabalic, symbols chalked on the city streets and tattooed on the shoulders of beings who ate cold steel; I rode with lunatics, moved from murderers to fallen women, accepted an inscribed photo from the fattest woman in the world, and one morning Van Mungo, the great Dodger pitcher, my hero long before I had come to Brooklyn, and my uncle's friend, rumpled my hair and autographed a baseball for me to take home, where I could varnish it to protect his signature and display it to the doubters of Dunkirk.

What is more, during Uncle Dan's office hours I lolled on the beach with *Official Detective* magazines from his waiting room that were forbidden me at home, surrounded by the undressed throngs come in their thousands from every stifling flat in New York, from every darkened corner of the world, actually, to sun themselves at my side; I learned the sweet subtleties of bluff and deception, kibitzing at the weekly session of my uncle's poker club, attended by the cadaverous dentist, Dr. Reinitz, and three Coney Island businessmen; and I was not just allowed but encouraged to stay up practically all night for the great flashy Mardi Gras parade, blinking sleepy-eyed at the red rows of fire engines rolling glossily along streets sparkling like Catherine wheels. It was the greatest week of my life.

But if my uncle graced my childhood, he also—one bitter wintry evening some ten years later—illumined my adulthood. When the destroyer escort on which I had been pitching miserably through the North Atlantic on wartime convoy duty paused in the dead of night in Gravesend Bay before nosing on up through the Narrows to the Navy Yard, I wangled my way ashore and hurried directly to my Uncle Dan. After all those black nights blinking at meandering merchant vessels groping toward their own destruction, Coney Island was startling, even in the dimout. But it had changed. Icy and inhospitable in the off-season, its faded invitations to dead pleasures creaked in the winter wind, and its empty, empty streets were rimmed with frost and frozen grime.

My uncle was not at home. "But you go on over to the Turkish bath," his housekeeper said to me. "You remember where it is, right down the block. He's playin' poker there with his club, Dr. Reinitz and all of them."

Already a little let down, I shivered along the barren streets and shouldered on into the hot, dank sanctuary of the bathhouse. There, seated around a card table messy with poker chips, sandwich ends, French fries on wax paper, and beer in paper cups, were my Uncle Dan and his fellow bachelors, their bare skulls and shoulders shining wetly under the brilliant light of a hundred-watt bulb that hung straight down from a cord. The cadaverous Dr. Reinitz was naked save for clogs and a Turkish towel across his lap, but I recognized him at once by his Adam's apple and his green eyeshade, which apparently he never discarded; instead of his swiveled drill he held three cards in his hand, but he had changed in no essential aspect.

Uncle Dan was half draped in a bed sheet, roughly like a Roman senator, except that you don't think of Romans as clenching cigars. The fringe of hair on his chest had turned white, and his paunch was twice what I had remembered it to be. He glanced up at me coolly, with a weary casualness more startling than the collapse of his looks.

"Look who's here. How are you, Charley boy? Gentlemen, you remember my nephew. Otto, Oscar—"

I nodded.

"Here, pull up a chair." The one named Oscar extended his hand and showed me two rings. "Hey, Jake, bring another corned beef. And a beer. Never saw a sailor didn't like beer."

"You been overseas?" Dr. Reinitz inquired incuriously.

"I've been back and forth," I muttered. "On convoy duty. Halifax. Scotland. Murmansk."

"You don't say. I was in Archangel once myself. Very

drab. You could see daylight right through the chinks in the log cabins."

"Well," said Uncle Dan, "main thing is you're back in New York safe and sound. What are you going to do with your leave—paint the town red?"

"Paint the town red?" I cried, hoping desperately that he would do for me, one last time, what he had when I was thirteen.

I had been seasick and frightened for a long time. I had been knocked off my feet by depth charges, I had been nauseated by the twilight farewell of a helpless wallowing Hog Island veteran of the first war, flaring briefly against the horizon like a struck match and then pointing its bow at the sky like an accusing finger before sinking beneath the sea, leaving nothing but a few screaming men and the junky debris of war.

Now I was appalled by these civilians and their unrationed self-satisfaction, and most of all by my uncle himself. I was heartsick with disappointment. Like a boy crudely misunderstood by a girl he has romanticized, I wanted only to flee. Then I saw that my uncle wore a queer expression that I would never have identified with him, and so found incomprehensible: At that moment I took it to be a look of envy, embedded in the puffy used-up features of one seemingly beyond anything but an evening of cards with his similars in a Turkish bath. And I could think of nothing to say except to repeat, "Paint the town red?"

He shook his head slowly. And slowly, as he turned the cigar between his lips, an old glint came back to his eyes. Passing his index finger across his whitening mustache to brush it into place, he murmured, "I know what you mean, Charley boy. But I wasn't worried about you for a minute. You're bigger now than I ever was. I'm the one that's been going down, here, little by little, and with no lifesaver either." Ignoring those about us, who had suddenly ceased to exist either as his friends or my antagonists, he paused for a moment in order that the words that followed, more shocking to me than his appearance, might bar the door forever to my childish demands on him. "I'm the one who could use some help now."

Bernard Malamud
(1914–1986)

Born and raised in Brooklyn, New York, where his father ran a small grocery, Bernard Malamud was educated at City College and Columbia University. For almost four decades he taught English, first at Erasmus Hall and other New York evening high schools, then at Oregon State University, and finally at Bennington College, where he taught creative writing and literature for more than twenty years. His novels include *The Natural* (1952), which was adapted in 1984 for a Hollywood film starring Robert Redford, *The Assistant* (1957), *A New Life* (1961), *The Fixer* (1967), which was awarded both the Pulitzer Prize and the National Book Award, *Pictures of Fidelman* (1969), which consists of stories about one central character, *The Tenants* (1971), *Dubin's Lives* (1979), and *God's Grace* (1982). He published four collections of stories, *The Magic Barrel* (1958), which won the National Book Award, *Idiots First* (1963), *Rembrandt's Hat* (1973), and *The Stories of Bernard Malamud* (1983), a retrospective collection.

MY SON THE MURDERER

He wakes to a feeling his father is in the hallway, listening. Listening to what? Listening to him sleep and dream. To him get up and fumble for his pants. To him not going to the kitchen to eat. Staring with shut eyes in the mirror. Sitting an hour on the toilet. Flipping the pages of a book he can't read. To his rage, anguish, loneliness. The father stands in the hall. The son hears him listen.

My son the stranger, he tells me nothing.

I open the door and see my father in the hall.

Why are you standing there, why don't you go to work?

I took my vacation in the winter instead of the summer like I usually do.

What the hell for if you spend it in this dark smelly hallway watching my every move. Guessing what you don't see. Why are you spying on me?

My father goes to his room and after a while comes out in the hallway again, listening.

I hear him sometimes in his room but he don't talk to me and I don't know what's what. It's a terrible feeling for a father. Maybe someday he'll write me a nice letter, Mr dear father. . . .

My dear son Harry, open up your door.

My son the prisoner.

My wife leaves in the morning to be with my married daughter who is having her fourth child. The mother cooks and cleans for her and takes care of the children. My daughter is having a bad pregnancy, with high blood pressure, and is in bed most of the time. My wife is gone all day. She knows something is wrong with Harry. Since he graduated college last summer he is nervous, alone, in his own thoughts. If you talk to him, half the time he yells. He reads the papers, smokes, stays in his room. Once in a while he goes for a walk.

How was the walk, Harry?

A walk.

My wife told him to go look for work and a few times he went, but when he got some kind of offer he didn't take the job.

It's not that I don't want to work. It's that I feel bad.

Why do you feel bad?

I feel what I feel. I feel what is.

Is it your health, sonny? Maybe you ought to go to a doctor?

Don't call me by that name. It's not my health. Whatever it is I don't want to talk about it. The work wasn't the kind I want.

So take something temporary in the meantime, she said.

He starts to yell. Everything is temporary. Why should I add more to what is already temporary? My guts feel temporary. The world is temporary. On top of that I don't want temporary work. I want the opposite of temporary, but where do you look for it? Where do you find it?

My father temporarily listens in the kitchen.

My temporary son.

She said I'd feel better if I work. I deny it. I'm twenty-two, since last December, a college graduate and you know where you can stick that. At night I watch the news broadcasts. I watch the war from day to day. It's a large war on a small screen. I sometimes lean over and touch the war with the flat of my hand. I'm waiting for my hand to die.

My son with the dead hand.

I expect to be drafted any day but it doesn't bother me so much anymore. I won't go. I'll go to Canada or somewhere, though the idea is a burden to me.

The way he is frightens my wife and she is glad to go off to my daughter's house in the morning to take care of the three children. I'm left alone, but he don't talk to me.

You ought to call up Harry and talk to him, my wife says to my daughter.

I will sometimes, but don't forget there's nine years' difference between our ages. I think he thinks of me as another mother around and one is enough. I used to like him, but it's hard to deal with a person who won't reciprocate.

She's got high blood pressure. I think she's afraid to call.

I took two weeks off from work. I'm a clerk at the stamps window in the Post Office. I told the superintendent I wasn't feeling so good, which is no lie, and he said I should take sick leave, but I said I wasn't that sick. I told my friend Moe Berk I was staying out because Harry had me worried.

I know what you mean, Leo. I got my own worries and anxieties about my kids. If you have two girls growing up you got hostages to fortune. Still in all, we got to live. Will you come to poker Friday night? Don't deprive yourself of a good form of relaxation.

I'll see how I feel by then, how it's coming. I can't promise.

Try to come. These things all pass away. If it looks better to you, come on over. Even if it don't look so good, come on over anyway because it might relieve the tension and worry that you're under. It's not good for your heart at your age if you carry that much worry around.

This is the worst kind of worry. If I worry about myself I know what the worry is. What I mean, there's no mystery. I can say to myself, Leo, you're a fool, stop worrying over nothing—over what, a few bucks? Over my health that always stood up pretty good although I've had my ups and downs? Over that I'm now close to sixty and not getting any younger? Everybody that don't die by age fifty-nine gets to be sixty. You can't beat time if it's crawling after you. But if the worry is about somebody else, that's the worst kind. That's the real worry because if he won't tell you, you can't get inside the other person and find out why. You don't know where's the switch to turn off. All you can do is worry more.

So I wait in the hallway.

Harry, don't worry about the war.

Don't tell me what to worry about.

Harry, your father loves you. When you were a little boy, every night when I came home you used to run to me. I picked you up and lifted you to the ceiling. You liked to touch it with your small hand.

I don't want to hear about that anymore. It's the very thing I don't want to hear about. I don't want to hear about when I was a child.

Harry, we live like strangers. All I'm saying is I remember better days. I remember when we weren't afraid to show we loved each other.

He says nothing.

Let me cook you an egg.

I don't want an egg. It's the last thing in the world I want.

So what do you want?

He put his coat on. He pulled his hat off the clothes tree and went downstairs into the street. Harry walked along Ocean Parkway in his long coat and creased brown hat. He knew his father was following him and it filled him with rage.

He didn't turn around. He walked at a fast pace up the broad avenue. In the old days there was a bridle path at the side of the walk where the concrete bicycle path was now. And there were fewer trees now, their black branches cutting the sunless sky. At the corner of Avenue X, just about where you begin to smell Coney Island, he crossed over and began to walk home. He pretended not to see his father cross over, although he was still infuriated. The father crossed over and followed his son home. When he got to the house he figured Harry was already upstairs. He was in his room with the door shut. Whatever he did in his room he was already doing.

Leo took out his key and opened the mailbox. There were three letters. He looked to see if one of them was, by any chance, from his son to him. My dear father, let me explain myself. The reason I act as I do is. . . . But there was no such letter. One of the letters was from the Post Office Clerks Benevolent Society, which he put in his coat pocket. The other two letters were for his son. One was from the draft board. He brought it up to his son's room, knocked on the door and waited.

He waited for a while.

To the boy's grunt he said, There is a draft board letter for you. He turned the knob and entered the room. Harry was lying on the bed with his eyes shut.

You can leave it on the table.

Why don't you open it? Do you want me to open it for you?

No, I don't want you to open it. Leave it on the table. I know what's in it.

What's in it?

That's my business.

The father left it on the table.

The other letter to his son he took into the kitchen, shut the door and boiled up some water in a kettle. He thought he would read it quickly and then seal it carefully with a little paste so that none leaked over the edge of the flap, then go downstairs and put it back in the mailbox. His wife would take it out with her key when she returned from their daughter's house and bring it up to Harry.

The father read the letter. It was a short letter from a girl. The girl said Harry had borrowed two of her books more than six months ago and since she valued them highly she would like him to send them back to her. Could he do that as soon as possible so that she wouldn't have to write again?

As Leo was reading the girl's letter Harry came into the kitchen and when he saw the surprised and guilty look on his father's face, he tore the letter out of his hands.

I ought to kill you the way you spy on me.

Leo turned away, looking out of the small kitchen window into the dark apartment-house courtyard. His face was a mottled red, his eyes dull, and he felt sick.

Harry read the letter at a glance and tore it up. He then tore up the envelope marked personal.

If you do this again don't be surprised if I kill you. I'm sick of you spying on me.

Harry left the house.

Leo went into his room and looked around. He looked in the dresser drawers and found nothing unusual. On the desk by the window was a paper Harry had written on. It said: Dear Edith, why don't you go fuck yourself? If you write another such letter I'll murder you.

The father got his hat and coat and left the house. He ran for a while, running then walking, until he saw Harry on the other side of the street. He followed him a half block behind.

He followed Harry to Coney Island Avenue and was in time to see him board a trolleybus going toward the Island. Leo had to wait for the next bus. He thought of taking a taxi and following the bus, but no taxi came by. the next bus came by fifteen minutes later and he took it all the way to the Island. It was February and Coney Island was cold and deserted. There were few cars on Surf Avenue and few people on the streets. It looked like snow. Leo walked on the boardwalk, amid snow flurries, looking for his son. The grey sunless beaches were empty. The hot-dog stands, shooting galleries, and bathhouses were shuttered up. The gunmetal ocean, moving like melted lead, looked freezing. There was a wind off the water and it worked its way into his clothes so that he shivered as he walked. The wind white-capped the leaden waves and the slow surf broke on the deserted beaches with a quiet roar.

He walked in the blow almost to Sea Gate, searching for his son, and then walked back. On his way toward Brighton he saw a man on the beach standing in the foaming surf. Leo went down the boardwalk stairs and onto the ribbed-sand beach. The man on the shore was Harry standing in water up to his ankles.

Leo ran to his son. Harry, it was my mistake, excuse me. I'm sorry I opened your letter.

Harry did not turn. He stayed in the water, his eyes on the leaden waves.

Harry, I'm frightened. Tell me what's the matter. My son, have mercy on me.

It's not my kind of world, Harry thought. It fills me with terror.

He said nothing.

A blast of wind lifted his father's hat off his head and carried it away over the beach. It looked as if it were going to land in the surf but then the wind blew it toward the boardwalk, rolling like a wheel along the ground. Leo chased after his hat. He chased it one way, then another, then toward the water. The wind blew the hat against his legs and he caught it. He pulled the freezing hat down tight on his head until it bent his ears. By now he was crying. Breathless, he wiped his eyes with icy fingers and returned to his son at the edge of the water.

He is a lonely man. This is the type he is, Leo thought. He will always be lonely.

My son who became a lonely man.

Harry, what can I say to you? All I can say to you is who says life is easy? Since when? It wasn't for me and it isn't for you. It's life, what more can I say? But if a person don't want to live what can he do if he's dead? If he doesn't want to live maybe he deserves to die.

Come home, Harry, he said. It's cold here. You'll catch a cold with your feet in the water.

Harry stood motionless and after a while his father left. As he was leaving, the wind plucked his hat off his head and sent it rolling along the sand.

My father stands in the hallway. I catch him reading my letter. He follows me at a distance in the street. We meet at the edge of the water. He is running after his hat.

My son stands with his feet in the ocean.

Henry Roth
(b. 1906)

Brought to the United States as an infant, Henry Roth was raised in New York City, first on the Lower East Side and later in Harlem. His classic novel about an immigrant Jewish boy's childhood in the ghettos of Brooklyn and New York City, *Call It Sleep*, was published in 1934 when the author was only twenty-eight. Suffering a severe writer's block during the following decades, he worked at such jobs as a toolmaker and an attendant in a mental hospital. He raised ducks and geese in Maine during the 1950s and 60s, and slowly returned to his writing. *Call It Sleep* was rediscovered during the 1960s, receiving high critical acclaim. In 1987 he published *Shifting Landscape*, a collection of his shorter writings, including excepts from letters and interviews edited by Mario Materassi.

FINAL DWARF

". . . the final dwarf of you
That is woven and woven and
waiting to be worn . . ."
—Wallace Stevens

He was so pleased with the reading glasses he had ordered through the catalog and he was so ingenuous in his enthusiasm that the woman behind the counter, the Sears mail-order clerk, asked his permission to try them on.

She was middle aged too, or past middle age, like himself, and wore bifocals, as he did. He tendered them to her, and she put them on; but apparently they didn't procure the same results for her that they did for him. She looked down at the invoice in her hand with a rather bewildered expression and handed the glasses back.

"Not strong enough?" Kestrel asked sympathetically.

"I don't know what they are." She took refuge behind her own bifocals as if she had been disturbed by what she had seen. "But they're not for me, that's for sure."

"I was told by an optician some time ago that my eyes were still fairly young according to my age. So I got the weaker ones: forty to forty-five age group instead of my own, fifty-five to sixty."

She no longer seemed to be listening and had begun totting up the price of the glasses, the shipping charge, and the sales tax. "That's four twenty-one, please."

He smiled, placed a five-dollar bill on the counter, and while she made change, he slipped the glasses into their case and pocketed them. At least fifteen bucks to the good, he thought triumphantly: that's how much more the unholy alliance of opticians and the American Optical Society would have soaked him. True, the lenses weren't prescription lenses and did nothing to correct his astigmatism. But that was a minor matter compared with the boon the glasses would be when he hunted up a word in a dictionary or read a carpenter's scale. He received his change, thanked the clerk, and folding the invoice, walked briskly through the center aisle of the store toward the doorway. Sears retail store, compact with merchandise and glistening under its many fluorescents, was always an interesting place to Kestrel, especially the hardware department, with its array of highly polished tools. But he had no time to stop and browse today; his father was waiting for him in the car.

The street he came out on was Water Street, the former commercial center of town. For many years Water Street had tried to keep abreast of the times by fusing new chromium trim onto old brick facades. With the advent of the shopping plaza, the street seemed to have given up and become dormant, as if waiting for a rebirth.

His car was on Haymarket Street, the next street west. He crossed with the WALK of the traffic light and made his way up the inclined sidewalk that led sharply around the corner. Haymarket Street served as a kind of ancillary to Water Street. It provided extra room for parking meters, ventilating ducts, and traffic circulation.

"Where to, Pop?" He opened the car door and slipped in behind the wheel. "My errand's all done. What are yours?" It was always necessary to shield Pop from the idea that the trip to town was being made on his behalf. Otherwise he would balk at going and then sulk.

His father continued to bow over his homemade cane. "I would like to go to the First National. First to the First National in the plaza. I need a little meat, a can tuna, a couple oranges. Then I want to go to the A & P and buy coffee." Pop always adopted a whimsical, placating drawl when he wanted a favor.

"Why the A & P?" Kestrel sensed an old ruse. "Why not the First National coffee?"

"I like A & P coffee better. I like better Eight O'Clock coffee. It ain't so strong."

"Oh, yes." Eight O'Clock coffee was a cent cheaper than any other brand in town. The usual guile was at work. "I think you'd better shop in one place, Pop. No sense running to two places just to buy a pound of coffee." Kestrel hoped that the gravel that had entered his voice was lost in the starting of the motor. "You get better trades at the A & P anyway."

"OK. You want A & P? So A & P."

Kestrel fastened his seat belt. The old boy would have him run all over town for a couple of cents. To save *him* a couple of cents, blind to the expense of running the car. As Norma said, Pop certainly had a knack of bringing out the worst in people. Kestrel smirked and steered right to cross the railroad tracks. Just a few days ago, before Pop arrived for the summer, she had proposed a scheme of levying a fifty-cent toll on everyone who accompanied them to town and then suspending the rule for everyone except Pop. And this coming from Norma, the most generous of women . . .

Behind them the bank and the abandoned theater, behind them the bowling alley and the car wash, they climbed Winslow Hill to the traffic light on the terrace and then drove on past the porticos and the fanlights, the prim round windows of the fine homes of another age, to the rear entrance of the A & P parking lot.

"OK, Pop?" Kestrel undid his seat belt and got out of the car on one side as his father got out, more slowly, on the other. "Norma didn't want anything special. Cigarettes. But I've got plenty of time. So shop for everything you need." He preceded the old man to the glass door and held it open. Pop hobbled in on arthritic legs. "You know where the car is. I'll be around somewhere."

"Yeh. Yeh." The old man dismissed him with a curt wave of the hand. "I'll find you." He hobbled over to the telescoped shopping carts in front of the brightly arranged aisles, separated one, and trundled it inside.

Kestrel debated with himself for a moment. It was just barely possible that Grant's in the shopping plaza across the avenue had the kind of lock he was looking for, a freezer lock. He hadn't thought of it while he was in Sears. On the impulse, he hurried to the edge of the A&P blacktop and crossed the highway to the immensity of the plaza parking area opposite. The First National where Pop had wanted to shop lay directly ahead, to the left of Grant's, and Kestrel realized he could as easily have stopped there as not. But it was the principle of the thing, he argued with himself. He resented being gulled, being cajoled into doing his father a service for the wrong reason, for spurious reasons. It came back to what Norma said: Pop brought out the worst in people.

Grant's had no freezer locks. They had bicycle locks with inordinately long hasps, but no freezer locks. Leaving the emporium, he hurried back toward the avenue, meanwhile trying to descry the car from a distance. Was his father already in it and observing his son's breach of faith? No, he had beaten the old boy to it. He waited impatiently at the curb for an opening in the flux of traffic, crossed in haste, and panting slightly with exertion, leaned against his car. "Oh, the cigarettes!" He started toward the A & P and reached the door just as his father emerged with a bag of groceries on his arm.

Kestrel hesitated. "Want a hand, Pop?"

"I don't need it." The old man elbowed the extended hand to one side. "Here." He pressed a batch of trading stamps into the empty palm.

"Why do you give me these?"

"I don't want them. You save them."

"I don't save them."

"Your wife saves them."

"OK." Kestrel followed his father to the car. "Now where?" They both got in.

"Maybe I could get a few day-old cookies down at Arlene's. I like a few cookies in the house."

"I suppose so." They had been on Water Street once, Kestrel was about to remind his father, but checked the impulse under a fleeting yet complex illumination of how the old man continually led away from any objection. Who could object to a few cookies in the house? "OK. Arlene's."

"We don't have to go if you ain't got time. If you're in a hurry to get home—"

"Oh, I'm in no hurry," Kestrel said resolutely. "No hurry at all. What else?"

"Onion sets." Pop took out his shopping list. "Onion sets at Russel's Hardware Store. One pound." He read the words as if the list shielded him from responsibility. "And that's all."

"Onion sets at Russel's." Kestrel started the motor.

"They had hamburg." The sign in the A & P window caught Pop's eye. "I didn't see that."

"That's the come-on for today. Do you want any?"

"That ain't bad. Forty-nine cents a pound. I could have used a little hamburg."

"I can still stop." Kestrel made a token thrust at the brake pedal.

"No. Too late. If I had more time to look around—" Pop sat back in regret.

"Who said you didn't have time?"

"You don't have to say. I can tell."

Kestrel took a firmer grip on the steering wheel.

"Instead I paid thirty-three cents a pound for chicken wings. Thirty-three cents," the old man intoned. "Nineteen cents a pound, twenty-one cents a pound, most twenty-five cents a pound they charge in New York. Here in your state where they raise chickens, thirty-three cents a pound!"

"Pop," Kestrel grated. "Your seat belt."

The old man felt behind him for the buckle and pushed it out of the way.

They drove back to the center of town. Arlene's was at the south end of Water Street. Kestrel spied an empty parking place, but it seemed too tight. He chose to drive on. "Best I can do, Pop," he said apologetically, and parked the car beside a twelve-minute meter in front of the post office.

"I saw back there a nice place near Arlene's."

"Too many cars behind me. I didn't want to hold up traffic."

"For them you got consideration," Pop muttered. "But for me—" He got out of the car and hobbled in the direction of Arlene's. There seemed to be a special emphasis about the way he hobbled, as though he were trying to impress the pain he felt on his son.

Oh, hell, Kestrel thought as he waited. He never could do anything to please his father. Ever since childhood it had been that way. Still, he had to get over it. It was ridiculous to bear a grudge against the old guy. There was nothing left of him. A little old dwarf in a baggy pair of pants. *The final dwarf.* Kestrel smiled.

The car door opened.

"That was snappy, Pop!" said Kestrel.

His father slid into the seat with a self-satisfied look, shut the door, and picked up his cane.

"What about the cookies?" Kestrel asked. His father seemed to be flaunting the fact that he had made no purchase.

"Another time," said Pop airily.

"Why? Didn't they have day-old cookies?"

"They had. They had."

"Were they too high?"

"No, they was the regular half price."

"Then for Pete's sake why didn't you get some?"

"There was only one girl behind the counter and maybe ten customers."

"Oh, please! I come down here for you to buy cookies, and now you come back empty handed." Kestrel was sure the old man was retaliating for the way his son had parked the car.

"*Noo, nischt gefehrlich.* I got yet a few cookies in the house."

"Wait a minute." Kestrel was loath to start the engine. "That isn't the point. You wanted to come down here to buy cookies. I brought you down. Now you tell me you've got a few in the house. Why don't you buy some while you have a chance? You're down here."

"I don't need them. You would have to wait a for-sure fifteen minutes."

"I don't care. I waited this long."

"I don't need them!" his father snapped. "Meantime the money is by me, no?"

"Well, for Christ sake!" Kestrel started the motor. "That's a fine trick. The whole trip down here is for nothing!"

"So you'll be home a few minutes later to your wife. She won't miss you." His voice reeked with contempt.

You son of a bitch! thought Kestrel. There it was again, the same mockery that had rankled so in childhood, in boyhood, in youth, disabling mockery against which there was no remedy and no redress. Furiously Kestrel steered into the near lane of traffic. Penney's clothing store passed on one side like a standard of his wrath and Woolworth's across the street like another. And so did McClellan's and Sears and the pawnshop. He made a right turn at the traffic light, crossed the low bridge over the river, and climbed the opposite hill. He had almost reached their destination before he could force himself to say, "Now you want onion sets."

"Yeh, if he's got," said his father.

Kestrel stopped the car. The hardware store was across the street. He shut off the ignition and waited. His father made no move to go. "Well?" Kestrel asked.

"There's so much traffic," said his father.

"Do you want me to go?" Compassion now made headway against his anger. "I suppose I can get across the street faster than you can."

"Go if you want to go. I'll pay you later."

Kestrel got out of the car. "Onion sets, right?"

"One pound, not more. You hear?"

Kestrel's lip curled. With his back turned to his father, he could safely sneer. As if he would deliberately buy more than a pound.

They were on their way home now. Kestrel had bought the onion sets—and the freezer lock too, even though he had taken a longer time to shop than his father had anticipated. When he came out of the store, Pop was sitting half turned around in his seat with a frown on his face, gazing fixedly in his direction. Fine, Kestrel had thought with a certain nervous malice as he quickened his step toward the car, it's your turn now. And he had made some remark about how few clerks there were in all the stores on a Tuesday.

"Oh, sure," was his father's neutral reply.

Town slipped past at a leisurely twenty-five miles an hour: shade tree and utility pole, service station and abandoned cemetery.

"This time I got my supply of matzos for the summer. I brought five pounds from New York."

"Five pounds! All that way on a bus?" Kestrel felt a little indulgent after his own retaliation. "You must really like them."

"Oh, for a matzo I'm crazy," said his father. "I eat matzos not only on Passover."

"That's evident."

"With a matzo you got a bite or you got a meal," Pop continued sententiously. "It's crisp, good, or you can dunk it in coffee. There's matzo-brei, matzo kugel, matzo pancakes. You can crumble it. Dip in it. It's better than cracker meal. A lot cheaper too, believe me, especially if you go down to the East Side to get the broken ones."

"Marvelous. Can you wipe up gravy with a matzo?"

"Of course you can wipe up gravy. You forgot already. You wet the matzo before you sit down to eat, and it becomes soft like bread."

"The stuff's universal," Kestrel twitted. "Khrushchev should have known better than to ban them."

"Oh, that dog!" said Pop.

The Gulf station was passing, with its used-car lot in front and its desolate auto graveyard in the rear. "You know, Pop—" Kestrel began, and then stopped. He had been on the point of remarking that matzos could be bought in the chain stores in town, but they would be more expensive. "Oh, well—"

"What?" his father asked.

"Nothing."

They drove on in silence. Some of the newly constructed houses slipped by, the cute little boxes, as Norma called them, gray and brown and red, that had begun to line the highway.

Pop fingered the onion sets in the bag, picked out a withered one, and let it fall back significantly. He still hadn't paid for them. "Noo, there was a big fuss here over this Kennedy?" He put the bag to one side.

"This Kennedy?" Kestrel was startled. "Which Kennedy?"

"Bobby Kennedy. About John Kennedy I'm not talking."

"Of course. Everyone was shocked, just as with John Kennedy. Why?"

His father leaned on his cane and smiled. "I'm only sorry the other one wasn't shot too before he became president."

Kestrel's face furrowed as he glanced into the rearview mirror. For a moment it seemed to him that the old man's tone of voice was almost solicitous, as though he wished John Kennedy had been spared the trials of the presidency. He turned to look at his father, still smiling ambiguously. "What do you mean, Pop?"

"I mean both of them should have been shot before they became president. We would all be better off."

"Why? I don't get you. I was no admirer of the Kennedys but— "

"Why?" The new sign advertising the Grand View Motel 6 Mi. vanished on the right among second-growth trees. "The Niggehs!" Pop said vehemently. Where the sheep had once ranged, the juniper-studded field on the left reeled about the corrugated-ironsheep cote in the distance. "The Niggehs, that's why."

"The Niggers?" Kestrel repeated stunned.

"Yeh, the Niggehs! What they made such a good friend from the Niggehs! You're such a good friend from the Niggehs? There!"

"What's that got to do with it?"

"Good for them!"

"But that's got nothing to do with it!" Kestrel's voice sharpened. "That wasn't why they were shot."

"No. But that's why I'm glad they was shot."

Whew, Kestrel whistled silently to himself; you goddamned venomous little worm!

"You know, you can't talk to a Niggeh no more since the Kennedys?" his father demanded. "Not to a man, not to a woman, not to a child. Even a child'll tell you: go to hell, you old white fool."

"I see. I wish you'd put your seat belt on, Pop." Kestrel tapped the buckle of his own.

"I don't like it."

"You'd like going through the windshield less."

"I don't wear that kind. I told you. When you get them so they go around the shoulder, then I'll wear them. They press me here." He rubbed his abdomen.

You damned idiot; Kestrel stared straight ahead.

"The Kennedys," said his father. "There's where the mugging and the robbing started. Only Kennedys. *Noo*, sure, they know a president is their friend. So whatever they do, he'll say: Nebich! It's a pity! So they rape," he slapped his hands together, "so they rob, so they mug, so they loot. That poor Jewish man what they hit him in the face with a bottle last week in the subway—a plain Jewish working man—the Kennedys is the cause of all that!"

The side road where they lived was only a short distance away, and peering deeply into the rearview mirror, Kestrel saw himself forbidding and ominous against the empty highway. Was the old man baiting him this last time in retaliation for having been made to wait, or were his own thoughts about his father of such force that they communicated? He could almost believe it. "Nobody is the cause," said Kestrel. "Nobody in particular. All of us."

"All of us? Go! You and the other *philosophes.* I had something to do with that Niggeh what he mugged me in the elevator and took away my watch and two hundred and eight dollars? And put me in the hospital? And who knows, gave me this arthritis? You should have seen that detective how he beat his fist on the wall when he seen my face. And the others what they get mugged and beat up—and raped. *They* the cause of it? With you *philosophes* you can't talk."

"OK."

"Come live in New York a few months, you'll see. Let's see how you'll be a *philosophe.*"

"OK." Kestrel braked the car gently, made his left turn into the side road with a minimum of swerve.

Pop glanced at the crowds of white cockerels behind the screen in the big doorways of the three-story broiler plant on the corner. "You should see them in the waiters' union, how they push us away when there's a good job—in the Waldorf or where. The best is for them. Old waiters like me, white waiters—throw them out and make jobs for *them*. They come first!"

Oh, shit. Kestrel pressed his foot down on the accelerator.

"Everything all at once," Pop continued. "More, more! Colleges and schools and beaches and motels. Regular princes make from them. And yesterday they was eating each other."

The stretch of road they were approaching had been cut through ledge—straightened out—leaving a few run-down buildings stranded in the bend on the left. On the right was the ledge. On top of it, in the gloom of over-hanging trees, he had once seen two pretty deer, a buck and a doe, poised for flight, and the memory of the sight always drew his gaze to the spot thereafter. Two inches to the right, he thought, two inches that way with the steering wheel, and it would all be over with the old fool. Just two inches *now;* he'd go through the windshield like a maul, he'd slam that rusty granite. And who would know? Instinctively Kestrel shied away from the rough shoulder of the road. "Don't you think that's enough of politics, Pop?"

"Sure. On another's behind it's good to smack, like they say. Here in the country you don't see a *schwartzer* face for I don't know. A mile. How will it be if they moved next door?"

"Oh, please!"

"Yeh," his father nodded. "You'll be just like me in a few years. Just wait. All I'm saying you'll say."

A truck came over the brow of the hill. Topheavy and loaded with logs, it picked up momentum as it rolled downhill toward them, lurched at the road's shoulder. And once again Kestrel heard himself urge: two inches on this wheel, a glancing blow, and the brakes. He skirted the other vehicle, glimpsed its driver, Reynolds, owner of a nearby lumber mill. "That was Reynolds," he said to Pop.

Pop rejected the overture with a slighting gesture. "You'll be just like me. Wait. I seen already *philosophes* like you. Your cousin Louis Cantor when he lived was a *philosophe*, a socialist. Every time he came to the house he brought the socialist *Call.* So what happened in the end? He laughed from it. 'What a fool I was,' he used to say."

The top of Turner's Hill was open on the left, open and sloping downward over sunlit boulders toward the woodland and the river valley. Almost inviting it seemed, inviting for a hideous spin and a rending of metal. Who would survive? Kestrel held the car grimly to the center of the road.

"And that's what you'll say," said Pop.

"You think so?"

"I know it."

"All right. Then let's drop it. I'm driving a car."

"Ah, if there only was a Verwoerd here like in South Africa," Pop lamented. "A Verwoerd. He should be like a bulldozer for those brutes. Even a Wallace. A Wallace I would vote for."

Kestrel could feel his jaw tremble. Christ, if the old fool didn't stop— They still had two miles to go. "That's enough!"

Pop hitched a scornful shoulder, crossed his legs over his cane. "So what did you get at Sears?"

"At Sears? Oh. Reading glasses."

"Reading glasses? At Sears?"

"Yes, they have them. I've been getting my bifocals chipped working around the place."

"How much did they cost?"

Brusquely Kestrel pulled the case out of his pocket, handed it to his father. "Here. You tell me."

The old man took the spectacles out of their sheath, appraised them, and adjusted them on his nose. "Oy!" He recoiled.

"What's the matter?"

"You're going right into the stone wall." Pop pulled the glasses off.

"I am?"

"Into a stone wall. I mean they look like it. Pheh! Only from Sears you can buy glasses like this." He slipped them into the case, handed the case to his son.

Kestrel sighed. He felt shriveled. He removed a hand from the wheel, replaced the glasses in his pocket.

"Boy, you gave me some scare!" The old man groped beside him for the seat-belt buckles.

Joanne Greenberg

(b. 1932)

A resident of Colorado, where she is a member of a paramedic emergency team, Joanne Greenberg published an early novel *I Never Promised You a Rose Garden* (1964) under the pseudonym "Hannah Green." The novel, which dramatizes the return to sanity of a sixteen-year-old girl who had created her own mad world to escape the painful real one, was made into a film in 1977. A graduate of American University in Washington, D.C., and the University of London, Greenberg is a registered interpreter of the deaf and has taught sign language. Among her works are three collections of short stories, *Summering* (1966), *Rites of Passage* (1972), and *High Crimes and Misdemeanors* (1980) as well as the novels *The King's Persons* (1963), *The Monday Voices* (1965), *In This Sign* (1970), which was adapted for a TV film, *Founder's Praise* (1976), *A Season of Delight* (1981), *The Far Side of Victory* (1983), *Simple Gifts* (1986), *Age of Consent* (1987), and *Of Such Small Differences* (1988).

AND SARAH LAUGHED

She went to the window every fifteen minutes to see if they were coming. They would be taking the new highway cutoff; it would bring them past the south side of the farm; past the unused, dilapidated outbuildings instead of the orchards and fields that were now full and green. It would look like a poor place to the new bride. Her first impression of their farm would be of age and bleached-out, dried-out buildings on which the doors hung open like a row of gaping mouths that said nothing.

All day, Sarah had gone about her work clumsy with eagerness and hesitant with dread, picking up utensils to forget them in holding, finding them two minutes later a surprise in her hand. She had been planning and working ever since Abel wrote to them from Chicago that he was coming home with a wife. Everything should have been clean and orderly. She wanted the bride to know as soon as she walked inside what kind of woman Abel's mother was—to feel, without a word having to be said, the house's dignity, honesty, simplicity, and love. But the spring cleaning had been late, and Alma Yoder had gotten sick—Sarah had had to go over to the Yoders and help out.

Now she looked around and saw that it was no use trying to have everything ready in time. Abel and his bride would be coming any minute. If she didn't want to get caught shedding tears of frustration, she'd better get herself under control. She stepped over the pile of clothes still unsorted for the laundry and went out on the back porch.

The sky was blue and silent, but as she watched, a bird passed over the fields crying. The garden spread out before her, displaying its varying greens. Beyond it, along the creek, there was a row of poplars. It always calmed her to look at them. She looked today. She and Matthew had planted those trees. They stood thirty feet high now, stately as figures in a procession. Once—only once and many years ago—she had tried to describe in words the sounds that the wind made as it combed those trees on its way west. The little boy to whom she had spoken was a grown man now, and he was bringing home a wife. *Married. . . .*

Ever since he had written to tell them he was coming with his bride, Sarah had been going back in her mind to the days when she and Matthew were bride and groom and then mother and father. Until now, it hadn't seemed so long ago. Her life had flowed on past her, blurring the early days with Matthew when this farm was strange and new to her and when the silence of it was sharp and bitter like pain, not dulled and familiar like an echo of old age.

Matthew hadn't changed much. He was a tall, lean man, but he had had a boy's spareness then. She remembered how his smile came, wavered and went uncertainly, but how his eyes had never left her. He followed everything with his eyes. Matthew had always been a silent man; his face was expressionless and his body stiff with reticence, but his eyes had sought her out eagerly and held her and she had been warm in his look.

Sarah and Matthew had always known each other—their families had been neighbors. Sarah was a plain girl, a serious "decent" girl. Not many of the young men asked her out, and when Matthew did and did again, her parents had been pleased. Her father told her that Matthew was a good man, as steady as any woman could want. He came from honest, hardworking people and he would prosper any farm he had. Her mother spoke shyly of how his eyes woke when Sarah came into the room, and how they followed her. If she married him, her life would be full of the things she knew and loved, an easy, familiar world with her parents' farm not two miles down the road. But no one wanted to mention the one thing that worried Sarah: the fact that Matthew was deaf. It was what stopped her from saying yes right away; she loved him, but she was worried about his deafness. The things she feared about it were the practical things: a fall or a fire when he wouldn't hear her cry for help. Only long after she had put those fears aside and moved the scant two miles into his different world, did she realize that the things she had feared were the wrong things.

Now they had been married for twenty-five years. It was a good marriage—good enough. Matthew was generous, strong, and loving. The farm prospered. His silence made him seem more patient, and because she became more silent also, their neighbors saw in them the dignity and strength of two people who do not rail against misfortune, who were beyond trivial talk and gossip; whose lives needed no words. Over the years of help given and meetings attended, people noticed how little they needed to say. Only Sarah's friend Luita knew that in the beginning, when they were first married, they had written yearning notes to each other. But Luita didn't know that the notes also were mute. Sarah had never shown them to anyone, although she kept them all, and sometimes she would go up and get the box out of her closet and read them over. She had saved every scrap, from questions about the eggs to the tattered note he had left beside his plate on their first anniversary. He had written it when she was busy at the stove and then he'd gone out and she hadn't seen it until she cleared the table.

The note said: "I love you derest wife Sarah. I pray you have happy day all day your life."

When she wanted to tell him something, she spoke to him slowly, facing him, and he took the words as they formed on her lips. His speaking voice was thick and hard to understand and he perceived that it was unpleasant. He didn't like to use it. When he had to say something, he used his odd, grunting tone, and she came to understand what he said. If she ever hungered for laughter from him or the little meaningless talk that confirms existence and affection, she told herself angrily that Matthew talked through his work. Words die in the air; they can be turned one way or another, but Matthew's work prayed and laughed for him. He took good care of her and the boys, and they idolized him. Surely that counted more than all the words—words that meant and didn't mean—behind which people could hide.

Over the years she seldom noticed her own increasing silence, and there were times when his tenderness, which was always given without words, seemed to her to make his silence beautiful.

She thought of the morning she had come downstairs feeling heavy and off balance with her first pregnancy—with Abel. She had gone to the kitchen to begin the day, taking the coffeepot down and beginning to fill it when her eye caught something on the kitchen table. For a minute she looked around in confusion. They had already laid away what the baby would need: diapers, little shirts and bedding, all folded away in the drawer upstairs, but here on the table was a bounty of cloth, all planned and scrimped for and bought from careful, careful study of the catalogue—yards of patterned flannel and plissé, coat wool and bright red corduroy. Sixteen yards of yellow ribbon for bindings. Under the coat wool was cloth Matthew had chosen for her; blue with a little gray figure. It was silk, and there was a card on which was rolled precisely enough lace edging for her collar and sleeves. All the long studying and careful planning, all in silence.

She had run upstairs and thanked him and hugged him, but it was no use showing delight with words, making plans, matching cloth and figuring which pieces would be for the jacket and which for sleepers. Most wives used such fussing to tell their husbands how much they thought of their gifts. But Matthew's silence was her silence too.

When he had left to go to the orchard after breakfast that morning, she had gone to their room and stuffed her ears with cotton, trying to understand the world as it must be to him, with no sound. The cotton dulled the outside noises a little, but it only magnified all the noises in her head. Scratching her cheek caused a roar like a downpour of rain; her own voice was like thunder. She knew Matthew could not hear his own voice in his head. She could not be deaf as he was deaf. She could not know such silence ever.

So she found herself talking to the baby inside her, telling it the things she would have told Matthew, the idle daily things: Didn't Margaret Amson look peaked in town? Wasn't it a shame the drugstore had stopped stocking lump alum—her pickles wouldn't be the same.

Abel was a good baby. He had Matthew's great eyes and gentle ways. She chattered to him all day, looking forward to his growing up, when there would be confidences between them. She looked to the time when he would have his own picture of the world, and with that keen hunger and hope she had a kind of late blooming into a beauty that made people in town turn to look at her when she passed in the street holding the baby in the fine clothes she had made for him. She took Abel everywhere, and came to know a pride that was very new to her, a plain girl from a modest family who had married a neighbor boy. When they went to town, they always stopped over to see Matthew's parents and her mother.

Mama had moved to town after Pa died. Of course they had offered to have Mama come and live with them, but Sarah was glad she had gone to a little place in town, living where there were people she knew and things happening right outside her door. Sarah remembered them visiting on a certain spring day, all sitting in Mama's new front room. They sat uncomfortably in the genteel chairs, and Abel crawled around on the floor as the women talked, looking up every now and then for his father's nod of approval. After a while he went to catch the sunlight that was glancing off a crystal nut dish and scattering rainbow bands on the floor. Sarah smiled down at him. She too had a radiance, and, for the first time in her life, she knew it. She was wearing the dress she had made from Matthew's cloth—it became her and she knew that too, so she gave her joy freely as she traded news with Mama.

Suddenly they heard the fire bell ringing up on the hill. She caught Matthew's eye and mouthed, "Fire engines," pointing uphill to the firehouse. He nodded.

In the next minutes there was the strident, off-key blare as every single one of Arcadia's volunteer firemen—his car horn plugged with a matchstick and his duty before him—drove hellbent for the firehouse in an ecstasy of bell and siren. In a minute the ding-ding-ding-ding careened in deafening, happy privilege through every red light in town.

"Big bunch of boys!" Mama laughed. "You can count two Saturdays in good weather when they don't have a fire, and that's during the hunting season!"

They laughed. Then Sarah looked down at Abel, who was still trying to catch the wonderful colors. A madhouse of bells, horns, screaming sirens had gone right past them and he hadn't cried, he hadn't looked, he hadn't turned. Sarah twisted her head sharply away and screamed to the china cats on the whatnot shelf as loud as she could, but Abel's eyes only flickered to the movement and then went back to the sun and its colors.

Mama whispered, "Oh, my dear God!"

Sarah began to cry bitterly, uncontrollably, while her husband and son looked on, confused, embarrassed, unknowing.

The silence drew itself over the season and the seasons layered into years. Abel was a good boy; Matthew was a good man.

Later, Rutherford, Lindsay, and Franklin Delano came. They too were silent. Hereditary nerve deafness was rare, the doctors all said. The boys might marry and produce deaf children, but it was not likely. When they started to school, the administrators and teachers told her that the boys would be taught specially to read lips and to speak. They would not be "abnormal," she was told. Nothing would show their handicap, and with training no one need know that they were deaf. But the boys seldom used their lifeless voices to call to their friends; they seldom joined games unless they were forced to join. No one but their mother understood their speech. No teacher could stop all the jumping, turning, gum-chewing schoolboys, or remember herself to face front from the blackboard to the sound-closed boys. The lip-reading exercises never seemed to make plain differences—"man," "pan," "began."

But the boys had work and pride in the farm. The seasons varied their silence with colors—crows flocked in the snowy fields in winter, and tones of golden wheat darkened across acres of summer wind. If the boys couldn't hear the bedsheets flapping on the washline, they could see and feel the autumn day. There were chores and holidays and the wheel of birth and planting, hunting, fishing, and harvest. The boys were familiar in town; nobody ever laughed at them, and when Sarah met neighbors at the store, they praised her sons with exaggerated praise, well meant, saying that no one could tell, no one could really tell unless they knew, about the boys not hearing.

Sarah wanted to cry to these kindly women that the simple orders the boys obeyed by reading her lips were not a miracle. If she could ever hear in their long-practiced robot voices a question that had to do with feelings and not facts, and answer it in words that rose beyond the daily, tangible things done or not done, *that* would be a miracle.

Her neighbors didn't know that they themselves confided to one another from a universe of hopes, a world they wanted half lost in the world that was; how often they spoke pitting inflection against meaning to soften it, harden it, make a joke of it, curse by it, bless by it. They didn't realize how they wrapped the bare words of love in gentle humor or wild insults that the loved ones knew were ways of keeping the secret of love between the speaker and the hearer. Mothers lovingly called their children crow-bait, mouse-meat, devils. They predicted dark ends for them, and the children heard the secrets beneath the words, heard them and smiled and knew, and let the love said-unsaid caress their souls. With her own bitter knowledge Sarah could only thank them for well-meaning and return to silence.

Standing on the back porch now, Sarah heard the wind in the poplars and she sighed. It was getting on to noon. Warm air was beginning to ripple the fields. Matthew would be ready for lunch soon, but she wished she could stand out under the warm sky forever and listen to birds stitching sounds into the endless silence. She found herself thinking about Abel again, and the bride. She wondered what Janice would be like. Abel had gone all the way to Chicago to be trained in drafting. He had met her there, in the school. Sarah was afraid of a girl like that. They had been married quickly, without family or friends or toasts or gifts or questions. It hinted at some kind of secret shame. It frightened her. That kind of girl was independent and she might be scornful of a dowdy mother-in-law. And the house was still a mess.

From down the road, dust was rising. Matthew must have seen it too. He came over the rise and toward the house walking faster than usual. He'd want to slick his hair down and wash up to meet the stranger his son had become. She ran inside and bundled up the unsorted laundry, ran upstairs and pulled a comb through her hair, put on a crooked dab of lipstick, banged her shin, took off her apron and saw a spot on her dress, put the apron on again and shouted a curse to all the disorder she suddenly saw around her.

Now the car was crunching up the thin gravel of the driveway. She heard Matthew downstairs washing up, not realizing that the bride and groom were already at the house. Protect your own, she thought, and ran down to tell him. Together they went to the door and opened it, hoping that at least Abel's familiar face would comfort them.

They didn't recognize him at first, and he didn't see them. He and the tiny bride might have been alone in the world. He was walking around to open the door for her, helping her out, bringing her up the path to the house, and all the time their fingers and hands moved and spun meanings at which they smiled and laughed; they were talking somehow, painting thoughts in the air so fast with their fingers that Sarah couldn't see where one began and the other ended. She stared. The school people had always told her that such finger-talk set the deaf apart. It was abnormal; it made freaks of them. . . . How soon Abel had accepted someone else's strangeness and bad ways. She felt so dizzy she thought she was going to fall, and she was more bitterly jealous than she had ever been before.

The little bride stopped before them appealingly and in her dead, deaf-rote voice, said, "Ah-am pliizd to meet'ou." Sarah put out her hand dumbly and it was taken and the girl's eyes shone. Matthew smiled, and this time the girl spoke and waved her hands in time to her words, and then gave Matthew her hand. So Abel had told that girl about Matthew's deafness. It had never been a secret, but Sarah felt somehow betrayed.

They had lunch, saw the farm, the other boys came home from their summer school and met Janice. Sarah put out cake and tea and showed Abel and Janice up to the room she had made ready for them, and all the time the two of them went on with love-talk in their fingers; the jokes and secrets knitted silently between them, fears told and calmed, hopes spoken and echoed in the silence of a kitchen where twenty-five years of silence had imprisoned her. Always they would stop and pull themselves back to their good manners, speaking or writing polite questions and answers for the family; but in a moment or two, the talk would flag, the urgent hunger would overcome them and they would fight it, resolutely turning their eyes to Sarah's mouth. Then the signs would creep into their fingers, and the joy of talk into their faces, and they would fall before the conquering need of their communion.

Sarah's friend Luita came the next day, in the afternoon. They sat over tea with the kitchen window open for the cool breeze and Sarah was relieved and grateful to hold to a familiar thing now that her life had suddenly become so strange to her. Luita hadn't changed at all, thank God—not the hand that waved her tea cool or the high giggle that broke into generous laughter.

"She's darling!" Luita said after Janice had been introduced, and, thankfully, had left them. Sarah didn't want to talk about her, so she agreed without enthusiasm.

Luita only smiled back. "Sarah, you'll never pass for pleased with a face like that."

"It's just—just her ways," Sarah said. "She never even wrote to us before the wedding, and now she comes in and—and changes everything. I'll be honest, Luita, I didn't want Abel to marry someone who was deaf. What did we train him for, all those special classes? . . . *not* to marry another deaf person. And she hangs on him like a wood tick all day . . ." She didn't mention the signs. She couldn't.

Luita said, "It's just somebody new in the house, that's all. She's important to you, but a stranger. Addie Purkhard felt the same way and you know what a lovely girl Velma turned out to be. It just took time. . . . She's going to have a baby, did she tell you?"

"Baby? Who?" Sarah cried, feeling cold and terrified.

"Why, *Velma*. A baby due about a month after my Dolores'."

It had never occurred to Sarah that Janice and Abel could have a baby. She wanted to stop thinking about it and she looked back at Luita whose eyes were glowing with something joyful that had to be said. Luita hadn't been able to see beyond it to the anguish of her friend.

Luita said, "You know, Sarah, things haven't been so good between Sam and me. . . ." She cleared her throat. "You know how stubborn he is. The last few weeks, it's been like a whole new start for us. I came over to tell you about it because I'm so happy, and I had to share it with you."

She looked away shyly, and Sarah pulled herself together and leaned forward, putting her hand on her friend's arm. "I'm so happy for you. What happened?"

"It started about three weeks ago—a night that neither of us could get to sleep. We hadn't been arguing; there was just that awful coldness, as if we'd both been frozen stiff. One of us started talking—just lying there in the dark. I don't even know who started, but pretty soon we were telling each other the most secret things—things we never could have said in the light. He finally told me that Dolores having a baby makes him feel old and scared. He's afraid of it, Sarah, and I never knew it, and it explains why he hates to go over and see them, and why he argues with Ken all the time. Right there beside me he told me so many things I'd forgotten or misunderstood. In the dark it's like thinking out loud—like being alone and yet together at the same time. I love him so and I came so close to forgetting it. . . ."

Sarah lay in bed and thought about Luita and Sam sharing their secrets in the dark. Maybe even now they were talking in their flower-papered upstairs room, moving against the engulfing seas of silence as if in little boats, finding each other and touching and then looking out in awe at the vastness all around them where they might have rowed alone and mute forever. She wondered if Janice and Abel fingered those signs in the dark on each other's body. She began to cry. There was that freedom, at least; other wives had to strangle their weeping.

When she was cried out, she lay in bed and counted all the good things she had: children, possessions, acres of land, respect of neighbors, the years of certainty and success. Then she conjured the little bride, and saw her standing in front of Abel's old car as she had at first—with nothing; all her virtues still unproven, all her fears still forming, and her bed in another woman's house. Against the new gold ring on the bride's finger, Sarah threw all the substance of her years to weigh for her. The balance went with the bride. It wasn't fair! The balance went with the bride because she had put that communion in the scales as well, and all the thoughts that must have been given and taken between them. It outweighed Sarah's twenty-five years of muteness; outweighed the house and barn and well-tended land, and the sleeping family keeping their silent thoughts.

The days went by. Sarah tortured herself with elaborate courtesy to Janice and politeness to the accomplice son, but she couldn't guard her own envy from herself and she found fault wherever she looked. Now the silence of her house was throbbing with her anger. Every morning Janice would come and ask to help, but Sarah was too restless to teach her, so Janice would sit for a while waiting and then get up and go outside to look for Abel. Then Sarah would decide to make coleslaw and sit with the chopping bowl in her lap, smashing the chopper against the wood with a vindictive joy that she alone could hear the sounds she was making, that she alone knew how savage they were and how satisfying.

At church she would see the younger boys all clean and handsome, Matthew greeting friends, Janice demure and fragile, and Abel proud and loving, and she would feel a terrible guilt for her unreasonable anger; but back from town afterwards, and after Sunday dinner, she noticed as never before how disheveled the boys looked, how ugly their hollow voices sounded. Had Matthew always been so patient and unruffled? He was like one of his own stock, an animal, a dumb animal.

Janice kept asking to help and Sarah kept saying there wasn't time to teach her. She was amazed when Matthew, who was very fussy about his fruit, suggested to her that Janice might be able to take care of the grapes and, later, work in the orchard.

"I haven't time to teach her!"

"Ah owill teeech Ja-nuss," Abel said, and they left right after dinner in too much of a hurry.

Matthew stopped Sarah when she was clearing the table and asked why she didn't like Janice. Now it was Sarah's turn to be silent, and when Matthew insisted, Sarah finally turned on him. "You don't understand," she shouted. "You don't understand a thing!" And she saw on his face the same look of confusion she had seen that day in Mama's fussy front room when she had suddenly begun to cry and could not stop. She turned away with the plates, but suddenly his hand shot out and he struck them to the floor, and the voice he couldn't hear or control rose to an awful cry, "Ah ahm dehf! Ah ahm dehf!" Then he went out, slamming the door without the satisfaction of its sound.

If a leaf fell or a stalk sprouted in the grape arbor, Janice told it over like a set of prayers. One night at supper, Sarah saw the younger boys framing those dumb-signs of hers, and she took them outside and slapped their hands. "*We* don't do that!" she shouted at them, and to Janice later she said, "Those . . . signs you make—I know they must have taught you to do that, but out here . . . well, it isn't our way."

Janice looked back at her in a confusion for which there were no words.

It was no use raging at Janice. Before she had come there had never been anything for Sarah to be angry about. . . . What did they all expect of her? Wasn't it enough that she was left out of a world that heard and laughed without being humiliated by the love-madness they made with their hands? It was like watching them undressing.

The wind cannot be caught. Poplars may sift it, a rising bird can breast it, but it will pass by and no one can stop it. She saw the boys coming home at a dead run now, and they couldn't keep their hands from taking letters, words, and pictures from the fingers of the lovers. If they saw an eagle, caught a fish, or got scolded, they ran to their brother or his wife, and Sarah had to stand in the background and demand to be told.

One day Matthew came up to her and smiled and said, "Look." He put out his two index fingers and hooked the right down on the left, then the left down gently on the right. "Fwren," he said, "Ja-nuss say, fwren."

To Sarah there was something obscene about all those gestures, and she said, "I don't like people waving their hands around like monkeys in a zoo!" She said it very clearly so that he couldn't mistake it.

He shook his head violently and gestured as he spoke. "Mouth eat; mouth kiss, mouth tawk! Fin-ger wohk; fin-ger tawk. E-ah" (and he grabbed his ear, violently), "e-ah dehf. *Mihn,*" (and he rapped his head, violently, as if turning a terrible impatience against himself so as to spare her) "*mihn not* dehf!"

Later she went to the barn after something and she ran into Lindsay and Franklin Delano standing guilty, and when she caught them in her eye as she turned, she saw their hands framing signs. They didn't come into the house until it was nearly dark. Was their hunger for those signs so great that only darkness could bring them home? They weren't bad boys, the kind who would do a thing just because you told them not to. Did their days have a hunger too, or was it only the spell of the lovers, honey-honeying to shut out a world of moving mouths and silence?

At supper she looked around the table and was reassured. It could have been any farm family sitting there, respectable and quiet. A glance from the father was all that was needed to keep order or summon another helping. Their eyes were lowered, their faces composed. The hands were quiet. She smiled and went to the kitchen to fix the shortcake she had made as a surprise.

When she came back, they did not notice her immediately. They were all busy talking. Janice was telling them something and they all had their mouths ridiculously pursed with the word. Janice smiled in assent and each one showed her his sign and she smiled at each one and nodded, and the signers turned to one another in their joy, accepting and begging acceptance. Then they saw Sarah standing there; the hands came down, the faces faded.

She took the dinner plates away and brought in the dessert things, and when she went back to the kitchen for the cake, she began to cry. It was beyond envy now; it was too late for measuring or weighing. She had lost. In the country of the blind, Mama used to say, the one-eyed man is king. Having been a citizen of such a country, she knew better. In the country of the deaf, the hearing man is lonely. Into that country a girl had come who, with a wave of her hand, had given the deaf ears for one another, and had made Sarah the deaf one.

Sarah stood, staring at her cake and feeling for that moment the profundity of the silence which she had once tried to match by stuffing cotton in her ears. Everyone she loved was in the other room, talking, sharing, standing before the awful, impersonal heaven and the unhearing earth with pictures of his thoughts, and she was the deaf one now. It wasn't "any farm family," silent in its strength. It was a yearning family, silent in its hunger, and a demure little bride had shown them all how deep the hunger was. She had shown Sarah that her youth had been sold into silence. She was too old to change now.

An anger rose in her as she stared at the cake. Why should they be free to move and gesture and look different while she was kept in bondage to their silence? Then she remembered Matthew's mute notes, his pride in Abel's training, his face when he had cried, "I am deaf!" over and over. She had actually fought that terrible yearning, that hunger they all must have had for their own words. If they could all speak somehow, what would the boys tell her?

She knew what she wanted to tell them. That the wind sounds through the poplar trees, and people have a hard time speaking to one another even if they aren't deaf. Luita and Sam had to have a night to hide their faces while they spoke. It suddenly occurred to her that if Matthew made one of those signs with his hands and she could learn that sign, she could put her hands against his in the darkness, and read the meaning—that if she learned those signs she could hear him. . . .

She dried her eyes hurriedly and took in the cake. They saw her and the hands stopped, drooping lifelessly again; the faces waited mutely. Silence. It was a silence she could no longer bear. She looked from face to face.

What was behind those eyes she loved? Didn't everyone's world go deeper than chores and bread and sleep?

"I want to talk to you," she said. "I want to talk, to know what you think." She put her hands out before her, offering them.

Six pairs of eyes watched her.

Janice said, "Mo-ther."

Eyes snapped away to Janice; thumb was under lip: the Sign.

Sarah followed them. "Wife," she said, showing her ring.

"Wife," Janice echoed, thumb under lip to the clasp of hands.

Sarah said, "I love. . . ."

Janice showed her and she followed hesitantly and then turned to Matthew to give and to be received in that sign.

Roberta Silman
(b. 1934)

Born in Brooklyn, New York, Roberta Silman grew up on Long Island, attended Lawrence High School, and was graduated Phi Beta Kappa from Cornell University. Her first short story was published in *The New Yorker* in 1973 while she was a student working on an MFA at Sarah Lawrence College. She has been awarded a Guggenheim Fellowship, a fellowship from the National Endowment for the Arts, and her story "The Education of Esther Eileen" won the National Magazine Award for fiction in 1984. Some of her stories, published in magazines such as *The Atlantic*, *Redbook*, and *McCall's*, are collected in *Blood Relations* (1979). In 1976 she published *Somebody Else's Child*, which won the Child Study Association award for the best children's book of that year. She has published two novels, *Boundaries* (1979) and *The Dream Dredger* (1986). Currently she lives in Westchester County in New York, where she recently completed a new novel about the lives of the families at Los Alamos during World War II, *Beginning the World Again*.

WEDDING DAY

The spider drops, then climbs again, high into the corner, then drops once more. Fascinated, I stop polishing my nails to watch the intricate process of making a web. I begin to hum; I once read that spiders have ears in their legs and like music. On one of her trips through the breakfast room my mother looks at me oddly. I want to grab her elbow and point to the web, but she will feel obligated to brush the fragile wonder down. This is no day to admire a spider's handiwork. Everything must be clean, shining.

I go back to my nails. I'm like a slow-motion movie. My mother noticed it after breakfast and each time she passes she mentions the heat. It isn't the heat, although it's ninety-two degrees at one o'clock. It's me. I'm a little lonely and that makes me tired and I can't hide it from her.

"I wish you would go to the beauty parlor," she said. But I have always done my own hair; the shampoo hurts when they dig their fingers into your scalp; the dryer gives me a headache. She knows all this but she wants me to be fussed over.

Instead I sit here, in everyone's way.

I cap the polish, holding it gingerly as I walk through the kitchen. Jean, our cleaning lady, says, "I thought you were on the porch with a book." That's where I've been for the last fifteen years. "If you go there and rest I'll bring you some lunch," she bribes me.

"And after you eat I want you to take a nap," Jean says and puts down the tray. She's known me since I was six years old; she doesn't approve of the rings under my eyes—she thinks graduating from college is enough excitement for one month. If I were hers, she told my mother, I would rest for the summer and get married in the fall. My mother no longer listens to Jean, but she knows Jean is disappointed that we aren't having a big wedding. The eldest daughter. Jean can't understand it. Sometimes, neither can my mother, I realize, as I watch the deepening frown between her eyes.

Lunch is a cold meat loaf sandwich, milk, half a cantaloupe. I feel odd having Jean wait on me. She never has before. I smile at her, but she's embarrassed and leaves quickly.

I'm in exile, I think ridiculously as tears climb the ducts up to my eyes. I consider calling Phil, but we have spoken to each other three times already this morning. I put down the sandwich uneaten and try the cantaloupe. It doesn't taste right.

The car flies into the driveway. My younger sisters Barbara and Erica come in carrying cigarettes, cocktail napkins, club soda—the things my mother always forgets.

"Well, well, if it isn't the birthday girl." Barbara is amused to see such a formal lunch. "Jean's work," she says. Erica nods.

"Sit down, ladies." I gesture grandly with a sweep of the hand. They drop wearily into the overstuffed chairs. I hand them each half a sandwich, they share the milk.

"Why did you have to decide to get married on the hottest day of the year?" Erica says. I shrug. They laugh.

Suddenly there's a crash. We go through the kitchen where Jean stares at us as if we were spies and then into the living room. Mother is directing two men who have enormous wire frames in their arms. On these will go the flowers for the bridal canopy, the *chupa*. It's huge. Even bigger than Mother anticipated, I can see, for she is beginning to chew the inside of her lower lip.

"There, that's fine," she says triumphantly as they hang the frame above the mantel. I move closer. My hair is in a ponytail and I'm wearing shorts. One of the men says, "Watch out, girlie."

"That's the bride," my mother announces coldly.

"How about some lunch, Mom?" I want to do something for her. Way back in her hazel eyes I see she's lonely, too. Because we're having such a small wedding we decided to have it on a Thursday. Maybe it was a mistake. If we had gotten married on a Sunday my father would have been around all day.

"Okay." She's pleasing me. I've been hard to please these days, but there has been so much talk, so much arranging.

In the kitchen Jean is annoyed. Mother wouldn't eat for her. I take a tray to my mother and we watch the men place white camellias into the wire frames. It will be a very beautiful *chupa*. And the house looks lovely—just painted and with new lush green carpeting.

"Now, darling, what else must we do?" My mother smiles.

"Not a thing, Mom, you did it all for me." I kiss her lightly, thinking of all the times she got me ready to go to camp, to college, to Europe. How many nights did she stay up hemming and packing, pretending she couldn't sleep?

"Okay, then, you do me a favor." She is bargaining now. "Please go up and take a nap."

I stare at her. Will no one understand that I cannot lie alone today in the room that Barbara and I have shared for more than fifteen years?

"I'll go to the porch and read," I tell her. She nods, preoccupied again, for the caterer has just arrived. The wedding must be catered because my grandparents insist on kosher food and my mother has never kept a kosher home. So everything will be done according to the silly, thousands-of-years-old rules. We will even have ice cream made without milk, a miracle of the modern world, the caterer has assured us.

It wasn't fair to my parents to have a small wedding. I knew it when we talked about it last winter. It snowed that Sunday. When my father came home with the *Times* and the Bialystok rolls there was mist on his thick gray eyebrows and moustache; he hunched his shoulders and rubbed his hands, glad to be in the warm house. Phil came over for breakfast and he told them what we wanted.

There were no interruptions, which is a sign of trouble in our house, but I was too busy agreeing with Phil to notice. When he finished my mother asked if we wouldn't like to have a small chapel wedding and invite our friends. That appealed to me, but Phil shook his head firmly; the immediate family at home was all he wanted.

Naturally, he forgot about the *minyan*. So, in addition to our parents, grandparents and sisters we are expecting my Aunt Helen and Uncle Nat (my mother's oldest sister and her husband) and Ruth and Max, my parents' closest friends.

"I never realized there would be such a fuss," I say to Erica when she walks through the porch.

"A wedding's a wedding," she says .

I pick up *Life*. Elsa Maxwell had a party, Yale's graduation was spectacular, dolphins are more intelligent than we are, Nero wasn't such a bad guy. This is just my speed now. I remember how my eyes ached two weeks ago while taking comprehensives. *The Magic Mountain* is upstairs on my night table but I haven't opened it.

I'll go for a walk. I plow through the dining room. I have the sense to know I should tell my mother. If she misses me today she will worry, as if I were two years old with an itchy foot and apt to be snatched by a kidnapper.

"I'm going for a walk," I tell her.

Sweat buds on her upper lip. I guess I look a little disheveled to be wandering around outside, although I've taken walks looking much worse before. But today is different, and though she is much too kind to say so I understand. I don't look like a bride!

"Okay, Mom, I'll help Barbara." Barbara is upstairs with a portable phonograph. She is trying to find the band on a record of popular classics that plays "Here Comes the Bride." Erica is in the shower. It's four-thirty; the wedding is set for seven.

"Hi, kiddly," Barbara says. By now she is convinced, her eyes tell me, that none of it is real; we are having a "play," just as we used to when we were children.

"We should have gone to a justice of the peace," I say.

"Uh-uh." she wags a finger at me. "Not at all kosher. Not even Jewish, and you would have had to have all this anyway, to keep Grandpa happy."

Grandpa is my father's father. He is an Orthodox rabbi who no longer has a pulpit in Borough Park, who reads all day long and publishes an occasional article in the Orthodox rabbinical literature. He is learned. And stubborn. And shrewd. Years and years ago he discovered the stock market and made a lot of money—how, no one knows.

Lately he has been crochety and so has my grandmother, but they are eighty-one and age gives them privileges they don't deserve. Besides, my father is a devoted son and I am the eldest grandchild in America, so this time we are letting them have their way.

Mother steps lightly into the upstairs den. She looks at the three of us sitting there and finally she is content.

"Are you all packed?" she asks redundantly. She closed my suitcases this morning. I nod.

The phone rings. We hear Jean begin the usual "She's terribly busy . . ." but it is the rabbi who is to marry us (with Grandpa also officiating, of course). Mother goes to her room and picks up the phone. I follow her and sit on the love seat, now frayed along the arms. I pull a loose thread and think of all the hours I have sat here, straining my eyes as I read in fading daylight.

Suddenly Mother's face is distorted with pain.

"George Bernstein had a heart attack this afternoon and just died," she says softly as she puts the telephone down. George is an old friend; he knew my father when they were young refugees on the East Side learning English at night at P.S. 6. He was here last night to play chess with Dad; later we had coffee and cake with him. He kissed me and wished me well, and before he left he pressed an envelope, which I still have not opened, into my hand. He was a dear man.

"The rabbi's at his house. Sylvia's very upset and the boys are flying home. The rabbi wants to stay there until the last minute, so I must call him when we're ready." My mother sits there, stunned, and I wonder what her faith tells her now. She believes unequivocally in God, which is more than my father and sisters and I do. I start to say, "If there's a God, why . . ." but she turns to me, her face gray.

"Not today, darling, please, not today." Then she cries tearlessly. I bring her a damp washcloth which she puts across her forehead as she lies down on the bed. Barbara goes to pick my father up at the station. I sit with my mother until he arrives.

Some of my friends are getting engaged, two are married and shopping for furniture, one just had a baby. My parents' friends are making weddings, watching over the births of grandchildren, and dying. I remember an old record player in my other grandmother's house; it had an enormous handle, and if we were good we could crank it. Round and round we turned and the music happened on our ears. Who cranks that bigger handle, I wonder as I gather my things to go take a shower.

After the hot water I turn on the cold. It clears my head a little, and when I step out of the shower I feel better. Just as I pull on a robe my father comes in. Without knocking, of course—such formalities are unheard of in our house—but instead of becoming annoyed I kiss him on the nose. He wants to shave and Barbara is using their bathroom. Mother is downstairs arranging porch furniture. He takes out his new electric razor and begins the process I have watched so often in awe. I smile and wave to him, for he can't hear me. The old manual razor was so much more civilized, but he can't resist gadgets.

When I next see him he is in his underwear, polishing his shoes in the hall near the linen closet. He always waits until the last minute to polish his shoes. The bald spot on top of his head glistens. He seems determined to treat this afternoon like any other.

"So?" he says tentatively.

"So?" I reply.

"So." Mother rescues us as she comes up the stairs, looking harried again. "Helen and Nat and Grandma and Grandpa are here."

Too early. Now Grandma will have time to go poking into the kitchen. My father finishes his shoes and almost runs into their room to get dressed.

Still avoiding my room, I go into my parents' bedroom and talk to my mother while she dresses. From the window I see Phil arrive with his parents. His intelligent face is sunburned and he is very handsome and I'm going to marry him in about an hour, but I have not the slightest idea what he is thinking. The eeriness of it sends a sudden tightness to my throat, and I stay at the window so Mom can't see. A little later Phil's sister Gail arrives with her husband. She is expecting her first child in a few days; her feet are so swollen she is wearing loafers cut open at the heel. We are cruel to make her come out, even for a wedding—especially for a wedding.

I zip my mother into a navy blue dress which is simple and not at all new and watch her put on a little powder and lipstick. She has forgotten George for the moment,

and her eyes glow with excitement for the first time all day. I kiss her quickly before she goes downstairs.

Finally I go to my room. In a corner my wedding dress stands propped by mounds of tissue paper; it is a delicate, headless, armless bride. The thermometer outside the window registers ninety-six. Once, when I was about seven, it read nine below zero. That was an important day!

So is this. Yet all I feel is out of sorts. If we can just get through this evening, by tomorrow we'll be settled in our apartment on the lake where we will spend the summer. Phil's smile in the photograph on my desk cheers me up. When Mother and Barbara come in I can see from their faces that I'm beginning to look like a bride.

"How's everything?" I ask.

"Fine," Barbara says, slightly surprised, which means that my grandparents are behaving. Just as I get into my dress we hear a scuffling. Here they are with Dad, who looks helpless. Before I have time to put on my shoes I am told to sit down, and my grandparents take out a white handkerchief knotted at the four corners. Then they walk around me murmuring a Hebrew prayer.

"It's supposed to be a purification rite," my father whispers. "The handkerchief represents the earth." But the explanation does not satisfy. I feel like witches' brew.

Then Grandpa disappears with Dad, but Grandma lingers to rub the stuff of my dress between her roughened fingers. She is shrunken now, but still pretty.

"Here, Ma." My mother hands her the veil and she places it on me and the photographer who appears from nowhere snaps a picture. Grandma sighs with pleasure. I wink at Mom, yet I'm a little hurt by my grandfather's cursory treatment of me. He is strange, but I like him.

Barbara senses how I feel.

"Grandpa had to make sure Phil signs the *ketubah,*" she says. Of course, the marriage contract, written in Hebrew. "Phil says it might be a conscription into the Israeli army for all he knows." We laugh, the photographer clicks away. I'm still not sure why we had to have a photographer. I recall saying, jokingly, that all we need is an album.

Barbara stays with me while we wait for Phil's grandmother. She is coming from the Bronx by subway and train. Someone has gone to meet her. As Barbara watches a purple finch duck its head in the big oak outside our window, I look at her thin shoulders. How grown up she is. The dress she is wearing was bought a year ago for me, but it never looked right; and now, seeing it look so well on her makes me feel old. Finished, somehow.

"Here they are," she says. But we hear only silence.

"Nana wasn't on the train," someone calls. A worried whispering emanates through the house. My mother decides to serve the hors d'oeuvres and drinks; the rabbi goes back to mourn with Sylvia Bernstein; one by one they ascend the stairs to visit me, exiled by tradition in my room.

Aunt Helen, a round bundle of a woman, takes my face in her hands and kisses me. She helps me take my dress off, gently, as if I were hurt. Then Mother enters. She and Helen look at each other, incredulous. In our family we don't let widowed, seventy-two-year-old grandmothers come from the Bronx to Long Island alone. This is now their family, they are thinking.

"She's very independent," I say. But they don't even bother to answer. And disappear.

Soon Dad arrives behind the largest fan in the house; the bride must be cool.

I lie down and the fan creates a breeze about my legs. Way down the block, near the big curve, some kids are playing baseball; near the chimney crickets ricochet in the grass; looking like Miss Muffets, the hollyhock along the side of the house push invisibly upward; plates clatter in the kitchen; Uncle Nat walks heavily down the hall. He feels guilty about being at my wedding while the rest of my aunts and uncles are cursing my parents at home. I pretend to doze and he goes away.

The next one is Max. I open one eye. We laugh.

"You look drunk that way," he says as I sit up in my slip, not at all embarrassed. He diapered me.

Suddenly I'm angry that they are all laughing and eating and drinking and I'm up here. "Isn't this ridiculous?"

"Yes," he says. "By the way, there was a wildcat subway strike at rush hour. We finally put on the radio."

The phone rings. It is almost nine. Max leaves. Barbara comes down the hall.

"Nana's at the station. Phil has gone to get her. Mom is calling the rabbi." She smoothes my hair. I get into the dress for the second time. On goes the veil.

From the hall I see pastel movement through the dark wood banisters. Then I am alone. The music starts. The wrong band. Inevitably. It begins again on the right spot. I walk down the stairs, Barbara walks ahead, Erica smiles, my mother holds out her arms as if to catch me, my father takes my arm. One of us, maybe both, is trembling, so I walk very close to him.

We stop. The rabbi smiles. I relax and smile back. But Grandpa's sharp blue eyes are severe. The rabbi assumes his pulpit manner, then begins. I don't hear a word. Phil steps forward and stands beside me. Now Grandpa is speaking in Yiddish, the fastest Yiddish spoken on this earth, then Phil places the ring on my fourth finger. Grandma jumps forward with a small cry and replaces it on my index finger. This is because the Talmud says it is more visible there, easier for the witnesses at a wedding to see. I can feel my mother stiffen behind me, but no one else cares where the ring is. Then there is the taste of the wine—too sweet—and the crunch of the broken glass, and Erica playing the wedding march on the piano while Phil kisses me, too tired of waiting to be shy about it.

The veil is whisked off me. Everyone kisses everyone else. My grandfather presses a pen into my hand and I sign the marriage contract. He looks at me, pleased, as if surprised I know how to write my own name. I place the ring back on my fourth finger, my grandmother frowns, someone slaps a bunch of telegrams into my hand. I greet Phil's grandma. She presses my arm and tears fill her eyes. "Am I glad to be alive!" she says.

Through dinner Phil and I scarcely talk. Despite all his careful plans it has been a long evening. In his eyes I see "Let's get out of here." I know it well; I have seen it for four years across lecture rooms, at parties, in stations, quadrangles, streets. But we can't move. Besides, we have years together. I see our life stretched out before me as clearly as the table, its settings, the food, the glasses. There will be lots of time.

"We must be patient," I whisper. He nods, but his eyes are still saying, "Let's get out of here."

It is getting cooler, the others are very gay. The photographer makes silly jokes so we smile, plates are rushed in laden and are taken away quietly, empty. Only Grandma won't eat. She nibbles some bread and drinks the champagne, but that's all. Mother has given up, I see, as she watches the old lady. Not even the dessert, the fabulous, chemically made ice cream will Grandma touch. I am filled with unreasonable hatred for her old, shriveled ways.

The cake is brought in, but I don't force myself to eat it; it can be frozen. "We can eat wedding cake all summer," I whisper to Phil, and this elicits the first real laugh from him all evening.

Spoons tinkle on glasses. My grandfather rises, holding an envelope. It is almost midnight, but he goes on and on. He is talking about the responsibilities of marriage, my father translates as he stands hunched behind us. Dad is proud of his vigorous father, and the old man's tactlessness doesn't surprise him. He has known his father for over fifty years.

Grandpa is finished. Finally. We get up from the table slowly, too full. Yet once up I revive. Just as I am beginning to enjoy myself Barbara draws me aside. It is time for us to leave. For the third time that evening she and Erica watch over me as I change and comb my hair and put on lipstick, and for the first time since we have known each other there is nothing to say. They kiss me very hard, then Mother comes upstairs. She isn't happy. Somewhere the wedding fell short of her ideal. But she is careful to let me know that I had nothing to do with it.

"You were beautiful, darling," she says, straightening my collar. I go into the kitchen to thank the caterer (why, I don't know, but we have been brought up to do such things) and kiss Jean, who has had a good cry. As I pass through the breakfast room I look up. The light shines through the spider's web; it is intact though the spider is gone. Then into the study, where Phil is getting the suitcases.

My father comes in. He looks confused. Put upon, almost, which is odd for him.

"Where is she going?" he asks my mother in a strange, harsh voice. She looks at him quizzically, and now I know why she has been so nervous all day. She starts to say something, but finally I am too impatient to wait for her explanation. I throw my arms around my parents and they kiss me, making a sandwich of me as they used to when I was little. Then we move apart, and as I take Phil's hand I see that his eyes are clear and filled with light.

Stephen Wolf
(b. 1947)

Born in Chicago, Stephen Wolf attended the University of Illinois, where he taught rhetoric and literature while working on his postgraduate degrees. His short stories have appeared in *Shenandoah, Ploughshares, Penthouse,* and *enclitic.* Presently he lives in Manhattan, where he has just completed a collection of fiction entitled *What the Early Harvest Brings.*

THE LEGACY OF BEAU KREMEL

So far, the visit was going fine. I hadn't been expected first of all, and so the initial surprise pleased my parents so much that any mention of our past difficulties dissolved in the affectionate air. Rather than asking—either pained or demandingly—why I haven't been home before this, they merely smiled, were grateful, and said, "It's been a long time."

"Too long" was the only complaint, but said by my mother, who threw her arms around me again. "It's good to have you home."

For nothing pleased my family—or so they believed—like a night that all of us spent together. And many nights were spent so. My brother still lived at home, for one thing, and though my sister was married and, allegedly, on her own, she could appear at my parents' door in just fifteen minutes—and did quite regularly. But my continual absence at their continual gatherings was not unnoticed, and punctuated, I imagined, with genuinely heartfelt sighs and the words "Don't you wish Stephen could be here?" directed at anyone save my father, who was—we all knew—as much responsible for that empty chair at the table as I was. But when the opportunity arose—and so unexpectedly—of having all of us together for a while, then let bygones be bygones, what's past is past, and it's out for dinner we all were to go.

"Where would you like to eat?" they asked me once we found ourselves hugged and kissed out with nothing jolly left to say.

"It doesn't matter," I replied complacently. "Anywhere is fine with me."

"How about the Ivanhoe?" my mother asked. "We haven't been there for so long and you like it so much."

"The Ivanhoe's fine."

"But it's so far," my father complained. "That's half way to the Loop. What about the Cork over here on Skokie Avenue," and his weighty arm gestured toward the closet.

"Fine."

"I hear the food is terrible," my mother declared.

"No!"

"*Ter*rible. Eileen ate there three days ago and nearly got food poisoning." But then she turned to me again and said eagerly, "Unless you'd like to eat there, dear."

"Doesn't matter. Any place is fine."

"How about Fanny's?" my father asked her.

"How *about* Fanny's?" she said to me.

"Fine."

"Should I call for a reservation?" inquired my father.

"Oh, we don't need one," she scoffed. "Unless we go late."

"Are you hungry?" he asked me.

"Starved."

"Why didn't you fix him something to eat?' he asked my mother irritably.

"Do you want me to fix you something to eat?" she asked.

"I can wait," I said to her.

"Wonderful," she exclaimed and scurried toward the telephone. "I'll call Susie and we'll all get ready and—"

Good idea: let's keep busy, for we can never be sure what ghosts will rise once families turn silent. And so upstairs I went, scanned the bedroom where I once lived and that my brother had completely usurped, cracked open my suitcase, grabbed my shaving kit, and headed for the Master Bath.

The bathroom had been redecorated into something vaguely resembling a science fiction movie. The wallpaper, which also spread across the ceiling, shined like paper mirrors. Little yellow butterflies, trapped and motionless, formed regular patterns throughout the paper, and the yellow window curtains and the yellow shower stall and the yellow toilet paper and the yellow kleenex box and—impossibly—even the yellow rosebud soaps in a yellow soap dish all matched the butterflies' color perfectly. On one entire wall and just above two separate, round-bowled, shiny sinks set in a black marble countertop, a large and glistening mirror reflected the sparkling yellow room. So sparkling and harmonious, in fact, that I had the distinct impression that I was the first person ever to set foot in here: I hoped that my farts would be hushed and odorless and that water would not bead in the sink.

"Hi," I said, turning to my father as he entered. "Quite a place you got here."

He frowned uncertainly at the room, then at me, and after tugging several times at the elastic of his boxer shorts he concentrated on the array of shaving utensils stored in a small drawer beside the sink. I kept watching him as I wet and lathered my face—he had gained more weight and his bulky body seemed resigned to it—and though his moody brooding often anticipated his erratic rage, he seemed preoccupied, as if something confusing and far away was eating at him. Not until I had rinsed my razor and started shaving did he finally speak.

"So how was the trip up here?" he asked tonelessly, his fingers and eyes still buried in the drawer.

"Fine," I said lightly and turned to him. "It's spring."

"Any trouble with the car?"

"None at all."

He frowned slightly as if his fingers came upon something that displeased him.

"Why don't you take the car over to Frank's tomorrow. Tell him to give you a grease and oil. Put it on my bill."

"I had a grease and oil less than two weeks ago. But thanks, Dad."

He pulled a razor from the drawer and studied it somberly: I knew he didn't believe me about the car and that nothing short of producing the receipt could convince him otherwise.

"Do you need anything while you're home?" he wondered.

"No," I replied seriously. "I don't think so."

"No underwear? Socks?"

"None."

"How about a few of those summer golf shirts I wear?" he asked, a wavering glimmer in his eyes.

"No, nothing, Dad. In fact, I think I still have shirts like that from last summer I haven't worn yet."

"No underwear? Socks?"

"I've got plenty," I replied. "But thank you."

He returned his focus to the razor, but I could see his expression and distrust swell in his eyes. I knew, from our past, what was happening here—how my refusals of what he offered denoted some rejection of what he had to give. This would anger him, and though the anger was only the underside of deep pain and frustration, that made it no less dangerous. I can remember, for example, when he grabbed me once, slammed me into the refrigerator and screamed, "Don't let me *ever* hear you say no one loves you in this house!"

And so, wanting to avoid a confrontation this early in the visit, I decided to finish shaving and do whatever else I had to do in here once my father was done. I hurried through the next few strokes with the razor as my father's ponderous silence filled the room more than the steam from my faucet, but once I rinsed my face and put my razor away, he exclaimed, "Good God, look at yourself!"

A dozen tiny cuts were scattered across my face, and a

deeper one below my chin dripped blood slowly down my neck.

"It's not as bad as it looks," I said bravely. "They're all surface cuts. I just put in a new blade."

With our eyes meeting in the mirror, he leaned forward suspiciously and asked, "What type of blades you use?"

I mentioned some brand—who knows which—then he turned quickly and reached into the small drawer, slapped something on the counter and shoved it toward me.

"Use these," he declared and revealed a packet of razor blades still in their cardboard wrapping. "They work just as well and they're not as sharp. Your face is still too soft to use tungsten."

He turned back to the mirror and began lathering his face aggressively.

"Will they last as long?" I wondered.

"Sure, why not?"

He ceased his lathering and turned to my reflection in the mirror.

"And if they don't, I'll buy you extras. I'd rather spend a few more pennies than have you walking around with your face sliced open."

Suddenly he grabbed the razors and held them an inch from my nose.

"They're better for you," he cried. "I'm telling you," then he slapped them down again.

I stared at the packet for a moment, conscious of him watching me in the mirror as he slashed away at the whiskers on his throat: whether I needed them or not—and regardless if they cut my face any less—these razors were going to leave this room with me.

I reached over and dropped them into my shaving kit.

"Thanks, I'll take them."

And if this were a movie then faint, sweet music would begin, for with my words the tension dissolved in his face and he shaved calmly; long, graceful strokes that left pink highways through the snow. I thought I even detected a smirk in the corner of his mouth.

"I'll tell you what I *could* use," I said, "Some hair tonic or something. My hair's been dry this winter."

"I've been telling you that for years," he announced triumphantly. Again he reached into the drawer beside the sink and this time set a little green jar on the counter. "This is just what you need."

"I'm not using that stuff," I cried.

"It's not greasy!"

"No," I insisted, sorry I had ever raised the subject at all. "I don't want to plaster it down. It's just a little dry."

He glared at me impatiently for a moment—he knew I had just betrayed him—then he shouldered me aside and reached into the cabinet below the sink. He brought out a tall bottle that had some yellowish liquid splashing about the bottom.

"This stuff isn't greasy at all," he declared, a husky insistence in his voice. "Dave at the barber shop gave it to me," and he pointed proudly to an ornate label. "For Professional Use Only" ran the inscription. "It's terrific stuff."

"Thanks, I'll use it," I said and took the bottle immediately, hoping to end this. "Sure you got enough?"

"Plenty. I've got another whole bottle."

Suddenly his head snapped back and his eyes went blank, then he hurried from the bathroom, leaned over the bannister and called to my mother downstairs.

"What is it?" she replied.

"Where's that other bottle of Beau Kremel?" he asked, straining forward to hear.

"In the linen closet."

He straightened up, reentered the bathroom, where he rinsed the lather from his partly shaven face, then said, "I just realized you can take some back with you," and hurried from the room, over to the closet. He opened the door, pushed sheets and towels aside—a few spilling to the floor in broken folds. His large body squeezed farther into the closet. Bottles were upended and I heard the faint rumbling of obscenities. Finally he emerged, his face red and his hair all disarranged, with an unopened bottle of the hair tonic he had just offered me. He picked up the sheets and towels, stuffed them back into the closet and slammed the door. While walking excitedly back to the bathroom, he ripped at the plastic seal around the neck of the new bottle.

"I'll put some in there," he said, indicating the other bottle with a glance. "There's not enough in there to do you any good."

He tossed the plastic seal at the wastebasket.

"I just want to give you a little more."

My father unscrewed the caps of both bottles, then carefully tipped the new one upside down so the spouts touched. But each spout had only a small hole and so just a solitary drop dangled from the spout and fell faintly to the liquid at the bottom. After a moment another drop appeared, hesitated, then slid reluctantly down the old bottle's side. He waited for a third drop, but one never appeared.

He turned the new bottle upright, glared at it reprimandingly, then, grabbing the old bottle, he squinted his eye as if taking aim. Quickly, he tipped the new bottle and the spouts clinked together, hair tonic squirting into my father's wrist. He tried again, but again he missed. He continued jerking at the bottle, repeatedly harder and harder, no longer taking aim but believing that hair tonic would find its way to the other spout simply because of his intense commitment.

"Dad, this'll take you all night," I said as little yellow drops dripped from the hair on his forearm and fell steadily to the countertop. "If the stuff works and I like it, I'll take more back with me the next time I'm home."

I reached over and took the old bottle, but he snatched it back and shoved it to the counter.

"You could be bald by then," he said darkly, then turned to the bottles with steadily angrying eyes. While he frowned at the bottles, the anger in his eyes spread throughout his face: these bottles, it seemed, had done him a great wrong, and now that he had them at his mercy he planned what way to show none. Finally, with a precise and concentrated gesture, he put his thumb on the spout of the new bottle and clutched it by its neck. He tipped the bottle upside down, gripped the old bottle with his other hand, then placed the spouts together with his thumb in between. He eased his thumb out, the spouts came together, then he shook both bottles simultaneously. The spouts separated, but he continued shaking them as hair tonic squirted all over the bottle, onto his fingers, squirting even to the countertop. That his plan wasn't working didn't stop him at all: it made him only angrier at the bottles and he shook them wildly until a spout banged a finger joint.

"Damn!" he cried and snapped the new bottle upright. He turned, ripped a towel from a rack, and wrapped half around the old bottle. He grabbed the new bottle and dumped it over so the spouts touched again, disregarding the hair tonic spurting out the hole. He wrapped the remaining towel around the neck of the new bottle, clutched both bottles by their thickened spouts and shook them until he resembled a man on a pneumatic drill. I could hear the muffled glass scratching together, and after several moments the towel around the spouts grew dark and wet. Hair tonic soon oozed from the towel between my father's fingers and began dripping to the countertop. Drops gathered, and a little yellow lake spilled over the side in a steady stream and was sponged up by the rug on the floor.

It wasn't working and he knew it, for he finally slammed the bottle to the countertop, tore off the towel, which he used to mop the counter, and flung it in the tub. His hand reached down and sucked up the rug and he flung that, too, in the same general direction. He turned back to the bottles: the new one was nearly half empty now, and the amount in the bottle he had given me had not visibly changed.

"Dad," I cried weakly, "this is *fine*, for God's sake, I've got *plenty* in this one," and I moved toward the bottles.

"Stay out of the mess!" he snapped. "We're going out for dinner, you know."

He turned and looked me in the face.

"You want hair tonic," he whispered, "you'll get hair tonic," and he stormed out the door.

Helpless, I tried thinking what to do before the visit splashed to the floor along with the hair tonic and our shaky reconciliation. Responsible for this and unable to prevent it from occurring, I felt that my car, even with the brakes on, was skidding unavoidably into the back of a truck. It was happening, I couldn't stop it, and—worse yet—I had time to watch it occur.

My father lunged into the bathroom, carrying a single sheet of paper. With his head bent down and taking large, heavy steps, he marched directly to the window and threw it open. His wet hands smudged the glass and left three dark stains on the curtain. He returned to the counter and rolled the sheet of paper into a tight funnel, an end of which he stuck into the spout of the bottle he had given me. He widened the lips at the top of the funnel, picked up the new bottle of hair tonic and frantically poured into the rolled paper. Streams of hair tonic jumped into the funnel with irregular spurts, making a damp "smack" as it hit. My father jerked at the bottle with hard, rapid strokes. More and more hair tonic streamed into the paper. He stopped, readjusted the funnel, then poured even harder and more rapidly, up and down, again and again. Tiny drops of perspiration ran down his forehead, hid in his eyebrows, reappeared above his lips. He began breathing furiously.

"Anything happening?" he gasped.

"Yes," I replied miserably. "The paper's soaking up all the hair tonic."

He banged the bottle to the countertop, directly onto the razor, which spun and jumped to the floor. He turned, kicked at the razor and sent it flying across the room.

"Do something for a change," he yelled. "Here," and he shoved the bottle into my chest. "You pour."

Exasperated and panting, he flicked thick fingers through his eyebrows, then across his lip, and, after taking one deep breath like he was diving underwater, he crouched toward the wet and already shedding funnel and cupped both hands around it. He froze in this position for an instant before yelling,

"Today, today, let's go!"

I jumped toward him while muttering apologies, then began pouring.

"It's working," he cried, his eyes following each drop falling into the bottle. "Pour a little faster."

With his hysterical eyes and half-shaven face, my father looked like the mad scientist whose creation lived.

"Good," he exclaimed. "Harder."

I pounded away, but then that funnel—having absorbed so much liquid—gave way entirely and melted over my father's hands just when hair tonic exploded from the spout, all over his belly, pressing hair wet and yellow against his pink skin.

"Shit!" he screamed and jumped back, his arm tipping the bottle, which fell and skidded to a stop in the sink. He grabbed for another towel and furiously scrubbed his belly while groping for the overturned bottle.

"Seymour," cried my mother from downstairs as hair tonic gurgled down the drain. "Seymour!"

"What do you want?" he shouted back, his body in a twist of contrary motions while his face strained toward her voice.

"What's that awful smell I smell?"

"Not a goddamn thing," he yelled, lurching from the bathroom and still rubbing his belly with a towel. "I'm giving your son a little hair tonic."

"Well I can smell it down *here*."

He was about to scream a reply, hesitated, then dragged the towel across his perspiring face.

"We're just having a little trouble," he said faintly. He returned to the bathroom, avoided my eyes, leaned heavily on the countertop and stared at the two bottles. Both were nearly empty, and when he reached for one, the decorative label shed into his hand.

Just then my mother appeared in the doorway with a worried face that transformed into astonishment: the mess in the bathroom had gathered enough force to knock her back a step, what with hair tonic across the countertop and streaming in puddles to her bare floor, the rug and towels limp in the tub, a razor in the corner, the windows smudged—and with her soaking husband, desperate and partly shaven, and my pathetic eyes.

"What's been going *on* in here?" she asked, amazed.

My father, not turning to her, waved a hand despairingly my way.

"His hair's dry."

His head swung back and forth and his mouth fidgeted like he was about to say more, but no words came and his confusion exhausted him. His excess weight sagged on him and he turned sad-eyed to my mother, who yanked in a breath, blew it out and began rolling up her sleeves.

"Alright, everybody out," she said nervously while moving through the room. "I'm cleaning this up *right now*."

She fussed with her sleeves a moment longer, picked up the razor, then pounced on the heap in the tub. She wrung and squeezed at something—I wasn't sure what, for just then my father folded his towel neatly, placed it beside the bottles on the counter and quietly left the room.

Gloria Naylor
(b. 1950)

After serving as a missionary for the Jehovah's Witnesses from 1968–75, Gloria Naylor, a native New Yorker, earned a B.A. at Brooklyn College of the City University of New York. While a student, she began writing the seven interconnected stories which form *The Women of Brewster Place* (1982), a collection which won an American Book Award for First Fiction and was made into a TV film starring Oprah Winfrey in 1989. She earned an M.A. in Afro-American Studies at Yale University, where she began work on *Linden Hills* (1985), a novel about the residents of an upper-middle-class black neighborhood. She has taught creative writing and American literature as a writer-in-residence at George Washington University. In 1988 she published *Mama Day*, a novel set on an island off the coast of South Carolina inhabited by the descendants of a white slave owner and a legendary slave, Sapphiria Wade.

KISWANA BROWNE

From the window of her sixth-floor studio apartment, Kiswana could see over the wall at the end of the street to the busy avenue that lay just north of Brewster Place. The late afternoon shoppers looked like brightly clad marionettes as they moved between the congested traffic, clutching their packages against their bodies to guard them from sudden bursts of the cold autumn wind. A portly mailman had abandoned his cart and was bumping into indignant window-shoppers as he puffed behind the cap that the wind had snatched from his head. Kiswana leaned over to see if he was going to be successful, but the edge of the building cut him off from her view.

A pigeon swept across her window, and she marveled at its liquid movements in the air waves. She placed her dreams on the back of the bird and fantasized that it would glide forever in transparent silver circles until it ascended to the center of the universe and was swallowed up. But the wind died down, and she watched with a sigh as the bird beat its wings in awkward, frantic movements to land on the corroded top of a fire escape on the opposite building. This brought her back to earth.

Humph, it's probably sitting over there crapping on those folks' fire escape, she thought. Now, that's a safety hazard. . . . And her mind was busy again, creating flames and smoke and frustrated tenants whose escape was being hindered because they were slipping and sliding in pigeon shit. She watched their cussing, haphazard descent on the fire escapes until they had all reached the bottom. They were milling around, oblivious to their burning apartments, angrily planning to march on the mayor's office about the pigeons. She materialized placards and banners for them, and they had just reached the corner, boldly sidestepping fire hoses and broken glass, when they all vanished.

A tall copper-skinned woman had met this phantom parade at the corner, and they had dissolved in front of her long, confident strides. She plowed through the remains of their faded mists, unconscious of the lingering wisps of their presence on her leather bag and black fur-trimmed coat. It took a few seconds for this transfer from one realm to another to reach Kiswana, but then suddenly she recognized the woman.

"Oh, God, it's Mama!" She looked down guiltily at the forgotten newspaper in her lap and hurriedly circled random job advertisements.

By this time Mrs. Browne had reached the front of Kiswana's building and was checking the house number against a piece of paper in her hand. Before she went into the building she stood at the bottom of the stoop and carefully inspected the condition of the street and the adjoining property. Kiswana watched this meticulous inventory with growing annoyance but she involuntarily followed her mother's slowly rotating head, forcing herself to see her new neighborhood through the older woman's eyes. The brightness of the unclouded sky seemed to join forces with her mother as it highlighted every broken stoop railing and missing brick. The afternoon sun glittered and cascaded across even the tiniest fragments of broken bottle, and at that very moment the wind chose to rise up again, sending unswept grime flying into the air, as a stray tin can left by careless garbage collectors went rolling noisily down the center of the street.

Kiswana noticed with relief that at least Ben wasn't sitting in his usual place on the old garbage can pushed against the far wall. He was just a harmless old wino, but Kiswana knew her mother only needed one wino or one teenager with a reefer within a twenty-block radius to decide that her daughter was living in a building seething with dope factories and hang-outs for derelicts. If she had seen Ben, nothing would have made her believe that practically every apartment contained a family, a Bible, and a dream that one day enough could be scraped from those meager Friday night paychecks to make Brewster Place a distant memory.

As she watched her mother's head disappear into the building, Kiswana gave silent thanks that the elevator was broken. That would give her at least five minutes' grace to straighten up the apartment. She rushed to the sofa bed and hastily closed it without smoothing the rumpled sheets and blanket or removing her nightgown. She felt that somehow the tangled bedcovers would give away the fact that she had not slept alone last night. She silently apologized to Abshu's memory as she heartlessly crushed his spirit between the steel springs of the couch. Lord, that man was sweet. Her toes curled involuntarily at the passing thought of his full lips moving slowly over her instep. Abshu was a foot man, and he always started his lovemaking from the bottom up. For that reason Kiswana changed the color of the polish on her toenails every week. During the course of their relationship she had gone from shades of red to brown and was now into the purples. I'm gonna have to start mixing them soon, she thought aloud as she turned from the couch and raced into the bathroom to remove any traces of Abshu from there. She took up his shaving cream and razor and threw them into the bottom drawer of her dresser beside her diaphragm. Mama wouldn't dare pry into my drawers right in front of me, she thought as she slammed the drawer shut. Well, at least not the *bottom* drawer. She may come up with some sham excuse for opening the top drawer, but never the bottom one.

When she heard the first two short raps on the door, her eyes took a final flight over the small apartment, desperately seeking out any slight misdemeanor that might have to be defended. Well, there was nothing she could do about the crack in the wall over that table. She had been after the landlord to fix it for two months now. And there had been no time to sweep the rug, and everyone knew that off-gray always looked dirtier than it really was. And it was just too damn bad about the kitchen. How was she expected to be out job-hunting every day and still have time to keep a kitchen that looked like her mother's, who didn't even work and still had someone come in twice a month for general cleaning. And besides . . .

Her imaginary argument was abruptly interrupted by a second series of knocks, accompanied by a penetrating, "Melanie, Melanie, are you there?"

Kiswana strode toward the door. She's starting before she even gets in here. She knows that's not my name anymore.

She swung the door open to face her slightly flushed mother. "Oh, hi, Mama. You know, I thought I heard a knock, but I figured it was for the people next door, since no one hardly ever calls me Melanie." Score one for me, she thought.

"Well, it's awfully strange you can forget a name you answered to for twenty-three years," Mrs. Browne said, as she moved past Kiswana into the apartment. "My, that was a long climb. How long has your elevator been out? Honey, how do you manage with your laundry and groceries up all those steps? But I guess you're young, and it wouldn't bother you as much as it does me." This long string of questions told Kiswana that her mother had no intentions of beginning her visit with another argument about her new African name.

"You know I would have called before I came, but you don't have a phone yet. I didn't want you to feel that I was snooping. As a matter of fact, I didn't expect to find you home at all. I thought you'd be out looking for a job." Mrs. Browne had mentally covered the entire apartment while she was talking and taking off her coat.

"Well, I got up late this morning. I thought I'd buy the afternoon paper and start early tomorrow."

"That sounds like a good idea." Her mother moved toward the window and picked up the discarded paper and glanced over the hurriedly circled ads. "Since when do you have experience as a fork-lift operator?"

Kiswana caught her breath and silently cursed herself for her stupidity. "Oh, my hand slipped—I meant to circle file clerk." She quickly took the paper before her mother could see that she had also marked cutlery salesman and chauffeur.

"You're sure you weren't sitting here moping and daydreaming again?" Amber specks of laughter flashed in the corner of Mrs. Browne's eyes.

Kiswana threw her shoulders back and unsuccessfully tried to disguise her embarrassment with indignation.

"Oh, God, Mama! I haven't done that in years—it's for kids. When are you going to realize that I'm a woman now?" She sought desperately for some womanly thing to do and settled for throwing herself on the couch and crossing her legs in what she hoped looked like a nonchalant arc.

"Please, have a seat," she said, attempting the same tones and gestures she'd seen Bette Davis use on the late movies.

Mrs. Browne, lowering her eyes to hide her amusement, accepted the invitation and sat at the window, also crossing her legs. Kiswana saw immediately how it should have been done. Her celluloid poise clashed loudly against her mother's quiet dignity, and she quickly uncrossed her legs. Mrs. Browne turned her head toward the window and pretended not to notice.

"At least you have a halfway decent view from here. I was wondering what lay beyond that dreadful wall—it's the boulevard. Honey, did you know that you can see the trees in Linden Hills from here?"

Kiswana knew that very well, because there were many lonely days that she would sit in her gray apartment and stare at those trees and think of home, but she would rather have choked than admit that to her mother.

"Oh, really, I never noticed. So how is Daddy and things at home?"

"Just fine. We're thinking of redoing one of the extra bedrooms since you children have moved out, but Wilson insists that he can manage all that work alone. I told him that he doesn't really have the proper time or energy for all that. As it is, when he gets home from the office, he's so tired he can hardly move. But you know you can't tell your father anything. Whenever he starts complaining about how stubborn you are, I tell him the child came by it honestly. Oh, and your brother was by yesterday," she added, as if it had just occurred to her.

So that's it, thought Kiswana. That's why she's here.

Kiswana's brother, Wilson, had been to visit her two days ago, and she had borrowed twenty dollars from him to get her winter coat out of layaway. That son-of-a-bitch probably ran straight to Mama—and after he swore he wouldn't say anything. I should have known, he was always a snotty-nosed sneak, she thought.

"Was he?" she said aloud. "He came by to see me, too, earlier this week. And I borrowed some money from him because my unemployment checks hadn't cleared in the bank, but now they have and everything's just fine." There, I'll beat you to that one.

"Oh, I didn't know that," Mrs. Browne lied. "He never mentioned you. He had just heard that Beverly was expecting again, and he rushed over to tell us."

Damn. Kiswana could have strangled herself.

"So she's knocked up again, huh?" she said irritably.

Her mother started. "Why do you always have to be so crude?"

"Personally, I don't see how she can sleep with Willie. He's such a dishrag."

Kiswana still resented the stance her brother had taken in college. When everyone at school was discovering their blackness and protesting on campus, Wilson never took part; he had even refused to wear an Afro. This had outraged Kiswana because, unlike her, he was dark-skinned and had the type of hair that was thick and kinky enough for a good "Fro." Kiswana had still insisted on cutting her own hair, but it was so thin and fine-textured, it refused to thicken even after she washed it. So she had to brush it up and spray it with lacquer to keep it from lying flat. She never forgave Wilson for telling her that she didn't look African, she looked like an electrocuted chicken.

"Now that's some way to talk. I don't know why you have an attitude against your brother. He never gave me a restless night's sleep, and now he's settled with a family and a good job."

"He's an assistant to an assistant junior partner in a law firm. What's the big deal about that?"

"The job has a future, Melanie. And at least he finished school and went on for his law degree."

"In other words, not like me, huh?"

"Don't put words into my mouth, young lady. I'm perfectly capable of saying what I mean."

Amen, thought Kiswana.

"And I don't know why you've been trying to start up with me from the moment I walked in. I didn't come here to fight with you. This is your first place away from home, and I just wanted to see how you were living and if you're doing all right. And I must say, you've fixed this apartment up very nicely."

"Really, Mama?" She found herself softening in the light of her mother's approval.

"Well, considering what you had to work with." This time she scanned the apartment openly.

"Look, I know it's not Linden Hills, but a lot can be done with it. As soon as they come and paint, I'm going to hang my Ashanti print over the couch. And I thought a big Boston Fern would go well in that corner, what do you think?"

"That would be fine, baby. You always had a good eye for balance."

Kiswana was beginning to relax. There was little she did that attracted her mother's approval. It was like a rare bird, and she had to tread carefully around it lest it fly away.

"Are you going to leave that statue out like that?"

"Why, what's wrong with it? Would it look better somewhere else?"

There was a small wooden reproduction of a Yoruba goddess with large protruding breasts on the coffee table.

"Well," Mrs. Browne was beginning to blush, "it's just that it's a bit suggestive, don't you think? Since you live alone now, and I know you'll be having male friends stop by, you wouldn't want to be giving them any ideas. I mean, uh, you know, there's no point in putting yourself in any unpleasant situations because they may get the wrong impressions and uh, you know, I mean, well . . ." Mrs. Browne stammered on miserably.

Kiswana loved it when her mother tried to talk about sex. It was the only time she was at a loss for words.

"Don't worry, Mama." Kiswana smiled. "That wouldn't bother the type of men I date. Now maybe if it had big feet . . ." And she got hysterical, thinking of Abshu.

Her mother looked at her sharply. "What sort of gibberish is that about feet? I'm being serious, Melanie."

"I'm sorry, Mama." She sobered up. "I'll put it away in the closet," she said, knowing that she wouldn't.

"Good," Mrs. Browne said, knowing that she wouldn't either. "I guess you think I'm too picky, but we worry about you over here. And you refuse to put in a phone so we can call and see about you."

"I haven't refused, Mama. They want seventy-five dollars for a deposit, and I can't swing that right now."

"Melanie, I can give you the money."

"I don't want you to be giving me money—I've told you that before. Please, let me make it by myself."

"Well, let me lend it to you, then."

"No!"

"Oh, so you can borrow money from your brother, but not from me."

Kiswana turned her head from the hurt in her mother's eyes. "Mama, when I borrow from Willie, he makes me pay him back. You never let me pay you back," she said into her hands.

"I don't care. I still think it's downright selfish of you to be sitting over here with no phone, and sometimes we don't hear from you in two weeks—anything could happen—especially living among these people."

Kiswana snapped her head up. "What do you mean, *these people*. They're my people and yours, too, Mama—we're all black. But maybe you've forgotten that over in Linden Hills."

"That's not what I'm talking about, and you know it. These streets—this building—it's so shabby and rundown. Honey, you don't have to live like this."

"Well, this is how poor people live."

"Melanie, you're not poor."

"No, Mama, *you're* not poor. And what you have and I have are two totally different things. I don't have a husband in real estate with a five-figure income and a home in Linden Hills—*you* do. What I have is a weekly unemployment check and an overdrawn checking account at United Federal. So this studio on Brewster is all I can afford."

"Well, you could afford a lot better," Mrs. Browne snapped, "if you hadn't dropped out of college and had to resort to these dead-end clerical jobs."

"Uh-huh, I knew you'd get around to that before long." Kiswana could feel the rings of anger begin to tighten around her lower backbone, and they sent her forward onto the couch. "You'll never understand, will you? Those bourgie schools were counterrevolutionary. My place was in the streets with my people, fighting for equality and a better community."

"Counterrevolutionary!" Mrs. Browne was raising her voice. "Where's your revolution now, Melanie? Where are all those black revolutionaries who were shouting and demonstrating and kicking up a lot of dust with you on that campus? Huh? They're sitting in wood-paneled offices with their degrees in mahogany frames, and they won't even drive their cars past this street because the city doesn't fix potholes in this part of town."

"Mama," she said, shaking her head slowly in disbelief, "how can you—a black woman—sit there and tell me that what we fought for during the Movement wasn't important just because some people sold out?"

"Melanie, I'm not saying it wasn't important. It was damned important to stand up and say that you were proud of what you were and to get the vote and other social opportunities for every person in this country who had it due. But you kids thought you were going to turn the world upside down, and it just wasn't so. When all the smoke had cleared, you found yourself with a fistful of new federal laws and a country still full of obstacles for black people to fight their way over—just because they're black. There was no revolution, Melanie, and there will be no revolution."

"So what am I supposed to do, huh? Just throw up my hands and not care about what happens to my people? I'm not supposed to keep fighting to make things better?"

"Of course, you can. But you're going to have to fight within the system, because it and these so-called 'bourgie' schools are going to be here for a long time. And that means that you get smart like a lot of your old friends and get an important job where you can have some influence. You don't have to sell out, as you say, and work for some corporation, but you could become an assemblywoman or a civil liberties lawyer or open a freedom school in this very neighborhood. That way you could really help the community. But what help are you going to be to these people on Brewster while you're living hand-to-mouth on file-clerk jobs waiting for a revolution? You're wasting your talents, child."

"Well, I don't think they're being wasted. At least I'm here in day-to-day contact with the problems of my people. What good would I be after four or five years of a lot of white brainwashing in some phony, prestige institution, huh? I'd be like you and Daddy and those other educated blacks sitting over there in Linden Hills with a terminal case of middle-class amnesia."

"You don't have to live in a slum to be concerned about social conditions, Melanie. Your father and I have been charter members of the NAACP for the last twenty-five years."

"Oh, God!" Kiswana threw her head back in exaggerated disgust. "That's being concerned? That middle-of-the-road, Uncle Tom dumping ground for black Republicans!"

"You can sneer all you want, young lady, but that organization has been working for black people since the turn of the century, and it's still working for them. Where are all those radical groups of yours that were going to put a Cadillac in every garage and Dick Gregory in the White House? I'll tell you where."

I knew you would, Kiswana thought angrily.

"They burned themselves out because they wanted too much too fast. Their goals weren't grounded in reality. And that's always been your problem."

"What do you mean, my problem? I know exactly what I'm about."

"No, you don't. You constantly live in a fantasy world—always going to extremes—turning butterflies into eagles, and life isn't about that. It's accepting what is and working from that. Lord, I remember how worried you had me, putting all that lacquered hair spray on your head. I thought you were going to get lung cancer—trying to be what you're not."

Kiswana jumped up from the couch. "Oh, God, I can't take this anymore. Trying to be something I'm not—trying to be something I'm not, Mama! Trying to be proud of my heritage and the fact that I was of African descent. If that's being what I'm not, then I say fine. But I'd rather be dead than be like you—a white man's nigger who's ashamed of being black!"

Kiswana saw streaks of gold and ebony light follow her mother's flying body out of the chair. She was swung around by the shoulders and made to face the deadly stillness in the angry woman's eyes. She was too stunned to cry out from the pain of the long fingernails that dug into her shoulders, and she was brought so close to her mother's face that she saw her reflection, distorted and wavering, in the tears that stood in the older woman's eyes. And she listened in that stillness to a story she had heard from a child.

"My grandmother," Mrs. Browne began slowly in a whisper, "was a full-bloodied Iroquois, and my grandfather a free black from a long line of journeymen who had lived in Connecticut since the establishment of the colonies. And my father was a Bajan who came to this country as a cabin boy on a merchant mariner."

"I know all that," Kiswana said, trying to keep her lips from trembling.

"Then, know this." And the nails dug deeper into her flesh. "I am alive because of the blood of proud people who never scraped or begged or apologized for what they were. They lived asking only one thing of this world—to be allowed to be. And I learned through the blood of these people that black isn't beautiful and it isn't ugly—black is! It's not kinky hair and it's not straight hair—it just is.

"It broke my heart when you changed your name. I gave you my grandmother's name, a woman who bore nine children and educated them all, who held off six white men with a shotgun when they tried to drag one of her sons to jail for 'not knowing his place.' Yet you needed to reach into an African dictionary to find a name to make you proud.

"When I brought my babies home from the hospital, my ebony son and my golden daughter, I swore before whatever gods would listen—those of my mother's people or those of my father's people—that I would use everything I had and could ever get to see that my children were prepared to meet this world on its own terms, so that no one could sell them short and make them ashamed of what they were or how they looked—whatever they were or however they looked. And Melanie, that's not being white or red or black—that's being a mother."

Kiswana followed her reflection in the two single tears that moved down her mother's cheeks until it blended with them into the woman's copper skin. There was nothing and then so much that she wanted to say, but her throat kept closing up every time she tried to speak. She kept her head down and her eyes closed, and thought, Oh, God, just let me die. How can I face her now?

Mrs. Browne lifted Kiswana's chin gently. "And the one lesson I wanted you to learn is not to be afraid to face anyone, not even a crafty old lady like me who can outtalk you." And she smiled and winked.

"Oh, Mama, I . . ." and she hugged the woman tightly.

"Yeah, baby." Mrs. Browne patted her back. "I know."

She kissed Kiswana on the forehead and cleared her throat. "Well, now, I better be moving on. It's getting late, there's dinner to be made, and I have to get off my feet—these new shoes are killing me."

Kiswana looked down at the beige leather pumps. "Those are really classy. They're English, aren't they?"

"Yes, but, Lord, do they cut me right across the instep." She removed the shoe and sat on the couch to massage her foot.

Bright red nail polish glared at Kiswana through the stockings. "Since when do you polish your toenails?" she gasped. "You never did that before."

"Well . . ." Mrs. Browne shrugged her shoulders, "your father sort of talked me into it, and, uh, you know, he likes it and all, so I thought, uh, you know, why not, so . . ." And she gave Kiswana an embarrassed smile.

I'll be damned, the young woman thought, feeling her whole face tingle. Daddy's into feet! And she looked at the blushing woman on her couch and suddenly realized that her mother had trod through the same universe that she herself was now traveling. Kiswana was breaking no new trails and would eventually end up just two feet away on that couch. She stared at the woman she had been and was to become.

"But I'll never be a Republican," she caught herself saying aloud.

"What are you mumbling about, Melanie?" Mrs. Browne slipped on her shoe and got up from the couch.

She went to get her mother's coat. "Nothing, Mama. It's really nice of you to come by. You should do it more often."

"Well, since it's not Sunday, I guess you're allowed at least one lie."

They both laughed.

After Kiswana had closed the door and turned around, she spotted an envelope sticking between the cushions of her couch. She went over and opened it up; there was seventy-five dollars in it.

"Oh, Mama, darn it!" She rushed to the window and started to call to the woman, who had just emerged from the building, but she suddenly changed her mind and sat down in the chair with a long sigh that caught in the upward draft of the autumn wind and disappeared over the top of the building.

Mary Hedin
(b. 1929)

Educated at the University of Minnesota and the University of California at San Francisco, where she received a master's degree, Mary Hedin has taught at the College of Marin in California for almost two decades. A recipient of the Iowa School of Letters Award for Short Fiction and the Great Lakes College Association Award for New Fiction, she has been writer-in-residence at the Robinson Jeffers Tor House Foundation. She has contributed short stories to *Redbook, McCall's, Southwest Review, South Dakota Review,* and *Ploughshares*; several of her stories have been included in the annual anthologies *Best American Short Stories* and *O. Henry Prize Stories. Fly Away Home* (1980) is a collection of her stories and *Direction* (1983) is a collection of her poems.

TUESDAYS

I park at the curb in front of the low white house set in the perfect center of its clipped yard. Patches of winter brown mar the green of the grass, but at the corner of the house, against the immaculate white wall, the camellia bush already holds knots of pink bloom in its thick dark green.

As I slide from behind the wheel, I see the curtains in the kitchen windows move. They are waiting, saying to one another, "She is here."

A small black boy, about eight, is sitting on the curb.

He wears stiff new blue jeans, a yellow sweat shirt. He tosses a stone into the air, catches it, his eyes sliding toward me when the stone drops neatly into his palm. I smile, he does not smile back. He watches me go around to the passenger door and take out the packages I have brought. My arms full, I bang the door shut, try another smile, say "Hello." He stares off down the avenue, does not answer. On the cross-street, other youngsters shout and run in a game of ball. Their voices are high and shrill, and they, too, are black.

I go up the walk and the five steps to the small portico in front of the door and push the bell. The door will not be opened until the two singing tones fall away on the inside air. Why? They know it is I. Why do they make me wait? A custom of manners? A masking of anticipation, of dependence?

When she is alone, she will not answer the door. Too many hippies, too many thieves. An old couple, not far away, were tied one night to chairs in their kitchen, beaten, burned with matches, robbed. Another old woman was murdered, and somehow worse, an old woman of eighty-three was raped.

And here in their own neighborhood: thefts, beatings. The petunia pots have been stolen from their front steps. The birdbath disappeared from the picket-fenced backyard. A strange muscular boy comes to their door, repeatedly, and asks for money. They give him dimes. They tell me this, smiling as if their coins were charity. But how will the boy respond if they refuse?

They should move, of course. But would anywhere be safe? And what can they afford? And how would they manage strange bathrooms, strange cupboards? And neighbors. What would the new neighbors be like?

Here Mrs. Compton is next door and known—arthritic, long-nosed, her friendship narrow and grudging. She rarely goes out anymore. Still, they know her. And across the street is Mr. Levine—humped as a camel, but his backyard full of dahlias. On a summer afternoon he hobbles over, a flower big as a dinner plate in his stained, gnarled hand. Grinning, he stays for a cup of Sanka in the secure kitchen. And down the avenue Mrs. Cavender survives.

She comes, asks a widow's favors: fix a faucet, a loose doorknob. He fixes, Mrs. Cavender brings grateful pastries, hard or raw, always inedible. But she, too, is known: that broad drooping bosom, thin blue legs.

Now slowly the bell-sounds fade away and the heavy green door swings back, stops at a twenty-degree angle. Around its edge he peers out at me, his cheeks flushed over the bone, his blue triangular eyes peeky. With shyness. Or shame. Proud, he cannot bear his old age. I make myself offer cheerfulness.

"Hello, Dad! How are you? Isn't it a beautiful day? That sun! The camellias, already! Beautiful."

He touches my shoulder, his hand heavy, clumsy. His smile is small. He draws me in, closes the door behind me. She is sitting in the green plastic Barcalounger in front of the empty fireplace. The footrest of the chair is raised, her legs, the ankles thickly swollen, extended. Her fingers turn crookedly the white thread, flashing hook. Through her thick inadequate glasses, she stares at me intently. The blue light of the television screen flickers over her face. She lifts her thin voice over the melodious voices issuing from the box. "Is that you, Marcie?" she wavers.

I answer, "Yes, Mother. How have you been?" I move toward her, lean down, kiss the soft wrinkled skin of her cheek, taking in the pale, aged, delicate smell.

She spies the packages in my hands. "My goodness, Marcie, what have you brought?" she sings, a bird flute. A social smile moves her mouth. Her head dips to one side, shakes genteelly. "You shouldn't have brought anything. My goodness, that's not necessary, bringing something every time you come."

The words ring from my childhood. She offered the same phrases to her friends, neighbors, bringing cookies or cake for afternoon coffee. Yes, old rituals, old modes. Had they not been correct always? Of course, of course. But now, when so much else is lost, they seem absurd.

"I brought the custard rolls you like, Mother," I report. "And a chicken for dinner."

Behind the glasses where light moves in deep rings, her

eyes widen. "Oh, are you staying for dinner? Oh my, that's nice, that's awfully nice of you."

Does she remember who I am? I always stay for dinner, cook for them. Once a week. Between us the television voices are rich with sorrow, intense with pain. "How is Charles, then?" she asks.

That, too, is merely miming convention. What I say she will not take in. But I reply. "He's fine, Mother. He's been terribly busy, there's so much flu around."

Her thin mouth turns downward, the rusty brows gather over the frames of her glasses. "I never get to see him anymore. I wish he could come over, once in a while, check my blood pressure sometimes. I have to have my blood pressure taken, you know."

"He was here last week," I remind her. "Last Sunday. He took it then. It was fine, Mother. Very low." But she will not remember, will believe again that she needs medical attention.

"No, it's been a long time," she grumbles. One shoulder pulls up toward the ear, and she looks sideways at me. She pushes a lumpy forefinger against her side, high up against the fifth rib. "I've got this terrible pain here. It hurts so I could scream. Just like a knife."

"Charlie will come soon," I tell her. "Next Sunday, maybe."

But the comfort is without function. She gives an inattentive nod, forgetting already what is being discussed. An image on the flickering screen has caught her interest. A young doctor, white-coated, frowning and tender, leans over a young woman in a hospital bed. His long fingers lightly hold her wrist. He whispers, "You're going to be all right, Melody." But the face against the pillow does not stir.

And she has moved into that fictional world, totally. Always she has loved medicine. The mysteries of disease. The magic of chemicals. Sick is more important than well. Suffering wins love. For her children she made illness a treat: a winter morning, sheets of snow outside the ice-rimmed window, snowy sheets where I lie in their wide downstairs bed. She comes with a tray: orange juice in dazzling cut glass, scrambled eggs golden on sheer, flowered china plate. Her hand a cool snowflake on hot forehead. Her voice offering music: tales of trolls, fairies, princes, magic. Who could wish to get well, princess in her caring; close, close in her love?

He has come to the archway, beckons, his crippled hand making a jerky sign. "Come and have coffee," he says. "She wants to watch her program now." Complicity gleams in his bright eye. Condescension, tolerance in his voice. The silly programs. The world of pretense.

Already he has set the table. Blue pottery dishes on the fringe flowered plastic cloth. Coffee cups, plates, forks, and spoons properly arranged. Sugar bowl, cream pitcher, paper napkins in plastic holder. The coffee warms on a low flame, giving off a dark rich odor. He is standing at the bread board covering slices of rye bread with a tuna-fish-egg-salad mix. He moves to the cupboard for a serving plate, his feet slow in brown slippers, heavy shoulders round under the blue coat-sweater. His trousers slip down past the push of paunch and are too long and fold over the instep. He goes to the cookie jar, lifts the lid, peers inside. He reaches in, pulls up a fistful of store-bought sugar cookies, drops them onto a plate. He shuffles back to the breadbox, takes out Svenhardt sweet rolls, puts them on the plate beside the cookies.

"Don't put out so much, Dad," I caution. "I'm not very hungry."

His chin jerks up, he shrugs. "You're always dieting," he answers crossly.

If there were fruit or green salad. But they do not eat those things. Nothing tart, nothing spicy. Nothing chewy, nothing hard. Not too much red meat, no fresh vegetables. Cans, frozen packages, mixes.

I eat half a sandwich, a cookie. He is offended. I give in, eat a sweet roll. We talk of weather, shootings in San Francisco, the teachers' strike. And then over a final cup of coffee I take the letter from my purse. "It's from Matt," I tell him. "It came yesterday."

Color deepens in his cheeks. He fumbles in his pocket for glasses, shoves them on. He reads the scrawled casual note. Air huffs through the high-boned nose, the glasses diffuse the angry eyes. Finished, he folds the paper, puts it on the table, runs his scarred thickened thumb over the fold. He cannot look at me. "I don't understand that kid," he mumbles.

I can offer no answer, I do not mean to sigh. His quick glance darts at me. He pulls off the glasses, waits for my tardy comment. I mumble back, "I don't understand him, either, Dad."

The letter crumbles a bit under the left hand where the second and third fingers are gone, lost long ago under an electric saw. "He's always full of plans, he never settles down." His sharp oblique glance follows his complaint. I watch his hands, smoothing the letter now, hard, repeatedly. "What's wrong with young men these days? They don't want to make anything of themselves. He's had every chance."

It's an old complaint. I think of them together mornings of World War II: in the pale dawn he comes to my war-widow bedroom, takes the fussing baby from his crib, carries him to the kitchen. Changes him, feeds him pablum, warms the bottle. Every morning the two of them alone, chuckling, chatting, the world going up in flame. Five forty-five A.M. he comes back to my room, thrusts the baby into my sleepy arms. Get up now, he commands, take care of Matthew. Matt wailing after him in loss.

"Why does he want to be a bum?" he asks, grief in his quick eye.

"Oh, he's not a bum," I protest. "He supports himself. He's not on welfare."

He drops bits of laughter. To him it is an outrage: the clothes from Goodwill, torn shoes, shabby jackets. Vagabonding: fishing in Mendocino, carpentering in Ann Arbor.

"He needs to explore," I argue. "In another time, he would have pioneered. He would have left home, wherever it was. Just like you did, leaving home at eighteen."

"I worked. I wanted to be something, make something of myself. I didn't want to be poor." The words are sharp. He knows the ugliness of poverty. "I wanted. . . ." His hands grow still on the table, his words fall away.

And that, too, I remember: him sitting in the dining room at the round oak table he had made himself, the great dictionary open before him, paper under his left hand, right hand making the high flourishes of the capitals, bold swellings of the lower loops, practicing the foreign words, practicing sentences. Left hand pushing through the thick hair, lower lip swelling with concentration. "Be quiet!" he shouted and we children retreated. Dunwoodie Institute, blue prints, perspectives, Sunday tours of new houses. Always making. Sawing pounding gluing. Yes, always. Making something. Plans, drawings, furniture. Houses. Himself.

And now his fist hits the table. The sugar bowl trembles, the cream shivers. "You gave him too much. They don't deserve what you give them." His mouth, shaking, seals to hardness, his chin pushes back against the folds of his neck. He stares a moment at his own crippled hand stopped on the table, his blue eyes wet.

"Oh, it isn't that. It's not that he's just spoiled," I say.

His gray head shakes negatively. "I don't meant that, I don't blame you, it's not just you. Or just him. All of them, all that education. That fellowship he could have had. What does he do? Throws it away. What do they want, anyway? They've had it too good, that's all."

She has come into the room, her feet moving cautiously along the waxed floor. She stands by the table, her eyes wide, holding to my chair for balance. "Oh, Matthew," she joins in, carolling. "He used to be with us so much, remember? It was Viet Nam ruined him." She smiles, appreciating her own sagacity.

His chair rasps backward. "Sit down," he orders loudly. "Eat something."

"I never eat till two o'clock," she informs him. "My pills, because of my pills." She watches to judge whether he understands as if she has given new facts. "I have to space my meals so my pills come out right." Behind her he shakes his head, despairing. The repetitions, repetitions! "Yes," she tells us again, "it was the war ruined Matthew."

"Ruined?" he bellows. "He isn't ruined!" He lurches away, goes to the stove, gets the coffee pot. But it is there between us, her word: ruined. Those wet jungles, mines, ambushes, night-time maneuvers. A young C.O.

medic, no gun. Friends killed, platoon wiped out, hepatitis. And we at home waiting without word, making our faith keep him alive. The silver star on the shelf. Ruined?

The long black stream of coffee fills our cups.

"Yah, and now that Ford." He gulps black coffee as if swallowing dark visions. "Hand-in-glove with the Wall Street crowd. He doesn't give a hoot about the poor people. And he can't manage anything. Look what happens in the U.N. A collection of bandits and murderers insulting us while they grab our aid. What they did to Israel! And what does Ford do? Nothing. Dances like Fred Astaire, bangs his head in a swimming pool!"

He cannot learn moderation. He is too old for such passions, ought to let go. At predictable times he suffers pains. His gut goes into spasm: nauseated, he cannot eat. He worries that there is something terribly wrong inside. He is hospitalized, tranquillized. Always his body's torments coincide with his grief: his beloved brother dies, Christmas bombings in Viet Nam, children starving in Africa, corruption in Washington, mass murders in California. And his stomach curdles with fury, despair.

"Dad, how are you feeling, how's your stomach?" I ask.

Red-cheeked, embarrassed, he thrusts back his chair, announces he has work to do in the garage. He is making a garden bench for a woman in Piedmont. "You visit with Mother for a while," he commands.

She is concentrating on the cookie plate, straightening the cookies, making a correct circle of them. I clear the dishes, begin to wash them. "Oh, don't bother with those, Marcia, I can do those," she says, another automatic convention. Only he does dishes now.

Then after I hang the damp towel on the oven bar we go to the living room. She lowers herself heavily into her chair. She pushes the lever, her legs ride up on the footpiece. Takes up her crocheting. "I like to crochet. It keeps my hands more limber." She does not look at me. "I've got this arthritis. My doctor says it's good to keep my fingers moving." Should I remind her I am her daughter, my husband is her doctor? No, nothing is required but that I listen. Dispute is pointless, facts have no function.

"Well." She sighs, "I've had a hard life. I had surgery twelve times." She is dreamy with old dramas. But twelve times? "Yes," I concede, "you've had some hard times."

"Have I told you about when Wendell was born?" her hands make jerky angles around the slender hook, the white chainings. Wendell, my brother.

"Yes, you've told me that story, many times, Mother."

"Have I?" Of course, she begins it again. "He thought I couldn't have children, that's why he married me. They tied my tubes, you know, when I was nineteen. On this side." Sad, negative nods. "The labor lasted three days. They walked me up and down the halls. Up and down, up and down. They threw the baby on the table. Dead." An audible inhaled breath, eyes profound with the past. "Another doctor came to help, went to the baby and worked on him. 'Forget the baby,' Doctor Schmidt said. 'Help me with this woman.' But the other one kept on with the baby. Three incisions in his head. Saved Wendell's life."

Why, out of the events of her seventy-six years of life, must she tell this story again and again? All terror, pain. When she forgets so much, why this one repeated tale? Does the deteriorating brain like our old slide projector stutter over some particular synapses, throw up a single frame, repeated, again and again?

"He." She is looking at me out of the corners of narrowed conspirator's eyes. "He never wanted children. How he yelled at me when I got that way. Once he threw me nearly across the room. . . ." The peaceful crocheting drops to her knees, one knobby arthritic hand grasping the other sweatered upper arm.

I need to stop her. "Mother, don't talk like that."

She huddles back into the chair, swift to sense rejection. Bitter, she gives it back. "Oh, you don't know. None of you know."

I get up, go to the television, pull the small brass button. The picture comes wavering into focus. "Look, isn't this your program now?"

She refuses distraction. "You don't know," she repeats brightly.

But my own memories defend. How he came home in work clothes pale with sawdust. His call, his laughter, lifting us up in strong arms, the cold winter breath of him against our faces. Turning us in somersaults, dancing us on his shoe-tops. Nights in the basement workshop, his singing saws, his hard hammers. Making things she needed, something she wanted.

"Mother, he was good, too. He worked all his life for his family."

"Ha." Her glance accuses me of disloyalty, ignorance. "The other day, he yelled and yelled at me."

"Hush, Mother, watch your program now."

"He writes all the time. He keeps writing things," she confides.

Yes, that is true. In his old age, he writes and writes. The letters fly to Sweden: his sister, his nephew. To Ann Arbor, Boston, Toledo, Hardwick—his grandchildren. To Minneapolis, his old friends. Sometimes they answer. Then he reads the letters aloud as we sit at the plastic-covered table in the sunshiney kitchen. Tears run down his cheeks.

"I found this letter he wrote. He thinks he is going to die." She scoffs as the idea. *He* die? He has never in his life been sick. It is *she* who is going to die.

"He is only thinking about you. He wants to provide for you." I turn back toward the television screen, pretend to watch. But she smiles, ironic disbelief. "Oh, he does terrible things. You don't know."

Can it be true? He is hot-tempered. She is stubborn, critical, difficult: she'd try anyone's patience. Does he yell in a frenzy of frustration? Give her a push now and then? Or is it a drama inside her head—confusion, dreams, paranoia? Why does she make him an enemy? He cleans her house, cooks her meals, washes her underwear.

I begin to talk without pause, narrate last week's small events, repeat old news about my children, her grandchildren, whom she cannot recall. Then at last the tv screen fills with a blue and green globe spinning in rich light. She smiles, wriggles back into the chair finding complete comfort, attends the screen. These are her people: these she remembers, these she loves.

I return to the kitchen and take out pots and pans, start the rice, wipe the chicken with a damp towel. He comes up from his workshop, watches. How much rice, how much onion, parsley, oregano? Salt? So: rice stuffing! How long does it bake? He found a good recipe in the paper, wants to share it. He goes through the cupboard drawer, finds the clipping. He copies the recipe on the back of an envelope. (That elegant hand, the loops and flourishes!) He hands it to me, grinning. Trading recipes! He is proud.

I am slicing carrots into a small pot. He makes that choppy, clumsy, beckoning gesture. Wants to show me something. He has taken a large black-covered book from the cupboard. A sort of ledger. I go sit at the table beside him.

"Look, what I've been doing." He turns back the stiff cover. On the pages of the book, photographs are fastened with bands of Scotch tape. Slowly he turns the pages. The photos are old, edges cracked, tones faded are mounted crookedly, clumsily, without regard for time or sequence. "I took all the pictures from all the drawers around here. I'm putting them all in here. Then we'll have them all in one place." He pushes one snapshot with a stained forefinger. "Look at this. Remember that trip we took?"

"Oh my gosh," I croon, tender over Wendell and me and him by a stone wall, the ranging high hills of pine in the distance. "When was that, nineteen-what?"

"Grand Marais, must have been 1937." He puts his finger on the lower edge of another. A color print. Of my mother. She stands before one of her rose bushes, one large peach-colored bloom cupped in her hand. The red tones of her auburn hair picked up by the ruddy, orange rose. She is plumped-cheeked, smiling. "Remember how she loved her flowers?" The calloused finger moves over the snapshot's surface, gentle. Another photo beside it, again she stands by her flower bed, several years later, a hat low on her brow. "She was a pretty woman," he mutters. "Smart, too. She sewed all your clothes, remember? Even your coats, Wendell's suits."

I study the photographs, hearing the choke in his words. I will not look at him.

"She wouldn't let me step inside the door with sawdust on my clothes, she was so fussy, so clean." His laugh is giddy, apologetic. He pushes knuckles against the wet trails on his cheeks. He finds a gruff tone. "That Wendell. Why can't he write? She looks for a letter every day." In the photograph, Wendell wears knickers, floppy cap, big front teeth. "Think, he's fifty now. At least a postcard."

The pages move again, giving irregular portions of our lives. Reminding of what we loved, of what we must remember to honor in the name of what was.

"This is a nice one," he points out. I have not seen the picture before. A young woman, small, her hair almost too heavy for the delicate head, stands in the curve of a young man's arm. Her white dress, blown by wind, curves around slender hips, lifts above slender ankles. His hair tumbles over a high brow, he is straight shouldered, lean. They look happy, perfectly confident, happy! "That was the year we got married. 1919."

In the seven o'clock evening, I lean over her chair, kiss her cheek. He follows to the door, steps out to the roofed-over entry. Dark is dropping into the dusk, and in its fall the street lamp on the corner brightens. In the antique light, he seems tired. He thanks me for coming. I say I will come next week. On Tuesday, as usual, he breathes deeply in, out, touches my shoulder. Then suddenly confesses, "Marcia, it can't go much longer, like this. With her like this."

Then we hold each other in a clumsy hug. What is there to do? The air is chilly, night has come. At home my family waits. He walks with me to the car and stands at the curb. Moving down the avenue I look back, and in the circle of light under the street lamp he is waving goodbye.

Ann Beattie
(b. 1947)

Born in Washington, D.C., Ann Beattie earned a B.A. at American University in Washington and an M.A. at the University of Connecticut. A recipient of a Guggenheim Fellowship and an award from the American Academy of Arts and Letters, she has taught creative writing at the University of Virginia and Harvard. Currently she lives in Charlottesville, Virginia, where she is at work on her fourth novel. Among her books are four collections of stories, *Distortions* (1976), *Secrets and Surprises* (1978), *The Burning House* (1982), and *Where You'll Find Me* (1986), and the novels *Chilly Scenes of Winter* (1976), *Falling in Place* (1980), and *Love Always* (1985). In the film adaptation of *Chilly Scenes of Winter*, which was titled *Head Over Heels*, she played the role of a waitress.

AFLOAT

Annie brings a hand-delivered letter to her father. They stand together on the deck that extends far over the grassy lawn that slopes to the lake, and he reads and she looks off at the water. When she was a little girl she would stand on the metal table pushed to the front of the deck and read the letters aloud to her father. If he sat, she sat. Later, she read them over his shoulder. Now she is sixteen, and she gives him the letter and stares at the trees or the water or the boat bobbing at the end of the dock. It has probably never occurred to her that she does not have to be there when he reads them.

Dear Jerome,

Last week the bottom fell out of the birdhouse you hung in the tree the summer Annie was three. Or something gnawed at it and the bottom came out. I don't know. I put the wood under one of the big clay pots full of pansies, just to keep it for old times' sake. (I've given up the fountain pen for a felt-tip. I'm really not a romantic.) I send to you for a month our daughter. She still wears bangs, to cover that little nick in her forehead from the time she fell out of the swing. The swing survived until last summer when—or maybe I told you in last year's letter—Marcy Smith came by with her "friend" Hamilton, and they were so taken by it that I gave it to them, leaving the ropes dangling. I mean that I gave them the old green swing seat, with the decals of roses even uglier than the scraggly ones we grew. Tell her to pull her bangs back and show the world her beautiful widow's peak. She now drinks spritzers. For the first two weeks she's gone I'll be in Ogunquit with Zack. He is younger than you, but no one will ever duplicate the effect of your slow smile. Have a good summer together. I will be thinking of you at unexpected times (unexpected to me, of course).

Love,
Anita

He hands the letter on to me, and then pours club soda and Chablis into a tall glass for Annie and fills his own glass with wine alone. He hesitates while I read, and I know he's wondering whether the letter will disturb me—whether I'll want club soda or wine. "Soda," I say. Jerome and Anita have been divorced for ten years.

In these first few days of Annie's visit, things aren't going very well. My friends think that it's just about everybody's summer story. Rachel's summers are spent with her ex-husband, and with his daughter by his second marriage, the daughter's boyfriend, and the boyfriend's best friend. The golden retriever isn't there this summer, because last summer he drowned. No one knows how. Jean is letting her optometrist, with whom she once had an affair, stay in her house in the Hamptons on weekends. She stays in town, because she is in love with a chef. Hazel's the exception. She teaches summer school, and when it ends she and her husband and their son go to Block Island for two weeks, to the house they always rent. Her husband has his job back, after a year in A. A. I study her life and wonder how it works. Of the three best friends I have, she blushes the most easily, is the worst dressed, is the least politically informed, and prefers AM rock stations to FM classical music. Our common denominator is that none of us was married in a church and all of us worried about the results of the blood test we had before we could get a marriage license. But there are so many differences. Say their names to me and what comes to mind is that Rachel cried when she heard Dylan's *Self Portrait* album, because, to her, that meant that everything was over; Jean fought off a man in a supermarket parking lot who was intent on raping her, and still has nightmares about the arugula she was going to the store to get; Hazel can recite Yeats's "The Circus Animals' Desertion" and bring tears to your eyes.

Sitting on the deck, I try to explain to Annie that there *should* be solidarity between women, but that when you look for a common bond you're really looking for a common denominator, and you can't do that with women. Annie puts down *My Mother/My Self* and looks out at the water.

Jerome and I, wondering when she will ever want to swim, go about our days as usual. She's gone biking with him, so there's no hostility. She has always sat at the foot of the bed while Jerome was showering at night and talked nonsense with me while she twisted the ends of her hair, and she still does. At her age, it isn't important that she's not in love, and she was once before anyway. When she pours for herself, it's sixty-forty white wine and club soda. Annie—the baby pushed in a swing. The bottom fell out of the birdhouse. Anita really knows how to hit below the belt.

Jerome is sulky at the end of the week, floating in the Whaler.

"Do you ever think that Anita's thinking of you?" I ask.

"Telepathy, you mean?" he says. He has a good tan. A scab by his elbow. Somehow, he's hurt himself. His wet hair is drying in curly strands. He hasn't had a haircut since we came to the summer house.

"No. Do you ever wonder if she just might be thinking about you?"

"I don't think about her," he says.

"You read the letter Annie brings you every year."

"I'm curious."

"Just curious for that one brief minute?"

Yes, he nods. "Notice that I'm always the one that opens the junk mail, too," he says.

According to Jerome, he and Anita gradually drifted apart. Or, at times when he blames himself, he says it's because he was still a child when he married her. He married her the week of his twentieth birthday. He says that his childhood wounds still weren't healed; Anita was Mama, she was the person he always felt he had to prove himself to—the stuff any psychiatrist will run down for you, he says now, trailing his hand in the water. "It's like there was a time in your life when you believed in paste," he says. "Think how embarrassed you'd be to go buy paste today. Now it's rubber cement. Or at least Elmer's glue. When I was young I just didn't know things."

I never had any doubt when things ended with my first husband. We knew things were wrong; we were going to a counselor and either biting our tongues or arguing because we'd loosened them with too much alcohol, trying to pretend that it didn't matter that I couldn't have a baby. One weekend Dan and I went to Saratoga, early in the spring, to visit friends. It was all a little too sun-dappled. Too *House Beautiful*, the way the sun, in the early morning, shone through the lace curtains and paled the walls to polka dots of light. The redwood picnic table on the stone-covered patio was as bright in the sunlight as if it had been waxed. We were drinking iced tea, all four of us out in the yard early in the morning, amazed at what a perfect day it was, how fast the garden was growing, how huge the heads of the peonies were. Then some people stopped by, with their little girl—people new to Saratoga, who really had no friends there yet. The little girl was named Alison, and she took a liking to Dan—came up to him without hesitation, the way a puppy that's been chastised will instantly choose someone in the room to cower by, or a bee will zero in on one member of a group. She came innocently, the way a child would come, fascinated by . . . by his curly hair? The way the sunlight reflected off the rims of his glasses? The wedding ring on his hand as he rested his arm on the picnic table? And then, as the rest of us talked, there was a squealing game, with the child suddenly climbing from the ground to his lap, some whispering, some laughing, and then the child, held around her middle, raised above his head, parallel to the ground. The game went on and on, with cries of "Again!" and "Higher!" until the child was shrill and Dan complained of numb arms, and for a second I looked away from the conversation the rest of us were having and I saw her raised above him, smiling down, and Dan both frowning and amused—that little smile at the edge of his lips—and the child's mouth, wide with delight, her long blond hair flopped forward. He was keeping her raised off the ground, and she was hoping that it would never end, and in that second I knew that for Dan and me it was over.

We took a big bunch of pink peonies back to the city with us, stuck in a glass jar with water in the bottom that I held wedged between my feet. I had on a skirt, and the flowers flopped as we went over the bumpy road and the sensation I felt was amazing: it wasn't a tickle, but a pain. When he stopped for gas I went into the bathroom and cried and washed my face and dried it on one of those brown paper towels that smell more strongly than any perfume. I combed my hair. When I was sure I looked fine I came back to the car and sat down, putting one foot on each side of the jar. He started to drive out of the gas station, and then he just drifted to a stop. It was still sunny. Late afternoon. We sat there with the sun heating us and other cars pulling around our car, and he said, "You are impossible. You are so emotional. After a perfect day, what have you been crying about?" Then there were tears, and since I said nothing, eventually he started to drive: out into the merging lane, then onto the highway, speeding all the way back to New York in silence. It was already over. The only other thing I remember about that day is that down by Thirty-fourth Street we saw the same man who had been there the week before, selling roses guaranteed to smell sweet and to be everlasting. There he was, in the same place, his roses on a stand behind him.

We swim, and gradually work our way back to the gunwale of the Whaler: six hands, white-knuckled, holding the rim. I slide along, hand over hand, then move so that my body touches Jerome's from behind. With my arms around his chest, I kiss his neck. He turns and smiles and kisses me. Then I kick away and go to where Annie is holding on to the boat, her cheek on her hands, staring at her father. I swim up to her, push her wet bangs to one side, and kiss her forehead. She looks aggravated, and turns her head away. Just as quickly, she turns it back. "Am I interrupting you two getting it on out here?" she says.

"I kissed both of you," I say, between them again, feeling the weightlessness of my legs dangling as I hold on.

She continues to stare at me. "Girls kissing girls is so dumb," she says. "It's like the world's full of stupid hostesses who graduated from Sweet Briar."

Jerome looks at her silently for a long time.

"I guess your mother's not very demonstrative," he says.

"Were you ever?" she says. "Did you love Anita when you had me?"

"Of course I did," he says. "Didn't you know that?"

"It doesn't matter what I know," she says, as angry and petulant as a child. "How come you don't feed me birdseed?" she says. "How come you don't feed the carrier pigeon?"

He pauses until he understands what she is talking about. "The letters just go one way," he says.

"Do you have too much *dignity* to answer them, or is it too risky to reveal anything?"

"Honey," he says, lowering his voice, "I don't have anything to say."

"That you loved her and now you don't?" she says. "That's what isn't worth saying?"

He's brought his knees up to his chin. The scab by his elbow is pale when he clasps his arm around his knees.

"Well, I think that's bullshit," she says. She looks at me. "And I think you're bullshit, too. You don't care about the bond between women. You just care about hanging on to him. When you kissed me, it was patronizing."

There are tears now. Tears that are ironic, because there is so much water everywhere. Today she's angry and alone, and I float between them knowing exactly how each one feels and, like the little girl Alison suspended above Dan's head, knowing that desire that can be more overwhelming than love—the desire, for one brief minute, simply to get off the earth.

David Low

(b. 1952)

A resident of the East Village in Manhattan, David Low grew up in the borough of Queens. Currently he is working on a novel about a Chinese-American family and editing travel guides. He earned a B.A. at Wesleyan University and an M.A. at Brown University, and has received a Wallace Stegner Creative Writing Fellowship from Stanford University, a National Endowment for the Arts Writing Fellowship, and a New York State CAPS Writing Grant. A fellow at Yaddo and the MacDowell Colony, he has published stories in *Ploughshares, Kansas Quarterly,* and *Mississippi Review*, as well as in a textbook titled *Elements of Literature.*

WINTERBLOSSOM GARDEN

I have no photographs of my father. One hot Saturday in June, my camera slung over my shoulder, I take the subway from Greenwich Village to Chinatown. I switch to the M local which becomes an elevated train after it crosses the Williamsburg Bridge. I am going to Ridgewood, Queens, where I spent my childhood. I sit in a car that is almost empty; I feel the loud rumble of the whole train through the hard seat. Someday, I think, wiping the sweat from my face, they'll tear this el down, as they've torn down the others.

I get off at Fresh Pond Road and walk the five blocks

from the station to my parents' restaurant. At the back of the store in the kitchen, I find my father packing an order: white cartons of food fit neatly into a brown paper bag. As the workers chatter in Cantonese, I smell the food cooking: spare ribs, chicken lo mein, sweet and pungent pork, won ton soup. My father, who has just turned seventy-three, wears a wrinkled white short-sleeve shirt and a cheap maroon tie, even in this weather. He dabs his face with a handkerchief.

"Do you need money?" he asks in Chinese, as he takes the order to the front of the store. I notice that he walks slower than usual. Not that his walk is ever very fast; he usually walks with quiet assurance, a man who knows who he is and where he is going. Other people will just have to wait until he gets there.

"Not this time," I answer in English. I laugh. I haven't borrowed money from him in years but he still asks. My father and I have almost always spoken different languages.

"I want to take your picture, Dad."

"Not now, too busy." He hands the customer the order and rings the cash register.

"It will only take a minute."

He stands reluctantly beneath the green awning in front of the store, next to the gold-painted letters on the window:

WINTERBLOSSOM GARDEN
CHINESE-AMERICAN RESTAURANT
WE SERVE THE FINEST FOOD

I look through the camera viewfinder.

"Smile," I say.

Instead my father holds his left hand with the crooked pinky on his stomach. I have often wondered about that pinky; is it a souvenir of some street fight in his youth? He wears a jade ring on his index finger. His hair, streaked with gray, is greased down as usual; his face looks a little pale. Most of the day, he remains at the restaurant. I snap the shutter.

"Go see your mother," he says slowly in English.

According to my mother, in 1929 my father entered this country illegally by jumping off the boat as it neared Ellis Island and swimming to Hoboken, New Jersey;

there he managed to board a train to New York, even though he knew no English and had not one American cent in his pockets. Whether or not the story is true, I like to imagine my father hiding in the washroom on the train, dripping wet with fatigue and feeling triumphant. Now he was in America, where anything could happen. He found a job scooping ice cream at a dance hall in Chinatown. My mother claims that before he married her, he liked to gamble his nights away and drink with scandalous women. After two years in this country, he opened his restaurant with money he had borrowed from friends in Chinatown who already ran their own businesses. My father chose Ridgewood for the store's location because he mistook the community's name for "Richwood." In such a lucky place, he told my mother, his restaurant was sure to succeed.

When I was growing up, my parents spent most of their days in Winterblossom Garden. Before going home after school, I would stop at the restaurant. The walls then were a hideous pale green with red numbers painted in Chinese characters and Roman numerals above the side booths. In days of warm weather huge fans whirred from the ceiling. My mother would sit at a table in the back where she would make egg rolls. She began by placing generous handfuls of meat-and-cabbage filling on squares of thin white dough. Then she delicately folded up each piece of dough, checking to make sure the filling was totally sealed inside, like a mummy wrapped in bandages. Finally, with a small brush she spread beaten eggs on the outside of each white roll. As I watched her steadily produce a tray of these uncooked creations, she never asked me about school; she was more concerned that my shirt was sticking out of my pants or that my hair was disheveled.

"Are you hungry?" my mother would ask in English. Although my parents had agreed to speak only Chinese in my presence, she often broke this rule when my father wasn't in the same room. Whether I wanted to eat or not, I was sent into the kitchen where my father would repeat my mother's question. Then without waiting for an answer, he would prepare for me a bowl of beef with snow peas or a small portion of steamed fish. My parents assumed that as long as I ate well, everything in my life would be fine. If I said "Hello" or "Thank you" in Chinese, I was allowed to choose whatever dish I liked; often I ordered a hot turkey sandwich. I liked the taste of burnt rice soaked in tea.

I would wait an hour or so for my mother to walk home with me. During that time, I would go to the front of the store, put a dime in the jukebox and press the buttons for a currently popular song. It might be D3: "Bye Bye, Love." Then I would lean on the back of the bench where customers waited for take-outs; I would stare out the large window that faced the street. The world outside seemed vast, hostile and often sad.

Across the way, I could see Rosa's Italian Bakery, the Western Union office and Von Ronn's soda fountain. Why didn't we live in Chinatown? I wondered. Or San Francisco? In a neighborhood that was predominantly German, I had no Chinese friends. No matter how many bottles of Coca-Cola I drank, I would still be different from the others. They were fond of calling me "Skinny Chink" when I won games of stoop ball. I wanted to have blond curly hair and blue eyes; I didn't understand why my father didn't have a ranch like the rugged cowboys on television.

Now Winterblossom Garden has wood-paneling on the walls, formica tables and aluminum Roman numerals over the mock-leather booths. Several years ago, when the ceiling was lowered, the whirring fans were removed; a huge air-conditioning unit was installed. The jukebox has been replaced by Muzak. My mother no longer makes the egg rolls; my father hires enough help to do that.

Some things remain the same. My father has made few changes in the menu, except for the prices; the steady customers know they can always have the combination plates. In a glass case near the cash register, cardboard boxes overflow with bags of fortune cookies and almond candies that my father gives away free to children. The first dollar bill my parents ever made hangs framed on the wall above the register. Next to that dollar, a picture of my parents taken twenty years ago recalls a time when they were raising four children at once, paying mortgages and putting in the bank every cent that didn't go toward bills. Although it was a hard time for them, my mother's face is radiant, as if she has just won the top prize at a beauty pageant; she wears a flower-print dress with a large white collar. My father has on a suit with wide lapels that was tailored in Chinatown; he is smiling a rare smile.

My parents have a small brick house set apart from the other buildings on the block. Most of their neighbors have lived in Ridgewood all their lives. As I ring the bell and wait for my mother to answer, I notice that the maple tree in front of the house has died. All that is left is a gray ghost; bare branches lie in the gutter. If I took a picture of this tree, I think, the printed image would resemble a negative.

"The gas man killed it when they tore up the street," my mother says. She watches television as she lies back on the gold sofa like a queen, her head resting against a pillow. A documentary about wildlife in Africa is on the screen; gazelles dance across a dusty plain. My mother likes soap operas but they aren't shown on weekends. In the evenings she will watch almost anything except news specials and police melodramas.

"Why don't you get a new tree planted?"

"We would have to get a permit," she answers. "The sidewalk belongs to the city. Then we would have to pay for the tree."

"It would be worth it," I say. "Doesn't it bother you, seeing a dead tree everyday? You should find someone to cut it down."

My mother does not answer. She has fallen asleep. These days she can doze off almost as soon as her head touches the pillow. Six years ago she had a nervous breakdown. When she came home from the hospital she needed to take naps in the afternoon. Soon the naps became a permanent refuge, a way to forget her loneliness for an hour or two. She no longer needed to work in the store. Three of her children were married. I was away at art school and planned to live on my own when I graduated.

"I have never felt at home in America," my mother once told me.

Now as she lies there, I wonder if she is dreaming. I would like her to tell me her darkest dream. Although we speak the same language, there has always been an ocean between us. She does not wish to know what I think alone at night, what I see of the world with my camera.

My mother pours two cups of tea from the porcelain teapot that has always been in its wicker basket on the kitchen table. On the side of the teapot, a maiden dressed in a jade-green gown visits a bearded emperor at his palace near the sky. The maiden waves a vermillion fan.

"I bet you still don't know how to cook," my mother says. She places a plate of steamed roast pork buns before me.

"Mom, I'm not hungry."

"If you don't eat more, you will get sick."

I take a bun from the plate but it is too hot. My mother hands me a napkin so I can put the bun down. Then she peels a banana in front of me.

"I'm not obsessed with food like you," I say.

"What's wrong with eating?"

She looks at me as she takes a big bite of the banana.

"I'm going to have a photography show at the end of the summer."

"Are you still taking pictures of old buildings falling down? How ugly! Why don't you take happier pictures?"

"I thought you would want to come," I answer. "It's not easy to get a gallery."

"If you were married," she says, her voice becoming unusually soft, "you would take better pictures. You would be happy."

"I don't know what you mean. Why do you think getting married will make me happy?"

My mother looks at me as if I have spoken in Serbo-Croatian. She always gives me this look when I say something she does not want to hear. She finishes the banana; then she puts the plate of food away. Soon she stands at the sink, turns on the hot water and washes dishes. My mother learned long ago that silence has a power of its own.

She takes out a blue cookie tin from the dining room cabinet. Inside this tin, my mother keeps her favorite photographs. Whenever I am ready to leave, my mother brings it to the living room and opens it on the coffee table. She knows I cannot resist looking at these pictures again; I will sit down next to her on the sofa for at least another hour. Besides the portraits of the family, my mother has images of people I have never met; her father who owned a poultry store on Pell Street and didn't get a chance to return to China before he died; my father's younger sister who still runs a pharmacy in Rio de Janeiro (she sends the family an annual supply of cough drops); my mother's cousin Kay who died at thirty, a year after she came to New York from Hong Kong. Although my mother has a story to tell for each photograph, she refuses to speak about Kay, as if the mere mention of her name will bring back her ghost to haunt us all.

My mother always manages to find a picture I have not seen before; suddenly I discover I have a relative who is a mortician in Vancouver. I pick up a portrait of Uncle Lao-Hu, a silver-haired man with a goatee who owned a curio shop on Mott Street until he retired last year and moved to Hawaii. In a color print, he stands in the doorway of his store, holding a bamboo Moon Man in front of him, as if it were a bowling trophy. The statue, which is actually two feet tall, has a staff in its left hand, while its right palm balances a peach, a sign of long life. The top of the Moon Man's head protrudes in the shape of an eggplant; my mother believes that such a head contains an endless wealth of wisdom.

"Your Uncle Lao-Hu is a wise man, too," my mother says, "except when he's in love. When he still owned the store, he fell in love with his women customers all the time. He was always losing money because he gave away his merchandise to any woman who smiled at him."

I see my uncle's generous arms full of gifts: a silver Buddha, an ivory dragon, a pair of emerald chopsticks.

"These women confused him," she adds. "That's what happens when a Chinese man doesn't get married."

My mother shakes her head and sighs.

"In his last letter, Lao-Hu invited me to visit him in Honolulu. Your father refuses to leave the store."

"Why don't you go anyway?"

"I can't leave your father alone." She stares at the pictures scattered on the coffee table.

"Mom, why don't you do something for yourself? I thought you were going to start taking English lessons."

"Your father thinks it would be a waste of time."

While my mother puts the cookie tin away, I stand up to stretch my legs. I gaze at a photograph that hangs on the wall above the sofa: my parents' wedding picture. My mother was matched to my father; she claims that if her own father had been able to repay the money that Dad spent to bring her to America, she might never have married him at all. In the wedding picture she wears a stunned expression. She is dressed in a luminous gown of ruffles and lace; the train spirals at her feet. As she clutches a bouquet tightly against her stomach, she might be asking, "What am I doing? Who is this man?" My father's face is thinner than it is now. His tuxedo is too small for him; the flower in his lapel droops. He hides his hand with the crooked pinky behind his back.

I have never been sure if my parents really love each other. I have only seen them kiss at their children's weddings. They never touch each other in public. When I was little, I often thought they went to sleep in the clothes they wore to work.

Before I leave, my mother asks me to take her picture. Unlike my father she likes to pose for photographs as much as possible. When her children still lived at home, she would leave snapshots of herself all around the house; we could not forget her, no matter how hard we tried.

She changes her blouse, combs her hair and redoes her eyebrows. Then I follow her out the back door into the garden where she kneels down next to the rose bush. She touches one of the yellow roses.

"Why don't you sit on the front steps?" I ask, as I peer through the viewfinder. "It will be more natural."

"No," she says firmly. "Take the picture now."

She smiles without opening her mouth. I see for the first time that she has put on a pair of dangling gold earrings. Her face has grown round as the moon with the years. She has developed wrinkles under the eyes, but like my father, she hardly shows her age. For the past ten years, she has been fifty-one. Everyone needs a fantasy to help them stay alive: my mother believes she is perpetually beautiful, even if my father has not complimented her in years.

After I snap the shutter, she plucks a rose.

As we enter the kitchen through the back door, I can hear my father's voice from the next room.

"Who's he talking to?" I ask.

"He's talking to the goldfish," she answers. "I have to live with this man."

My father walks in, carrying a tiny can of fish food.

"You want a girlfriend?" he asks, out of nowhere. "My friend has a nice daughter. She knows how to cook Chinese food."

"Dad, she sounds perfect for you."

"She likes to stay home," my mother adds. "She went to college and reads books like you."

"I'll see you next year," I say.

That evening in the darkroom at my apartment, I develop and print my parents' portraits. I hang the pictures side by side to dry on a clothesline in the bathroom. As I feel my parents' eyes staring at me, I turn away. Their faces look unfamiliar in the fluorescent light.

II

At the beginning of July my mother calls me at work.

"Do you think you can take off next Monday morning?" she asks.

"Why?"

"Your father has to go to the hospital for some tests. He looks awful."

We sit in the back of a taxi on the way to a hospital in Forest Hills. I am sandwiched between my mother and father. The skin of my father's face is pale yellow. During the past few weeks he has lost fifteen pounds; his wrinkled suit is baggy around the waist. My mother sleeps with her head tilted to one side until the taxi hits a bump on the road. She wakes up startled, as if afraid she has missed a stop on the train.

"Don't worry," my father says weakly. He squints as he turns his head toward the window. "The doctors will give me pills. Everything will be fine."

"Don't say anything," my mother says. "Too much talk will bring bad luck."

My father takes two crumpled dollar bills from his jacket and places them in my hand.

"For the movies," he says. I smile, without mentioning it costs more to go to a film these days.

My mother opens her handbag and takes out a compact. She has forgotten to put on her lipstick.

The hospital waiting room has beige walls. My mother and I follow my father as he makes his way slowly to a row of seats near an open window.

"Fresh air is important," he used to remind me on a sunny day when I would read a book in bed. Now after we sit down, he keeps quiet. I hear the sound of plates clattering from the coffee shop in the next room.

"Does anyone want some breakfast?" I ask.

"Your father can't eat anything before the tests," my mother warns.

"What about you?"

"I'm not hungry," she says.

My father reaches over to take my hand in his. He considers my palm.

"Very, very lucky," he says. "You will have lots of money."

I laugh. "You've been saying that ever since I was born."

He puts on his glasses crookedly and touches a curved line near the top of my palm.

"Be patient," he says.

My mother rises suddenly.

"Why are they making us wait so long? Do you think they forgot us?"

While she walks over to speak to a nurse at the reception desk, my father leans toward me.

"Remember to take care of your mother."

The doctors discover that my father has stomach cancer. They decide to operate immediately. According to them, my father has already lost so much blood that it is a miracle he is still alive.

The week of my father's operation, I sleep at my parents' house. My mother has kept my bedroom on the second floor the way it was before I moved out. A square room, it gets the afternoon light. Dust covers the top of my old bookcase. The first night I stay over I find a pinhole camera on a shelf in the closet; I made it when I was twelve from a cylindrical Quaker Oats box. When I lie back on the yellow comforter that covers my bed, I see the crack in the ceiling that I once called the Yangtze River, the highway for tea merchants and vagabonds.

At night I help my mother close the restaurant. I do what she and my father have done together for the past forty-three years. At ten o'clock I turn off the illuminated white sign above the front entrance. After all the customers leave and the last waiter says goodbye, I lock the front door and flip over the sign that says "Closed." Then I shut off the radio and the back lights. While I refill the glass case with bottles of duck sauce and packs of cigarettes, my mother empties the cash register. She puts all the money in white cartons and packs them in brown paper bags. My father thought up that idea long ago.

In the past when they have walked the three blocks home, they have given the appearance of carrying bags of food. The one time my father was attacked by three teenagers, my mother was sick in bed. My father scared the kids off by pretending he knew kung fu. When he got home, he showed me his swollen left hand and smiled.

"Don't tell your mother."

On the second night we walk home together, my mother says:

"I could never run the restaurant alone. I would have to sell it. I have four children and no one wants it."

I say nothing, unwilling to start an argument.

Later my mother and I eat jello in the kitchen. A cool breeze blows through the window.

"Maybe I will sleep tonight," my mother says. She walks out to the back porch to sit on one of the two folding chairs. My bedroom is right above the porch; as a child I used to hear my parents talking late into the night, their paper fans rustling.

After reading a while in the living room, I go upstairs to take a shower. When I am finished, I hear my mother calling my name from downstairs.

I find her dressed in her bathrobe, opening the dining room cabinet.

"Someone has stolen the money," she says. She walks nervously into the living room and looks under the lamp table.

"What are you talking about?" I ask.

"Maybe we should call the police," she suggests. "I can't find the money we brought home tonight."

She starts to pick up the phone.

"Wait. Have you checked everywhere? Where do you usually put it?"

"I thought I locked it in your father's closet but it isn't there."

"I'll look around," I say. "Why don't you go back to sleep?"

She lies back on the sofa.

"How can I sleep?" she asks. "I told your father a long time ago to sell the restaurant but he wouldn't listen."

I search the first floor. I look in the shoe closet, behind the television, underneath the dining room table, in the clothes hamper. Finally after examining all the kitchen cupboards without any luck, I open the refrigerator to take out something to drink. The three cartons of money are on the second shelf, next to the mayonnaise and the strawberry jam.

When I bring the cartons to the living room, my mother sits up on the sofa, amazed.

"Well," she says, "how did they ever get *there*?"

She opens one of them. The crisp dollar bills inside are cold as ice.

The next day I talk on the telephone to my father's physician. He informs me that the doctors have succeeded in removing the malignancy before it has spread. My father will remain in intensive care for at least a week.

In the kitchen my mother irons a tablecloth.

"The doctors are impressed by Dad's willpower, considering his age," I tell her.

"A fortune teller on East Broadway told him that he will live to be a hundred," she says.

That night I dream that I am standing at the entrance to Winterblossom Garden. A taxi stops in front of the store. My father jumps out, dressed in a bathrobe and slippers.

"I'm almost all better," he tells me. "I want to see how the business is doing without me."

In a month my father is ready to come home. My sister Elizabeth, the oldest child, picks him up at the hospital. At the house the whole family waits for him.

When Elizabeth's car arrives my mother and I are already standing on the front steps. My sister walks around the car to open my father's door. He cannot get out by himself. My sister offers him a hand but as he reaches out to grab it, he misses and falls back in his seat.

Finally my sister helps him stand up, his back a little stooped. While my mother remains on the steps, I run to give a hand.

My father does not fight our help. His skin is dry and pale but no longer yellow. As he walks forward, staring at his feet, I feel his whole body shaking against mine. Only now, as he leans his weight on my arm, do I begin to understand how easily my father might have died. He seems light as a sparrow.

When we reach the front steps, my father raises his head to look at my mother. She stares at him a minute, then turns away to open the door. Soon my sister and I are leading him to the living room sofa, where we help him lie back. My mother has a pillow and a blanket ready. She sits down on the coffee table in front of him. I watch them hold each other's hands.

III

At the beginning of September my photography exhibit opens at a cooperative gallery on West 13th Street. I have chosen to hang only a dozen pictures, not much to show for ten years of work. About sixty people come to the opening, more than I expected; I watch them from a corner of the room, now and then overhearing a conversation I would like to ignore.

After an hour I decide I have stayed too long. As I walk around the gallery, hunting for a telephone, I see my parents across the room. My father calls out my name in Chinese; he has gained back all his weight and appears to be in better shape than many of the people around him. As I make my way toward my parents, I hear him talking loudly in bad English to a short young woman who stares at one of my portraits.

"That's my wife," he says. "If you like it, you should buy it."

"Maybe I will," the young woman says. She points to another photograph. "Isn't that you?"

My father laughs. "No, that's my brother."

My mother hands me a brown paper bag.

"Leftover from dinner," she tells me. "You didn't tell me you were going to show my picture. It's the best one in the show."

I take my parents for a personal tour.

"Who is that?" my father asks. He stops at a photograph of a naked woman covered from the waist down by a pile of leaves as she sits in the middle of a forest.

"She's a professional model," I lie.

"She needs to gain some weight," my mother says.

A few weeks after my show has closed, I have lunch with my parents at the restaurant. After we finish our meal, my father walks into the kitchen to scoop ice cream for dessert. My mother opens her handbag. She takes out a worn manila envelope and hands it to me across the table.

"I found this in a box while I was cleaning the house," she says. "I want you to have it."

Inside the envelope, I find a portrait of my father, taken when he was still a young man. He does not smile but his eyes shine like wet black marbles. He wears a polka-dot tie; a plaid handkerchief hangs out of the front pocket of his suit jacket. My father has never cared about his clothes matching. Even when he was young, he liked to grease down his hair with brilliantine.

"Your father's cousin was a doctor in Hong Kong," my mother tells me. "After my eighteenth birthday, he came to my parents' house and showed them this picture. He said your father would make the perfect husband because he was handsome and very smart. Grandma gave me the picture before I got on the boat to America."

"I'll have it framed right away."

My father returns with three dishes of chocolate ice cream balanced on a silver tray.

"You want to work here?" he asks me.

"Your father wants to sell the business next year," my mother says. "He feels too old to run a restaurant."

"I'd just lose money," I say. "Besides, Dad, you're not old."

He does not join us for dessert. Instead, he dips his napkin in a glass of water and starts to wipe the table. I watch his dish of ice cream melt.

When I am ready to leave, my parents walk me to the door.

"Next time, I'll take you uptown to see a movie," I say as we step outside.

"Radio City?" my father asks.

"They don't show movies there now," my mother reminds him.

"I'll cook dinner for you at my apartment."

My father laughs.

"We'll eat out," my mother suggests.

My parents wait in front of Winterblossom Garden

until I reach the end of the block. I turn and wave. With her heels on, my mother is the same height as my father. She waves back for both of them. I would like to take their picture, but I forgot to bring my camera.

Bobbie Ann Mason

(b. 1940)

Raised on a dairy farm near Mayfield, Kentucky, Bobbie Ann Mason received a B.A. from the University of Kentucky, an M.A. from the State University of New York at Binghamton, and a doctorate from the University of Connecticut. A recipient of a Guggenheim fellowship and grants from the National Endowment for the Arts and American Academy and Institute for Arts and Letters, she has taught English and journalism at Mansfield State College. Her stories, which have appeared in magazines such as *Atlantic Monthly, Ascent, The New Yorker, Redbook,* and *Vanity Fair,* have been selected for inclusion in the *Pushcart Prize* and *Best American Short Stories* series. They are collected in *Shiloh and Other Stories* (1982), which received the Ernest Hemingway Foundation Award for the Best Short Fiction of that year, and in *Love Life* (1989). She is the author of two novels: *In Country* (1985) and *Spence & Lila* (1988).

OLD THINGS

Cleo Watkins makes invisible, overlapping rings on the table with her cup as she talks.

"The kids just got off to school and I'm still in one piece," she says. "Last night we was up till all hours watching that special and my eyes is pasted together this morning. After the weekend we've been through, now everybody's going off and I'll be so lonesome all day!"

Cleo puts her elbow on the kitchen table and switches the receiver to the other ear. Her friend Rita Jean Wiggins says she had trouble getting her car started yesterday in time for church; it flooded and she had to let it sit for a while. Rita Jean is worried sick about her cat Dexter and is going to take him to the vet again. As Cleo listens, she notices that Tom Brokaw is introducing a guest who is going to talk about men as single parents. Cleo doesn't know whether to listen to Tom or Rita Jean. For a minute she loses the train of Rita Jean's story.

"Just a minute, I better turn this television down." Cleo crosses the kitchen and lowers the volume. "This house is such a mess," says Cleo, sitting down again. "And you don't know how embarrassing it all is—Linda's car here all the time, the kids going in and out. She's making an old woman out of me."

"Did she bring much from home?" Rita Jean asks.

"Mostly things the kids needed, and a lot of her clothes," Cleo says, watching the faces move on the television screen. "I told her wasn't no use carrying all that over here, they'd be going back before long, but she wouldn't listen. You can't walk here."

Rita Jean's voice is sympathetic. "I'm sure she'll get straightened out with Bob in no time."

"I don't know. Looks like she's moved in. She went to trade day out here at the stockyard, and she came back with the awfulest conglomeration you ever saw."

"What all did she get?"

"A rocking chair she's going to refinish, and a milk glass lamp, and some kind of whatnot, and a big grabbag —a box of junk you buy for a dollar and then there might be one thing in it you want. I never saw such par'phenalin."

"Was there anything in it she could use?" asks Rita Jean. Rita Jean, who has no children, is always intensely concerned about Cleo's family.

"She found a wood spoon she said was antique."

"People are antique-crazy."

"You're telling me." Cleo has spent years trying to get rid of things she has collected. After her husband died, she moved to town, to a little brick house with a dishwasher and wall-to-wall carpet. Cleo's two sons haven't mentioned it, but Linda says it's awful that Cleo has gotten rid of every reminder of Jake. There is nothing but the picture album left. All his suits were given away, and the rest of his things boxed up and sold. She gave away all his handkerchiefs, neatly washed and ironed. They were monogrammed with the initials RJW, for Robert Jacob Watkins. And now somebody with totally different initials is carrying them around and blowing his nose on them. Linda reminds her of this every so often but Cleo isn't sorry. She doesn't want to live in the past.

After talking to Rita Jean, Cleo cleans the house with unusual attention. The kids have scattered their things everywhere. Cleo hangs up Tammy's clothes and puts Davey's toys in the trunk Linda has brought. The trunk is yellow enamel with thin black swirls that make it look old. Linda has antiqued it.

Cleo pins patterns down on the length of material laid on the table. She is cutting out a set of cheerleader outfits that have to be done by next week. The cheerleader outfits are red and gray, made like bib overalls, with shorts. Everything is double seams, and the bibs have pockets with flaps.

"Get down from there, Prissy-Tail!" The cat has attacked the flimsy pattern and torn it. "You know you're not supposed to be on Mama's sewing." Cleo waves the scissors at Prissy-Tail, who scampers onto Cleo's shoulder. Cleo sets her down on a pillow, saying, "I can't cut out with you dancing on my shoulder." Prissy-Tail struts around on the divan, purring.

"I could tell you things that would sizzle your tailfeathers," Cleo says.

Cleo backs in the front door, pulling the storm door shut with her foot. On TV there is a wild west shoot-out, and the radio is blaring out an accompanying song with a heavy, driving beat. Tammy is talking on the telephone.

"What do you mean, what do I mean? Oh, you know what I mean. Anyway, we're at my grandmother's and my mother's going out tonight—Davey, quit it!—that was my little brother. He's a meanie. I just stuck my tongue out at him. Anyway, do you think he'll ask you or what? Unh-huh. That's what I thought."

Cleo stands in the hallway, adjusting to the sounds. Tammy's patter on the phone is meaningless to her. Linda had never done that. Linda had been such a quiet child. She hears Tammy speaking in a knowing tone.

"You know what April told Kevin? I nearly died! Kevin was going to ask her for her homework? And he said to her could she meet him at the Dairy Queen and she said she might and she might not, and he said to her could she carry him because his car was broke down? And she said he had legs, he could walk! I think he's mad at her."

"Watch out, Tammy, I'm coming through," says Cleo. Davey has returned to the television, and Tammy is sprawled out in the kitchen doorway. Tammy is wearing ripped bluejeans and a velour pullover with stripes down the sleeves. Tammy bends her knees so half the doorway is clear, and Cleo squeezes by, balancing the groceries on her hip.

Tammy hangs up and pokes into the grocery sack. "Chicken! Not again!"

"Chicken was ninety-nine cents a pound," says Cleo. "You better be glad you're where there's food on the table, kid."

"Ick! All that yellow fat."

"The yellower a chicken is, the better it is. That's how you tell when they're good. If they're blue they're not any 'count. Or if they've got spots."

"Oooh!" Tammy makes a twisted face. "Why can't you just buy it already fried!"

"Hah! We're lucky we don't have to pull the feathers off. I used to kill chickens, you know. Whack their heads off, dip 'em in boiling water, pick off the feathers. I'd like to see you pick a chicken!"

Cleo reaches around Tammy and hugs her. Tammy squeals. "Hey, why don't we just eat the cat?"

"Now you're going to hurt somebody's feelings," says Cleo, as Tammy squirms away from her.

Tammy prances out of the room and the noises return. The television; the radio; the buzz of the electric clock;

the whir of the furnace making its claim for attention. The kids never hear the noises. Kids never seem to care about anything anymore, Cleo thinks. Tammy had a complete toy kitchen, with a stove and refrigerator, when she was five, and she didn't care anything about it. It cost a fortune. Linda's children always make Cleo feel old.

"I'm old enough to be a grandmother," Rita Jean said early in their acquaintance. Rita Jean had lost her husband too.

"I think of you as a spring chicken," Cleo told her.

"You're not that much older than me. Louise Brown is two years younger than me, and she's a grandmother. Imagine, thirty-five and a grandmother."

"That makes me feel old."

"I feel old," said Rita Jean. "To think that the war could be that long ago."

Rita Jean's husband was twenty-one when he left for Vietnam. It was early in the war and nobody thought it would turn out so bad. She has a portrait on her dresser of a young man she hardly knew, a child almost. Now Rita Jean is old enough to be the mother of a boy like that.

Cleo told Rita Jean she could still get married and have a baby. She could start all over again.

"If anybody would have me," said Rita Jean.

"You don't try."

"Sometimes I think I'm just waiting to get into Senior Citizens."

"Listen to yourself," said Cleo. "That's the most ridiculous thing I ever heard. Why, *I'm* not but fifty-two."

"They say that's the prime of life," said Rita Jean.

"Where are you going, Mama? Tell me where you're going." Davey is pulling at Linda's belt.

"Oh, Davey, look. You're going to mess up Mama's outfit. I told you seven times, Shirley and me's going to Paducah to hear some music. It's not anything you're interested in, so don't be saying you want to go too."

Linda has washed her hair and put on a new pants suit, a tangerine color. Cleo knows Linda cannot afford it, but Linda always has to have the best.

Tammy, sitting with her legs propped up on the back of the divan, says, with mock surprise, "You mean you're going to miss *Charlie's Angels*? You ain't *never* missed *Charlie's Angels*!"

"Them younguns want you to stay home," Cleo says as Linda combs her hair. It is wet and falls in skinny black ringlets.

"I can't see what difference it makes." Linda lights a cigarette.

"These children need a daddy around."

"You're full of prunes if you think I'm going back to Bob!" Linda says, turning on the blow dryer. She raises her voice. "I don't feel like hanging around the same house with somebody that can go for three hours without saying a word. He might as well not be there."

"Hush. The children might hear you."

Linda works on her hair, holding out damp strands and brushing them under with the dryer to style them. Cleo admires the way her daughter keeps up her appearance. She can't imagine Bob would ever look at another woman when he has Linda. Cleo cannot believe Bob has mistreated Linda. It is just as though she has been told some wild tale about outer space, like something on a TV show.

Cleo says, "I bet he's just held in and held in till he's tight as a tick. People do that. I know you—impatient. Listen. A man takes care of a woman. But it works the other way round too. If he thinks you're not giving him enough loving, he'll draw up—just like a morning glory at evening. You think he's not paying any attention to you, but maybe you've been too busy for him."

Cleo knows Linda thinks she is silly. Daughters never believe their mothers. "You have to remember to give each other some loving," she says, her confidence fading. "Don't take each other for granted."

"Bob's no morning glory." Linda puts on lip gloss and works her lips together.

"You'll be wondering how to buy them kids fine things. You'll be off on your own, girl."

Linda says nothing. She examines her face in the mirror and picks at a speck on her cheek.

* * *

Davey gets his lessons on the floor in front of the television. He is learning a new kind of arithmetic Cleo has never heard of. Later, Cleo watches *Charlie's Angels* with Tammy, and after Tammy goes to bed, she watches the *10 O'Clock Report.* She tells herself that she has to wait up to unlock the doors for Linda. She has put a chain on the door, because young people are going wild, breaking in on defenseless older women. Cleo is afraid Linda's friend Shirley is a bad influence. Shirley had to get married and didn't finish school. Now she is divorced. She even let her husband have her kids, while she went gallivanting around. Cleo cannot imagine a mother giving her kids away. Shirley's husband moved to Alabama with the kids, and Shirley sees them only occasionally. On TV, Johnny Carson keeps breaking into the funny dance he does when a joke flops. Cleo usually gets a kick out of that, but it doesn't seem funny this time, with him repeating it so much. Johnny has been divorced twice, but now he is happily married. He is the stay-at-home type, she has read.

Cleo is well into the *Tomorrow* show, which is a disturbing discussion of teenage alcoholism, when Linda returns. Linda's cheeks are glowing and she looks happy.

"I thought Duke Ellington was dead," says Cleo, when Linda tells her about the concert.

"He is. But his brother leads the band. He directs the band like this." Linda makes her hands dive in fishlike movements. "He danced around, with his back to the audience, swaying along in a trance. He had on this dark pink suit the exact same color of Miss Imogene's panties that time in fifth grade—when she fell off the desk?"

Cleo groans. Everything seems to distress her, she notices. She is afraid Linda has been drinking.

"And the band had this great singer!" Linda goes on. "She wore a tight skullcap with sequins on it? And a brown tuxedo, and she sounded for all the world like Ella Fitzgerald. Boy, was she sexy. She had a real deep voice, but she could go real high at times."

Linda unscrews the top of a quart of Coke and pours herself a glass. She drinks the Coke thirstily. "I wouldn't be explaining all this to you if you had gone. I tried to get you to go with me."

"And leave the kids here?" Cleo turns off the TV.

"Shirley had on the darlingest outfit. It had these pleats—what do you want, Davey?"

Davey is trailing a quilt into the living room. "I couldn't sleep," he whines. "The big girls was going to get me."

"He means Charlie's Angels," says Cleo. "We were watching them and they kept him awake."

"He's had a bad dream. Here, hon." Linda hugs Davey and takes him back to bed.

"I worked myself to death yesterday getting this house in shape and it looks like a cyclone hit it," Cleo says to Rita Jean on the telephone the next morning. "First, tell me how's Dexter."

Cleo listens to Rita Jean's account of Dexter's trip to the vet. "He said there's nothing to do now but wait. He's not suffering any, and the vet said it would be all right if I keep him at home. He's asleep most of the time. He's the pitifulest thing."

Rita Jean's cat is thirteen. After the news came from Vietnam, Rita Jean got a cat and then another cat when the first one got run over. The present cat she has kept in the house all its life.

"The one thing about cats," says Cleo, trying to sound comforting, "is that there's more where that one come from. You'll grieve, but you'll get over it and get you another cat."

"I guess so."

Cleo tells about Linda's night out. "She was dolled up so pretty, she looked like she was going out on a date. It made me feel so funny. She had on a new pants suit. The kids didn't want her to go, either. They know something's wrong. They never miss a thing."

"Kids don't miss much," Rita Jean agrees.

"And how in the world does she think they can afford to keep on like they've been doing? But I think they'll get back together."

"Surely they will."

"Knock on wood." Cleo has to stretch to reach the door facing. She is getting a headache. Absently, she watches the *Today* credits roll by as Rita Jean tells about her brother's trip out West. He tried to get her to go along, but she couldn't think of closing her house up and she wouldn't leave Dexter. "They went to the Grand Canyon and Yosemite and a bunch of other places," Rita Jean says. "You should see the load of pictures they took. They must of takened a bushel."

"It must be something to be able to take off like that," Cleo says. "I never had the chance when we lived on the farm, but now there are too many maniacs on the road." Cleo sips her coffee, knowing it will aggravate her headache. "The way things are going around here, I think maybe I ought to go out West. I think I'll just get me a wig and go running around!" Cleo laughs at herself, but a pain jabs at her temple. Rita Jean laughs, and Cleo goes on, "I think Linda's going to have it out with Bob finally. They're going to meet over at the lake one day next week. It wasn't none of my business, but I tried to tell her she ought to simmer down and think it over."

"I think they'll patch it up, Cleo. I really do."

"That Bob Isbell was always the best thing!" Cleo leans back in her chair, almost dreamily. "I tell you, girl, I couldn't have survived if it hadn't been for him when Jake passed away. He was here every hour; he seen to it that we all got to where we was going; he took care of the house here and then went back and took care of their house. He was even washing dishes. Davey was little-bitty then. Of course, none of us could think straight and we didn't see right then all he was doing, but don't you know we appreciated it. I never will forget how good he was."

"He always was good to the kids."

"They had to pinch them pennies, but those kids never did without. He makes good at the lumberyard, and with what Linda brings in from the K Mart, they're pretty well off. That house is just as fine as can be—and Linda walks off and leaves it! You just can't tell me he done her that way, the way she said. And she don't seem to care!"

"She's keeping it in."

"I keep halfway expecting Bob to pull in the driveway, but he hasn't called or said boo to the kids or anything. I don't want to run them out, but I'll be glad when they get this thing worked out! They're tearing up jack! There's always something a-going. A washing machine or the dishwasher. The television, of course. I never saw so many dishes as these younguns can mess up. I never aimed to be feeding Coxey's Army! And they just strow like you've never seen. Right through the middle of the living room. Here comes one dropping this and that, and then right behind here comes the other one. Prissy-Tail's got her tail tied up in knots with all the combustion here!"

Cleo stands up. She has to get an aspirin. "Well, I'll let you get back to your doodling!"

When Cleo starts toward the refrigerator to get ice water, Prissy-Tail bounds straight out of the living room and beats her to the refrigerator.

"You're going to throw me down," she cries.

She gives Prissy-Tail some milk and takes two aspirins. Phil Donahue is talking to former dope addicts. Cleo turns off the TV and finishes her coffee. She looks around at all the extra objects that have accumulated. A tennis racket. Orange-and-blue-striped shoes. Bluejeans in heaps like rag dolls. Tammy's snapshots scattered around on the divan and end tables. A collapsible plaid suitcase. Tote bags with dirty clothes streaming out the tops. Davey's Star Wars toys and his red computer toy that resembles a Princess phone. Tammy's Minute Maker camera. Cleo has forgotten how to move effortlessly through the clutter children make. She pours more coffee and looks at the mail. She looks at a mail-order catalog which specializes in household gadgets. She is impressed with the number of things you can buy to help you organize things, items such as plastic pockets for grocery coupons and accessory chests for closets. She spends a long time then studying the luxurious compartments of a Winnebago in a magazine ad. She imagines traveling out West in it, doing her cooking in the tiny kitchen, but she can't think why she would be going out West by herself.

The cheerleaders' outfits are taking a week. Everything has to be done over. Cleo puts zippers in upside down, allows too much on seams, has to cut plackets out twice. The cheerleaders come over for a fitting and everything is the wrong size. Cleo tells the cheerleaders, "I'm just like a wiggleworm in hot ashes." In comparison to the overalls, the blouses are easy, but she has trouble with the interfacing.

"You don't charge enough," Linda tells her. "You should charge twenty-five dollars apiece for those things."

"People here won't pay that much," Cleo says.

Linda is in and out. The kids visit Bob at home during the weekend. It is more peaceful, but it makes Cleo worry. She is almost glad when they return Sunday evening, carrying tote bags of clothes and playthings. Bob has taken them out for pizza every meal, and they turn up their noses at what she has on the table—fried channel cat and hush puppies. Linda doesn't eat either. She is going out with Shirley. Cleo gives Prissy-Tail more fish than she can eat.

"Smile, Grandma."

"Well, hurry up," Cleo says, her body poised as if about to take off and fly. "I can't hold like this all day."

"Just a minute." Tammy moves the camera around. It looks like the mask on a space suit. "Say cheese!"

Cleo holds her smile, which is growing halfhearted and strained. The camera clicks, and the flashbulb flares. Together, they watch the picture take shape. Like the dawn, it grows in intensity until finally Cleo's features appear. The Cleo in the picture stands there vacantly, like a scared cat.

"I look terrible," says Cleo.

"You look old, Grandma."

On the cheerleader outfits, Cleo is down to finger work. As she whips the facings, she imagines Bob alone in the big ranch house. What would a man do in a house like that by himself? Linda had left him late one night and brought Tammy and Davey over, right in the middle of *The Tonight Show* (John Davidson was the guest host). The children were half asleep. Cleo imagines them groggy and senseless, one day hooked on dope.

* * *

The cheerleader outfits are finished. There are some flaws, Cleo knows, where she has had to take out and put in again so many times, but she tells herself that only somebody who sews will notice them. She pulls out bright blue basting thread.

She does some wash, finishes this week's *Family Circle* and cuts out a hamburger casserole recipe she thinks the kids might like. She throws away the *Family Circle* and the old *TV Guide*. She carries out trash. Then she straightens up her sewing corner and sorts her threads. She collects Tammy's scattered pictures and puts them in a pile. As she tries to find a box they will fit in, she accidentally steps on the cat's tail. "Oh, I'm sorry!" she cries, shocked. Prissy-Tail hides under the couch. Cleo can't find a box the right size.

When the cheerleaders try on their new outfits, Cleo spots bits of blue basting thread she has missed. Embarrassed, she pulls out the threads. She knows the cheerleaders will go to the ball game and someone will see blue basting thread sticking out.

Later, thinking she will go to the show if there is a decent one on, Cleo drives to the shopping center. There isn't. An invasion from outer space and Jane Fonda. Cleo parks and goes to the K Mart. She waves at Linda, who is busy with a long line of people at her register. Cleo walks around the store and finds a picture album with plastic pockets for Tammy. She will pay for it with some of the money she collected from the cheerleaders. Davey will want something too, but she doesn't know what to buy that he will like. After rejecting all the toys she sees, she buys a striped turtleneck sweater on sale. The album and sweater are roughly the same price. She doesn't see Linda when she goes through the checkout line.

Cleo sits in the parking lot of the shopping center for a long time and then she goes home and makes the hamburger recipe.

"You all go on about your cats like they was babies," says Linda. Linda is sanding a rocking chair, which is upside down on newspapers in the hall.

"They're a heap sight less trouble," says Cleo, who is dusting. Rita Jean has called to say Dexter is home from the hospital, but there isn't much hope.

"Stop fanning doors, Tammy," Linda says. "Grandma's got a present for you."

Cleo brings out the picture album and the sweater.

"Now I want you to keep all them pictures in this," she tells Tammy. "Here, squirt," she says to Davey. "Here's something else for me to pick up."

The children take the presents wordlessly, examining them. Tammy turns the pages and pokes her fingers into the picture pockets. Davey rips the plastic wrapper off the sweater and holds it up. "It fits!" he says.

Davey turns on the television and Tammy sits on the divan, turning the empty pages of the picture album.

"You didn't have to do that," says Linda to Cleo.

"I'm just keeping up with the times," Cleo says. "Spend spend, spend."

"Nothing wrong with keeping up with the times," says Linda.

"I see you are. With all that old-timey stuff you're collecting. Explain that."

"Everybody's going back to old-timey stuff. Furniture like yours is out of style."

"Then maybe one day it'll be antique. If I live that long." Cleo pokes the dusting broom at the ceiling.

"We're getting on your nerves," says Linda. "We're going to be getting out before long."

"I hope you mean going back home where you belong. Not that I mean to kick you out. You know what I mean."

"We're going back home, all right," Linda says. "This is the big night—I'm going to meet Bob at Kenlake. I'm going to have it out with him. I can't wait." She wipes the rocker with a rag and turns it right side up. "There, I think that's enough. What a job. If I could just find a twin to it. Tammy, turn that radio down; you're bothering Grandma."

Cleo has to sit down. She is out of breath. The broom falls to the floor as she sinks onto the divan. "I'm not sixteen anymore," she says. "I give out too quick."

"Mama, there's not a thing wrong with you. You just don't do anything with yourself."

"What do you mean?"

"Look at you; you're still a young woman. You could go to school, make a nurse or something. That Mrs. Smith over yonder is sixty-eight and flies an airplane. By herself too."

"I can see me doing that." Cleo clutches a needlepoint pillow. Tammy and Davey are arguing, sounding like wild Indians, but the racket is losing its definition around her. She finds it hard to pick out individual sounds. It is just a racket, something like a prolonged, steady snore—with lots of tuneful snorts and snuffles and puffs. Jake used to snore like that, but she could always tug the covers or kick at him gently and he would stop.

"Rita Jean said I was in the prime of life," says Cleo.

"Rita Jean should talk. Look at her. She petted that cat to death, if you ask me. And I never heard anything so ridiculous as her not wanting to go out West when she had the chance! I'd be gone in a minute!"

"People can't just have everything they want, all the time," Cleo says.

"I'm not mad at you, Mama. But people don't have to do what they don't want to as much now as they used to."

"I should know that," Cleo says. "It's all over television. You make me feel awful."

"I don't mean to. It's for your own good."

Prissy-Tail jumps up on the divan and Cleo grabs her. She squirms up onto Cleo's shoulder.

"You sure are lucky, Prissy-Tail, that you don't have to worry," Cleo says.

Linda pulls the rocker through the doorway into the living room. It scrapes the paint on the door facing.

Cleo is behind on supper. She is making a blackberry cobbler and she is confused about the timing. The children's favorite show comes on before supper is ready. They take their plates into the living room. *Mork and Mindy* is the one thing Tammy and Davey agree on. Cleo fills her plate and watches it with them. It isn't one of her regular stories, and it seems strange to her. Mork is from outer space and drinks through his finger. Otherwise, he is like a human being. Cleo finds his nonstop wisecracks hard to follow. Also, he wears galluses and sleeps hanging upside down. Jake used to wear galluses, Cleo thinks suddenly. Mork lives with Mindy, but Davey and Tammy seem to think nothing of it. Cleo is pleased that they eat the hamburger casserole without complaining. During the commercial she gets them large helpings of hot blackberry cobbler.

In the light she sees that Tammy is wearing blue eye shadow. "It makes you look holler-eyed," Cleo tells her, but Tammy shrugs.

When Tammy and Davey are asleep, Cleo gets out her family picture album. It has few pictures, compared to the way people take pictures nowadays, she thinks. The little black corners are coming loose, and some of the pictures are lying at crazy angles. She tries to put them back in place, knowing they won't stay. She looks through the pictures of her parents' wedding trip to Biloxi. Her parents look so young. Her mother looks like Linda in the picture. She is wearing a long baggy dress in style at the time. Cleo's father is a slim, dark-haired man in the picture. He is smiling. He always smiled. Cleo's parents are both dead. She turns the pages to her own honeymoon pictures. One, in which she and Jake look like children, was taken by a stranger in front of the Jefferson Davis monument. She looks carefully at Jake's face, realizing that the memory of the snapshots is more real than the memory of his actual face. As she turns the pages she sees herself and Jake get slightly older. A picture of Linda shows a stubborn child with bangs.

Cleo looks at a picture of Jake on the tractor. He is grinning into the sun. That was Jake when he was happy. He was a quiet man. Cleo studies a picture taken the year he died, and she wonders suddenly if Jake had ever cheated on her. He could have that time he went to the state fair, she thinks. When he returned he acted strangely, bringing back a red ribbon he had won, and talking in a peculiar way about the future of the family farm. Jake would never forgive her for selling the farm. It was surely her way of cheating on him, she thinks uncomfortably, but she never would have thought of divorcing him, just as she has not been able later to think of remarrying.

On the last pages of the album she sees a surprise, a picture she does not recognize at first. It is dim figures on a television screen. Then she remembers. Tammy took pictures of *Charlie's Angels* the night Linda missed it.

"Here, Mama, that's you." Tammy had pointed to the dark-haired actress, whose face was no bigger than a pencil eraser and hard to make out.

"Just give me her money and I'll do without her looks," Linda had replied.

Tammy has put this picture in Cleo's family album. Cleo cannot think why Tammy would do this. Then she sees on the next page that Tammy has also put in the picture she took of Cleo. The picture is the last one in the scrapbook. Again, Cleo sees herself, looking scared and old.

"The roof fell in," Cleo tells Rita Jean the next day. "Linda says she's not going back to Bob. She says she wants a separation and he's agreed to move out. Them children will be packed from pillar to post. I didn't sleep a wink all night last night."

Cleo is at Rita Jean's. Cleo has driven over, skipping the *Today* show and her morning phone conversation. Now she feels more comfortable at Rita Jean's than at home. The house is brightly decorated with handmade objects. Rita belongs to a mail-order craft club which sends a kit every month. She has made a new embroidered wall hanging of an Arizona sunset. Cleo admires it and says, as she gazes at a whipstitch, "What I don't understand is how my daughter can carry on like she does. She chirps like a bird!"

"I just don't know," says Rita Jean. "Don't look at this mess," she says as she leads Cleo to the back room, where Dexter is sleeping in a box. "The vet said there's not a thing wrong with him. He's just wearing out. He said keep him warm, have food for him whenever he wants it, and pet him and talk to him. It might be that I kept him in too long and he's just pined away. Do you think that was right, to keep him in like that all this time?"

"If you had let him out he would have just got run over," says Cleo. She strokes Dexter and he stirs slightly. His fur is dull and thin.

"I'll just have to accept it," says Rita Jean.

"Maybe it will be good for you," says Cleo, more harshly than she intends. "I've about decided there's no use trying to hang on to anything. You just lose it all in the end. You might as well just not care."

"Don't talk that way, Cleo."

"I must be getting old." Cleo laughs. "I'm saying what I think more. Or younger, one. Old people and children—they always say what they think."

Over coffee, Cleo talks Rita Jean into going to trade day at the stockyard.

"Linda said we've got to get out, keep up with the times," Cleo says. "Just what I need—more junk. But it's the style."

"Maybe it will take our minds off of everything," says Rita Jean, getting her scarf.

Most of the traders at the stockyard are farmers who trade in secondhand goods on the side. Cleo is shocked to realize this, though she knows nobody can make a living on a farm these days. She recognizes some of the farmers, behind their folding tables of dusty old objects. Even at the time of Jake's death, feeding the cows was costing almost as much as the milk brought. She cannot imagine Jake in a camper, peddling some old junk from the barn. That would kill him if the heart attack hadn't.

Cleo and Rita Jean drift from table to table, touching Depression glass, crystal goblets, cracked china, cast-off egg beaters and mixers, rusted farm implements, and greasy wooden boxes stuffed with buttons and papers.

"I never saw so much old stuff," says Cleo.

"Look at this," says Rita Jean, pointing to a box of plastic jump ropes. "These aren't old."

They look at hand-tooled leather belts and billfolds, made by prisoners. And paintings of bright scenes on black velvet—bullfights and skylines and sunsets. A man in a cowboy hat displays the paintings from a fancy camper called a Sports Coach.

"He must have come from far away," says Rita Jean.

"I used to have a set of these." Cleo holds a tiny crystal salt shaker, without the pepper. There is a syrup holder to match.

"You could spend all day here," says Rita Jean, looking around like a lost child.

Cleo doesn't hear her. All of a sudden her blood is rushing to her head and her stomach is churning. She is looking at a miniature Early American whatnot, right in front of her. It is imitation mahogany. She holds it, touching it, turning it, amazed.

"If it had been a snake it would have bit me!" cries Cleo, astonished. But Rita Jean is intent on examining a set of enamel canisters with cat decals on them and doesn't notice.

The whatnot cannot be the same one. Cleo cannot remember what happened to the little whatnot that sat on the dresser, the box in which Jake kept his stamps, his receipts, and his bankbook.

This whatnot has a door held in place by a wooden button, and on the top, like books on a shelf, is a series of tiny boxes, with sliding covers like match boxes. The little boxes have names: Book Plates, Mending Tape, Gummed Patches, Rubber Bands, Gummed Labels, Mailing Labels. There are pictures on the spines of the boxes, together forming a scene—an old-fashioned train running through a meadow past a river, with black smoke trailing across three of the boxes and meeting a distant mountain. A steamboat is in the background. The curved track extends from the first box to the last. The scene is faded green and yellow, and there are lacy ferns and a tree in the foreground. The boxes are a simple picture puzzle to put in order. Cleo's children played with the puzzle when they were small, but her grandchildren were never interested in it. It cannot be the very same whatnot, she thinks.

"I'm going to buy this!" Cleo says.

"That's high," says Rita Jean, fingering the price sticker. The whatnot is three dollars.

Cleo looks at the train. Two of the pictures are out of order, and she rearranges them so that the caboose is at the end. For a moment she can see the train gliding silently through the pleasant scene, as quietly as someone dreaming, and she can imagine her family aboard the train as it crosses a fertile valley—like the place down by the creek that Jake loved—on its way out West. On the train, her well-behaved sons and their children are looking out the windows, and Linda and Bob are driving the train, guiding the cowcatcher down the track, while Tammy and Davey patiently count telephone poles and watch the passing scenery. Cleo is following unafraid in the caboose, as the train passes through the golden meadow and they all wave at the future and smile perfect smiles.

Marian Thurm
(b. 1952)

Born in New York City, where she now lives, Marian Thurm was educated at Vassar College and Brown University. She has worked for *Esquire, Redbook, Partisan Review,* and *Family Circle,* and has published fiction in *The Atlantic, The New Yorker, The Boston Globe Magazine,* and *Mademoiselle.* Her stories, which have been selected for such anthologies as *Best American Short Stories* and *Editor's Choice,* are collected in *Floating* (1984) and *These Things Happen* (1988). Her first novel, *Walking Distance*, was published in 1987, and she is currently working on her new novel, titled *Henry in Love.*

STARLIGHT

Elaine and her mother had spent the day shopping, going from one department store to the next—from Lord & Taylor to Saks to Jordan Marsh to Burdines. It was Elaine's third day in Florida, and they had been looking for gifts for her two boys: Jesse, who was nine, and Matthew, who was eleven. Elaine hadn't seen either of them in months, and she hoped the shirts and sweaters she had bought were the right sizes. The last time she saw them was in early December, when she left their house in New Jersey with three large suitcases crammed with her winter clothes. At first she had felt an overwhelming grief when the boys told her they preferred to live with their father; the humiliation had come later, along with a sudden cold anger. She got over her anger soon enough—how could you be angry at children who were too young to know they had hurt you? The grief stayed with her much longer, but she was finally over that, too. It was the humiliation that lingered. As her mother and father had said more than once since Elaine's arrival, "Who ever heard of young children like that just coming right out and picking their father over their mother, no two ways about it?"

Even Peter, Elaine's husband, had been amazed at the boys' decision. He hadn't been all that pleased about it, either. Keeping Jesse and Matthew meant keeping the house and finding someone to take care of things until he got home from work. It wasn't anything like what he had envisioned for himself. He didn't go into details, but Elaine knew that whatever it was he wanted was going to be harder to get now that there were two children to be looked after. When he first told her why he wanted out, she stared at him in disbelief. She was boring, he said. Nothing she did or said or wanted was interesting anymore. They were on their way back from the city, where they had had dinner with a friend of Peter's from college—a criminal lawyer who specialized in defending celebrities who'd been arrested on drug charges. He had asked them to a big party he was giving, where there was sure to be plenty of really good dope, and Elaine wanted to know why Peter had said they'd love to come, why he'd said it sounded like a great way to spend an evening. We're not college kids anymore, she yelled at him in the car as they crossed the George Washington Bridge. You really are a drag, he said quietly, and he didn't let up until they pulled into the driveway of their house. They sat in the car for what seemed to be hours, Elaine shivering as they talked. What did he want her to do, she asked him. Take up skydiving? Get a job as a trapeze artist? Put a ring through her nose? That's when he told her he wanted out and gave his reasons. Her own reasons, at least, made sense; it was impossible to love someone who criticized her at every opportunity, who belittled her in front of her children, her friends, strangers, the whole world. After thirteen years, she had had enough. Even so, Peter had the last word. Whenever Elaine heard a book or a movie or a TV program described as boring, her skin prickled with goose bumps, as if she were in danger.

"You had a phone call," her father said. He had just unlocked the apartment's four locks to let Elaine and her mother inside.

"Who was it?" her mother said.

"Sweetie, did I say I was talking to you?" her father said.

"Who was it, Daddy?" Elaine said.

"It was Peter. He said the airport in Newark was snowed in, and the kids wouldn't be down until tomorrow. Or maybe the day after. It all depends on the weather."

"Was he civil to you, at least?" Elaine's mother said. She and Elaine put their shopping bags down in the foyer. The apartment was the perfect size for two people, with an L-shaped living room and a kitchen that could only take a small round table. Elaine had been sleeping in the second bedroom her parents used as a den, but once the boys arrived she'd have to camp out in the living room. The three of them went out onto the screened-in terrace. The terrace overlooked the Intracoastal Waterway; just as they sat down, a motorboat went by, buzzing so loudly neither of them caught her father's answer. "Well, was he or wasn't he?" her mother said.

"Bastards," her father said. "I wish those creeps would stay out of my backyard."

"What else did he say?" Elaine asked her father.

"Peter? He was very polite. He asked how all of us were. He said the boys were very disappointed about the trip's being postponed. They can't wait to see all of us. Especially you, Lainie Bug, needless to say."

"Needless to say." Elaine knew her father was lying—his voice sounded unnaturally hearty, as if he were speaking to someone too old or too young to be told anything close to the truth.

"Well," her mother said, "disappointed though we all may be, you can't do anything about the weather, and that's that."

"Thank you, Mother, for your wit and wisdom in these trying times," Elaine's father said.

"Please don't talk to her like that," Elaine said.

"Your mother knows I like to kid around. That's the way I am."

"I don't mind. Or most of the time I don't. After forty years—"

"Well, you should mind," Elaine said. She stood up and looked out over the water at the condominiums that seemed to take up every last square foot of land. Just across the way, a hundred yards in the distance, she could see men and women lounging around a long rectangular swimming pool, and a diver poised on the board, ready to take off. She watched as he flew into the water and disappeared. It was a mistake to have come to Florida, she realized. But the boys had never been here before, and she had wanted to meet them on neutral ground, to vacation with them far enough from home so that she wouldn't have to worry about their calling for their father to come and get them in the middle of the night. And she had wanted to be among allies, people she could count on for comfort if things went disastrously with her children. What she hadn't counted on was her parents' making her feel worse than she'd felt all winter long. Her father was especially hard to take. Since his retirement, he'd mellowed, but she never knew what to expect. It was easy enough to be fond of him from a distance; living with him in such close quarters these past few days, she'd begun to wonder if she'd last the week or end up running out to find herself a motel.

The telephone rang.

Her mother said, "Arthur?"

"Don't look at me," her father said. "I'm just sitting here enjoying the view from my terrace."

"If it's for you, I may just hang up."

"Suit yourself."

Her mother picked up a phone that was on the terrace floor, next to a seven-foot-tall cactus. "Brenda," she said after a moment. "It's not bad news, is it?" She carried the phone past the sliding glass door into the living room, rolling her eyes as she went.

"Who's Brenda?" Elaine said, running her hand along the spines of the cactus.

"One of your mother's friends from OA."

"I give up," Elaine said. Her fingertips were bleeding; she put them in her mouth.

"Overeaters Anonymous. Your mother can be on the phone day and night with those people. If any of them feel like they're about to go stuff their faces with a nice Sara Lee cake, for example, they call someone in this network they've got set up and talk their heads off instead of finishing the cake. Mommy lost fifteen pounds, by the way. Looks great, doesn't she?"

"Terrific." Elaine turned around in her chair so she could see her mother. "Wonderful," she said.

"You, on the other hand—"

"I'm fine."

"Feel like talking your head off to your old father?"

"About what?"

"Whatever. How about what you're going to do to get the boys back."

"This is the last time I'm going to repeat this," Elaine said, "so pay attention: they're perfectly happy where they are. Perfectly."

"They can't be. Children belong with their mother. That's the way it works in this world."

"It seems to me I've heard that before—twice yesterday and once the day before that."

"Does it sound any better today?"

"Worse," Elaine said.

Her mother came back out onto the terrace, eating the largest carrot Elaine had ever seen, and she was reminded of Jesse and Matthew, aged three and five, dressed in their Popeye pajamas, holding carrots in their hands as they sat on their knees in front of the television set watching some dopey program—"Gilligan's Island," she thought it was. They were young enough then that their heads smelled sweet when she bent to kiss them. She hadn't noticed when the sweetness disappeared; one day, it was simply gone.

She couldn't explain why her children had done what they had. The morning after she and Peter had driven home from the city, they had just finished breakfast and Jesse and Matthew were about to leave the table when Peter said, "Sit still a minute." They listened to him talk, staying silent until Peter said it was all up to them, whatever they wanted to do was fine. "Think carefully. Take your time," Elaine started to warn them, but already Matthew was saying he would stay with his father and Jesse was nodding his head up and down, saying that was what he wanted, too. They shrugged their shoulders when she questioned them, and she didn't have the heart to press the issue. If they had been daughters, it might have been different; she just didn't know.

After she left, she settled herself into an apartment in Fort Lee and found a job as a secretary in a private school in Manhattan—the first job she'd ever had. She stayed away from the house in Fair Lawn and talked to Peter briefly now and then. She spoke to Matthew and Jesse only once; she was near tears throughout the conversation and couldn't wait to hang up. They talked about school—book reports, and new gym uniforms, and the science teacher who made Matthew come in at the end of the day and stare at the clock on the wall for half an hour as punishment for talking in class. The boys talked easily, as if it had been hours rather than months that had passed since they heard her voice. At the end, she told them she missed them, then hung up before she could hear their response.

It was spring vacation and she was ready to see them, finally; to see what would happen. She wouldn't expect too much of them—if they were stiff as strangers at first, she was prepared to draw back and let them approach her at their own pace. Maybe, after their week together in Florida was up, they would decide to see each other every weekend, or every other weekend. Beyond that, she couldn't speculate. She certainly wasn't about to ask them to come and live with her, to set herself up for being kicked in the teeth again. That was what it had felt like this winter—a swift hard blow that left her so weak she could hardly move.

Her parents kept wanting to know what she had done. It's easy enough to be a lousy mother, her mother told her. You think you're doing everything right and then one day it turns out you were all wrong.

Elaine knew what her mother had done wrong. She

had been a mother who couldn't wait for her children to grow up. Elaine and Philip, her younger brother, were always treated like adults; whenever there was trouble, they were expected to act calmly and reason things out. Once, at the train station, when they were on their way to the city to see *My Fair Lady*, Philip, who was terrified of escalators, couldn't bring himself to put one foot in front of the other and step onto the moving stair. "Just get a grip on yourself," their mother had shouted, while Elaine, who was twelve, ran down the other escalator to Philip and took his hand. It was the middle of the winter, but Philip's hand was moist and warm. Elaine promised him that it didn't matter whether they ever got to the city to see *My Fair Lady* that day, she only wanted him to stop crying. After the train left without them, their mother came down from the platform. "Get away from him," she said to Elaine. "I don't want you feeling sorry for him. The whole world knows how to deal with escalators. What's so special about him?" Elaine watched her brother lick tears from the corners of his mouth, and she wanted to lift him off the ground and fly him high above the escalator all the way to the city, leaving her mother behind with a look of absolute astonishment on her face. But Philip finally made it up the escalator and was forgiven. It was her mother who was never forgiven—not by Elaine, anyway.

"Do I care that Brenda has to put her mother into a nursing home?" her father was saying. "Does Elaine care?"

"What?" Elaine said.

"Tell your mother you couldn't care less."

"All right, I get the picture," her mother said.

"Can't we talk about something pleasant for a change?"

"What should we talk about? The weather? Even that kind of talk gets me in trouble."

"Talk to your daughter. Find out what's on her mind."

"I'm going to take a nap," Elaine said. "That's what's on my mind."

"Are you tired?" her mother said. "I'm not surprised. A long day of shopping can be very exhausting."

"I'm a people-watcher," Elaine's mother announced in the airport coffee shop the following afternoon. During breakfast they'd got a call from Peter saying the boys would be arriving at three fifty-five. After the call, Elaine had gone alone to the beach in Fort Lauderdale, taken a quick swim, then slept in the sun for an hour and returned to the apartment feeling fairly self-possessed. (It was the one time she'd been away from both her parents—the one time she'd successfully avoided them.) Now it was almost three thirty, and she was close to panic.

"People fascinate me. I could look at them for hours," her mother went on. "Look at the couple over there." She motioned toward a man with a cowboy hat and a big red mustache, and the black woman who sat opposite him. Their baby was asleep in a plastic infant seat they had placed on the table. "Now, what do you think motivates people like that?"

"What do you think motivates your mother?" Elaine's father asked. He smiled at her. "Plain old-fashioned nosiness?"

Elaine smiled back, but her hand shook as she reached for her water glass.

"Go ahead and laugh," her mother said. "I guarantee you ninety-nine percent of the people in this world would understand my point."

"I think," her father said, "the time has come for me to make my speech."

"If it's the one about mothers and children and who belongs with whom, you can cancel it," Elaine said.

"Give me a chance," her father said. "I just want to give you a little piece of advice, that's all. You listen to what I'm going to say to you and you'll have those children eating out of the palm of your hand one-two-three."

"Excuse me," Elaine said, and pushed back her chair.

"You can't afford to make any more mistakes, Lainie Bug," her father called after her as she headed for the rest rooms at the back of the coffee shop.

Inside, she rushed past a teenage girl who was tweezing her eyebrows in front of a large mirror over a row of sinks. She locked herself into a stall, dropped the seat cover, and sat down at the very edge. She closed her eyes. The stall reeked of strawberry-scented air freshener; still, it was easier to breathe now that she was alone.

In the dark she told herself who she was: a grown woman scared to death of two little boys. Her own children. She had always wanted to be a mother, had always wanted babies. You couldn't go wrong with babies; there was no possibility of disappointment. You could hold them as close as you needed to, tell them all day long how much you loved them, and never feel foolish.

One night last summer, already suspecting her marriage was lost, Elaine had led the boys into her darkened bedroom, and in their pajamas Jesse and Matthew stretched themselves out on the floor and stared in amazement at the hundred glow-in-the-dark stars and planets she had stuck on her ceiling that afternoon—a whole galaxy that shimmered endlessly above them. Peter was away in Japan on a business trip, on the other side of the world; there was no one to question what she had done with her day. After the boys were settled, Elaine got down on the floor, concentrating on nothing except the perfect faces of her children. When she awoke two hours later, her neck was stiff and the boys were gone. There was a light summer blanket covering her; someone, Jesse or Matthew, or maybe both of them, had bent over her while she slept.

"We thought you fell in and drowned," her father said when Elaine made her way back to the table. "Like that time at the World's Fair when you and your friend what's-her-name disappeared into the bathroom for a nice relaxing smoke. I couldn't imagine what you two were doing in there for so long. Of course, as soon as I got a whiff of you I knew what it was all about."

"You all right?" her mother said. She touched her lips to Elaine's forehead. "Nice and cool."

"Do you want a Coke or something?" her father said.

"Not me," Elaine said. "We really should get a move on. I don't even know why I sat down again."

They got to the gate just as the first passengers from Newark appeared. Matthew and Jesse were right up front, dressed identically in tweed jackets, tan pants with cuffs, and Weejuns. Jesse was wearing glasses and had a flesh-colored patch over his right eye. Elaine ran to him. "What's the matter with your eye? When did you start wearing glasses?" she said. She kissed him and then she kissed Matthew. Neither of them kissed her back, though Jesse hugged her and Matthew shook her hand.

"Can't you give your mother a kiss?" her mother said.

"I'm in seventh grade," Matthew said. "I shake hands."

"And what about your brother?"

"Me?" Jesse said. "I hug, but I don't kiss."

Elaine said, "What's the patch for? Tell me what's wrong." She sat down in a padded chair opposite the check-in counter. Everyone else stood around her.

"It's just a lazy eye," Jesse said cheerfully. "It won't do any work unless I force it to. With a patch over the other eye, the lazy eye has to do all the work. You understand what I'm saying?"

"Why didn't your father tell me?" Elaine said. "Why didn't you tell me?"

"He says 'Hi,' " Matthew said. "I forgot all about it."

"You know what? His girlfriend bought us Star Wars costumes, even though it wasn't Halloween," Jesse said.

"God, what a jerk." Matthew put his hand over his brother's mouth.

"It's all right." Leaning forward, Elaine took Matthew's hand away from Jesse and held it. "Your father can have as many girlfriends as he wants. It makes no difference to me whatsoever."

"Well, he doesn't have one anymore. She dumped him."

Jesse said, "She used to make breakfast for us a lot on Saturdays and Sundays. She'd be there real early in the morning, like seven o'clock. She was a real early bird, Dad said."

"This kid is unbelievable," Matthew said.

Quickly Elaine's mother said, "Who would like to go for a midnight swim tonight? The water will be nice and warm, and we'll have the whole pool to ourselves."

"If it's really summertime here, can we have a barbecue?" Jesse asked.

"Sorry, guys," her father said. "No barbecuing allowed. Those are the rules of the condominium."

Jesse tried again. "Instead of a barbecue, can we go to Disney World?"

"You don't want to go to Disney World," her father

said. "It's a four-hour drive each way. And you've already been to Disneyland, haven't you?"

"Are we going to have fun on this trip, or what?" Matthew said. "What did we come down here for?"

"What do you mean? You came down here to be with your mother," Elaine's mother said. "That's the main thing."

Elaine studied her shoes, yellow espadrilles that she had bought just for the trip. The little toe on each foot had already worn holes through the canvas, she noticed. When she looked up, Jesse was dancing, shifting his weight back and forth from one foot to the other, his arms in the air, his elbows and wrists bent at right angles. Some sort of Egyptian dance, Elaine thought.

"Look at me. I'm Steve Martin," Jesse yelled. " 'Born in Arizona, moved to Babylonia, King Tut.' "

"Terrific," Elaine said, and clapped her hands.

"Oh, Jesus," Matthew said.

Ignoring her mother's warning and her father's dire predictions, Elaine took the boys everywhere they wanted to go: Monkey Jungle, Parrot Jungle, and the Seaquarium. The boys seemed excited and happy, though often they would run ahead of her, too impatient to stay by her side. Once, from a distance, Elaine saw Jesse casually rest his arm on his brother's shoulder as the two of them stood watching a pair of orangutans groom each other; she kept waiting for Matthew to shake Jesse off, but it never happened. Two nights in a row, they went to see the movie *Airplane!* A couple of nights, they played miniature golf. At the end of each day, Jesse and Matthew told Elaine they had had "the best time." She supposed that this meant the trip was a success, that they would have nothing to complain about to their father when they went back home. She had kept them entertained, which was all they seemed to have wanted from her. She might have been anyone—a camp counselor, a teacher leading them on class trips, a friend of the family put in charge while their parents were on vacation. There was plenty of time to talk, and they told her a lot—long involved stories about the fight Jesse had recently had with his best friend, the rock concert Matthew had gone to with two thirteen-year-olds, the pair of Siamese fighting fish with beautiful flowing fins they'd bought for the new fish tank in their bedroom—all about the things that had happened to them in the four months they had been out of touch. But she still didn't know if they were really all right, if they loved their father, loved her. You couldn't ask questions like that. When, several years ago, her brother had started seeing a shrink, he'd complained that his parents were always asking him if he was happy. It's none of their business, the shrink told him—if you don't feel you want to give them an answer, don't. As simple as that.

It was nearly midnight; the boys had just gone to bed. Elaine went into her parents' room, where her mother and father were sitting up in their king-size bed watching "Columbo" on a small color TV. Dick Van Dyke was tying his wife to a chair. He took two Polaroid pictures of her and then he picked up a gun. His wife insisted he was never going to get away with it; he aimed the gun at her and pulled the trigger.

"Wait a minute," Elaine's mother said. "Is this the one where Columbo tricks him into identifying his camera at the—"

"Thanks a lot," her father said. "You know how I love Peter Falk."

"Who knows, maybe I'm wrong."

"You're not," Elaine said. "I saw this one, too."

"Well, it's nice to be right about something."

Elaine lay down on her stomach at the foot of the bed, facing the TV set. She yawned and said, "Excuse me."

"All that running around," her mother said. "Who wouldn't be tired?"

"It's not necessary to run like that all day long," her father said. "Didn't those two kids ever hear of sleeping around the pool, or picking up a book or a newspaper? Maybe they're hyperactive or something."

"They're kids on vacation. What do they want to read the newspaper for?" her mother said.

Elaine sat up and swung her legs over the side of the bed. "It's my fault," she said. "I couldn't bring myself to say no to them about anything."

"Did you accomplish anything all those hours you were running?" her mother asked. "Do you feel like you made any headway?"

Elaine was watching an overweight woman on TV dance the cha-cha with her cat along a shining kitchen floor. "What?" she said.

"Of course, if they really are just fine there with Peter and his sleep-over girlfriends, that's another story," her father said.

"Quiet," her mother said. "Look who's here."

Jesse stood in the doorway, blinking his eyes. "There's a funny noise in my ears that keeps waking me up," he said. He sat down on the floor next to the bed and put his head in Elaine's lap. "You know," he said, "like someone's whistling in there."

Elaine hesitated, then kissed each ear. "Better?"

"A little."

"More kisses?"

Jesse shook his head.

"Let me take you back to bed." Elaine walked him to the little den at the other end of the apartment, where Matthew was asleep on his side of the convertible couch. Jesse got onto the bed. On his knees, he sat up and looked out the window. "I can't go to sleep right now," he said quietly. Beneath them, the water was black; above, the palest of moons appeared to drift by. There were clouds everywhere, and just a few dim stars.

"Did you want to tell me something?" Elaine waited; she focused on the sign lit up on top of the Holiday Inn across the Waterway.

"We're getting a new car. A silver BMW," Jesse said dreamily. "We saw it in the showroom." He moved away from the window and slipped down on the bed. "We might drive it over to Fort Lee and come and see you. And when Matthew has his license, the two of us will pick you up every day and take you anywhere you want to go."

Elaine still faced the window; she did not turn around. "To the moon," she said. "Will you do that for me?"

Jesse didn't answer for a long time. "We can do that," he said finally, and when she turned to look at him he was asleep.

E. L. Doctorow

(b. 1931)

Born in New York City, where he now lives and works, E(dgar) L(aurence) Doctorow earned a B.A. at Kenyon College. Following a decade during which he became a senior editor at one publishing house and, later, editor-in-chief and vice president at another, he joined the faculty of Sarah Lawrence College. He has received a Guggenheim Fellowship, a National Book Critics Circle Award, and the Arts and Letters Award of The American Academy and Institute of Arts and Letters. He is the author of seven novels: *Welcome to Hard Times* (1960), *Big as Life* (1966), *The Book of Daniel* (1971), *Ragtime* (1975), *Loon Lake* (1980), *World's Fair* (1985), and *Billy Bathgate* (1989), as well as a collection of stories, *Lives of the Poets* (1984). Two of his novels, *Welcome to Hard Times* and *Ragtime,* were made into Hollywood films, and his play *Drinks Before Dinner* (1978) was produced at The New York Shakespeare Festival Theater.

THE WRITER IN THE FAMILY

In 1955 my father died with his ancient mother still alive in a nursing home. The old lady was ninety and hadn't even known he was ill. Thinking the shock might kill her, my aunts told her that he had moved to Arizona for his bronchitis. To the immigrant generation of my grandmother, Arizona was the American equivalent of the Alps, it was where you went for your health. More accurately, it was where you went if you had the money. Since my father had failed in all the business enterprises of his life, this was the aspect of the news my grandmother dwelled on, that he had finally had some success. And so it came about that as we mourned him at home in our stocking feet, my grandmother was bragging to her cronies about her son's new life in the dry air of the desert.

My aunts had decided on their course of action without consulting us. It meant neither my mother nor my brother nor I could visit Grandma because we were supposed to have moved west too, a family, after all. My brother Harold and I didn't mind—it was always a nightmare at the old people's home, where they all sat around staring at us while we tried to make conversation with Grandma. She looked terrible, had numbers of ailments, and her mind wandered. Not seeing her was no disappointment either for my mother, who had never gotten along with the old woman and did not visit when she could have. But what was disturbing was that my aunts had acted in the manner of that side of the family of making government on everyone's behalf, the true citizens by blood and the lesser citizens by marriage. It was exactly this attitude that had tormented my mother all her married life. She claimed Jack's family had never accepted her. She had battled them for twenty-five years as an outsider.

A few weeks after the end of our ritual mourning my Aunt Frances phoned us from her home in Larchmont. Aunt Frances was the wealthier of my father's sisters. Her husband was a lawyer, and both her sons were at Amherst. She had called to say that Grandma was asking why she didn't hear from Jack. I had answered the phone. "You're the writer in the family," my aunt said. "Your father had so much faith in you. Would you mind making up something? Send it to me and I'll read it to her. She won't know the difference."

That evening, at the kitchen table, I pushed my homework aside and composed a letter. I tried to imagine my father's response to his new life. He had never been west. He had never traveled anywhere. In his generation the great journey was from the working class to the professional class. He hadn't managed that either. But he loved New York, where he had been born and lived his life, and he was always discovering new things about it. He especially loved the old parts of the city below Canal Street, where he would find ships' chandlers or firms that wholesaled in spices and teas. He was a salesman for an appliance jobber with accounts all over the city. He liked to bring home rare cheeses or exotic foreign vegetables that were sold only in certain neighborhoods. Once he brought home a barometer, another time an antique ship's telescope in a wooden case with a brass snap.

"Dear Mama," I wrote. "Arizona is beautiful. The sun shines all day and the air is warm and I feel better than I have in years. The desert is not as barren as you would expect, but filled with wildflowers and cactus plants and peculiar crooked trees that look like men holding their arms out. You can see great distances in whatever direction you turn and to the west is a range of mountains maybe fifty miles from here, but in the morning with the sun on them you can see the snow on their crests."

My aunt called some days later and told me it was when she read this letter aloud to the old lady that the full effect of Jack's death came over her. She had to excuse herself and went out in the parking lot to cry. "I wept so," she said. "I felt such terrible longing for him. You're so right, he loved to go places, he loved life, he loved everything."

We began trying to organize our lives. My father had borrowed money against his insurance and there was very little left. Some commissions were still due but it didn't look as if his firm would honor them. There were a couple of thousand dollars in a savings bank that had to be maintained there until the estate was settled. The lawyer involved was Aunt Frances' husband and he was very proper. "The estate!" my mother muttered, gesturing as if to pull out her hair. "The estate!" She applied for a job part-time in the admissions office of the hospital where my father's terminal illness had been diagnosed, and where he had spent some months until they had sent him home to die. She knew a lot of the doctors and staff and she had learned "from bitter experience," as she told them, about the hospital routine. She was hired.

I hated that hospital, it was dark and grim and full of tortured people. I thought it was masochistic of my mother to seek out a job there, but did not tell her so.

We lived in an apartment on the corner of 175th Street and the Grand Concourse, one flight up. Three rooms. I shared the bedroom with my brother. It was jammed with furniture because when my father had required a hospital bed in the last weeks of his illness we had moved some of the living-room pieces into the bedroom and made over the living room for him. We had to navigate bookcases, beds, a gateleg table, bureaus, a record player and radio console, stacks of 78 albums, my brother's trombone and music stand, and so on. My mother continued to sleep on the convertible sofa in the living room that had been their bed before his illness. The two rooms were connected by a narrow hall made even narrower by bookcases along the wall. Off the hall were a small kitchen and dinette and a bathroom. There were lots of appliances in the kitchen—broiler, toaster, pressure cooker, counter-top dishwasher, blender—that my father had gotten through his job, at cost. A treasured phrase in our house: *at cost.* But most of these fixtures went unused because my mother did not care for them. Chromium devices with timers or gauges that required the reading of elaborate instructions were not for her. They were in part responsible for the awful clutter of our lives and now she wanted to get rid of them. "We're being buried," she said. "Who needs them!"

So we agreed to throw out or sell anything inessential. While I found boxes for the appliances and my brother tied the boxes with twine, my mother opened my father's closet and took out his clothes. He had several suits because as a salesman he needed to look his best. My mother wanted us to try on his suits to see which of them could be altered and used. My brother refused to try them on. I tried on one jacket which was too large for me. The lining inside the sleeves chilled my arms and the vaguest scent of my father's being came to me.

"This is way too big," I said.

"Don't worry," my mother said. "I had it cleaned. Would I let you wear it if I hadn't?"

It was the evening, the end of winter, and snow was coming down on the windowsill and melting as it settled. The ceiling bulb glared on a pile of my father's suits and trousers on hangers flung across the bed in the shape of a dead man. We refused to try on anything more, and my mother began to cry.

"What are you crying for?" my brother shouted. "You wanted to get rid of things, didn't you?"

A few weeks later my aunt phoned again and said she thought it would be necessary to have another letter from Jack. Grandma had fallen out of her chair and bruised herself and was very depressed.

"How long does this go on?" my mother said.

"It's not so terrible," my aunt said, "for the little time left to make things easier for her."

My mother slammed down the phone. "He can't even die when he wants to!" she cried. "Even death comes second to Mama! What are they afraid of, the shock will kill her? Nothing can kill her. She's indestructible! A stake through the heart couldn't kill her!"

When I sat down in the kitchen to write the letter I found it more difficult than the first one. "Don't watch me," I said to my brother. "It's hard enough."

"You don't have to do something just because someone wants you to," Harold said. He was two years older than me and had started at City College; but when my father became ill he had switched to night school and gotten a job in a record store.

"Dear Mama," I wrote. "I hope you're feeling well. We're all fit as a fiddle. The life here is good and the people are very friendly and informal. Nobody wears suits and ties here. Just a pair of slacks and a short-sleeved shirt. Perhaps a sweater in the evening. I have bought into a very successful radio and record business and I'm doing very well. You remember Jack's Electric, my old place on Forty-third Street? Well, now it's Jack's

Arizona Electric and we have a line of television sets as well."

I sent that letter off to my Aunt Frances, and as we all knew she would, she phoned soon after. My brother held his hand over the mouthpiece. "It's Frances with her latest review," he said.

"Jonathan? You're a very talented young man. I just wanted to tell you what a blessing your letter was. Her whole face lit up when I read the part about Jack's store. That would be an excellent way to continue."

"Well, I hope I don't have to do this anymore, Aunt Frances. It's not very honest."

Her tone changed. "Is your mother there? Let me talk to her."

"She's not here," I said.

"Tell her not to worry," my aunt said. "A poor old lady who has never wished anything but the best for her will soon die."

I did not repeat this to my mother, for whom it would have been one more in the family anthology of unforgivable remarks. But then I had to suffer it myself for the possible truth it might embody. Each side defended its position with rhetoric, but I, who wanted peace, rationalized the snubs and rebuffs each inflicted on the other, taking no stands, like my father himself.

Years ago his life had fallen into a pattern of business failures and missed opportunities. The great debate between his family on the one side, and my mother Ruth on the other, was this: who was responsible for the fact that he had not lived up to anyone's expectations?

As to the prophecies, when spring came my mother's prevailed. Grandma was still alive.

One balmy Sunday my mother and brother and I took the bus to the Beth El cemetery in New Jersey to visit my father's grave. It was situated on a slight rise. We stood looking over rolling fields embedded with monuments. Here and there processions of black cars wound their way through the lanes, or clusters of people stood at open graves. My father's grave was planted with tiny shoots of evergreen but it lacked a headstone. We had chosen one and paid for it and then the stonecutters had gone on strike. Without a headstone my father did not seem to be honorably dead. He didn't seem to me properly buried.

My mother gazed at the plot beside his, reserved for his coffin. "They were always too fine for other people," she said. "Even in the old days on Stanton Street. They put on airs. Nobody was ever good enough for them. Finally Jack himself was not good enough for them. Except to get them things wholesale. Then he was good enough for them."

"Mom, please," my brother said.

"If I had known. Before I ever met him he was tied to his mama's apron strings. And Essie's apron strings were like chains, let me tell you. We had to live where we could be near them for the Sunday visits. Every Sunday, that was my life, a visit to mamaleh. Whatever she knew I wanted, a better apartment, a stick of furniture, a summer camp for the boys, she spoke against it. You know your father, every decision had to be considered and reconsidered. And nothing changed. Nothing ever changed."

She began to cry. We sat her down on a nearby bench. My brother walked off and read the names on stones. I looked at my mother, who was crying, and I went off after my brother.

"Mom's still crying," I said. "Shouldn't we do something?"

"It's all right," he said. "It's what she came here for."

"Yes," I said, and then a sob escaped from my throat. "But I feel like crying too."

My brother Harold put his arm around me. "Look at this old black stone here," he said. "The way it's carved. You can see the changing fashion in monuments—just like everything else."

Somewhere in this time I began dreaming of my father. Not the robust father of my childhood, the handsome man with healthy pink skin and brown eyes and a mustache and the thinning hair parted in the middle. My dead father. We were taking him home from the hospital. It was understood that he had come back from death. This was amazing and joyous. On the other hand, he was terribly mysteriously damaged, or, more accurately, spoiled and unclean. He was very yellowed and debilitated by his death, and there were no guarantees that he wouldn't soon die again. He seemed aware of this and his entire personality was changed. He was angry and impatient with all of us. We were trying to help him in some way, struggling to get him home, but something prevented us, something we had to fix, a tattered suitcase that had sprung open, some mechanical thing: he had a car but it wouldn't start; or the car was made of wood; or his clothes, which had become too large for him, had caught in the door. In one version he was all bandaged and as we tried to lift him from his wheelchair into a taxi the bandage began to unroll and catch in the spokes of the wheelchair. This seemed to be some unreasonableness on his part. My mother looked on sadly and tried to get him to cooperate.

That was the dream. I shared it with no one. Once when I woke, crying out, my brother turned on the light. He wanted to know what I'd been dreaming but I pretended I didn't remember. The dream made me feel guilty. I felt guilty *in* the dream too because my enraged father knew we didn't want to live with him. The dream represented us taking him home, or trying to, but it was nevertheless understood by all of us that he was to live alone. He was this derelict back from death, but what we were doing was taking him to some place where he would live by himself without help from anyone until he died again.

At one point I became so fearful of this dream that I tried not to go to sleep. I tried to think of good things about my father and to remember him before his illness. He used to call me "matey." "Hello, matey," he would say when he came home from work. He always wanted us to go someplace—to the store, to the park, to a ball game. He loved to walk. When I went walking with him he would say: "Hold your shoulders back, don't slump. Hold your head up and look at the world. Walk as if you meant it!" As he strode down the street his shoulders moved from side to side, as if he was hearing some kind of cakewalk. He moved with a bounce. He was always eager to see what was around the corner.

The next request for a letter coincided with a special occasion in the house: My brother Harold had met a girl he liked and had gone out with her several times. Now she was coming to our house for dinner.

We had prepared for this for days, cleaning everything in sight, giving the house a going-over, washing the dust of disuse from the glasses and good dishes. My mother came home early from work to get the dinner going. We opened the gateleg table in the living room and brought in the kitchen chairs. My mother spread the table with a laundered white cloth and put out her silver. It was the first family occasion since my father's illness.

I liked my brother's girlfriend a lot. She was a thin girl with very straight hair and she had a terrific smile. Her presence seemed to excite the air. It was amazing to have a living breathing girl in our house. She looked around and what she said was: "Oh, I've never seen so many books!" While she and my brother sat at the table my mother was in the kitchen putting the food into serving bowls and I was going from the kitchen to the living room, kidding around like a waiter, with a white cloth over my arm and a high style of service, placing the serving dish of green beans on the table with a flourish. In the kitchen my mother's eyes were sparkling. She looked at me and nodded and mimed the words: "She's adorable!"

My brother suffered himself to be waited on. He was wary of what we might say. He kept glancing at the girl—her name was Susan—to see if we met with her approval. She worked in an insurance office and was taking courses in accounting at City College. Harold was under a terrible strain but he was excited and happy too. He had bought a bottle of Concord-grape wine to go with the roast chicken. He held up his glass and proposed a toast. My mother said: "To good health and happiness," and we all drank, even I. At that moment the phone rang and I went into the bedroom to get it.

"Jonathan? This is your Aunt Frances. How is everyone?"

"Fine, thank you."

"I want to ask one last favor of you. I need a letter from Jack. Your grandma's very ill. Do you think you can?"

"Who is it?" my mother called from the living room.

"OK, Aunt Frances," I said quickly. "I have to go now, we're eating dinner." And I hung up the phone.

"It was my friend Louie," I said, sitting back down. "He didn't know the math pages to review."

The dinner was very fine. Harold and Susan washed the dishes and by the time they were done my mother and I had folded up the gateleg table and put it back against the wall and I had swept the crumbs up with the carpet sweeper. We all sat and talked and listened to records for a while and then my brother took Susan home. The evening had gone very well.

Once when my mother wasn't home my brother had pointed out something: the letters from Jack weren't really necessary. "What is this ritual?" he said, holding his palms up. "Grandma is almost totally blind, she's half deaf and crippled. Does the situation really call for a literary composition? Does it need verisimilitude? Would the old lady know the difference if she was read the phone book?"

"Then why did Aunt Frances ask me?"

"That is the question, Jonathan. Why did she? After all, she could write the letter herself—what difference would it make? And if not Frances, why not Frances' sons, the Amherst students? They should have learned by now to write."

"But they're not Jack's sons," I said.

"That's exactly the point," my brother said. "The idea is *service*. Dad used to bust his balls getting them things wholesale, getting them deals on things. Frances of Westchester really needed things at cost. And Aunt Molly. And Aunt Molly's husband, and Aunt Molly's ex-husband. Grandma, if she needed an errand done. He was always on the hook for something. They never thought his time was important. They never thought every favor he got was one he had to pay back. Appliances, records, watches, china, opera tickets, any goddamn thing. Call Jack."

"It was a matter of pride to him to be able to do things for them," I said. "To have connections."

"Yeah, I wonder why," my brother said. He looked out the window.

Then suddenly it dawned on me that I was being implicated.

"You should use your head more," my brother said.

Yet I had agreed once again to write a letter from the desert and so I did. I mailed it off to Aunt Frances. A few days later, when I came home from school, I thought I saw her sitting in her car in front of our house. She drove a black Buick Roadmaster, a very large clean car with whitewall tires. It was Aunt Frances all right. She blew the horn when she saw me. I went over and leaned in at the window.

"Hello, Jonathan," she said. "I haven't long. Can you get in the car?"

"Mom's not home," I said. "She's working."

"I know that. I came to talk to you."

"Would you like to come upstairs?"

"I can't, I have to get back to Larchmont. Can you get in for a moment, please?"

I got in the car. My Aunt Frances was a very pretty white-haired woman, very elegant, and she wore tasteful clothes. I had always liked her and from the time I was a child she had enjoyed pointing out to everyone that I looked more like her son than Jack's. She wore white gloves and held the steering wheel and looked straight ahead as she talked, as if the car was in traffic and not sitting at the curb.

"Jonathan," she said, "there is your letter on the seat. Needless to say I didn't read it to Grandma. I'm giving it back to you and I won't ever say a word to anyone. This is just between us. I never expected cruelty from you. I never thought you were capable of doing something so deliberately cruel and perverse."

I said nothing.

"Your mother has very bitter feelings and now I see

she has poisoned you with them. She has always resented the family. She is a very strong-willed, selfish person."

"No she isn't," I said.

"I wouldn't expect you to agree. She drove poor Jack crazy with her demands. She always had the highest aspirations and he could never fulfill them to her satisfaction. When he still had his store he kept your mother's brother, who drank, on salary. After the war when he began to make a little money he had to buy Ruth a mink jacket because she was so desperate to have one. He had debts to pay but she wanted a mink. He was a very special person, my brother, he should have accomplished something special, but he loved your mother and devoted his life to her. And all she ever thought about was keeping up with the Joneses."

I watched the traffic going up the Grand Concourse. A bunch of kids were waiting at the bus stop at the corner. They had put their books on the ground and were horsing around.

"I'm sorry I have to descend to this," Aunt Frances said. "I don't like talking about people this way. If I have nothing good to say about someone, I'd rather not say anything. How is Harold?"

"Fine."

"Did he help you write this marvelous letter?"

"No."

After a moment she said more softly: "How are you all getting along?"

"Fine."

"I would invite you up for Passover if I thought your mother would accept."

I didn't answer.

She turned on the engine. "I'll say good-bye now, Jonathan. Take your letter. I hope you give some time to thinking about what you've done."

That evening when my mother came home from work I saw that she wasn't as pretty as my Aunt Frances. I usually thought my mother was a good-looking woman, but I saw now that she was too heavy and that her hair was undistinguished.

"Why are you looking at me?" she said.

"I'm not."

"I learned something interesting today," my mother said. "We may be eligible for a V.A. pension because of the time your father spent in the Navy."

That took me by surprise. Nobody had ever told me my father was in the Navy.

"In World War I," she said, "he went to Webb's Naval Academy on the Harlem River. He was training to be an ensign. But the war ended and he never got his commission."

After dinner the three of us went through the closets looking for my father's papers, hoping to find some proof that could be filed with the Veterans Administration. We came up with two things, a Victory medal, which my brother said everyone got for being in the service during the Great War, and an astounding sepia photograph of my father and his shipmates on the deck of a ship. They were dressed in bell-bottoms and T-shirts and armed with mops and pails, brooms and brushes.

"I never knew this," I found myself saying. "I never knew this."

"You just don't remember," my brother said.

I was able to pick out my father. He stood at the end of the row, a thin, handsome boy with a full head of hair, a mustache, and an intelligent smiling countenance.

"He had a joke," my mother said. "They called their training ship the S.S. *Constipation* because it never moved."

Neither the picture nor the medal was proof of anything, but my brother thought a duplicate of my father's service record had to be in Washington somewhere and that it was just a matter of learning how to go about finding it.

"The pension wouldn't amount to much," my mother said. "Twenty or thirty dollars. But it would certainly help."

I took the picture of my father and his shipmates and propped it against the lamp at my bedside. I looked into his youthful face and tried to relate it to the Father I knew. I looked at the picture a long time. Only gradually did my eye connect it to the set of Great Sea Novels in the bottom shelf of the bookcase a few feet away. My father had given that set to me: it was uniformly bound in green with gilt lettering and it included works by Melville, Conrad, Victor Hugo and Captain Marryat. And lying across the top of the books, jammed in under the sagging shelf above, was his old ship's telescope in its wooden case with the brass snap.

I thought how stupid, and imperceptive, and self-centered I had been never to have understood while he was alive what my father's dream for his life had been.

On the other hand, I had written in my last letter from Arizona—the one that had so angered Aunt Frances—something that might allow me, the writer in the family, to soften my judgment of myself. I will conclude by giving the letter here in its entirety.

Dear Mama,

This will be my final letter to you since I have been told by the doctors that I am dying.

I have sold my store at a very fine profit and am sending Frances a check for five thousand dollars to be deposited in your account. My present to you, Mamaleh. Let Frances show you the passbook.

As for the nature of my ailment, the doctors haven't told me what it is, but I know that I am simply dying of the wrong life. I should never have come to the desert. It wasn't the place for me.

I have asked Ruth and the boys to have my body cremated and the ashes scattered in the ocean.

Your loving son,
Jack

Tobias Wolff

(b. 1945)

Born in Birmingham, Alabama, Tobias Wolff was raised in Chinook, Washington, and educated at Oxford University and Stanford University. A veteran of Vietnam, he became a reporter for *The Washington Post*, and subsequently taught at Stanford University, Goddard College, Arizona State University, and—since 1980—has taught literature and creative writing at Syracuse University each fall. He has published a novel, *The Barracks Thief* (1984), which won a PEN/Faulkner Award for Fiction, two collections of short stories, *In the Garden of the North American Martyrs* (1981) and *Back in the World* (1985), and a memoir of youth titled *This Boy's Life* (1989). He is a recipient of a Wallace Stegner Fellowship at Stanford University, a National Endowment for the Arts Fellowship, a Guggenheim Fellowship, and the St. Lawrence Award for Fiction.

THE RICH BROTHER

There were two brothers, Pete and Donald.

Pete, the older brother, was in real estate. He and his wife had a Century 21 franchise in Santa Cruz. Pete worked hard and made a lot of money, but not any more than he thought he deserved. He had two daughters, a sailboat, a house from which he could see a thin slice of the ocean, and friends doing well enough in their own lives not to wish bad luck on him. Donald, the younger brother, was still single. He lived alone, painted houses when he found the work, and got deeper in debt to Pete when he didn't.

No one would have taken them for brothers. Where Pete was stout and hearty and at home in the world, Donald was bony, grave, and obsessed with the fate of his soul. Over the years Donald had worn the images of two different Perfect Masters around his neck. Out of devotion to the second of these he entered an ashram in Berkeley, where he nearly died of undiagnosed hepatitis. By the time Pete finished paying the medical bills Donald had become a Christian. He drifted from church to church, then joined a pentecostal community that met somewhere in the Mission District to sing in tongues and swap prophecies.

Pete couldn't make sense of it. Their parents were both dead, but while they were alive neither of them had found it necessary to believe in anything. They managed to be decent people without making fools of themselves, and Pete had the same ambition. He thought that the whole thing was an excuse for Donald to take himself seriously.

The trouble was that Donald couldn't content himself with worrying about his own soul. He had to worry about everyone else's, and especially Pete's. He handed down his judgments in ways that he seemed to consider subtle: through significant silence, innuendo, looks of mild despair that said, *Brother, what have you come to*? What Pete had come to, as far as he could tell, was prosperity. That was the real issue between them. Pete prospered and Donald did not prosper.

At the age of forty Pete took up sky diving. He made his first jump with two friends who'd started only a few months earlier and were already doing stunts. They were both coked to the gills when they jumped but Pete wanted to do it straight, at least the first time, and he was glad that he did. He would never have used the word *mystical*, but that was how Pete felt about the experience. Later he made the mistake of trying to describe it to Donald, who kept asking how much it cost and then acted appalled when Pete told him.

"At least I'm trying something new," Pete said. "At least I'm breaking the pattern."

Not long after that conversation Donald also broke the pattern, by going to live on a farm outside of Paso Robles. The farm was owned by several members of Donald's community, who had bought it and moved there with the idea of forming a family of faith. That was how Donald explained it in the first letter he sent. Every week Pete heard how happy Donald was, how "in the Lord." He told Pete that he was praying for him, he and the rest of Pete's brothers and sisters on the farm.

"I only have one brother," Pete wanted to answer, "and that's enough." But he kept this thought to himself.

In November the letters stopped. Pete didn't worry about this at first, but when he called Donald at Thanksgiving Donald was grim. He tried to sound upbeat but he didn't try hard enough to make it convincing. "Now listen," Pete said, "you don't have to stay in that place if you don't want to."

"I'll be all right," Donald answered.

"That's not the point. Being all right is not the point. If you don't like what's going on up there, then get out."

"I'm all right," Donald said again, more firmly. "I'm doing fine."

But he called Pete a week later and said that he was quitting the farm. When Pete asked him where he intended to go, Donald admitted that he had no plan. His car had been repossessed just before he left the city, and he was flat broke.

"I guess you'll have to stay with us," Pete said.

Donald put up a show of resistance. Then he gave in. "Just until I get my feet on the ground," he said.

"Right," Pete said. "Check out your options." He told Donald he'd send him money for a bus ticket, but as they were about to hang up Pete changed his mind. He knew that Donald would try hitchhiking to save the fare. Pete didn't want him out on the road all alone where some head case could pick him up, where anything could happen to him.

"Better yet," he said, "I'll come and get you."

"You don't have to do that. I didn't expect you to do that," Donald said. He added, "It's a pretty long drive."

"Just tell me how to get there."

But Donald wouldn't give him directions. He said that the farm was too depressing, that Pete wouldn't like it. Instead, he insisted on meeting Pete at a service station called Jonathan's Mechanical Emporium.

"You must be kidding," Pete said.

"It's close to the highway," Donald said. "I didn't name it."

"That's one for the collection," Pete said.

The day before he left to bring Donald home, Pete received a letter from a man who described himself as "head of household" at the farm where Donald had been living. From this letter Pete learned that Donald had not quit the farm, but had been asked to leave. The letter was written on the back of a mimeographed survey form asking people to record their response to a ceremony of some kind. The last question said:

What did you feel during the liturgy?
a) Being
b) Becoming
c) Being and Becoming
d) None of the Above
e) All of the Above

Pete tried to forget the letter. But of course he couldn't. Each time he thought of it he felt crowded and breathless, a feeling that came over him again when he drove into the service station and saw Donald sitting against a wall with his head on his knees. It was late afternoon. A paper cup tumbled slowly past Donald's feet, pushed by the damp wind.

Pete honked and Donald raised his head. He smiled at Pete, then stood and stretched. His arms were long and thin and white. He wore a red bandanna across his forehead, a T-shirt with a couple of words on the front. Pete couldn't read them because the letters were inverted.

"Grow up," Pete yelled. "Get a Mercedes."

Donald came up to the window. He bent down and said, "Thanks for coming. You must be totally whipped."

"I'll make it." Pete pointed at Donald's T-shirt. "What's that supposed to say?"

Donald looked down at his shirt front. "Try God. I guess I put it on backwards. Pete, could I borrow a couple of dollars? I owe these people for coffee and sandwiches."

Pete took five twenties from his wallet and held them out the window.

Donald stepped back as if horrified. "I don't need that much."

"I can't keep track of all these nickels and dimes," Pete said. "Just pay me back when your ship comes in." He waved the bills impatiently. "Go on—take it."

"Only for now." Donald took the money and went into the service station office. He came out carrying two orange sodas, one of which he gave to Pete as he got into the car. "My treat," he said.

"No bags?"

"Wow, thanks for reminding me," Donald said. He balanced his drink on the dashboard, but the slight rocking of the car as he got out tipped it onto the passenger's seat, where half its contents foamed over before Pete could snatch it up again. Donald looked on while Pete held the bottle out the window, soda running down his fingers.

"Wipe it up," Pete told him. "Quick!"

"With what?"

Pete stared at Donald. "That shirt. Use the shirt."

Donald pulled a long face but did as he was told, his pale skin puckering against the wind.

"Great, just great," Pete said. "We haven't even left the gas station yet."

Afterwards, on the highway, Donald said, "This is a new car, isn't it?"

"Yes. This is a new car."

"Is that why you're so upset about the seat?"

"Forget it, okay? Let's just forget about it."

"I said I was sorry."

Pete said, "I just wish you'd be more careful. These seats are made of leather. That stain won't come out, not to mention the smell. I don't see why I can't have leather seats that smell like leather instead of orange pop."

"What was wrong with the other car?"

Pete glanced over at Donald. Donald had raised the hood of the blue sweatshirt he'd put on. The peaked hood above his gaunt, watchful face gave him the look of an inquisitor.

"There wasn't anything wrong with it," Pete said. "I just happened to like this one better."

Donald nodded.

There was a long silence between them as Pete drove on and the day darkened toward evening. On either side of the road lay stubble-covered fields. A line of low hills ran along the horizon, topped here and there with trees black against the grey sky. In the approaching line of cars a driver turned on his headlights. Pete did the same.

"So what happened?" he asked. "Farm life not your bag?"

Donald took some time to answer, and at last he said, simply, "It was my fault."

"What was your fault?"

"The whole thing. Don't play dumb, Pete. I know they wrote to you." Donald looked at Pete, then stared out the windshield again.

"I'm not playing dumb."

Donald shrugged.

"All I really know is they asked you to leave," Pete went on. "I don't know any of the particulars."

"I blew it," Donald said. "Believe me, you don't want to hear the gory details."

"Sure I do," Pete said. He added, "Everybody likes the gory details."

"You mean everybody likes to hear how someone else messed up."

"Right," Pete said. "That's the way it is here on Spaceship Earth."

Donald bent one knee onto the front seat and leaned against the door so that he was facing Pete instead of the windshield. Pete was aware of Donald's scrutiny. He waited. Night was coming on in a rush now, filling the hollows of the land. Donald's long cheeks and deep-set eyes were dark with shadow. His brow was white. "Do you ever dream about me?" Donald asked.

"Do I ever dream about you? What kind of a question is that? Of course I don't dream about you," Pete said, untruthfully.

"What do you dream about?"

"Sex and money. Mostly money. A nightmare is when I dream I don't have any."

"You're just making that up," Donald said.

Pete smiled.

"Sometimes I wake up at night," Donald went on, "and I can tell you're dreaming about me."

"We were talking about the farm," Pete said. "Let's finish that conversation and then we can talk about our various out-of-body experiences and the interesting things we did during previous incarnations."

For a moment Donald looked like a grinning skull; then he turned serious again. "There's not that much to tell," he said. "I just didn't do anything right."

"That's a little vague," Pete said.

"Well, like the groceries. Whenever it was my turn to get the groceries I'd blow it somehow. I'd bring the groceries home and half of them would be missing, or I'd have all the wrong things, the wrong kind of flour or the wrong kind of chocolate or whatever. One time I gave them away. It's not funny, Pete."

Pete said, "Who did you give the groceries to?"

"Just some people I picked up on the way home. Some fieldworkers. They had about eight kids with them and they didn't even speak English—just nodded their heads. Still, I shouldn't have given away the groceries. Not all of them, anyway. I really learned my lesson about that. You have to be practical. You have to be fair to yourself." Donald leaned forward, and Pete could sense his excitement. "There's nothing actually wrong with being in business," he said. "As long as you're fair to other people you can still be fair to yourself. I'm thinking of going into business, Pete."

"We'll talk about it," Pete said. "So, that's the story? There isn't any more to it than that?"

"What did they tell you?" Donald asked.

"Nothing."

"They must have told you something."

Pete shook his head.

"They didn't tell you about the fire?" When Pete shook his head again Donald regarded him for a time, then said, "I don't know. It was stupid. I just completely lost it." He folded his arms across his chest and slumped back into the corner. "Everybody had to take turns cooking dinner. I usually did tuna casserole or spaghetti with garlic bread. But this one night I thought I'd do something different, something really interesting." Donald looked sharply at Pete. "It's all a big laugh to you, isn't it?"

"I'm sorry," Pete said.

"You don't know when to quit. You just keep hitting away."

"Tell me about the fire, Donald."

Donald kept watching him. "You have this compulsion to make me look foolish."

"Come off it, Donald. Don't make a big thing out of this."

"I know why you do it. It's because you don't have any purpose in life. You're afraid to relate to people who do, so you make fun of them."

"Relate," Pete said softly.

"You're basically a very frightened individual," Donald said. "Very threatened. You've always been like that. Do you remember when you used to try to kill me?"

"I don't have any compulsion to make you look foolish, Donald—you do it yourself. You're doing it right now."

"You can't tell me you don't remember," Donald said. "It was after my operation. You remember that."

"Sort of." Pete shrugged. "Not really."

"Oh yes," Donald said. "Do you want to see the scar?"

"I remember you had an operation. I don't remember

the specifics, that's all. And I sure as hell don't remember trying to kill you."

"Oh yes," Donald repeated, maddeningly. "You bet your life you did. All the time. The thing was, I couldn't have anything happen to me where they sewed me up because then my intestines would come apart again and poison me. That was a big issue, Pete. Mom was always in a state about me climbing trees and so on. And you used to hit me there every chance you got."

"Mom was in a state every time you burped," Pete said. "I don't know. Maybe I bumped into you accidentally once or twice. I never did it deliberately."

"Every chance you got," Donald said. "Like when the folks went out at night and left you to baby-sit. I'd hear them say good night, and then I'd hear the car start up, and when they were gone I'd lie there and listen. After a while I would hear you coming down the hall, and I would close my eyes and pretend to be asleep. There were nights when you would stand outside the door, just stand there, and then go away again. But most nights you'd open the door and I would hear you in the room with me, breathing. You'd come over and sit next to me on the bed—you remember, Pete, you have to—you'd sit next to me on the bed and pull the sheets back. If I was on my stomach you'd roll me over. Then you would lift up my pajama shirt and start hitting me on my stitches. You'd hit me as hard as you could, over and over. And I would just keep lying there with my eyes closed. I was afraid that you'd get mad if you knew I was awake. Is that strange or what? I was afraid that you'd get mad if you found out that I knew you were trying to kill me." Donald laughed. "Come on, you can't tell me you don't remember that."

"It might have happened once or twice. Kids do those things. I can't get all excited about something I maybe did twenty-five years ago."

"No maybe about it. You did it."

Pete said, "You're wearing me out with this stuff. We've got a long drive ahead of us and if you don't back off pretty soon we aren't going to make it. You aren't, anyway."

Donald turned away.

"I'm doing my best," Pete said. The self-pity in his own voice made the words sound like a lie. But they weren't a lie! He was doing his best.

The car topped a rise. In the distance Pete saw a cluster of lights that blinked out when he started downhill. There was no moon. The sky was low and black.

"Come to think of it," Pete said, "I did have a dream about you the other night." Then he added, impatiently, as if Donald were badgering him, "A couple of other nights too. I'm getting hungry," he said.

"The same dream?"

"Different dreams. I only remember one of them well. There was something wrong with me, and you were helping out. Taking care of me. Just the two of us. I don't know where everyone else was supposed to be."

Pete left it at that. He didn't tell Donald that in this dream he was blind

"I wonder if that was when I woke up," Donald said. He added, "I'm sorry I got into that thing about my scar. I keep trying to forget it but I guess I never will. Not really. It was pretty strange, having someone around all the time who wanted to get rid of me."

"Kid stuff," Pete said. "Ancient history."

They ate dinner at a Denny's on the other side of King City. As Pete was paying the check he heard a man behind him say, "Excuse me, but I wonder if I might ask which way you're going?" and Donald answer, "Santa Cruz."

"Perfect," the man said.

Pete could see him in the fish-eye mirror above the cash register: a red blazer with some kind of crest on the pocket, little black moustache, glossy black hair combed down on his forehead like a Roman emperor's. A rug, Pete thought. Definitely a rug.

Pete got his change and turned. "Why is that perfect?" he asked.

The man looked at Pete. He had a soft ruddy face that was doing its best to express pleasant surprise, as if this new wrinkle were all he could have wished for, but the eyes behind the aviator glasses showed signs of regret. His lips were moist and shiny. "I take it you're together," he said.

"You got it," Pete told him

"All the better, then," the man went on. "It so happens I'm going to Santa Cruz myself. Had a spot of car trouble down the road. The old Caddy let me down."

"What kind of trouble?" Pete asked.

"Engine trouble," the man said. "I'm afraid it's a bit urgent. My daughter is sick. Urgently sick. I've got a telegram here." He patted the breast pocket of his blazer.

Pete grinned. Amazing, he thought, the old sick daughter ploy, but before he could say anything Donald got into the act again. "No problem," Donald said. "We've got tons of room."

"Not that much room," Pete said.

Donald nodded. "I'll put my things in the trunk."

"The trunk's full," Pete told him.

"It so happens I'm traveling light," the man said. "This leg of the trip anyway. In fact I don't have any luggage at this particular time."

Pete said, "Left it in the old Caddy, did you?"

"Exactly," the man said.

"No problem," Donald repeated. He walked outside and the man went with him. Together they strolled across the parking lot, Pete following at a distance. When they reached Pete's car Donald raised his face to the sky, and the man did the same. They stood there looking up. "Dark night," Donald said.

"Stygian," the man said.

Pete still had it in mind to brush him off, but he didn't do that. Instead he unlocked the door for him. He wanted to see what would happen. It was an adventure, but not a dangerous adventure. The man might steal Pete's ashtrays but he wouldn't kill him. If Pete got killed on the road it would be by some spiritual person in a sweatsuit, someone with his eyes on the far horizon and a wet Try God T-shirt in his duffel bag.

As soon as they left the parking lot the man lit a cigar. He blew a cloud of smoke over Pete's shoulder and sighed with pleasure. "Put it out," Pete told him.

"Of course," the man said. Pete looked into the rear-view mirror and saw the man take another long puff before dropping the cigar out the window. "Forgive me," he said. "I should have asked. Name's Webster, by the way."

Donald turned and looked back at him. "First name or last?"

The man hesitated. "Last," he said finally.

"I know a Webster," Donald said. "Mick Webster."

"There are many of us," Webster said.

"Big fellow, wooden leg," Pete said.

Donald gave Pete a look.

Webster shook his head. "Doesn't ring a bell. Still, I wouldn't deny the connection. Might be one of the cousinry."

"What's your daughter got?" Pete asked.

"That isn't clear," Webster answered. "It appears to be a female complaint of some nature. Then again it may be tropical." He was quiet for a moment, and added: "If indeed it *is* tropical, I will have to assume some of the blame myself. It was my own vaulting ambition that first led us to the tropics and kept us in the tropics all those many years, exposed to every evil. Truly I have much to answer for. I left my wife there."

Donald said quietly, "You mean she died?"

"I buried her with these hands. The earth will be repaid, gold for gold."

"Which tropics?" Pete asked.

"The tropics of Peru."

"What part of Peru are they in?"

"The lowlands," Webster said.

Pete nodded. "What's it like down there?"

"Another world," Webster said. His tone was sepulchral. "A world better imagined than described."

"Far out," Pete said.

The three men rode in silence for a time. A line of trucks went past in the other direction, trailers festooned with running lights, engines roaring.

"Yes," Webster said at last, "I have much to answer for."

Pete smiled at Donald, but Donald had turned in his

seat again and was gazing at Webster. "I'm sorry about your wife," Donald said.

"What did she die of?" Pete asked.

"A wasting illness," Webster said. "The doctors have no name for it, but I do." He leaned forward and said, fiercely, "*Greed.*" Then he slumped back against his seat. "My greed, not hers. She wanted no part of it."

Pete bit his lip. Webster was a find and Pete didn't want to scare him off by hooting at him. In a voice low and innocent of knowingness, he asked, "What took you there?"

"It's difficult for me to talk about."

"Try," Pete told him.

"A cigar would make it easier."

Donald turned to Pete and said, "It's okay with me."

"All right," Pete said. "Go ahead. Just keep the window rolled down."

"Much obliged." A match flared. There were eager sucking sounds.

"Let's hear it," Pete said.

"I am by training an engineer," Webster began. "My work has exposed me to all but one of the continents, to desert and alp and forest, to every terrain and season of the earth. Some years ago I was hired by the Peruvian government to search for tungsten in the tropics. My wife and daughter accompanied me. We were the only white people for a thousand miles in any direction, and we had no choice but to live as the Indians lived—to share their food and drink and even their culture."

Pete said, "You knew the lingo, did you?"

"We picked it up." The ember of the cigar bobbed up and down. "We were used to learning as necessity decreed. At any rate, it became evident after a couple of years that there was no tungsten to be found. My wife had fallen ill and was pleading to be taken home. But I was deaf to her pleas, because by then I was on the trail of another metal—a metal far more valuable than tungsten."

"Let me guess," Pete said. "Gold?"

Donald looked at Pete, then back at Webster.

"Gold," Webster said. "A vein of gold greater than the Mother Lode itself. After I found the first traces of it nothing could tear me away from my search—not the sickness of my wife nor anything else. I was determined to uncover the vein, and so I did—but not before I laid my wife to rest. As I say, the earth will be repaid."

Webster was quiet. Then he said, "But life must go on. In the years since my wife's death I have been making the arrangements necessary to open the mine. I could have done it immediately, of course, enriching myself beyond measure, but I knew what that would mean—the exploitation of our beloved Indians, the brutal destruction of their environment. I felt I had too much to atone for already." Webster paused, and when he spoke again his voice was dull and rushed, as if he had used up all the interest he had in his own words. "Instead I drew up a program for returning the bulk of the wealth to the Indians themselves. A kind of trust fund. The interest alone will allow them to secure their ancient lands and rights in perpetuity. At the same time, our investors will be rewarded a thousandfold. Two-thousandfold. Everyone will prosper together."

"That's great," Donald said. "That's the way it ought to be."

Pete said, "I'm willing to bet that you just happen to have a few shares left. Am I right?"

Webster made no reply.

"Well?" Pete knew that Webster was on to him now, but he didn't care. The story had bored him. He'd expected something different, something original, and Webster had let him down. He hadn't even tried. Pete felt sour and stale. His eyes burned from cigar smoke and the high beams of road-hogging truckers. "Douse the stogie," he said to Webster. "I told you to keep the window down."

"Got a little nippy back here."

Donald said, "Hey, Pete. Lighten up."

"Douse it!"

Webster sighed. He got rid of the cigar.

"I'm a wreck," Pete said to Donald. "You want to drive for a while?"

Donald nodded.

Pete pulled over and they changed places.

Webster kept his counsel in the back seat. Donald hummed while he drove, until Pete told him to stop. Then everything was quiet.

Donald was humming again when Pete woke up. Pete stared sullenly at the road, at the white lines sliding past the car. After a few moments of this he turned and said, "How long have I been out?"

Donald glanced at him. "Twenty, twenty-five minutes."

Pete looked behind him and saw that Webster was gone. "Where's our friend?"

"You just missed him. He got out in Soledad. He told me to say thanks and good-bye."

"Soledad? What about his sick daughter? How did he explain her away?" Pete leaned over the seat. Both ashtrays were still in place. Floor mats. Door handles.

"He has a brother living there. He's going to borrow a car from him and drive the rest of the way in the morning."

"I'll bet his brother's living there," Pete said. "Doing fifty concurrent life sentences. His brother and his sister and his mom and his dad."

"I kind of liked him," Donald said.

"I'm sure you did," Pete said wearily.

"He was interesting. He'd been places."

"His cigars had been places, I'll give you that."

"Come on, Pete."

"Come on yourself. What a phony."

"You don't know that."

"Sure I do."

"How? How do you know?"

Pete stretched. "Brother, there are some things you're just born knowing. What's the gas situation?"

"We're a little low."

"Then why didn't you get some more?"

"I wish you wouldn't snap at me like that," Donald said.

"Then why don't you use your head? What if we run out?"

"We'll make it," Donald said. "I'm pretty sure we've got enough to make it. You didn't have to be so rude to him," Donald added.

Pete took a deep breath. "I don't feel like running out of gas tonight, okay?"

Donald pulled in at the next station they came to and filled the tank while Pete went to the men's room. When Pete came back, Donald was sitting in the passenger's seat. The attendant came up to the driver's window as Pete got in behind the wheel. He bent down and said, "Twelve fifty-five."

"You heard the man," Pete said to Donald.

Donald looked straight ahead. He didn't move.

"Cough up," Pete said. "This trip's on you."

Donald said, softly, "I can't."

"Sure you can. Break out that wad."

Donald glanced up at the attendant, then at Pete. "Please," he said. "Pete, I don't have it anymore."

Pete took this in. He nodded, and paid the attendant.

Donald began to speak when they left the station but Pete cut him off. He said, "I don't want to hear from you right now. You just keep quiet or I swear to God I won't be responsible."

They left the fields and entered a tunnel of tall trees. The trees went on and on. "Let me get this straight," Pete said at last. "You don't have the money I gave you."

"You treated him like a bug or something," Donald said.

"You don't have the money," Pete said again.

Donald shook his head.

"Since I bought dinner, and since we didn't stop anywhere in between, I assume you gave it to Webster. Is that right? Is that what you did with it?"

"Yes."

Pete looked at Donald. His face was dark under the hood but he still managed to convey a sense of remove, as if none of this had anything to do with him.

"Why?" Pete asked. "Why did you give it to him?" When Donald didn't answer, Pete said, "A hundred dollars. Gone, Just like that. I *worked* for that money, Donald."

"I know, I know," Donald said.

"You don't know! How could you? You get money by holding out your hand."

"I work too," Donald said.

"You work too. Don't kid yourself, brother."

Donald leaned toward Pete, about to say something, but Pete cut him off again.

"You're not the only one on the payroll, Donald. I don't think you understand that. I have a family."

"Pete, I'll pay you back."

"Like hell you will. A hundred dollars!" Pete hit the steering wheel with the palm of his hand. "Just because you think I hurt some goofball's feelings. Jesus, Donald."

"That's not the reason," Donald said. "And I didn't just *give* him the money."

"What do you call it, then. What do you call what you did?"

"I *invested* it. I wanted a share, Pete." When Pete looked over at him Donald nodded and said again, "I wanted a share."

Pete said, "I take it you're referring to the gold mine in Peru."

"Yes," Donald said.

"You believe that such a gold mine exists?"

Donald looked at Pete, and Pete could see him just beginning to catch on. "You'll believe anything," Pete said. "Won't you? You really will believe anything at all."

"I'm sorry," Donald said, and turned away.

Pete drove on between the trees and considered the truth of what he had just said—that Donald would believe anything at all. And it came to him that it would be just like this unfair life for Donald to come out ahead in the end, by believing in some outrageous promise that would turn out to be true and that he, Pete, would reject out of hand because he was too wised up to listen to anybody's pitch anymore except for laughs. What a joke. What a joke if there really was a blessing to be had, and the blessing didn't come to the one who deserved it, the one who did all the work, but to the other.

And as if this had already happened Pete felt a shadow

move upon him, darkening his thoughts. After a time he said, "I can see where all this is going, Donald."

"I'll pay you back," Donald said.

"No," Pete said. "You won't pay me back. You can't. You don't know how. All you've ever done is take. All your life."

Donald shook his head.

"I see exactly where this is going," Pete went on. "You can't work, you can't take care of yourself, you believe anything anyone tells you. I'm stuck with you, aren't I?" He looked over at Donald. "I've got you on my hands for good."

Donald pressed his fingers against the dashboard as if to brace himself. "I'll get out," he said.

Pete kept driving.

"Let me out," Donald said. "I mean it, Pete."

"Do you?"

Donald hesitated. "Yes," he said.

"Be sure," Pete told him. "This is it. This is for keeps."

"I mean it."

"All right. You made the choice." Pete braked the car sharply and swung it to the shoulder of the road. He turned off the engine and got out. Trees loomed on both sides, shutting out the sky. The air was cold and musty. Pete took Donald's duffel bag from the back seat and set it down behind the car. He stood there, facing Donald in the red glow of the taillights. "It's better this way," Pete said.

Donald just looked at him.

"Better for you," Pete said.

Donald hugged himself. He was shaking. "You don't have to say all that," he told Pete. "I don't blame you."

"Blame me? What the hell are you talking about? Blame me for what?"

"For anything," Donald said.

"I want to know what you mean by blame me."

"Nothing. Nothing, Pete. You'd better get going. God bless you."

"That's it," Pete said. He dropped to one knee, searching the packed dirt with his hands. He didn't know what he was looking for; his hands would know when they found it.

Donald touched Pete's shoulder. "You'd better go," he said.

Somewhere in the trees Pete heard a branch snap. He stood up. He looked at Donald, then went back to the car and drove away. He drove fast, hunched over the wheel, conscious of the way he was hunched and the shallowness of his breathing, refusing to look at the mirror above his head until there was nothing behind him but darkness.

Then he said, "A hundred dollars," as if there were someone to hear.

The trees gave way to fields. Metal fences ran beside the road, plastered with windblown scraps of paper. Tule fog hung above the ditches, spilling into the road, dimming the ghostly halogen lights that burned in the yards of the farms Pete passed. The fog left beads of water rolling up the windshield.

Pete rummaged among his cassettes. He found Pachelbel's Canon and pushed it into the tape deck. When the violins began to play he leaned back and assumed an attentive expression as if he were really listening to them. He smiled to himself like a man at liberty to enjoy music, a man who has finished his work and settled his debts, done all things meet and due.

And in this way, smiling, nodding to the music, he went another mile or so and pretended that he was not already slowing down, that he was not going to turn back, that he would be able to drive on like this, alone, and have the right answer when his wife stood before him in the doorway of his home and asked, Where is he? Where is your brother?

Don Zacharia
(b. 1933)

Born in Mount Vernon, New York, Don Zacharia was graduated from New York University School of Journalism. For almost three decades he has pursued two careers, one as a wine merchant and proprietor of Zachys, a well-known liquor store in Scarsdale, New York, and the other as a novelist and short story writer. His stories have appeared in *Epoch, Partisan Review, Kenyon Review,* and *Pushcart Press,* and in 1982 his first novel, *The Match Trick,* was published. Currently he is working on the screenplay for a Hollywood film based on *The Match Trick* and on another novel, *Dying in Miami,* which depicts an upper-middle-class businessman's bizarre midlife crisis.

MY LEGACY

For many years my father was a communist, an atheist, and a *great* intellectual. When other boys my age were being slipped crisp five-dollar bills for bar mitzvah presents, I was out ringing door bells collecting quarters for the Spanish War Relief. My mother and older sister were also communists, atheists, and intellectuals. I was a communist for a while, an atheist for a while, but never, I mean *never,* an intellectual.

More than anything, I liked playing baseball, and none of the boys who were members my YCL, Young Communist League, knew or cared about baseball.

They all looked alike: very intense, very skinny, with

stringy black hair and double thick myopic glasses that looked like wrong-way binoculars perched on their noses. I always had a feeling if I ever threw them a baseball, they would put their hands up and the ball would smack them in the face. My comrades looked upon me with suspicion. My dedication toward the movement was not what it should have been, I was told, and I'm sure, if it hadn't been for my father, I would have been kicked out of the group. We met once a week at night and made plans for America when the revolution took over. The best part of the meetings was when they ended, and we were joined by our sister YCL group for soda, cake, and Chesterfield cigarettes. Everybody, including me, smoked like a fiend in those days. Young communist girls looked a million times better than young communist boys.

I played baseball with a bunch of local Italian kids in Mount Vernon, New York, where I grew up. I never discussed the U.S.S.R. with any of them. I'm sure if they had known what I was doing one night a week they would have kicked me off the team. One of the boys we played with was Ralph Branca. In those days he pitched and played third base. I played first base. Ralph would whistle the ball to me across the diamond so fast that some nights my left hand would swell up to twice its size, and I would have to soak my hand in warm salt water for hours. I knew my ball playing displeased my father. He never said it in so many words, but I could see the disappointment etched in his face. More than anything, my father wanted me to read. "Not to read," he would say, pausing deep in thought, "is not to have eyesight." I never answered him. What could I possibly say to that? Almost every day my father handed me books—not one book, but six, seven, eight, ten: Faulkner, Hemingway, Steinbeck, Dos Passos, William Carlos Williams, Sandburg, Whitman, Jack Reed. "Here," he would say, "read these and we'll talk about them tomorrow."

I tried. I really did. I would have liked to please my father, but with the exception of Ring Lardner and Jack London, I found them boring.

What My Father Did for a Living

Work interfered with my father's life, so he worked only three hours a day, selling newspapers to the morning commuters in a nearby affluent suburb. Could those people who thrust a nickel at my father for the morning *New York Daily Mirror,* waiting impatiently for their two cents change, possibly know that within the hour this short unshaven man, who some people thought looked like Lenin, would be working on translating a Chekhov story from Russian to Yiddish? My father was fluent in Russian, Polish, French, Italian, German, Hebrew, Yiddish and English. With Mrs. Redka as a Spanish teacher, I failed the only language I ever took, Beginning Spanish, three consecutive years.

Besides his income from his newspaper stand, my father made a modest amount of money translating an author's work from language to language, usually into Yiddish. When I say modest, I mean *modest.* For translating a Kafka novel from German to Yiddish, my father was paid sixty dollars. For translating ten Shalom Aleichem stories from Yiddish to Italian, he was paid forty dollars. I remember that particularly, because he kept complaining that Shalom Aleichem in Italian made as much sense as Baudelaire in Swahili.

Besides selling newspapers, and besides his work as a translator, my father wrote Yiddish poetry. As far as I know, he never received a nickel for his poetry. On the contrary, in a sense he paid for their publication. There were three Yiddish newspapers published in New York in the late thirties and early forties: the *Forward,* which my father and many of his friends considered a right-wing newspaper; the *Day* or *Tog,* a middle-of-the-road newspaper; and the *Freiheit,* a left-wing and, some people thought, communist paper.

My father had two arrangements: one with the *Freiheit* and one with the *Tog.* With the *Freiheit,* for every ten poems they published, he would arrange for three lifetime subscriptions. With the *Tog,* it was a one-on-one basis: for every poem—a lifetime subscription. He published most of his poetry in the *Freiheit.* A lifetime subscription to the *Freiheit* cost twelve dollars and fifty cents. So for thirty-seven dollars and fifty cents, my father published ten poems, or three dollars and fifty cents a poem. I'm sure he never thought of it in this way, but after translating ten Shalom Aleichem stories from Yiddish to Italian, net income forty dollars, and "selling" ten poems to the *Freiheit,* net outlay thirty-seven dollars and fifty cents, he showed a net profit of two dollars and fifty cents.

My House

Culture seeped through my house. It came at you from everywhere. The walls were infused with it; the floors exhaled it; the ceilings inhaled it. Every room looked like a library. Books everywhere: floor to ceiling, wall to wall, sitting on shelves, and, where there were no shelves, vertically stacked from the floor up. There were books in the kitchen, the bathroom, the hallways, and on every windowsill. We had a large oak table in the dining room. I do not recall a single meal served there because the dining room table always had at least a thousand books stacked on it. That was my father's desk: where he worked, read, translated, and wrote his poetry. My mother never had to worry about cleaning the walls, because there were no walls. If they weren't covered by books and bookcases, there were paintings—Picasso, Chagall, Matisse, Weber, Ernst, Walkowitz—paintings everywhere. Using a double-edged razor with black tape on one side, my father would carefully slit his favorite paintings out of the art books, put them in a simple frame, and exchange them for a painting already hanging. A Utrillo went up, a Picasso came down. One week Chagall would replace Matisse, only to be replaced the following week by Mondrian. It was a process without end. Besides the books, besides the art, there was classical music on from the moment he came home until he went to sleep. It was not unusual to see him abruptly stand up and conduct the last portion of Beethoven's Fifth or a Brahms violin concerto.

With the exception of my sister's boyfriends, the only people who came into my house were friends of my father: other intellectuals, poets and writers and would-be poets and would-be writers, communists and almost-communists. Quite often you could hear five languages being spoken simultaneously in my home. But more than anything, there were arguments: loud, shouting fist-thumping arguments. Was Ezra Pound a fascist? Was Leon Trotsky a socialist? What direction should the movement take? Was John Dos Passos truly a greater writer?

In the wintertime our radiators hissed not steam, but Theodore Dreiser. The hum from our refrigerator, the verses of Whitman. The whirr from the washing machine, the voice of Scott Fitzgerald. The sound of running water in the kitchen, the poetry of Sandburg. The way the wind rattled our front screen door, the stories of Shalom Aleichem. And I—I walked about my home from room to room flipping a baseball from hand to hand.

My Older Sister

My sister was twelve years older. Her name was Sarah. I don't know why my parents waited so long to have a second child. I am very grateful to my sister for many reasons, but more than anything else, for my name. When I was born, I was named Ivan Tukhachevshy Roth after the great Russian general. When I was three, Sarah began lobbying my parents to change my name. Her arguments were simple and sound: nobody could spell it, and nobody could pronounce it. Neither argument convinced my parents. "I can spell it," my father said, "and I can pronounce it, and so can my friends. Who else is there?"

The good old Central Committee of the U.S.S.R. saved me from a life of Ivan who? when it had a slight shift of policy (history?) in 1937 and decided that Ivan Tukhachevshy wasn't a hero after all but a neo-Trotskyite, and he was purged. My father, with the weight of this new evidence, relented and a search for a new name began. My father came up with names like Sholem, after Shalom Aleichem or Sholem Asch; Karl or Carl, after Karl Marx or Carl Sandburg; Ezra, after Ezra Pound; and Lincoln, after Lincoln Steffens or Abraham Lincoln. My sister came up with names like Joe, Bill, Bob, and Jim. My mother came up with Chaim, after her grandfather from Smolensk, and they compromised on Noel with three middle names. Don't ask me how Noel came up. A new birth certificate was officially issued, and at the age of three I became Noel Ezra Karl Sholem Roth. One thing you can be sure of, Ivan Tukhachevshy never could have played first base for the Mount Vernon Scarlets—even if he batted left-handed.

My sister Sarah was my go-between. Whenever I had a problem, I went to her, and she went to my father. When I wanted a bike, a radio, a baseball glove, it was Sarah who asked my father. Every request was a storm.

"A bike? A radio? A baseball glove??? For what? What is he going to do? Become a hooligan? Tell him when he reads Chekhov I will consider a *small* radio. A bike is out of the question, and he'll get a baseball thing when Tolstoy sneezes."

Somehow, Sarah arranged for me to get everything I needed.

My sister always had a lot of boyfriends. My father used to say that Sarah had as many boyfriends as he had books, which was an exaggeration. She was tall and attractive and bright and knew how to dress smartly and put on makeup. She was certainly the best-looking communist in Mount Vernon, which confused my father. I think it is safe that my father neither liked nor trusted any of my sister's suitors.

"What they want from her," he said, "has nothing to do with the People's Revolution."

Sarah would occasionally bring her current beau home to meet my father and mother. I never understood why she did it until I was in my late teens.

The tableau was always the same: early 1940s, the young suitor would be sitting nervously in the corner of the couch, Sarah demurely in the other corner, my father in *his* chair, me on the floor squeezing a baseball, and my mother, when not in the kitchen, sitting in *her* chair. My mother would bring in cookies that she made and hot chocolate that Sarah made. My father smoking one Camel cigarette after the other, stared at the young man the way Bob Feller looked at a two-hundred hitter who just got a scratch single off of him. After the brief introductions, there was always an enforced period of silence. If one of the young men ever chanced in a timorous voice, "Nice day today, Mr. Roth," my father would blow smoke in his direction.

Finally, my father would speak. "Do you like my wife's cookies?" he demanded.

"Oh, yes, sir, they're excellent. I'll even have another."

My father nodded. Another long pause. "Do you like my daughter's hot chocolate?" Again the demand.

"Oh, yes, sir. It's truly excellent." A smile toward Sarah.

Another long pause. "I have a slight favor to ask of you." Was that a twinkle I detected in my father's voice? "A very slight favor."

"Anything, Mr. Roth," the boyfriend said, sitting straight up, ready for action. "Anything."

My father handed a book to my sister's soon to be ex-suitor. "I would like you to read *out loud* from Eliot's 'Prufrock,' the first two pages up until the line—'I have measured out my life with coffee spoons'—and when you are finished, tell *me,* what *you* think *Mr. Eliot* was trying to tell *us.*"

Well, that always was the end of that. Interestingly enough, everybody (except the boyfriend) got what he or she wanted. My sister got rid of her boyfriend, which pleased her; my mother and my father and I got my mother's cookies, filled with rich pieces of chocolate and pecan nuts, that were delicious.

Songs We Used to Sing

On Sundays we would get into my father's 1938 Dodge truck and drive to the country, to the Kensico Dam in Valhalla, for a picnic lunch. In the picnic hamper there were a foot-long salami, thick chunks of liverwurst, a meat loaf, hard-boiled eggs, rolls of every type, pickles, a bag of fruit, a thermos filled with punch, and beer for my father. He always gave me a couple of swallows despite my mother's admonishings. The drive from Mount Vernon to Kensico Dam took an hour and a half, I think. It's only fourteen miles, and today I have a friend who *jogs* it on Sunday mornings and *he* does it in an *hour and a half.* I know it sounds crazy, but I *swear,* at least in my memory, that's how long it took us to drive fourteen miles. We would leave early in the morning so we would get a good spot for our picnic, and we would sing songs the entire trip.

Lenin is our Leader
We shall not be moved
Lenin is our Leader

We shall not be moved
Just like a tree
Standing by the water
We shall not be moved.

Tell me comrade
Do you read
The Daily Worker—Yes indeed
If you do then dance with me
True comrades—we'll always be.

I dreamed I saw Joe Hill last night
Alive as you and me
Says I to Joe
You're ten years dead
I never died says he
I never died says he.

Far and wide as the eye can wander
Heath and bog are everywhere
Not a bird sings out to cheer us
Oaks are standing gaunt and bare
We are The Peat Bog Soldiers
We are marching with our spades
To the bogs.

One Day I Played Catch with the Great Paul Robeson

During World War Two my parents had many fund-raisers for the Russian War Relief. It was a good time to be a communist in America. The U.S.S.R. and America had a common enemy, and you didn't have to hum the Soviet National Anthem under your breath. Little did we know what was to come. My father had somehow managed to get the great Paul Robeson for a brief appearance. There were at least a hundred people crowding our small house beyond capacity. My father said that he wouldn't be surprised if they raised as much as a thousand dollars. I was in the backyard playing catch with myself when Paul Robeson walked out.

"Throw me the ball, son."

I was big for my age, but Paul Robeson was a giant. I couldn't help but stare at him. Nineteen forty-four was before the era of six-foot-six black basketball players, and I had never seen anyone so big or so dark.

"I said 'throw me the ball,' son."

Everyone in the house was staring at us from the porch and windows. "It's a hardball," I said, holding up my taped-over Spaulding for him to see.

"I've caught many a hardball bare-handed." He held his hands up. They looked like they could crush a stone.

I underhanded him the ball and he whistled it back to me. He moved across the yard. "Your father tells me you're quite a ball player."

I was speechless. It was the last thing I would expect my father to talk about to Paul Robeson. The second front, the battle of Stalingrad, the heroic Russian soldier, the Scottsboro boys, the problems of being a Negro in America, *anything* but my ball playing prowess. "My father said that?" I said weakly. I threw him a lazy overhand. He flung it back to me over my head and I caught it gracefully in the web of my mitt.

"I used to play baseball," he said. "I could hit a ball so high it would disappear in the clouds, but the real player in my family was my brother Bill. Bill Robeson hit a ball so hard that if you caught it, your hand would sting for a week."

I wanted to tell him about Ralph Branca, that we were on the same team and he had major league scouts looking at him, but something stopped me. He threw me ground balls—to my left, my right. I handled them easily. He threw me a short hop that I muffed but kept in front of me.

"That's good," he said, "that's good."

He threw me a couple more short hops that I handled cleanly. All the time I kept on throwing the ball back to him with more and more velocity. I had a feeling he could have caught Dizzy Dean bare-handed. I sensed my father waiting impatiently for our game to stop, but I certainly wasn't going to be the one to quit. After thirty minutes, with a hundred startled American communists watching me and Paul Robeson playing catch on a Sunday afternoon in Mount Vernon, New York, he walked over and handed me the ball.

"You're pretty good," he said.

"Thanks." Should I have said more? Should I have said *at least* that he was pretty good also?

"How long have you had this ball?"

"About a year."

"It's pretty beat-up."

"I play in the street with it a lot. I bang it up against the curb and practice fielding grounders that way."

"It's awfully lumpy."

I shrugged.

"What's your first name?"

"Noel."

"How old are you?"

"Fifteen."

"I have a son. He's fifteen also." Paul Robeson nodded. He seemed deep in thought. I wanted so much to say something, anything, about his son, about how much I admired his singing, but I didn't say a word. To this day I'm sorry for that.

He was studying the ball, turning it around in his gigantic hand, gripping it, squeezing it, still deep in his own thoughts. "Mr. Roth," he finally spoke, calling up to my father who was on the porch. "Comrade Roth," he raised his voice, his bass filling our yard up as if he were in a concert hall, "I would like to make a suggestion, a motion if need be. After our collection today for our Russian brothers, I would like to peel off one dollar and fifty cents from whatever monies we take in and give it to your son for a new Spaulding baseball. Does anyone have any objections?"

I looked up at the dozens of openmouthed faces. My sister was smiling. My father showed no expression. Shapiro, the leader of the local Communist Party who had a head like a pin, was violently shaking his face no, but didn't dare say a word to the great Paul Robeson.

"Do you think we have to get Premier Stalin's permission?" Robeson's voice thundered out.

"I think it's an excellent idea," I heard my father say, "and I second the motion."

"Well, let's get started." Paul Robeson flipped me the ball and bounded up the stairs.

The next day, with three of my friends, I bought a shiny new Spaulding baseball and promised myself to use it only where, if someone didn't catch it, it would land on grass.

My Father's Favorite Joke

An immigrant is walking down Orchard Street in lower Manhattan and sees a sign in the window of a dry-cleaning store.

What do you think
My name is Fink
I press your pants
For nothing.

He goes into the store and asks about the sign. The man behind the counter points to the sign and says:

What do you think
My name is Fink
I press your pants
For nothing.

The immigrant gives him a pair of pants and is told they will be ready on Tuesday. On Tuesday, when he comes back, the man behind the counter tells him that he owes fifty cents for having his pants pressed. "What do you mean?" the immigrant says angrily. He points to the sign in the window and reads out loud:

What do you think
My name is Fink
I press your pants
For nothing.

"I'm not Fink," the man behind the counter says, "I'm Goldstein."

I Become a Capitalist—Almost

When I was fourteen, my father put me into business for myself. He opened up another newsstand in Bronxville, about three blocks from his, and put me in charge of it. I didn't get the morning commuters the way he did, but I was on a main street that led to a highway and drivers would stop and buy their papers. My father provided the money to get me started, and I gave him a percentage of the profits and kept everything else for myself. I bought my newspapers from a man my father introduced me to whose name was Al Sharkey. Al got paid every three days and carried a pistol in his glove compartment. I know, because he showed it to me the first time I paid him. Al took a liking to me and would spend time by my stand, sometimes helping me out, and even came to a couple of my baseball games. He had a lot of stories about gangsters, and was always hinting at some close connection of his who could get him, or any friend of his, *anything*. I had no idea what he was talking about. After a while, Al started asking me about girls. He wanted to know if I knew any girls. If I wanted to meet any girls. How far did I ever go with a girl? At the end of every sentence, Al would wink at me. "Remember kid," he had a low husky voice, "if you ever need anything," he winked at me, "ask Big Al." He winked at me. "If Big Al can't do it," he winked again, "nobody can."

I really didn't know what to make of Al. He was different from anyone I had ever met before, but I liked him.

My business flourished. People took kindly to me, many of them going out of their way to buy their morning papers at my stand. I began to develop regular customers whose names I learned. Some of them would buy all four morning papers from me: the *Mirror*, the *News*, the *Tribune*, and the *New York Times*, which was a sixteen-cent sale. I had a couple of regulars who gave me a quarter and waved off the change. Not a bad profit.

I started to handle magazines—the *Saturday Evening Post*, *Collier's*, *Look* and *Life*—and my business soared. Many of my customers began to learn *my* name and when picking up their papers would ask how I was doing in baseball. After I had been open for two months, I was taking home twenty dollars a week after all expenses. None of my friends made that kind of money.

My father was proud of my success. He didn't tell me so directly, but he boasted to his friends how well his son the entrepreneur was doing. I began to know him in a different way. He would wake me every morning at four-thirty, and we would have breakfast together at a local diner. He had been eating there for years, and the owners knew him well. My father introduced me to them: three Greeks, all of whom needed shaves. We always ordered exactly the same thing: two scrambled egg sandwiches with bacon on buttered hard rolls. I had milk and my father had tea. On cold mornings, rubbing the sleep from my eyes, blowing into my hands for warmth, sitting next to my father, I could feel his pleasure.

I was doing so well in my stand, I began looking around for other spots to open up. All of the railroad stations were taken, but there were two street corners in Mount Vernon where I thought a stand like mine would succeed. I spoke to my father about it one morning, showed him the location after work, and told him how easy it would be for me to get school friends to run them. "More and more people are driving to work," I said, "and the only place there are newspaper stands are at railroad stations. Look how well I'm doing after being open only a few months."

My father was impressed. We shook hands on it. He told me to speak to Al Sharkey before I did anything. That night I could hardly sleep as fifty-dollar bills danced in front of my eyes.

The next day I presented my plan to Al. "It could be a gold mine," I said excitedly. "I got two kids lined up and if these spots work as well as mine, I'm going to start looking in White Plains for spots. In a year I could have ten stands, Al."

When Al didn't like something he had a way of looking at you like you were nuts, and that's the way he was looking at me.

"What's wrong?" I said.

"Let me give it to you straight, kid, forget it."

"Why?"

"Because I said so. You are what we call, very na-ive, kid." He winked at me.

"But you said you could do anything for me. 'Anything. Just ask Big Al.' " I mimicked him angrily.

"I was talking about girls, kid. Girls." He winked at me.

"I don't want girls, Al. I want those two corners in Mount Vernon."

Al stared at me. "You're not only na-ive, kid. You're stupid. You can't open a stand in another town. Now let's forget this pipe dream and go over your account—"

"Suppose I just do it, Al. Who's going to stop me?"

"Kid, you're not only na-ive and stupid, but you're dumb besides. If you open up a stand in Mount Vernon, some friend of mine is going to open up a stand next to your father's." Al didn't wink at me.

"Oh," I said, "now I get it."

"I knew you would, kid."

"I thought you were my friend."

"I am, kid."

"If you were my friend, you wouldn't do that."

Al looked hurt. "Boy, you really don't understand. Very na-ive. It's the American way. Someday you'll get it." He winked at me.

The Mount Vernon Scarlets

My baseball team was named The Mount Vernon Scarlets. We were *excellent.* All the boys, except me, were fifteen or sixteen. At fourteen, I was the youngest. I was also the only one who was not Italian. Tony Daniello was our captain, and because of him I was on the team. He pitched and played the outfield. Today he owns a fruit stand. Sal Mosca was our catcher. Sal was a catcher because he looked like a catcher; short and squat, he could fire a ball to second base from the kneeling position. Very few people could steal against him. He reads meters for Con Edison now. Jackie Campanella played second base. No relation. A wonderful fielder but couldn't hit the ball out of the infield. He batted ninth, and was killed in Korea. Fishman played shortstop. I don't remember his real name. His father owned a fish store, so everybody called him Fishman. Fishman and I didn't get along. He always called me Rothman, instead of Roth, made snide cracks about me being Jewish, and—even worse—would purposely throw me short hops to make me look bad. We got into a fist fight once that Sal Mosca broke up, but not until Fishman broke my nose with a left hook I never saw. Today, Fishman owns a fish store, and I occasionally see him. The Rico Brothers, Frank and Anthony, played left and right field. Anthony had the better arm, but Frank was our clean-up hitter. Today they are both electricians. Anthony Pelligrino was our center fielder. He was the fastest boy on the team. I never recall a fly ball being hit over his head. Anthony works in Tony Daniello's fruit stand.

Ralph Branca pitched and played third base. We all knew that Ralph was going to make it in the major leagues. We just knew it. It was the kind of thing we just knew. I played first base. I batted second. I was tall and rangy for my age and had a natural, whippy swing that produced a lot of line drives. One of the scouts for the Philadelphia Athletics who came to watch Ralph Branca pitch once told me that it was too bad I wasn't left-handed. I own a men's clothing store.

I played for the Scarlets for two years until the team

broke up. In that time we never lost a game. We played other sandlot teams from surrounding towns, and we scrimmaged the local high school team, kids that were three and four years older, and we always beat them. We were—great. But, with the exception of Ralph Branca, not one of us ever played high school baseball.

My Father Has a Crisis and I Come to His Aid

One day my father stopped writing poetry because he ran out of friends. Everybody he knew, every single person he could think of, was now receiving a lifetime subscription to the *Freiheit* or the *Tog*. It didn't make sense to me, but no more friends to offer free subscriptions, no more poetry. He became despondent and depressed. I tried talking to him about it in the mornings when we were having breakfast at the Greeks', usually a good time for us, but he looked upon me with a combination of disdain and compassion. I pressed the issue.

"Couldn't you continue to write poetry?" I asked him one morning.

"And do what with it?"

"Give the *Freiheit* whatever you normally give them and let them do with the money what they want. Make a contribution. What difference does it make?"

He slammed his fist on the table. "You mean I should pay to have my poetry published?" he shouted. "Is that what you are telling me? Is that my son's *great* advice? I should pay to have my poetry published. Where is your sensitivity? How can you tell me about my poetry? That kind of advice is like a blob of snot. My poetry is everything to me. Do you think I obtain pleasure from selling Mr. Big Shot the *New York Times,* with his gloved hand waiting for pennies change? Do you think this is my pleasure? Or perhaps you think your ability to throw a ball is my pleasure? Or even better, perhaps you think that one day I will come to one of your games and cheer, and afterward you imagine the two of us playing catch?"

My father never hit me, but each word he said to me that morning was like a slap in the face. I fought back the tears. I wanted to tell him that just because I didn't read poetry didn't mean I couldn't understand his pain, and yes, very much, I would like to play catch with him. Would that be so terrible? To throw a ball with your son? But I was fourteen, and sentences like that did not form in my mouth.

My father's depression got worse. He stopped reading. He stopped translating and he stopped talking to me except for an occasional monosyllable.

"Look," I said one morning. "I have a way that you can start writing your poetry again."

"I'm not interested. Let it rest. I'm not interested. When the day comes that I need advice from my son who can't read past the sports pages, I'm in trouble."

"I think I can help you," I persisted.

"You cannot help me. Now stop talking. That would help me."

"Will you do me a favor?"

"No."

"Will you go to the library with me after work?"

"The library?" My father showed some emotion. "I didn't know you knew where it was."

"Will you?"

"Why? What are we going to do there?"

"I'm not going to tell you." I knew if I told him my idea he wouldn't go. "Will you do it?"

"All right. My son wants to take me to the library? In America, wonders never cease."

That morning, after work, we went to the Mount Vernon library. "Sit here," I told my father. "I'll be right back." I returned in a moment with my arms loaded down with twenty or so phone books from Montana, Idaho, and Wyoming.

"What are those?"

"They're phone books."

My father closed his eyes. "We are in a library," he took a deep breath. "I am in a library with my son, a library where the shelves are filled with Stendhal and Proust and Dostoyevsky and Tolstoy and my son, my son brings me a phone book."

Paying no attention to him I opened the Idaho book at random. "Look at this."

"What am I looking at?"

"In Idaho there is a town called Kimberly. It can't be very big. There are only two pages of phone numbers. Here." I pointed to a name in the middle of a page and wrote it down on a pad. "Ralph Sanders, that's a nice name, County Road 16, Kimberly, Idaho." I skipped a few pages to another town. "Tremont. This is bigger. There are six pages. How's this one? Frank Mace. County road 21, Tremont, Idaho." I wrote it down.

"What are you doing?" My father said. "Why did you shlep me here? Is this funny? Am I to laugh?"

"These names, Pop, names of people you can send lifetime subscriptions to the *Freiheit.*"

"Are you mad?"

"Why? What's wrong with it? Why not?"

There was a half a minute of silence. My father nodded.

"Let me help you pick the names," he said.

My father started writing poetry again. To this day there is a vision that slips in front of my eyes of Farmer Sanders riding to his mailbox on his tractor, opening it, and there is the morning *Freiheit,* every morning, forever.

My Son

Much has happened. The world has changed. My days as a young man are shadows. When I tell my wife and son that once I was a member of the Communist Party they look at me with skepticism.

My father died a few years ago. He was eighty-six. Although I was angry at him for many years, my anger has dissipated since his death, and now I remember most of all this tough little man who wanted more than anything in the world for his son to read a book.

I have been trying in vain to find some of his poetry with the idea of publishing a collection with a vanity press. (I'm sure it would cost me more than three dollars and fifty cents a poem.) It is inconceivable, but he never kept copies of his work. I suppose my father thought the

Tog and especially the *Freiheit* were as immortal as the *New York Times*. The *Tog* has long since stopped publishing, and the *Freiheit* publishes a tabloid once a week that bears little resemblance to the paper I knew. Almost everybody from that world is gone, and I have not been able to uncover a single poem that my father wrote. I have asked everyone there is to ask, but in 1982 no one has copies of Yiddish newspapers from forty-five years ago.

When my father died, his entire estate consisted of books: thousands and thousands of books. On a rainy Sunday afternoon my sister and I divided them up. Half of them sit in my house now, and my son, who is sixteen, reads them. I don't think my son has ever held a baseball in his hand, but he reads books with a passion and voracity that is astonishing. "I want," he told me, "to read every book ever written."

Besides the books, my father had bound all of the literary magazines that were being published in the twenties and thirties: *Dial, Poetry, Hound and Horn, Pagany, Exile, Quarterly* and *Transition,* to mention just a few. When my son first discovered them in dusty cartons, he acted a little bit like a young man in love. A few days later, he came to me with a copy of a 1928 issue of *Dial.* "Look what I found," he said. In the middle of the magazine, in a William Carlos Williams poem, was a yellowed piece of paper folded over twice. It was an eight-line poem of my father's, written in Yiddish. I don't know why it was there.

"What is it?" my son asked.

"It's your legacy," I answered.

Mary Gordon
(b. 1949)

Born in Far Rockaway, New York, where she was raised in a devoutly Catholic home, Mary Gordon was educated at Barnard College and Syracuse University. She has taught at Amherst College and Barnard. Her short stories, which have appeared in magazines such as *The Virginia Quarterly Review*, *Atlantic*, *Redbook*, *Harper's*, and *Ms.*, are collected in *Temporary Shelter* (1987). She has published three novels: *Final Payments* (1978), *The Company of Women* (1981), and *Men and Angels* (1985), and is presently at work on a novel about Irish immigration titled *The Other Side.*

VIOLATION

I suppose that in a forty-five-year life, I should feel grateful to have experienced only two instances of sexual violation. Neither of them left me physically damaged and I cannot in truth say they have destroyed my joy of men. I have been happily married for fifteen years before which I had several blissful and some ordinary disappointing times with lovers. In addition, I am the mother of two sons, my passion for whom causes me to draw inward, away, when I hear the indiscriminate castigation of all males, so common and so understandable within the circles I frequent. I rarely think of my two experiences, and I'm grateful for that, for I don't like what they suggest to me about a world which I must, after all, go on inhabiting. And I don't like it when I start to feel in danger in my house, the Federalist house we've been so careful in restoring, in the town not far from Hartford where we've lived now for ten years, and when I wonder if, perhaps, safety is a feeling open to men alone. It is then, especially, that I am glad to be the mother only of sons.

I am thinking of all that now as I stand at the wooden counter cutting celery, carrots, water chestnuts, so unvegetative in their texture, radishes that willingly compose themselves in slices decorative as shells. Courageously, we've kept the kitchen faithful to its period: We have not replaced the small windows by large sheets of glass that would allow a brightness our ancestors would have shunned. Leaves make a border at the windows; farther out—beech, locust—they become a net that breaks up the white sky. I arrange the vegetables, green, orange white, white circled by a ring of red on the dark wood of the chopping board, as if I had to make decisions like a painter, purely on the basis of looks. As I handle the slices of vegetable, cool and admirably dry, I think about myself as a young woman, traveling abroad or "overseas" as my parents then called it, truly away from home for the first time.

At twenty-two, I must have thought myself poetical. This is the only thing I can surmise when I look at the itinerary of that trip—my parents' present to me after college graduation—that I took with my college roommate and best friend. Lydia had majored in economics like me, although like me she had adopted it as a practical measure, rejecting a first love (for her it had been Art History, for me English). But we both prided ourselves on being tough-minded and realistic; we knew the value of a comfortable life, and we didn't want to feel we had to be dependent on a lucky marriage to achieve it. We'd both got jobs, through our fathers' connections, at large Manhattan banks; we'd take them up in the fall, and the knowledge of this gave us a sense of safety. We could be daring and adventurous all summer, have experiences, talk to people (men) we never would have talked to at home, reap the rewards of our secret devotion to the art and poetry we hadn't quite the confidence to give our lives to. We considered ourselves in the great line of student pilgrims admiring ourselves for our self-denial, traveling as we did with backpacks and hostel cards and a few volume of poetry. Not for a moment did we understand the luxury of a journey made on money we had never had to earn, and that the line we followed was that of young people on the grand tour: a look at the best pictures, the best buildings, some introduction to Continental manners, the collision of which with our young natures would rub off the rough edges but leave our idealism smooth. We would return then to the place that had been held for us in the real life that had been going on without us, not forgetting us, but not requiring us yet.

Our plane landed in Amsterdam. We saw the Rembrandts and Vermeers, and the Van Goghs my friend thought, by comparison, jejune, and then we took an all-night train to Florence. We stayed in a cheap *pensione* with marble floors and huge mirrors and painted ceilings above the iron cots that were our beds. And in Piazzole Michaelangelo, I met Giovanni, who sold Electrolux vacuum cleaners. Poor Italian, he was over-mastered by the consonants of his employer's name and pronounced his product E-LAY-TRO-LOO. Luckily, he worked all day so my friend and I could see the *Ufizzi*, the *Palazzo Pitti*, the *Duomo*, the *Museo San Marco*, and I need leave her alone only at night when Giovanni drove me around Florence at breakneck speed and snuck me into his *pensione* until midnight, then miraculously got me back into mine. (Now I see he must have bribed the concierge.) He agreed to drive us to Ravenna, where I could do homage to Dante and my friend to the mosaics, but even after he'd done this nice thing for the both of us and paid for both our lunches, my friend was put out with me. She felt that I'd abandoned her for a man. She hadn't met anybody possible, the friends that Giovanni had introduced her to were coarse, she said, and she was afraid to go out alone at night, she was always being followed by soldiers. It wasn't her idea of a vacation, she said, sitting in her room reading Kenneth Clark. Punitively, she suggested that when we got to England, where we both could speak the language, we should split up and travel alone. It would open us up to experiences, she said. Clearly she felt she hadn't had hers yet, and I'd had more than my share.

I left Giovanni tearfully, vowing to write. He bought us chocolates and bottles of *acqua minerale* for the train. Then we were off, heartlessly, to our next adventure. We were both sick crossing the channel; it made us tenderer to each other as we parted at Dover and hugged each other earnestly, awkward in our backpacks. She would go to Scotland, I to Ireland; in two weeks we would meet in London, stay there for a week, then travel home.

I decided to cross the Irish Sea from Wales, the home of poets. I would spend the day in Swansea and cross over at Fishguard to Rosslare. From Dylan Thomas' home, I would proceed on a pilgrimage to Yeats'. I felt ennobled but a bit lonely. It might be a long time, I knew, before I found someone to talk to.

Swansea was one of the least prepossessing cities I had ever seen: it might, despite the hints left by the poets, have been some place in Indiana or worse, Ohio, where I was from. I decided to look for a pub where Thomas must have got his inspiration. I found one that looked appropriate, ordered bread and sausages and beer and read my Yeats.

So I was not entirely surprised to hear an Irish voice ask if it could join me, and was pleased to look up and see a red-haired sailor standing with a pint of beer. I was abroad, after all, for experience, to do things I wouldn't do at home. I would never have spoken to a sailor in Cleveland, but then he wouldn't have been Irish. I thought he'd noticed me because he saw that I was reading Yeats.

"Yer American, then," he said.

"Yes."

"Great place, America. What yer doin' in this part of the world?"

"I'm traveling," I said.

"On yer own?"

"Yes."

"Brave, aren't ye?"

"No, not especially," I said. "I just don't see that

much to be afraid of. And an awful lot that's fun and exciting. I'd hate to think I'd let fear hold me back."

"It's a great attitude. Great. Ye have people over here in Swansea?"

"No."

"What brings ye here?"

"Dylan Thomas, the poet. You've heard of him?"

"I have, of course. You're a great poetry lover, aren't ye? I seen ye with the Yeats. I'm from the Yeats country myself."

"That's where I'm going," I said, excitedly. "To Sligo."

"Yer takin' the ferry?"

"Nine o'clock."

"What a shame. I won't have much time to show ye Swansea. But we could have a drink or two."

"Okay," I said, anxious for talk. "You must have traveled a lot of places."

"Oh, all over," he said. "It's a great life, the sailor's."

He brought us drinks and I tried to encourage him to talk about himself, his home, his travels. I don't remember what he said, only that I was disappointed that he wasn't describing his life more colorfully, so I was glad when he suggested going for a walk to show me what he could of the town.

There really wasn't much to see in Swansea; he took me to the Catholic Church, the post office, the city hall. Then he suggested another pub. I said I had to be going, I didn't want to be late for the boat. He told me not to worry, he knew a shortcut; we could go there now.

I don't know when I realized I was in danger, but at some point I knew the path we were on was leading nowhere near other people. When he understood that I was not deceived, he felt no more need to hesitate. He must have known I would not resist, he didn't have to threaten. He merely spoke authoritatively, as if he wanted to get on with things.

"Sit down," he said. "And take that thing off your back."

I unbuckled my backpack and sat among the stalky weeds.

"Now take yer things off on the bottom."

I did what he said, closing my eyes. I didn't want to look at him, I could hear the clank of his belt as it hit the ground.

"What's this," he said. "One of yer American tricks?"

I had forgotten I was wearing a Tampax. Roughly, he pulled it out. I was more embarrassed by the imagination of it lying on the grass, so visible, than I was by my literal exposure.

"Yer not a virgin?" he said worriedly.

I told him I was not.

"All right then," he said, "then you know what's what."

In a few seconds, everything was finished, and he was on his feet. He turned his back to me to dress.

"I want ye to know one thing," he said. "I've just been checked out by the ship's doctor. Ye won't get no diseases from me, that's for sure. If ye come down with something, it's not my fault."

I thanked him.

"Yer all right?" he said.

"Yes," I told him.

He looked at his watch.

"Ye missed yer ferry."

"It's all right," I said, trying to sound polite. "There's another one in the morning." I was afraid that if I showed any trace of fear, any sense that what had happened was out of the ordinary, he might kill me to shut my mouth.

"I'll walk ye to the town."

I thanked him again.

"I'm awful sorry about yer missing the boat. It's too bad ye'll have to spend the night in this godforsaken town." He said this with genuine unhappiness, as though he had just described what was the genuine offense.

We walked on silently, looking at hotels blinking their red signs FULL.

"I'll be fine now," I said, hoping now we were in public, I could safely get him to leave.

"As long as yer all right."

"I'm fine, thank you."

"Would you give me yer name and address in the States? I could drop you a line. I'm off to South America next."

I wrote a false name and address on a page in my notebook, ripped it out and handed it to him.

He kissed me on the cheek. "Now don't go on like all these American ladies about how terrible we are to ye. Just remember, treat a man right, he'll treat you right."

"Okay," I said.

"Adios," he said, and waved.

I stepped into the foyer of the hotel we were standing in front of and stood there a while. Then I looked out onto the street to be sure he was gone. There was no sign of him, so I asked the hotel clerk for a room. I wanted one with a private bath, and he told me the only room available like that was the highest priced in the house. I gladly paid the money. I couldn't bear the idea of sharing a bathtub. It wasn't for myself I minded; I cared for the other people. I knew myself to be defiled, and I didn't want the other innocent, now sleeping guests, exposed to my contamination.

I traveled through Ireland for ten days, speaking to no one. It wasn't what I had expected, a country made up of bards and harpists and passionate fine-limbed women tossing their dark red hair. Unlike the other countries of Europe, there was nothing one really *had* to look at, and the beauty of the landscape seemed to wound, over and over, my abraded feelings; it made me feel even more alone. The greasy banisters of the urban hotels I stayed in sickened me; the glowing pictures of the Sacred Heart in the rooms of the private houses that, in the country, took in guests, disturbed my sleep. I felt that I was being stared at and found out.

And that, of course, was the last thing I wanted, to be found out. I've never said anything about the incident to anyone, not that there's much reason to keep it from people. Except, I guess, my shame at having been ravished, my dread of the implication, however slight, that I had "asked for what had happened," that my unwisdom was simply a masked desire for a coupling anonymous and blank. And so I have been silent about that time without good cause; how, then, could I ever speak of the second incident, which could, if I exposed it, unravel the fabric of my family's life?

My Uncle William was my father's only brother. He was two years older, handsomer, more flamboyant, more impatient, and it was said that though he lacked my father's steadiness, my father hadn't got his charm. Their mother had died when they were children, and their father drowned before their eyes when my father was seventeen and William nineteen. They agreed between them, teenage orphans, that my father should go off to college—he would study engineering at Purdue—and my uncle would stay home and run the family business, a successful clothing store my grandfather had built up and expanded as the town's prosperity increased and its tastes became more daring. When my father left for school it was a thriving business and it was assumed that with William's way with people, women especially (he planned to build his line of women's clothing; his first move was to enlarge the millinery department) it could only flourish. But in two years, everything was lost and my father had to leave college. The truly extraordinary aspect of the affair, to my mind, is that it was always my father who was apologetic about the situation. He felt it had been unfair, a terrible position to put Uncle William in, making him slave alone in the hometown he had never liked, while my father had been able to go away. William was really smarter, my father always said. (It wasn't true; even my mother, a great fan of Uncle William's and a stark critic of my father, corrected him, always, at this point in the story.) My father and my uncle agreed that it would be better for my uncle to go away; he'd put in his time and it was my father's turn; there was no reason for Uncle William to stick around and endure the petty insults and suspicions of uncomprehending minds.

In five years, my father had paid all the debts, a feat that so impressed the president of the local bank that he offered him a job. His rise in the bank was immediate, and it led to his move to Cleveland and his continued steady climb and marriage to my mother, the daughter of a bank president. I've never understood my father's success; he seems to trust everyone; wrongdoing not only shocks but seems genuinely to surprise him; yet he's made a career lending people money. I can only imagine that inside those cool buildings he always worked in, he assumed a new identity; the kind eyes grew steely, the tentative, apologetic yet protective posture hardened into something wary and astute. How else can I explain the fact that somebody so lovable made so much money?

In the years that my father was building his career, my uncle was traveling. We got letters from around the country; there was a reference in one, after the fact, to a failed marriage that lasted only sixteen months. And occasionally, irregularly, perhaps once every five years, there would be a visit, sudden, shimmering, like a rocket illuminating our ordinary home and lives, making my father feel he had made all the right decisions, he was safe, yet not removed from glamour. For here it was, just at his table, in the presence of the brother whom he loved.

I, too, felt illuminated by the visits. In middle age, William was dapper, anecdotal and offhand. He could imitate perfectly Italian tailors, widows of Texas oilmen, Mexican Indians who crossed the border every spring. In high school, my friends were enchanted by him; he was courtly and praising and gave them a sense of what they were going away to college for. But by the time we had all been away a couple of years, his stories seemed forced and repetitious, his autodidact's store of information suspect, his compliments something to be, at best, endured. For my father, however, my Uncle William never lost his luster. He hovered around his older brother, strangely maternal, as if my uncle were a rare, invalid *jeune fille,* possessed of delicate and special talents which a coarse world would not appreciate. And while my father hovered, my mother leaned toward my uncle, flirtatious and expectant and alight.

Once, when I was living in New York, his visit and my visit to Ohio coincided. I was put on the living-room couch to sleep since my uncle had inhabited my room for two weeks and I would be home for only three days. At twenty-five, any visit home is a laceration, a gesture meanly wrought from a hard heart and an ungiving spirit. No one in town did I find worth talking to, my parents were darlings, but they would never understand my complicated and exciting life. Uncle William, in this context, was a relief; I had, of course, to condescend to him, but then he condescended to my parents, and he liked to take me out for drinks and hear me talk about my life.

One night, I had gone to dinner at a high school friend's. She had recently married, and I had all the single woman's contempt for her Danish Modern furniture, her silver pattern, her china with its modest print of roses. But it was one of those evenings that is so boring it's impossible to leave; one is always afraid that in rising from the chair, one is casting too pure a light on the whole fiasco. I drove into my parents' driveway at one-thirty, feeling ill-used and restless, longing for my own bed in my own apartment and the sound of Lexington Avenue traffic. In five minutes, I was crankily settling onto the made-up couch, and I must have fallen instantly to sleep. I have always been a good sleeper.

It was nearly four when I realized there was someone near me, kneeling on the floor. Only gradually, I understood that it was my Uncle William, stroking my arm and breathing whiskey in my face.

"I couldn't sleep," he said. "I was thinking about you."

I lay perfectly still; I didn't know what else to do. I couldn't wake my parents, I could see behind my eyes years of my father's proud solicitude for the man now running his hand toward my breast, scene after scene of my mother's lively and absorbed attentions to him. As I lay there, I kept remembering the feeling of being a child sitting on the steps watching my parents and their guests below me as they talked and held their drinks and nibbled food I didn't recognize as coming from my mother's kitchen or her hand. A child transgressing, I was frozen into my position: any move would mean exposure and so punishment. At the same time that the danger of my situation stiffened me into immobility, I was paralyzed by the incomprehensibility of the behavior that went on downstairs. Could these be people I had known, laughing in these dangerous, sharp, unprovoked ways, leaning so close into one another, singing snatches of songs, then breaking off to compliment each other on their looks, their clothes, their business or community success. My childish sense of isolation from the acts of these familiars now grown strangers made me conscious of the nerves that traveled down my body's trunk, distinct, electric, and my eyes, wide as if they were set out on stalks, now lidless and impossibly alert. Twenty years later as I lay, desperately strategizing, watching my uncle I knew the memory was odd, but it stayed with me as I simulated flippancy, the only tactic I could imagine that would lead to my escape. My uncle had always called me his best audience when I'd forced laughter at one of his jokes; he'd say I was the only one in the family with a sense of humor.

"Well, unlike you, Uncle William, I *could* sleep, I *was* sleeping," I said, trying to sound like one of those thirties comedy heroines, clever in a jam. "And that's what I want to do again."

"Ssh," he said, running his hand along my legs. "Don't be provincial. Have some courage, girl, some imagination. Besides I'm sure I'm not the first to have the privilege. I just want to see what all the New York guys are getting."

He continued to touch me, obsessive now and furtive, like an animal in a dark box.

"I'm not going to hurt you," he said. "I could make you happy. Happier than those young guys."

"What would make me really happy is to get some sleep," I said, in a tone I prayed did not reveal all my stiff desperation.

But, miraculously, he rose from his knees. "You really are a little prude at heart, aren't you? Just like everybody else in this stinking town."

And suddenly, he was gone. In the false blue light of four o'clock, I felt the animal's sheer gratitude for escape. I kept telling myself that nothing, after all, had happened, that I wasn't injured, it was rather funny really, I'd see that in time.

My great fear was that I would betray, by some lapse of warmth or interest in the morning, my uncle's drunken act. I longed for my parents' protection, yet I saw that it was I who must protect them. It had happened, that thing between parents and children: the balance had shifted; I was stronger. I was filled with a clean, painful love for them, which strikes me now each time I see them. They are gallant; they are innocent, and I must keep them so.

And I must do it once again today. They are coming to lunch with my Uncle William. I will be alone with them: my husband is working; my children are at school. In twenty years, I've only seen him twice, both times at my parents' house. I was able to keep up the tone: jocular, tough-minded, that would make him say, "You're my best audience," and make my father say, "They're cut from the same cloth, those two." It was one of those repayments the grown middle-class child must make, the overdue bill for the orthodontists, the dance lessons, the wardrobe for college, college itself. No one likes repayment; it is never a pure act, but for me it was a possible one. Today, though, it seems different. Today they are coming to my house, they will sit at my table. And as I stand at the kitchen window where I have been happy, where I have nurtured children and a husband's love and thought that I was safe, I rage as I look at the food I'd planned to serve them. The vegetables which minutes ago pleased me look contaminated to me now. Without my consent it seems, the side of my hand has moved toward them like a knife and shoved them off the cutting board. They land, all their distinction gone, in a heap in the sink. I know that I should get them out of there; I know I will; for I would never waste them, but for now it pleases me to see them ugly and abandoned and in danger, as if their fate were genuinely imperiled and unsure.

What is it that I want from Uncle William? I want some hesitation at the door, as if he isn't sure if he is welcome. I want him to take me aside and tell me he knows that he has done me harm. I want him to sit, if he must sit, at my table, silent and abashed. I don't demand that he be hounded; I don't even want him to confess. I simply want him to know, as I want the Irish sailor to know, that a wrong has been done me. I want to believe that they remember it with at the least regret. I know that things cannot be taken back, the forced embraces, the caresses brutal underneath the mask of courtship, but what I do want taken back are the words, spoken by those two men, that suggest that what they did was all right, no different from what other men had done, that it is all the same, the touch of men and women; nothing of desire or consent has weight, body parts touch body parts; that's all there is. I want them to know that because of them I cannot ever feel about the world the way I might have felt had they never come near me.

But the Irishman is gone and Uncle William, here before me, has grown old and weak. I can see him from the window, I can see the three of them. Him and my parents. They lean on one another, playful, tender; they have been together a lifetime. In old age, my parents have taken to traveling; I can hear them asking my uncle's advice about Mexico, where they will go this winter, where he once lived five years. They are wearing the youth-endowing clothing of the comfortably retired: windbreakers, sneakers, soft, light-colored sweaters, washable dun-colored pants. They have deliberately kept their health, my parents, so that they will not be a burden to me; for some other reason my uncle has kept his. Groaning, making exaggerated gestures, they complain about the steepness of my steps. But it is real, my father's muscular uncertainty as he grabs for the rail. They stand at my front door.

What happened happened twenty years ago. I've had a good life. I am a young and happy woman. And now I see the three of them, the old ones, frail, expectant, yearning toward me. So there is nothing for it; I must give them what they want. I open my arms to the embrace they offer. Heartily, I clap my uncle on the back.

"Howdy, stranger," I say in a cowboy voice. "Welcome to these parts."

Sue Miller
(b. 1943)

Born in Chicago, Illinois, Sue Miller received a B.A. from Radcliffe College, an M.A.T. from Wesleyan University, and an M.A. from Boston University. She has taught writing at M.I.T., Tufts University, Brandeis, and Boston University. Her novel *The Good Mother* (1986) was the basis of a Hollywood film of the same title, which starred Diane Keaton. *Inventing the Abbotts,* a collection of short stories, was published in 1987.

APPROPRIATE AFFECT

Grandma Frannie was a tall, slim woman, stooped now, who had been pretty before all her children were born. She still had a beautiful smile, with all her own teeth. It was sweet and sad, perhaps even reproachful, and she had used it for years to shame the family into orderly compliance. She had met Henry Winter before she finished library school, and brought to her marriage all the passion she had once lavished on the Dewey decimal system. In passion, she was disappointed. Henry was a rigid and unimaginative man, though a dutiful lover. She was pregnant within two months of the wedding, and within five years she had four daughters, Maggie, Laura, Frieda and Martha.

No one escaped the bright beam of Grandma Frannie's love. At eighty-six, she still sent birthday presents to every grandchild and great-grandchild. She remembered who was married to whom, and even who was living with whom, what his name was, and what he did. Although it didn't really matter what anyone did. Her love leapt all hurdles. Her oldest grandson, Martin, who had a coming out party within a month of moving to San Francisco, had dedicated his first volume of poetry to Frannie. His mother cried when he told her he'd sent Frannie a copy, but Frannie kept it in plain view, on the coffee table in the living room. When Martin's mother saw it there, she didn't comment. She figured Frannie probably didn't even know what it was about. And the Christmas after Fred showed up at a family Thanksgiving party with a black stripper, Frannie sent a card that brought love "to that pretty Tanya" and a gift (small, because she wasn't family) from the church bazaar.

"Christ," said Louisa, Frieda's youngest and a graduate student in psychology, "you can't be a black sheep in this family even if you want." It was true. The steady pressure of Grandma's love reduced them all, eventually, to gray normality. Even Julian, who was in prison in Joliet, Illinois, for forgery, wrote her regularly.

Frannie and Henry lived in Connecticut in a large frame house built on a hill. It had once overlooked an abandoned orchard where wizened little apples grew. Ten years before, a developer had leveled the field and built row on row of identical two-story gray town houses with fake mansard roofs.

Henry and Frannie's house was a faded salmon pink that was gently peeling, and here and there a shutter had fallen off and never been replaced. It was darkened by overgrown cedars in the front yard which reached above the roof for sunlight. The front porch listed slightly, but Bob Hancock, Laura's son-in-law, had jumped up and down on it and it held. It was pronounced safe for Frannie and Henry for the time being.

All the children wanted them to move to the retirement community nearby, but Henry couldn't bear to think of it. He loved the ornate woodwork and soot-streaked wallpaper, the dark furniture inherited from his mother, and the threadbare Oriental rugs.

One Sunday afternoon, an hour or so after their return

from the Congregational church, Henry was watching football on television. Frannie came into the living room to tell him that dinner was ready. It was in the middle of the third quarter and that irritated Henry. Because he was slightly deaf and had the television on loud, he didn't hear her coming and that irritated him even more. She stepped suddenly into his line of vision and turned the set off. She shouted, "Dinner, Henry," at him, and smiled her warm, browbeaten smile.

Henry stood up. "There's no need to shout," he said. "What's more, I'm not ready for dinner and I won't be for a good long while. The Sabbath was made for man, madam, not man for the Sabbath." And he walked right over to the TV set and turned it back on.

She said something to him, but he ignored her, so she started her long, slow shuffle back to the kitchen.

Henry turned the set off about forty-five minutes later and started toward the kitchen himself. His walk was brisker and more steady than Frannie's. He stopped abruptly when he rounded the doorway to the dining room. Frannie's legs were sticking straight out from behind the highboy on the floor. He felt a numbed panic as he approached her. She was sitting up, wedged in the corner between the highboy and the wall. Her face was white and agonized. Her mouth had dropped open and her eyes were closed.

"My dear!" Henry said, bending over her stiffly from the waist. He saw her lips move slightly as though she were trying to talk. Her left arm rested uselessly on the floor and her right was somehow bent behind her. Henry reached down and tried to lift her up, but he only managed to slide her forward slightly. Her head lolled back and smacked the wall. Henry cried out. He straightened and started into the kitchen. Halfway to the telephone, with his arms already lifting to take off the receiver and dial, he turned and went back to her. He bent down again.

"I'll be right back, my darling," he said very loudly and clearly, as though she were the deaf one. She made no sign that she'd heard. He went back and placed the call.

* * *

No one answered when the ambulance driver rang the bell, so the men walked in with the stretcher. They looked around the dark, empty front hall and then heard a murmuring voice from the room on their right, the dining room. Henry had pulled a chair over next to Frances, and he was sitting in it, holding her hand across his knees and patting it, talking softly to her.

When the ambulance driver was only a few steps away, Henry saw him and stopped talking. He stood up. "Sir, my name is Henry Winter and this is my wife," he said. He began to explain the circumstances under which he'd found her, but the men were already lifting her onto the stretcher and strapping her in, giving loud instructions to each other.

"You coming in the ambulance, Pop?" the driver asked as he picked up his end of the stretcher.

"What say?" asked Henry, turning his head so his good ear was nearer the driver.

"Are you coming with us?" the driver yelled.

"Ah! Much obliged, but I'll follow in my car," said Henry, and he went to get his hat and coat.

"Christ!" the driver said a minute later as they hoisted Frannie into the truck. "Can you imagine them letting an old guy like that have a license?"

In the days following Frannie's stroke, different children, grandchildren and great-grandchildren came and went in the house. As though it were an old country hotel getting ready for the season, rooms that had been shut up for years were opened, mouse droppings and dead insects were swept up and mattresses turned over. Frannie's daughters ransacked the bedding box and clucked to each other about the down puffs and heavy linen sheets with hand stitching that you would think Mother might have handed down by now.

For the first three days they took turns going in one at a time to sit by Frannie in intensive care. They got permission to have a member of the family stay by her straight through the night. The third night it was her granddaughter Charlotte's turn.

The overhead lights were off in the hospital room, but a white plastic nipple plugged into the wall socket next to Frannie's bed glowed like a child's night light and Charlotte could see the shape of her grandmother's skinny body under the bedclothes. She didn't like to look at Gram's face, so embryonic and naked without her glasses, her hair uncombed for three days and her mouth slack. Instead she looked at the sac of IV fluid with its plastic umbilicus running into Gram's bruised arm. Or she held Gram's freckled hand, which lay alongside the mound of bones under the sheets; or she slept; or wept. She rubbed her hands up and down her slightly thickening waist and cried as she thought of life and death; of Gram about to die, and of the baby, her third, taking life inside her own body.

She had tried to talk about this to her younger sister, Louisa, the afternoon before at Frannie and Henry's house, but Louisa had been irritable. Louisa was always irritable when Charlotte cried. "Oh, spare us, why don't you," she'd said, chopping onions for stew. Her knife whacked the board rapidly, like a burst of gunfire. "Next you'll be going on about reincarnation."

Charlotte blew her nose loudly into a Kleenex, and wiped her lower lids carefully so the mascara wouldn't smear. Grandma Frannie stirred slightly and swung her head toward Charlotte. Her mouth closed with a smacking sound and opened again. Charlotte leaned toward the bed, grabbing the steel railings that boxed her grandmother in.

"Gram?" she whispered. She cleared her throat. "Gram?" Her grandmother's eyes snapped open and stared wildly for a second. Then the lids seemed to grow heavy and they drooped again.

Charlotte stood up and put one hand on her grandmother's shoulder. The other hand rested on her own belly. At her touch, her grandmother's eyes opened again and she frowned and seemed to try to fix Charlotte in focus with the anxious intensity of a newborn.

"Gram? Do you hear me?" Charlotte said. "Do you hear me?"

After a few seconds' pause, Grandma Frannie nodded, a slow swaying of her frizzy head.

"Do you know me?" asked Charlotte. Gram shut her lips and tightened them and frowned hard at Charlotte.

"It's Charlotte, Grandma," she said, and started to weep again. Her right hand was furiously rubbing her belly. She was already thinking of how she would tell the others of this moment. She leaned over and put her face close to her grandmother's.

"It's Charlotte, Grandma. Do you know me?"

Again her grandmother moved her head slightly, up and down. Her lips quivered with some private effort.

"Oh, Grandma, I wanted you to know. I'm going to have a baby." Tears ran down Charlotte's face and plopped onto the neatly folded sheet covering her grandmother's chest. "I'm going to have another baby, Gram."

There was no change in the intense frown on Grandma Frannie's face, but her mouth opened. Charlotte leaned closer still and Grandma Frannie's breath was horrible in her face. Frannie's lips worked and her breathing was shallow and fast.

"The. Nasty. Man," she whispered.

Charlotte reported to the doctors and the family that Grandma Frannie had waked in the night and had spoken. When they asked, as they did eagerly and repeatedly, what she had said, Charlotte would only say that she hadn't been herself. Her cousin Elinore thought Charlotte was being "a bit of a snot" not to tell, trying to rivet all that attention on herself. Charlotte felt everyone's irritation with her all the next day. Frannie was fluttering delicately in and out of consciousness and muttered only incoherent phrases as the nurses changed her bedding or inserted another IV. But Charlotte still tearfully refused to tell what it was Grandma had said to her, although she insisted that Grandma had spoken clearly. "God, you'd think it was her mantra," Louisa said.

After Charlotte heard Grandma Frannie speak, the family came by twos and threes for several days. Slowly Frannie began to recognize them, calling out their names as they walked in. Sometime she couldn't seem to say the name and then she'd spell it aloud, carefully and often correctly. It was a small hospital, and the doctors and nurses came to know the family as they sat in little clusters in the lounge or cafeteria, waiting for a turn to see Frannie.

In the evening at the house, there were always nine or ten around the dinner table. Henry felt an almost unbearable joy sometimes when he was called in to the extended table covered with a white linen cloth. The china and glassware glittered. The tureens and platters that had come down from his parents were heaped with food like creamed onions and scalloped potatoes, food Henry hadn't eaten at home in years, except at Thanksgiving or Christmas.

They talked animatedly at the table of what Gram had said or done that day. Everyone had a favorite story he liked to tell. Frannie had asked Elinore to get the bedpan, but called it a perambulator. She had clearly asked Maggie if she was going to die and cried when Maggie told her she would not, that she was getting better. She rambled on and on to Emily, her youngest grandchild, who was down from Smith for the weekend. She talked about apple trees and she had said, "I think of all those trees gone, don't you know, the apples, all cut down. Well, that's the way. All those trees." Emily had sat in the darkened room and stroked her hand. "Why would they do a thing like that?" Grandma Frannie had asked, and Emily had said, honestly, that she didn't know. Then Grandma Frannie had said, "Those assholes!" but Emily was sure she had meant to say "apples," so she didn't repeat that part.

Henry told over and over how he had found her and called for the ambulance. He didn't tell the whole truth. He said, "My dearest was in the kitchen making dinner. I sat in the corner of the living room, you see, watching football—it was, I believe, the Los Angeles Rams that day, but I could be wrong—and when the game was over, I walked back towards the kitchen to inquire about dinner, and as I came around the corner, what do you think I saw?" He would wait here however long it took some listener to ask, "What?"

"*There* was my darling sitting on the floor with her legs protruding out from behind the highboy that Auntie gave us for a wedding present." He would go on, detailing every step of the process of getting Frannie to the hospital, and making himself sound very heroic.

The group staying at the house shrank and stabilized somewhat after it became clear that Frannie was going to survive. Maggie stayed on with Henry to take care of him, and Charlotte, who lived nearby, often came for part of the day while her children were in school. Sometimes she returned later with them and her husband, to have dinner with Maggie and Henry.

Frequently, one of the other children or grandchildren would arrive for a day or two. Michael stopped in one night with his entire band, Moonshot, and a few of their girlfriends on the way to a gig in the Berkshires. Maggie told everyone later, "Who knows who was with whom. I just told them where the bedrooms were and shut my eyes."

Grandma Frannie made extraordinary progress. She was having therapy with a walker and physically she had recovered almost completely, except for a dragging in her left leg. Most of her powers of speech had returned. But she still had trouble with an occasional word and when she was tired she would lose track of where she was and to whom she was speaking and drift off to other places and times. Like a baby, she napped three or four times a day.

One afternoon, Henry went in alone to visit her. She was asleep. Her mouth puffed out with each exhalation and she snored faintly. Henry stood in the open doorway and tried to engage some of the passing hospital staff in conversation. His loud voice woke Frannie up.

"Henry!" she called to him.

He turned. "Oh, my dear, now you're awake, and looking so well today, so very well." He leaned over and kissed her cheek.

"Graphics," she said.

"Eh?"

She bit her lip and looked angry. "Now I didn't mean that," she said, "Fetch me my . . . you know." She pointed to her nose. The marks of her glasses were like permanent bluish stains on either side of the bridge. "They're somewhere or other in that coffin there," and she gestured at the stand by her bed.

Henry opened the drawer and got her glasses out. He started to help her put them on, but she waved his hands away and hooked them over her ears herself.

"My love," Henry began, seating himself by her bed.

But she cut him off. "Where *were* you?" she asked.

"Why, my dear, I just arrived, but you were asleep so I stood by the door."

"Not likely!" she snapped, and behind her glasses her eyes glinted malevolently at him.

"Very well, my love," he said in an injured tone, resolved to be patient. The doctors had told him it was a miracle she had survived at all, and besides, Henry couldn't forget the shame of his behavior to her in the moments before her stroke. Worse yet, he found himself hoping she would never recover fully enough to recall it herself, to blame him or tell the children.

"I heard you down there in that other room," Frannie said, slowly and carefully.

"Now, Frannie, you must stay calm."

She shut her eyes and seemed for a moment to relax or to be asleep. Then her eyes opened and she smiled. "Yes, I'm not well. Not a bit well."

"But you're getting better."

Her lips labored, as though choosing the exact position they needed to be in to form the next word. "The children were here."

"That's right, dear."

"Maggie. And Frieda. And Martha. And that other."

"Laura? She couldn't come. She wasn't here."

"Not Laura," She said irritably. "Not one of mine. That other."

"Louisa? Charlotte?"

"Yes! That one." She smiled in satisfaction. A moment later she said, "Did I tell you the children were here?"

"Yes, you just did, my love. You just said that." And he laughed loudly at her.

Her eyes narrowed behind the bifocals. Her mouth tensed into an angry line. A nurse walked in briskly.

"Ah, here comes that . . ." She stopped.

"It's Nurse Gorman, Mrs. Winter. Just checking your blood pressure again."

"Again? You have nothing superior to do?" Something funny in her sentence made Frannie shake her head angrily.

"I just wanted to get another reading 'cause it's been a few hours, honey." She pumped up the band around Frannie's skinny arm, squeezing the loose flesh close to the bone. "Your wife is my favorite patient, Mr. Winter. She's a doll."

"Eh?" said Henry.

"Your wife is doing well," yelled the nurse. She was tall and wore glasses and very red lipstick.

"Oh, I know, yes, thanks," said Henry.

After the nurse left, Frannie closed her eyes for a while and seemed to sleep again. Henry looked at a copy of *Newsweek* he'd picked up in the lobby.

"Oh, you're still here." She labored over the words.

"Yes, my love," he said, and patted her hand.

"Why don't you just go down there. If you want to. Go right on down. To your little nurse."

Henry frowned.

"I heard you down there. Yes. The children, probably. Thought it was just me again. Making that noise. But I knew just what it was with that Mrs. Sheffield." She said this very slowly and precisely. "Fuck-ing Mrs. Sheffield."

Henry started and withdrew his hand.

"Always that. Mrs. Sheffield. When I wanted some other nurse, but oh, no, you had to have her. Again. Sneaking off down the hall. Did you think I couldn't hear? You? I knew just what it was. I heard you."

"You're upset, Frances. You—you should sleep."

"Yes. Sleep. Don't you wish. I saw you looking at her. As soon as I sleep you'll go off. Down the hall again. Why couldn't we have some other nurse? I didn't want Mrs. Sheffield again." Her voice had become plaintive.

Henry stood up.

Frances began to cry. Her face crumpled into bitter

lines. "I don't want her. There's too many children here, and you. Always sneaking around with her, making those noises down the hall. Yes, go. Go on. I know where you're . . . you're going."

Henry drove home slowly. He didn't notice the line of cars forming behind him and he didn't hear the honking. The sun was low and pink in the Connecticut sky. He was remembering Mrs. Sheffield, whose eyes had bulged out slightly so that the whites showed all the way around the iris and made Henry think of nipples sitting round and staring in the middle of her breasts. She was quiet and solemn as she performed her duties after Maggie's birth and she wouldn't sit with him at meals. He had known what he wanted from her when he wrote to hire her again for the second child. After that she had come and stayed with them at each birth, and Frannie, he thought, had never known. Mrs. Sheffield was small and plump, with dark hair, and he had been right, her nipples did sit exactly in the middle of her small breasts, unlike his wife's, which drooped down and leaked milk at his mouth's pull for years on end.

When he got home, Henry called the doctor and explained that he thought his presence was distressing to his wife, and with his permission Henry wouldn't come in for a bit. The doctor was surprised that Henry thought he needed permission to stay away.

And now each person who visited Frannie came to a point in telling how she was doing where he or she would fall silent and then say in a perplexed tone that Grandma Frannie was still not really herself. In little groups of two and three they discussed her and they agreed that they wouldn't have believed Grandma Frannie even knew the meaning of half the words she was using. She told Charlotte's husband that Henry didn't know the first thing about fucking. She said "fucking." "In and out," she said. "That was his big idea. I hope you take a little more time and care. And if you don't know what's up," she said, "there's no shame in asking."

She told Maggie that she had thought she would die when they were all little. She said she'd spent fifteen years "up to my elbows in runny yellow shit. Not one of you children turned out a well-formed stool until you were doing it on your own."

Maggie had blushed and spoken to her as though she were a child, "Be nice, Mother," she'd said, nervously smiling.

"Oh, nice, nice!" said Grandma Frannie. "I know very well how to be nice."

Like Henry, the children and grandchildren began to think of reasons why they couldn't visit. Maggie still went once a day, but most of the time the others stayed away. Late one night Maggie called her husband long-distance in Pennsylvania. She stood in her flannel nightgown in the hall and sobbed softly into the phone so Henry wouldn't hear her. "I can't imagine where she ever heard that kind of language. I almost wished she'd died rather than end up like this."

A few weeks after this, when Frannie began to get better, the doctors called it the return of "appropriate affect." Maggie sent out a family letter saying: "Mother's coming around. She's practically back to normal except for forgetting a few words and we're planning on a home-coming party soon."

And later: "Mother seems just about okay now. Sends her love to everyone and asks about you all. She can't remember who visited and who didn't, but she's talking normally now, thank goodness. For those who can come, we'll bring her home February 16 in the early afternoon and the doctor says a very short party would be all right."

Snow had fallen the night of the fifteenth, but the sixteenth was bright and cold. Frannie's daughters and granddaughters took charge of lunch. One of the sons-in-law put the extra leaf in the table again and took three of the smaller children out to shovel the walk. They ran in and out all morning, bringing cold air and snow into the front hall. "Here, here," Henry said crossly. "In or out. I'm not paying to heat all outdoors."

Someone brought a towel and left it by the front door to mop up the puddles of melting snow. Charlotte's husband lugged two high chairs up from the basement, washed off the dust and cobwebs, and set them at corners of the table.

The chime of the metal shovel ringing on concrete outside, the banging of the front door, the good smells from the kitchen, the table gleaming with silver, made it seem like a dozen Christmases they'd shared in the past. But there was a subdued anxiousness among the adults and several tense abbreviated conversations. Maggie said over and over to people, "Really, she's quite all right now." Henry was surly and spent the morning watching TV or scolding his great-grandchildren.

At one o'clock, Bob Hancock's car swung up the driveway. His oldest boy, Nick, jumped out from the far side and extracted a walker from the back seat. He brought it around to the door Bob was opening at the foot of the walk. Frannie rose slowly out of the car and Nick put the walker down in front of his great-grandmother. The children who were outside danced around her and their muffled shouts brought the family in the house to the windows. "She's home! She's home!" they cried. Henry rose and went to the window.

Slowly, with Nick at one elbow and Bob at the other, Frannie made her way across the shoveled, sanded walk. Her entourage of great-grandchildren in bright nylon snowsuits leapt around her. She was watching her feet, so Henry couldn't see her face. Charlotte had gone to the hospital two days before to give her a permanent, and her hair was immobilized in rigid waves on her head, though the wind made her coat flap.

She turned at the bottom of the porch stairs and Bob came to face her. Holding each other's hands like partners in some old court dance, they stepped sideways up the stairs. Then the children burst open the front door, yelling and stomping the snow off their feet and taking advantage of the excitement to dance around in the front hall without having to remove their boots. Frannie shuffled in and looked around at her family gathered in an irregular circle in the hallway. Charlotte fished a Kleenex out of her maternity smock and several others wiped at their eyes.

"Where's Henry?" Frannie asked. Henry felt a slight constriction in his chest, but he pushed past his children and grandchildren and stood before her. "Here I am, my darling," he said. She looked at him a moment. Then she smiled her sad smile and raised her face to be kissed. Gratefully, he put his lips to hers.

The children yelled and danced, the adults broke into applause. Henry said softly, "It's wonderful to see you yourself again, Frances."

Grandma Frannie looked at him and then at her clapping family. She raised her hands slightly as though to ward off the noise, and for a moment her face registered confusion. But the applause continued.

Then she seemed to realize what they wanted from her. Unassisted and shaky, she stepped forward and smiled again. Slowly she bowed her head, as though to receive the homage due a long and difficult performance.

Lynne Sharon Schwartz
(b. 1939)

Born in New York City, Lynne Sharon Schwartz was graduated from Barnard College, received an M.A. from Bryn Mawr, and studied Comparative Literature at New York University. She has taught creative writing at Columbia University, the University of Iowa, Rice University, and Boston University, as well as holding positions in which she did editing, writing publicity for a civil rights–fair housing organization, translating from French and Italian, and directing a spoken records firm. Her stories, which have been selected for inclusion in *The Best American Short Stories,* the *O. Henry Prize Stories,* and *The Pushcart Prize,* are collected in *Acquainted With the Night* (1984) and *The Melting Pot and Other Subversive Stories* (1987). She has published four novels: *Rough Strife* (1980), nominated for an American Book Award and a PEN/Hemingway First Novel Award, *Balancing Acts* (1981), *Disturbances in the Field* (1983), and *Leaving Brooklyn* (1989). In 1985 she published *We Are Talking About Homes,* a nonfiction book. She has received grants from the Guggenheim Foundation, the National Endowment for the Arts, and the New York State Foundation for the Arts.

WHAT I DID FOR LOVE

Together with Carl I used to dream of changing the power structure and making the world a better place. Never that I could end up watching the ten o'clock news with a small rodent on my lap.

He was the fourth. Percy, the first, was a bullet-shaped dark brown guinea pig, short-haired as distinct from the long-haired kind, and from the moment he arrived he tried to hide, making tunnels out of the newspapers in his cage until Martine, who was just eight then, cut the narrow ends off a shoebox and made him a real tunnel, where he stayed except when food appeared. I guess she would have preferred a more sociable pet, but Carl and I couldn't walk a dog four times a day, and the cat we tried chewed at the plants and watched us in bed, which made us self-conscious, and finally got locked in the refrigerator as the magnetic door was closing, so after we found it chilled and traumatized we gave it to a friend who appreciated cats.

Percy had been living his hermit life for about a year when Martine noticed he was hardly eating and being unusually quiet, no rustling of paper in the tunnel. I made an appointment with a vet someone recommended. On the morning of the appointment, after I got Martine on the school bus, I saw Percy lying very still outside the tunnel. I called the vet before I left for work to say I thought his patient might be dead.

"Might be?"

"Well . . . how can I tell for sure?"

He clears his throat and with this patronizing air doctors have, even vets, says, "Why not go and flick your finger near the animal's neck and see if he responds?'

Since I work for a doctor I'm not intimidated by this attitude, it just rolls off me. "Okay, hold on a minute. . . ." I went and flicked. "He doesn't seem to respond, but still . . . I just don't feel sure."

"Raise one of his legs," he says slowly, as if he's talking to a severely retarded person, "wiggle it around and see if it feels stiff." He never heard of denial, this guy. What am I going to tell Martine?

"Hang on. . . ." I wiggled the leg. "It feels stiff," I had to admit.

"I think it's safe to assume," he says, "that the animal is dead."

"I guess we won't be keeping the appointment, then?"

I'm not retarded. I said it on purpose, to kind of rile him and see what he'd say.

"That will hardly be necessary."

To get ready for the burial, I put Percy in a shoebox (a new one, not the tunnel one), wrapped the tissue paper from the shoes around him, and added some flowers I bought on the way home from work, then sealed it up with masking tape. Carl and I kept the coffin in our room that night so Martine wouldn't have to be alone in the dark with it. She didn't cry much, at least in front of us. She keeps her feelings to herself, more like me in that way than Carl. But I knew she was very attached to Percy, hermit that he was. The next morning, a Saturday, the three of us set out carrying the box and a spade and shovel we borrowed from the super of the building. Carl's plan was to bury him in the park, but it was the dead of winter, February, and the ground was so frozen the spade could barely break it.

"This isn't going to work," he said.

Martine looked tragic. She's always been a very beautiful child, with a creamy-skinned face and an expression of serene tragic beauty that, depending on the situation, can make you want to laugh or cry. At that moment I could have done either. We were huddled together, our eyes and noses running from the cold, Martine clutching the shoebox in her blue down mittens.

"I know what," Carl said. "We'll bury him at sea."

Martine's face got even more tragic, and I gave him a funny look too. What sea? It was more than an hour's drive to Coney Island and I had a million things to do that day.

"The river. It's a very old and dignified tradition," he told her. "For people who die on ships, when it would take too long to reach land. In a way it's nicer than an earth burial—in the course of time Percy's body will drift to the depths and mingle with coral and anemone instead of being confined in—"

"Okay," she said.

So we walked up to the 125th Street pier on the Hudson River. This is a desolate place just off an exit of the West Side Highway, where the only buildings are meat-processing plants and where in the daytime a few lone people come to wash their cars, hauling water up in buckets, and even to fish, believe it or not, and at night people come to buy and sell drugs. I looked at Martine. She handed me the box like she couldn't bear to do it herself, so I knelt down and placed it in the river as gently as I could. I was hoping it would float for a while, at least till we could get her away, but my romantic Carl was saying something poetic and sentimental about death and it began to sink, about four feet from where we stood. It was headed south, though, towards the Statue of Liberty and the open sea, I pointed out to her. Free at last.

We got her another guinea pig, a chubby buff-colored one who did not hide and was intelligent and interested in its surroundings, as much as a guinea pig can be. We must have had it—Mooney, it was called—for around a year and a half when Carl began talking about changing his life, finding a new direction. He was one of those people—we both were—who had dropped out of school because it seemed there was so much we should be doing in the world. I was afraid he would be drafted, and we had long searching talks, the way you do when you're twenty, about whether he should be a conscientious objector, but at the last minute the army didn't want him because he had flat feet and was partially deaf in one ear. Those same flat feet led all those marches and demonstrations. Anyhow, he never managed to drop back in later on when things changed. Not that there was any less to do, but somehow no way of doing it anymore and hardly anyone left to do it with, not to mention money. You have to take care of your own life, we discovered. And if you have a kid . . . You find yourself doing things you never planned on.

He started driving a cab when Martine was born and had been ever since. It's exhausting, driving a cab. He spent less and less time organizing demonstrations and drawing maps of the locations of nuclear stockpiles. Now he spent his spare time playing ball with the guys he used to go to meetings with, or reading, or puttering with his plants, which after me, he used to say, where his great passion. It was not a terrible life, he was not harming anyone, and as I often told him, driving a cab where you come in contact with people who are going places was more varied than what I do all day as an X-ray technician, which you could hardly call upbeat. Most of the time, you find the patients either have cancer or not, and while you naturally hope for the best each time, you can't help getting to feel less and less, because a certain percentage are always doomed regardless of your feelings. Well, Carl was not satisfied, he was bored, so I said, "Okay, what would you do if you had a totally free choice?"

"I would like to practice the art of topiary."

"What's that?"

"Topiary is the shaping of shrubberies and trees into certain forms. You know, when you drive past rich towns in Westchester, you sometimes see bushes on the lawns trimmed to spell a word or the initials of a corporation? You can make all sorts of shapes—animals, statues. Have you ever seen it?"

"Yes." I was a little surprised by this. You think you know all about a person and then, topiary. "Well, maybe there's someplace you can learn. Take a course in, what is it, landscape gardening?"

"It's not very practical. You said totally free choice. I don't think that there could be much of a demand for it in Manhattan."

"We could move."

"Where, Chris?" He smiled, sad and sweet and sexy. That was his kind of appeal. "Beverly Hills?"

"Well, maybe there's something related that you can do. You know those men who drive around in green trucks and get hoisted into the trees in little metal seats? I think they trim branches off the ones with Dutch elm disease. Or a tree surgeon?"

This didn't grab him. We talked about plants and trees, and ambition, and doing something you cared about that also provided a living. Finally he said it was a little embarrassing, but what he really might like, in practical terms, was to have a plant store, a big one, like the ones he browsed in down in the Twenties.

"Why should that be embarrassing?"

"When you first met me I was going to alter the power structure of society and now I'm telling you I want to have a plant store. Are you laughing at me, Chris? Tell the truth."

"I haven't heard you say anything laughable yet. I didn't really expect you to change the world, Carl."

"No?"

"I mean, I believed you meant it, and I believed in you, but that's not why I married you." Lord no. I married him for his touch, it struck me, and the sound of his voice, and a thousand other of those things I thought I couldn't exist without. It also struck me that I had never truly expected to change the power structure but that I had liked hanging out with people who thought they could. It was, I would have to say, inspiring.

"Do you think I'm having a mid-life crisis?"

"No. You're only thirty-three. I think you want to change jobs."

So we decided he should try it. He could start by getting a job in a plant store to learn about it, and drive the cab at night. That way we could save some money for a small store to begin with. He would have less time with me and Martine, but it would be worth it in the long run. Except he didn't do it right away. He liked to sit on things for a while, like a hen.

That summer we scraped together the money to send Martine to a camp run by some people we used to hang out with in the old days, and since it was a camp with animals, sort of a farm camp, she took Mooney along. Her third night away she called collect from Vermont and said she had something very sad to tell us. From her tragic voice for an instant I thought they might have discovered she had a terminal disease like leukemia, and how could they be so stupid as to tell her—they were progressive types, maybe they thought it was therapeutic to confront your own mortality—but the news was that Mooney was dead. Someone had left the door of the guinea pigs' cage open the night before and he got out and was discovered in the morning in a nearby field, most likely mauled by a larger animal. I sounded relieved and not tragic enough, but fortunately Carl had the right tone throughout. At the age of eleven she understood a little about the brutalities of nature and the survival of the fittest and so on, but it was still hard for her to accept.

Martine is a peacefully inclined, intuitive type. She would have felt at home in our day, when peace and love were respectable attitudes. We named her after Martin Luther King, which nowadays seems a far-out thing to have done. Not that my estimation of him has changed or that I don't like the name, only it isn't the sort of thing people do anymore. Just as, once we stayed up nights thinking of how to transform the world and now I'm glad I have a job, no matter how boring, and can send her to camp for a few weeks.

Anyway, the people running the camp being the way they were, they immediately bought her a new guinea pig. Aside from her tragedy she had a terrific time, and she came home with a female pig named Elf, who strangely enough looked exactly like Mooney, in fact if I hadn't known Mooney was dead I would have taken Elf for Mooney. I remember remarking to Carl that if things were reversed, if Mooney had been left at home with us and died and we had managed to find an identical bullet-shaped replacement, I might have tried to pass it off as Mooney, in the way mothers instinctively try to protect their children from the harsher facts of life. But Carl said he wouldn't have, he would have told her the truth, not to make her confront harsh reality but because Martine would be able to tell the difference, as mothers can with twins, and he wouldn't want her catching him in a lie. "You know she has such high standards," he said.

In the dead of winter, even colder than in Percy's era, Martine told us Elf wasn't eating. Oh no, I thought. *Déjà vu.* The stillness, then the stiffness, wrapping it in the shoebox, burial at sea . . . Nevertheless, what can yo do, so I made an appointment with the vet, the same old arrogant vet—I didn't have the energy to look for a new one. I was feeling sick when the day arrived, so Carl took off from work and went with Martine and Elf.

"There's good news and bad news," he said when they

got home. "The good news is that she doesn't have a dread disease. What's wrong with her is her teeth."

I was lying in bed, trying to sleep. "Her teeth?"

"You've got it. Her top and bottom teeth are growing together so she can't eat. She can't separate them to chew." He gave me a demonstration of Elf's problem, stretching his lips and straining his molars.

"Please, this is no time to make me laugh. My stomach is killing me."

"What is it? Your period?"

"No. I don't know what."

"Well, listen—the bad news is that she needs surgery. Oral surgery. It's a hundred twenty-five including the anesthetic."

"This is not the least bit funny. What are we going to do?" Martine was putting Elf back in her cage, otherwise we would have discussed this with more sensitivity.

"Is there a choice? You know how Martine feels—Albert Schweitzer Junior. I made an appointment for tomorrow. She'll have to stay overnight."

"I presume you mean Elf, not Martine."

"Of course I mean Elf. Maybe I should call a doctor for you too."

"No, I'll be okay. What's a stomachache compared to oral surgery?"

"I don't want you getting all worked up over this, Chris." He joined me on the bed and started fooling around. "Thousands of people each year have successful oral surgery. It's nothing to be alarmed about."

"I'll try to deal with it. Ow, you're leaning right where it hurts." Martine came into the room and Carl sat up quickly.

"She's looking very wan," she said.

"Two days from now she'll be a new person," Carl said.

"She's never been a person before. How could she be one in two days?"

"Medical science is amazing."

"I have no luck with guinea pigs." She plopped into a chair, stretched out her legs, and sat gazing at her sneakers. I noticed how tall she was growing. She was nearly twelve and beginning to get breasts. But she wasn't awkward like most girls at that stage; she was stunning, willowy and auburn-haired, with green eyes. There was sometimes a faint emerald light in the whites of her eyes that would take me by surprise, and I would stare and think, What a lucky accident.

"Maybe none of them live long," I said. "I doubt if yours are being singled out."

"They have a four-to-six-year life span. I looked it up in the encyclopedia. But in four years I've gone through almost three."

That night I had such terrible pains in my stomach that Carl took me to the emergency room, where after a lot of fussing around—they tried to send me home, they tried to get me to sleep—they found it was my appendix and it had to come out right away. It was quite a few days before I felt like anything resembling normal, and I forgot completely about Elf's oral surgery.

"Chris, before we go inside, I'd better tell you something." Carl switched off the engine and reached into the back seat for my overnight bag. He was avoiding my eyes.

"What happened? I spoke to her on the phone just last night!" I was about to leap out of the car, but he grabbed my arm.

"Hold it a minute, will you? You're supposed to take it easy."

"Well what's wrong, for Chrissake?"

He looked at me. "Not Martine. Jesus! Elf."

"Elf." I thought I would pass out. I was still pretty drugged.

"She got through the surgery all right. We brought her home the next day. But . . . I don't know whether she was too weak from not eating or what, but she never started eating again. And so . . ."

"I never liked that doctor. How did Martine take it this time?"

"Sad but philosophical. I think she's used to it by now. Besides, she was more concerned about you."

"I'm glad to hear that. So where is the corpse? At sea again?"

"Well, no, actually. That's why I wanted to tell you before you went in the apartment. The temperature has been near zero. The river is frozen."

"Just give it to me straight, Carl."

"She's wrapped in some plastic bags on the bathroom windowsill. Outside. The iron grating is holding her in place. I was going to put her in the freezer with the meat, but I thought you might not care for that."

"Couldn't you find a shoebox?"

"No. I guess nobody's gotten new shoes lately."

"And how long is she going to stay there?"

"They're predicting a thaw. It's supposed to get warm, unseasonably warm, so in a few days we'll take her out to the park. Anyway, welcome home. Oh, there's another thing."

"I hope this is good."

It was. He had found a job working in the greenhouse at the Botanical Garden.

Since Martine never brought the subject up again after the thaw and the park burial, I assumed the guinea pig phase of her life was over. Two weeks after she returned from camp that summer, the super who had loaned us the spade and shovel for Percy came up to say there was a family in the next building with a new guinea pig, but their baby was allergic to it and couldn't stop sneezing. Maybe we wanted to do them a favor and take it off their hands?

Martine and I turned to each other. "What do you think?" I said.

"I'm not sure. They're a lot of expense, aren't they?"

"Not so bad. I mean, what's a little lettuce, carrots . . ."

"The medical expenses. And you don't like them too much, do you, Mom?"

I tried to shrug it of with a blank smile. I looked at Mr. Coates—what I expected I'll never know, since he stood there as if he had seen and heard everything in his lifetime and was content to wait for this discussion to be over. I wondered how much of a tip he would get for the deal. Nothing from us, I vowed.

"I've noticed," Martine said. "You don't like to handle them. You don't like small rodents."

"Not a whole lot, frankly." They looked to me like rats, fat tailless rats. For Martine's sake I had wished them good health and long life, but I tried not to get too close. When she was out with her friends and I had to feed them, I used to toss the lettuce in and step back as they lunged for it. I didn't like the eager squeaks they let out when they smelled the food coming, or the crunching sounds they made eating it. And when I held them—at the beginning, when she would offer them to me to stroke, before she noticed how I felt about small rodents—I didn't like the nervous fluttery softness of them, their darting squirmy little movements, the sniffing and nipping and the beat of the fragile heart so close to the surface I could feel it in my palms. "But they don't bother me so long as they're in the cage in your room." Which was true.

"You could go over and take a look," said Mr. Coates finally. "I'll take you over there if you want."

"Maybe I'll do that, Mom. Do you want to come too?"

"No. I know what guinea pigs look like by now."

"What color is it?" Martine was asking him on the way out.

"I don't know the color. I ain't seen it myself yet."

I didn't pay any more attention to Rusty, named for his color, than I had to the others. I made sure to be in another room while Martine and Carl cut his nails, one holding him down, the other clipping—they took turns. Martine started junior high and got even more beautiful, breasts, hips, the works, with a kind of slow way of turning her head and moving her eyes. She also started expressing intelligent opinions on every subject in the news, test tube babies, airplane hijackings, chemicals in packaged foods, while Carl and I listened and marveled, with this peculiar guilty relief that she was turning out so well—I guess because we were not living out our former ideals, not changing the world or on the other hand being particularly upwardly mobile either. Carl was happier working in the greenhouse, but we still hadn't managed to save enough to rent a store or qualify for a bank loan.

At Martine's thirteenth birthday party in May, we got to talking in the kitchen with one of the mothers who came to pick up her kid. I liked her. She was about our age, small and blonde, and she had dropped out of school too but had gone back to finish and was even doing graduate work.

"What field?" I asked. I was scraping pizza crusts into the garbage while Carl washed out soda cans—he was very big on recycling. In the living room the kids were dancing to a reggae song called "Free Nelson Mandela," and the three of us had been remarking, first of all, that Nelson Mandela had been in prison since we were about their age and in the meantime we had grown up and were raising children and feeling vaguely disappointed with ourselves, and secondly, that dancing to a record like that wouldn't have been our style even if there had been one back then, which was unlikely. Singing was more our style. And the fact that teen-agers today were dancing to this "Free Nelson Mandela" record at parties made their generation seem less serious, yet at this point who were we to judge styles of being serious? The man was still in prison, after all.

"Romance languages," she said. She was playing with the plastic magnetic letters on the refrigerator. They had been there since Martine was two. Sometimes we would use them to write things like Merry Xmas or, as tonight, Happy Birthday, and sometimes to leave real messages, like Skating Back at 7 M. The messages would stay up for the longest time, eroding little by little because we knocked the letters off accidentally and stuck them back any old place, or because we needed a letter for a new message, so that Happy Birthday could come to read Hapy Birda, and at some point they would lose their meaning altogether, like Hay irda, which amused Martine no end. This woman wrote, "Nel mezzo del cammin di nostra vita."

"What does that mean?" Carl asked her.

" 'In the middle of the journey of our life.' It's the opening of *The Divine Comedy*. What it means is, here I am thirty-five years old and I'm a graduate student."

"There's nothing wrong with that," said Carl. "I admire your determination. I'm driving a cab, but one day before I die I'm going to learn to do topiary, for the simple reason that I want to."

She said what I knew she would. "What's topiary?"

He stopped rinsing cans to tell her.

I never read *The Divine Comedy*, but I do know Dante goes through Hell and Purgatory and eventually gets to Paradise. All the parts you ever hear about, though, seem to take place in Hell, and so a small shiver ran up my spine, seeing that message on the refrigerator above Happy Birthday. Then I forgot about it.

In bed that night I asked Carl if he was serious about learning topiary. He said he had been thinking it over again. Since he had gotten a raise at the greenhouse, maybe he might give up the cab altogether, he was so sick of it, and use the money we'd saved for the store to study landscape gardening

"Well, okay. That sounds good. I can work a half day Saturdays, maybe."

"No, I don't want you to lose the little free time you have. We'll manage. Maybe there's something you want to go back and study too."

"I'm not ambitious. Why, would I be more attractive, like, if I went to graduate school?"

"Ha! Did I hear you right?" He let out a comic whoop. "I don't even remember her name, Chris. Listen, you want me to prove my love?"

That was the last time. The next day he came down with the flu, then Martine and I got it, and just when we were beginning to come back to life he had a heart attack driving the cab. He might have made it, the doctor said, except he was alone and lost control of the wheel. They told me more details about it, just like a news report, more than I could bear to listen to, in fact. I tried to forget the words the minute I heard them, but no amount of trying could make me stop seeing the scene in my mind. They offered me pills, all through those next insane days, but I wasn't interested in feeling better. Anyhow, what kind of goddamn pill could cure this? I asked them. I also kept seeing in my mind a scene on the Long Island Expressway when Martine was a baby and we were going to Jones Beach. About three cars ahead of us over in the right lane, a car started to veer, and as we got closer we could see the driver slumping down in his seat. Before we could even think what to do, a state trooper appeared out of nowhere and jumped in on the driver's side to grab the wheel. Sirens started up, I guess they took him to the hospital, and a huge pile-up was averted. Watching it, I felt bad about how we used to call cops pigs. That sounds a little simpleminded, I know, but so was calling them pigs. And now I wondered how come a miracle in the form of a cop happened for that person and not for Carl, which is a question a retarded person might ask—I mean, an out-of-the-way street in Queens at eleven at night . . . It happened the way it happened, that's all. A loss to all those who might have enjoyed his topiary. I do think he would have done it in his own good time. If only we had had a little more time, I could have taken care of him. I wouldn't have been a miracle, but I would have done a good job. The way he vanished, though, I couldn't do a thing, not even say goodbye or hold his hand in the hospital or whatever it is old couples do—maybe the wife whispers that she'll be joining him soon, but I have no illusions that I'll ever be joining him, soon or late. I just got a lot less of him than I expected. Another thing is that the last time we made love I was slightly distracted because of the graduate student he admired for her determination, not that anything transpired between them except some ordinary conversation, but it started me wondering in general. Stupid, because I know very well how he felt, he told me every night. Those words I don't forget. I let them put me to sleep. I lie there remembering how it felt with his arms and legs flung over me and can't believe I'm expected to get through decades without ever feeling that again.

So I did end up working half days on Saturdays. In July Martine was supposed to go back to the camp run by the progressives and pacifists, where she had always had such a great time except for her tragedy with Mooney, and I didn't want to begin my life alone by asking for help.

"I don't have to go," she said, "If we don't have the money it's all right. I don't think I even feel like going anymore." My beautiful child with the tragic face. Now she had something worthy of that face.

"You should go, however you feel. When you get there you'll be glad."

"Except there's a slight problem," she said.

"What's that?"

"Rusty. I'm not taking him. Not after what happened to Mooney."

"No," I agreed.

"Which means . . ."

"Oh God! All right, I can do it. How bad can it be? A little lettuce, cabbage, right? A few handfuls of pellets . . ."

"There's the cage to clean too."

"The cage. Okay."

It was hard, her going off on the bus, with the typical scene of cheery mothers and fathers crowding around waving brown lunch bags, but I forced myself through it and so did she. I would force myself through the rest of my life if I had to.

First thing every morning and before I went to bed I put a handful of pellets in Rusty's bowl and fresh water in his bottle, and when I left for work and came home I dropped a few leaves of something green into the cage. Since I never really looked at him I was shocked, the fourth night after Martine left, when Mr. Coates, who had come up to fix the window lock in her room, said in his usual unexcited way, "Your pig's eye's popping out."

The right eye was protruding half an inch out of the socket and the cylindrical part behind it was yellow with gummy pus, a disgusting sight. "Jesus F. Christ," I said.

"He won't be no help to you. You need a vet."

The thought of going back to that arrogant vet who I always suspected had screwed up with Elf was more than I could take, so I searched the yellow pages till I found a woman vet in the neighborhood. When I walked in the next day carrying Rusty in a carton, I knew I had lucked out. She had curly hair like a mop, she wore jeans and a white sweatshirt, and she seemed young, maybe twenty-nine or thirty. Her name was Doctor Dunn. Very good, Doctor Dunn, so there won't be all that other shit to cope with.

To get him on the examining table I had to lift him up by his middle and feel all the squirminess and the beat of the scared delicate heart between my palms.

"It looks like either a growth of some kind pushing it forward, or maybe an abscess. But in either case I'm afraid the eye will have to go. It's badly infected and unless it's removed it'll dry up and the infection will spread and . . . uh . . ."

"He'll die?"

"Right."

Seventy-five dollars, she said, including his overnight stay, plus twenty-five for the biopsy. Terrific, I thought, just what I need. It was lower than the other vet's rates, though.

"I want to explain something about the surgery. He's a very small animal, two pounds or so, and any prolonged anesthesia is going to be risky. What this means is, I can't make any guarantees. I'd say his chances are . . . seventy-thirty, depending on his general condition. Of course, we'll do everything we can. . . ."

"And if I don't do it he'll die anyhow?"

"Right."

Squirming there on the table was this orange rat whose fate I was deciding. I felt very out of sync with reality, as if I was in a science fiction movie and how did I ever arrive at this place. "Okay. I guess we'd better do it."

The receptionist I left him with told me to call around four the next day to see how he came through the surgery. *If* was what she meant. That evening out of habit I almost went in to toss him some celery, then I remembered the cage was empty. There was no reason to go into Martine's room. But I decided to take the opportunity to clean the cage and the room both. I had found that the more I moved around the more numb I felt, which was what I wanted.

On the dot of four, I called from work. Doctor Dunn answered herself.

"He's fine! What a trouper, that Rusty! We had him hooked up to the EKG the whole time and monitored him, and he was terrific. I'm really pleased."

"Thank you," I managed to say. "Thank you very

much." In one day she had established a closer relationship with him than I had in a year. That was an interesting thought. I mean, it didn't make me feel emotionally inadequate; I simply realized that's why she went through years of veterinary school, because she really cared, the way Carl could have about topiary, I guess.

"Can you come in and pick him up before seven? Then I can tell you about the post-op care."

Post-op care? I had never thought of that. I had never even thought of how the eye would look. Would it be a hole, or just a blank patch of fur? Would there be a bandage on it, or maybe she could fix him up with a special little eye patch?

I found Rusty in his carton on the front desk, with the receptionist petting him and calling him a good boy. "We're all crazy about him," she said. "He's quite a fella, aren't you, Rusty-baby?"

Where his right eye used to be, there was a row of five black stitches, and the area around it was shaved. Below the bottom stitch, a plastic tube the diameter of a straw and about an inch long stuck out. That was a drain for the wound, Doctor Dunn explained. He had a black plastic collar around his neck that looked like a ruff, the kind you see in old portraits of royalty. To keep him from poking himself, she said.

"Was he in good condition otherwise?" I thought I should sound concerned, in this world of animal-lovers.

"Oh, fine. Now . . . The post-operative care is a little complicated, so I wrote it down." She handed me a list of instructions:

1. Cold compresses tonight, 5–10 minutes.
2. Oral antibiotics, 3× a day for at least 7 days.
3. Keep collar on at all times.
4. Feed as usual.
5. Call if any excessive redness, swelling, or discharge develops.
6. Come in 3–4 days from now to have drain pulled.
7. Call early next week for biopsy results.
8. Make appointment for suture removal, 10–14 days.

9. Starting tomorrow, apply warm compresses 5–10 minutes, 2× a day for 10 days.

"Here's a sample bottle of antibiotics. Maybe I'd better do the first dose to show you how." She held him to her chest with one hand, while with the other she nudged his mouth open using the medicine dropper and squeezed the drops in, murmuring, "Come on now, that's a good boy, there you go." As she wiped the drips off his face and her sweatshirt with a tissue, I thought, Never. This is not happening to me. But I knew it was, and that I would have to go through with it.

When I went to get some ice water for the cold compress that night, I saw the message the graduate student mother had left on the refrigerator near Happy Birthday, which was now Happ Brhday. "Ne mezz I camn di nstr vita," it read. I knew some letters were missing though not which ones, and those that were left were crooked, but I remembered well enough what it meant. I sat down to watch the ten o'clock news with Rusty on my lap and put the compress on his eye, or the place where his eye used to be, but he squirmed around wildly, clawing at my pants. Ice water oozed onto my legs. I told him to cut it out, he had no choice. Finally I tried patting him and talking to him like a baby, to quiet him. Don't worry, kiddo, you're going to be all right—stuff like that, the way Carl would have done without feeling idiotic. It worked. Only hearing those words loosened me a little out of my numbness and I had this terrible sensation of walking a tightrope in pitch darkness, though in fact I was whispering sweet nothings to a guinea pig. I even thought of telling him what I'd been through with my appendix, a fellow sufferer, and God knows what next, but I controlled myself. If I freaked out, who would take care of Martine?

I figured seven and a half minutes for the compress was fair enough—Doctor Dunn had written down 5–10. Then I changed my mind and held it there for another minute so if anything happened I would have a clear conscience when I told Martine. I held him to my chest with a towel over my shirt, feeling the heart pulsing against me, and squirted in the antibiotic. I lost a good bit, but I'd have plenty of chances to improve.

In the morning I found the collar lying in the mess of shit and cedar chips in his cage. I washed it and tried to get it back on him, but he fought back with his whole body—each time I fitted it around his neck he managed to squirm and jerk his way out, till beyond being repelled I was practically weeping with frustration. Two people could have done it easily. Carl, I thought, if ever I needed you . . . Finally after a great struggle I got it fastened in back with masking tape so he wouldn't undo it. But when I came home from work it was off again and we wrestled again. The next morning I rebelled. The drops, the compresses, okay, but there was no way I was going to literally collar a rodent morning and night for ten days. There are limits to everything, especially on a tightrope in the dark. I called Doctor Dunn from work.

"Is he poking himself around the eye?" she asked. "Any bleeding or discharge? Good. Then forget it. You can throw the collar away."

I was so relieved.

"How is he otherwise? Is he eating?"

"Yes. He seems okay. Except he's shedding." I told her how when I lifted him up, orange hair fluttered down into his cage like leaves from a tree. When leaves fell off Carl's plants, which I was also trying to keep alive though that project wasn't as dramatic, it usually meant they were on their way out. I had already lost three—I didn't have his green thumb. It seemed my life had become one huge effort to keep things alive, with death hot on my trail. I even had nightmares about what could be happening to Martine at camp. When I wrote to her, though, I tried to sound casual, as if I was fine, and I wrote that Rusty was fine too. Maybe Carl would have given her all the gory details, but I didn't mind lying. He was going to be fine. I was determined that pig would live even if it was over my dead body. Luckily I wasn't so far gone as to say all this to Doctor Dunn. "Is that a bad sign?"

"Shedding doesn't mean anything," she said. "He doesn't feel well, so he's not grooming himself as usual. It'll stop as he gets better."

I also noticed, those first few days, he would do this weird dance when I put the food in his cage. It dawned on me that he could smell it but not see it. While he scurried around in circles, I kept trying to shove it towards his good side—kind of a Bugs Bunny routine. Then after a while he developed a funny motion, turning his head to spot it, and soon he was finding it pretty well with his one eye. I told Doctor Dunn when I brought him in to have the drain removed. She said yes, they adapt quickly. They compensate. She talked about evolution and why eyes were located where they were. Predators, she said, have close-set eyes in the front of their heads to see the prey, and the prey have eyes at the sides, to watch out for the predators. How clever, I thought, the way nature matched up the teams. You couldn't change your destiny, but you had certain traits that kept the game going and gave you the illusion of having a fighting chance. We talked about it for a good while. She was interesting, that Doctor Dunn.

A few days later she plucked out the stitches with tweezers while I held him down.

"I have to tell you," she said, "not many people would take such pains with a guinea pig. Some people don't even bother with dogs and cats, you'd be amazed. They'd rather have them put away. You did a terrific job. You must really love animals."

I didn't have the heart to tell her that although it didn't turn my stomach anymore to hold him on my lap and stroke him for the compresses, he was still just a fat rat as far as I was concerned, but a fat rat which fate had arranged I had to keep alive. So I did.

"Well, you could say I did it for love."

She laughed. "Keep applying the warm compresses for another day or two, to be on the safe side. Then that's it. Case closed."

"What about the biopsy?"

"Oh yes, the lab report. It's not in yet, but I have a feeling it wasn't malignant. He doesn't look sick to me. Call me on it next week."

In eleven days Martine will be back. Beautiful Martine, with her suntan making her almost the color of Rusty. I'll warn her about the eye before she sees him. It doesn't look too gruesome now, with the stitches out and the hair growing back—soon it'll be smooth blank space. In fact, if not for the missing eye she would never have to know what he went through. The house will feel strange to her all over again without Carl, because whenever you're away for a while you expect to come home to some pure and perfect condition. She'll be daydreaming on the bus that maybe it was all a nightmare and the both of us are here waiting for her. But it'll be an altogether different life, and the worst thing is—knowing us, sensible, adaptable types—that one remote day we'll wake up and it'll seem normal this way, and in years to come Carl will turn into the man I had in my youth instead of what he is now, my life. I even envy her—he'll always be her one father.

So I'm applying the warm compresses for the last time, sitting here with a one-eyed guinea pig who is going to live out his four-to-six year life span no matter what it takes, in the middle of the journey of my life, stroking him as if I really loved animals.

John Updike

(b. 1932)

At the age of twenty-two, John Updike had graduated summa cum laude from Harvard, won a fellowship to the Ruskin School of Drawing and Fine Art in Oxford, England, sold his first short story, "Friends from Philadelphia," to *The New Yorker,* and had been offered a job on the magazine's staff for the following year. In 1957, after two years as a staff reporter, he left New York for Ipswich, Massachusetts. Among his novels are *The Poorhouse Fair* (1958), *Rabbit Run* (1961), *Couples* (1968), *Rabbit Redux* (1971), *Rabbit Is Rich* (1981), *The Witches of Eastwick* (1984), which was adapted for a film starring Jack Nicholson, *Roger's Version* (1986), and *S* (1987). His collections of short fiction include *The Same Door* (1959), *Pigeon Feathers* (1962), *The Music School* (1966), *Bech: A Book* (1970) a collection of linked stories, *Too Far to Go* (1979), *Bech Is Back* (1982), and *Trust Me* (1987). Some of his essays, criticism and literary reviews are collected in *Assorted Prose* (1965), *Picked-Up Pieces* (1975), and *Hugging the Shore* (1983); a memoir titled *Self-Conscious* was published in 1989.

STILL OF SOME USE

When Foster helped his ex-wife clean out the attic of the house where they had once lived and which she was now selling, they came across dozens of forgotten, broken games. Parcheesi, Monopoly, Lotto; games aping the strategies of the stock market, of crime detection, of real-estate speculation, of international diplomacy and war; games with spinners, dice, lettered tiles, cardboard spacemen, and plastic battleships; games bought in five-and-tens and department stores feverish and musical with Christmas expectations; games enjoyed on the afternoon of a birthday and for a few afternoons thereafter and then allowed, shy of one or two pieces, to drift into closets and toward the attic. Yet, discovered in their bright flat boxes between trunks of outgrown clothes and defunct appliances, the games presented a forceful semblance of value: the springs of their miniature launchers still reacted, the logic of their instructions would still generate suspense, given a chance. "What shall we do with all these games?" Foster shouted, in a kind of agony, to his scattered family as they moved up and down the attic stairs.

"Trash 'em," his younger son, a strapping nineteen, urged.

"Would the Goodwill want them?" asked his ex-wife, still wife enough to think that all of his questions deserved answers. "You used to be able to give things like that to orphanages. But they don't call them orphanages anymore, do they?"

"They call them normal American homes," Foster said.

His older son, now twenty-two, with a cinnamon-colored beard, offered, "They wouldn't work anyhow; they all have something missing. That's how they got to the attic."

"Well, why didn't we throw them away at the time?" Foster asked, and had to answer himself. Cowardice, the answer was. Inertia. Clinging to the past.

His sons, with a shadow of old obedience, came and looked over his shoulder at the sad wealth of abandoned playthings, silently groping with him for the particular happy day connected to this and that pattern of colored squares and arrows. Their lives had touched these tokens and counters once; excitement had flowed along the paths of these stylized landscapes. But the day was gone, and scarcely a memory remained.

"Toss 'em," the younger decreed, in his manly voice. For these days of cleaning out, the boy had borrowed a pickup truck from a friend and parked it on the lawn beneath the attic window, so the smaller items of discard could be tossed directly into it. The bigger items were lugged down the stairs and through the front hall; already the truck was loaded with old mattresses, broken clock-radios, obsolete skis and boots. It was a game of sorts to hit the truck bed with objects dropped from the height of the house. Foster flipped game after game at the target two stories below. When the boxes hit, they exploded, throwing a spray of dice, tokens, counters, and cards into the air and across the lawn. A box called Mousetrap, its lid showing laughing children gathered around a Rube Goldberg device, drifted sideways, struck one side wall of the truck, and spilled its plastic components into a flower bed. A set of something called Drag Race! floated gently as a snowflake before coming to rest, much diminished, on a stained mattress. Foster saw in the depth of downward space the cause of his melancholy: he had not played enough with these games. Now no one wanted to play.

Had he and wife wife avoided divorce, of course, these boxes would have continued to gather dust in an undisturbed attic, their sorrow unexposed. The toys of his own childhood still rested in his mother's attic. At his last visit, he had crept up there and wound the spring of a tin Donald Duck; it had responded with an angry clack of its bill and a few stiff strokes on its drum. A tilted board with concentric grooves for marbles still waited in a bushel basket with his alphabet blocks and lead airplanes—waited for his childhood to return.

His ex-wife paused where he squatted at the attic window and asked him, "What's the matter?"

"Nothing. These games weren't used much."

"I know. It happens fast. You better stop now; it's making you too sad."

Behind him, his family had cleaned out the attic, the slant-ceilinged rooms stood empty, with drooping insulation. "How can you bear it?" he asked, of the emptiness.

"Oh, it's fun," she said, "once you get into it. Off with the old, on with the new. The new people seem nice. They have *little* children."

He looked at her and wondered whether she was being brave or truly hardhearted. The attic trembled slightly. "That's Ted," she said.

She had acquired a boy friend, a big athletic accountant fleeing from domestic embarrassments in a neighboring town. When Ted slammed the kitchen door two stories below, the glass shade of a kerosene lamp that, though long unused, Foster hadn't had the heart to throw out of the window vibrated in its copper clips, emitting a thin note like a trapped wasp's song. Time for Foster to go. His dusty knees creaked when he stood. His ex-wife's eager steps raced ahead of him down through the emptied house. He followed, carrying the lamp, and set it finally on the bare top of a bookcase he had once built, on the first-floor landing. He remembered screwing the top board, a prize piece of knot-free pine, into place from underneath, so not a nailhead marred its smoothness.

After all the vacant rooms and halls, the kitchen seemed indecently full of heat and life. "Dad, want a beer?" the bearded son asked. "Ted brought some." The back of the boy's hand, holding forth the dewy can, blazed with fine ginger hairs. His girl friend, wearing gypsy earrings and a NO NUKES sweatshirt, leaned against the disconnected stove, her hair in a bandanna and a black smirch becomingly placed on one temple. From the kind way she smiled at Foster, he felt this party was making room for him.

"No, I better go."

Ted shook Foster's hand, as he always did. He had a thin pink skin and silver hair whose fluffy waves seemed mechanically induced. Foster could look him in the eye no longer than he could gaze at the sun. He wondered how such a radiant brute had got into such a tame line of work. Ted had not helped with the attic today because he had been off in his old town, visiting his teen-aged twins. "I hear you did a splendid job today," he announced.

"They did," Foster said. "I wasn't much use. I just sat there stunned. All these things I had forgotten buying."

"Some were presents," his son reminded him. He passed the can his father had snubbed to his mother, who took it and tore up the tab with that defiant-sounding *pssff*. She had never liked beer, yet tipped the can to her mouth.

"Give me one sip," Foster begged, and took the can from her and drank a long swallow. When he opened his eyes, Ted's big hand was cupped under Mrs. Foster's chin while his thumb rubbed away a smudge of dirt along her jaw which Foster had not noticed. This protective gesture made her face look small, pouty, and frail. Ted, Foster noticed now, was dressed with a certain comical perfection in a banker's Saturday outfit—softened blue jeans, crisp tennis sneakers, lumberjack shirt with cuffs folded back. The youthful outfit accented his age, his hypertensive flush. Foster saw them suddenly as a touching, aging couple, and this perception seemed permission to go.

He handed back the can.

"Thanks for your help," his former wife said.

"Yes, we do thank you," Ted said.

"Talk to Tommy," she unexpectedly added, in a lowered voice. She was still sending out trip wires to slow Foster's departures. "This is harder on him than he shows."

Ted looked at his watch, a fat, black-faced thing he could swim under water with. "I said to him coming in, 'Don't dawdle till the dump closes.' "

"He loafed all day," his brother complained, "mooning over old stuff, and now he's going to screw up getting to the dump."

"He's very sensi-tive," the visiting gypsy said, with a strange chiming brightness, as if repeating something she had heard.

Outside, the boy was picking up litter that had fallen wide of the truck. Foster helped him. In the grass there were dozens of tokens and dice. Some were engraved with curious little faces—Olive Oyl, Snuffy Smith, Dagwood—and others with hieroglyphs—numbers, diamonds, spades, hexagons—whose code was lost. He held out a handful for Tommy to see. "Can you remember what these were for?"

"Comic-Strip Lotto," the boy said without hesitation. "And a game called Gambling Fools there was a kind of slot machine for." The light of old payoffs flickered in his eyes as he gazed down at the rubble in his father's hand. Though Foster was taller, the boy was broader in the shoulders, and growing. "Want to ride with me to the dump?" Tommy asked.

"I would, but I better go." He, too, had a new life to lead. By being on this forsaken property at all, Foster was in a sense on the wrong square, if not *en prise*. He remembered how once he had begun to teach this boy chess, but in the sadness of watching him lose—the little furry bowed head frowning above his trapped king—the lessons had stopped.

Foster tossed the tokens into the truck; they rattled to rest on the metal. "This depresses you?" he asked his son.

"Naa." The boy amended, "Kind of."

"You'll feel great," Foster promised him, "coming back with a clean truck. I used to love it at the dump, all that old happiness heaped up, and the seagulls."

"It's changed since you left. They have all these new rules. The lady there yelled at me last time, for putting stuff in the wrong place."

"She did?"

"Yeah. It was scary." Seeing his father waver, he added, "It'll only take twenty minutes." Though broad of build, Tommy had beardless cheeks and, between thickening eyebrows, a trace of that rounded, faintly baffled blankness babies have, that wrinkles before they cry.

"O.K.," Foster said. "You win. I'll come along. I'll protect you."

Raymond Carver
(1939–1988)

Born in Clatskanie, Oregon, Raymond Carver grew up in Yakima, Washington, where his father worked as a logger. After graduating from Humboldt State College in California, he studied at the University of Iowa's Writers' Workshop. His collections of stories include: *Put Yourself in My Shoes* (1974), *Will You Please Be Quiet, Please?* (1976), *Furious Seasons and Other Stories* (1977), *What We Talk About When We Talk About Love* (1981), *The Pheasant* (1982), *Cathedral* (1983), *If It Please You* (1984), *The Stories of Raymond Carver* (1985) and *Where I'm Calling From* (1988). In addition he published three collections of poems in small press editions: *Near Klamath* (1968), *Winter Insomnia* (1970), *At Night the Salmon Move* (1976), as well as *Where Water Comes Together with Other Water* (1985) and *Ultramarine* (1986). A recipient of a Guggenheim Fellowship in 1979, Carver received a National Endowment for the Arts Discovery Award for Poetry and was elected in 1988 to the American Academy and Institute of Arts and Letters.

ELEPHANT

I knew it was a mistake to let my brother have the money. I didn't need anybody else owing me. But when he called and said he couldn't make the payment on his house, what could I do? I'd never been inside his house—he lived a thousand miles away, in California; I'd never even *seen* his house—but I didn't want him to lose it. He cried over the phone and said he was losing everything he'd worked for. He said he'd pay me back. February, he said. Maybe sooner. No later, anyway, than March. He said his income-tax refund was on the way. Plus, he said, he had a little investment that would mature in February. He acted secretive about the investment thing, so I didn't press for details.

"Trust me on this," he said. "I won't let you down."

He'd lost his job last July, when the company he worked for, a fiberglass-insulation plant, decided to lay off two hundred employees. He'd been living on his unemployment since then, but now the unemployment was gone, and his savings were gone, too. And he didn't have health insurance any longer. When his job went, the insurance went. His wife, who was ten years older, was diabetic and needed treatment. He'd had to sell the other car—her car, an old station wagon—and a week ago he'd pawned his TV. He told me he'd hurt his back carrying the TV up and down the street where the pawnshops did business. He went from place to place, he said, trying to get the best offer. Somebody finally gave him a hundred dollars for it, this big Sony TV. He told me about the TV, and then about throwing his back out, as if this ought to cinch it with me, unless I had a stone in place of a heart.

"I've gone belly up," he said. "But you can help me pull out of it."

"How much?" I said.

"Five hundred. I could use more, sure, who couldn't?" he said. "But I want to be realistic. I can pay back five hundred. More than that, I'll tell you the truth, I'm not so sure. Brother, I hate to ask. But you're my last resort. Irma Jean and I are going to be on the street before long. I won't let you down," he said. That's what he said. Those were his exact words.

We talked a little more—mostly about our mother and her problems—but, to make a long story short, I sent him the money. I had to. I felt I had to, at any rate—which amounts to the same thing. I wrote him a letter when I sent the check and said he should pay the money back to our mother, who lived in the same town he lived in and who was poor and greedy. I'd been mailing checks to her every month, rain or shine, for three years. But I was thinking that if he paid her the money he owed me it might take me off the hook there and let me breathe for a while. I wouldn't have to worry on that score for a couple of months, anyway. Also, and this is the truth, I thought maybe he'd be more likely to pay her, since they lived right there in the same town and he saw her from time to time. All I was doing was trying to cover myself some way. The thing is, he might have the best intentions of paying me back, but things happen sometimes. Things get in the way of best intentions. Out of sight, out of mind, as they say. But he wouldn't stiff his own mother. Nobody would do that.

I spent hours writing letters, trying to make sure everybody knew what could be expected and what was required. I even phoned out there to my mother several times, trying to explain it to her. But she was suspicious over the whole deal. I went through it with her on the phone step by step, but she was still suspicious. I told her the money that was supposed to come from me on the first of March and on the first of April would instead come from Billy, who owed the money to me. She'd get her money, and she didn't have to worry. The only difference was that Billy would pay it to her those two months instead of me. He'd pay her the money I'd normally be sending to her, but instead of him mailing it to me and then me having to turn around and send it to her he'd pay it to her directly. On any account, she didn't have to worry. She'd get her money, but for those two months it'd come from him—from the money he owed me. My God, I don't know how much I spent on phone calls. And I wish I had fifty cents for every letter I wrote, telling him what I'd told her and telling her what to expect from him—that sort of thing.

But my mother didn't trust Billy. "What if he can't come up with it?" she said to me over the phone. "What then? He's in bad shape, and I'm sorry for him," she said. "But, son, what I want to know is, what if he isn't about to pay me? What if he can't? Then what?"

"Then I'll pay you myself," I said. "Just like always. If